JUDY BEEZLEY

Amanda

Secrets in the neighborhood

The Reading Glass Books
1-888-420-3050
www.readingglassbooks.com
fulfillment@readingglassbooks.com

Contents

Chapter 1

"Did you hear that?" The cat didn't even bother to look up, let alone answer me. I went to the dining room window and ever so cautiously moved the drapes to look out. Nothing. I knew that I had heard something so I moved on to the kitchen to peer out. It didn't take long to discover that the culprit had a black mask on, wore a bushy tail and was raiding the garbage can. These raccoons may be cute, but they have become real pests in the neighborhood, and they aren't that friendly. So much for an intruder. I went back to the living room to reclaim my place on the couch, but the cat had already moved in. There is simply something regal about an 18-pound, cream color female Burmese, with chocolate markings that resemble a cougar, that makes her difficult to ignore. I chose her when I returned to Edgartown, and she was just 4 weeks old and had her since she was weened. She loves me, but she doesn't want me to know it. Rather than argue with her (which is basically useless anyway) I moved to the chair to finish my project. My nerves had been a bit jumpy ever since the break-in at the house across the street last week. I picked up the family album again and started thumbing through it looking for the best photographs of my ancestors. January marked Edgartown's Annual Celebration. I knew that my ancestors, on both sides, had settled in Massachusetts in the early 1700s. However, I didn't have photos or rock-solid information any further back than my 2x great grandparents. Townspeople were asked to provide photographs, when available, and offer either a short bio or a story on each ancestor. I had decided to start there and work my way forward.

JONATHAN AND HILDA (STENNES) BRADLEY –
Amanda's Paternal 2x Great Grandparents

Jonathan was an Episcopalian Minister. He was a quiet man, not much for idle chit chat. He was a good husband and a fine father. He was not a demonstrative man, but his wife and children knew that he loved and cared about them.

Hilda was a homemaker. She was a joyful lass who loved to laugh and had a good time being rowdy with her children. She loved to sew and make all the children's clothing. She had fallen in love with Jonathan shortly after meeting him and loved him dearly until the day she died.

JAMES AND HELEN (SCHMIDT) BRADLEY –
Amanda's Paternal Great Grandparents

James Bradley was destined for success. Even as a child he had an ambition that nobody in his family seemed to understand. He loved politics and used to practice giving State of the Union speeches to the children in the neighborhood. Being from a small town like Edgartown, Massachusetts, you know everyone. He would walk up and down the streets waving and yelling hello to everyone he met. He was a smart lad. He loved to read, and he learned quickly. His memory was extraordinary. It seemed that everything he read or was told logged into his mind forever. James was tall, around 6-foot, and he kept an even weight for all his life. He wasn't particularly interested in food so only ate when it was necessary or pushed him on. He was class president and graduated valedictorian from his high school. He attended Boston University and later graduated with a law degree from Harvard. He met and married Helen Schmidt while they were both in college. He was just 22 and she was 21 when they got married. When James' passed the Massachusetts bar they returned to Edgartown, and he opened a small law firm where he specialized in employment law. He was always working to help those less fortunate than he was. They started a family right away as they both wanted a large family. They managed to have 6 boys and 2 girls in 10 years! Because of James' love of politics, he threw his hat in the ring for the Mayor of Edgartown. He won that election and served as Mayor until he retired. From retirement until his death James worked tirelessly for the people of Edgartown to be sure that they received fair pay for a day's work.

Helen Schmidt was a Boston girl. She was an only child born to German immigrants. She strived to make the best possible grades and to speak the English language without any hint of an accent. It wasn't that she was ashamed of her heritage or didn't love her parents because she did. She simply wanted to fit in and be the best that she could be. She loved to read and loved languages. She graduated from high school with honors and received several scholarships for college tuition. She applied for two jobs and was selected for both so she could afford books and other incidentals. Her parents tried to help the best they could, but it wasn't much. She enrolled at Boston University where she majored in Education. She worked at the library three nights each week and as a waitress at a local café whenever they needed her. She met James Bradley in the library and was immediately smitten. He was so tall and handsome and had impeccable manners. One evening while returning books that he had borrowed he asked if she might like to have a soda with him after her work hours were complete. She was thrilled and immediately answered yes. They were totally comfortable with one another from the beginning of their courtship. James met and won over Helen's parents. And shortly after their courtship began James asked Helen to marry him and she accepted. She earned her degree and taught school, while raising 8 children, in James' hometown of Edgartown. They remained devoted to each other and very much in love until they passed.

JOHN AND AMANDA (O'MALLEY) BRADLEY –
Amanda's Paternal Grandparents

John Bradley was the eldest son of James & Helen Bradley. He had 5 brothers and 2 sisters that followed him in quick succession. 8 children in 10 years! John was sent off to college but hated it. He didn't like studying and if he didn't like something, he found it difficult to retain it. He dropped out of school and returned to Edgartown and joined the police department. He was a good cop. He believed in law and order, and he did whatever it took to enforce the law. He was a handsome man. Bigger than any of the other Bradley's ancestors and siblings alike. He was over 6'2" tall and weighed 225 pounds. He worked out regularly. He lifted weights and ran track during school and was still a weekend runner into his 40s. He met a local girl named **Amanda O'Malley** when he was about 23 or 24 years old. She was a nurse at the local hospital. She was tall, slender and had the most beautiful auburn color hair he'd ever seen. She had bright blue eyes that twinkled when she found something humorous. She had a lovely lilt to her voice when she spoke. Probably because her parents were Irish immigrants and spoke Gaelic at home. He fell head over heels for Amanda in about the first 5 minutes of meeting her. He invited her to dinner; she turned him down. He invited her to lunch; she turned him down. After being turned down so many times he finally asked her point blank why she didn't like him. "I like you just fine, John Bradley," she said. Where'd you get the idea I didn't like you?" "You won't dine with me, he said, no matter how many times I ask." "Well, she said, not one time have you mentioned meeting my parents and asking to court me. What kinda' girl do you take me for?" John apologized for having overlooked this matter and asked if he might have her home address so he could talk with her parents. She gladly gave him the address and told him she'd be off duty tomorrow night at 5pm sharp. If he were to show up at her home and her parents were satisfied with the likes of him then he could buy her supper. John showed up on her doorstep promptly at 5:30 giving her time to get off shift and get home. Her father answered the door and invited him in. He introduced himself to her parents and her two brothers and voiced his hopes that he might court their daughter. Her father asked what his intentions were, and John answered without hesitation that he'd like to buy her dinner tonight and then get her a ring and ask her to be his wife. Her parents couldn't help but smile at the quick response but liked the young man for his honesty. They gave John their blessings to court their daughter and her brothers reminded him that she was a good girl; a good Catholic girl and that there'd be no messing around, or they would come to find him. He told them that he was an honorable man; a police officer and promised to be the gentleman that she deserved. They were married 2 months later. To this union one son and three daughters were born. They named the baby boy Gordon and they doted on him all their lives. He was a wonderful boy and an even more wonderful man. Their daughters were Mary Margaret (called Meg) who died when she was just 20 years old, Sarah Jane and Savannah Jo were the twin girls. Their marriage was a happy one that was full of laughter. Amanda stopped working full time when Gordon was born. She would occasionally sub for someone's vacation or illness but loved being home with her son. Her husband built them a beautiful home just a few blocks from the house he'd grown up in. He always fought to be independent in all things.

GORDON AND REBECCA (Athearn) BRADLEY –
Amanda's parents

Gordon Bradley was the only son of John and Amanda Bradley. His parents doted on him, and he was a very happy child. He loved school, church, his friends, his family and most of all, he loved Edgartown. He excelled at school and received high marks and was presented with several scholarships that would more than pay for his tuition at Boston University. While at University he met Rebecca Athearn of Tisbury. They dated off and on and then became acquainted again after graduation. They married soon after. Gordon excelled at the police department and was soon a detective. He continued to move up through the ranks and was Chief of Police for 15 years when he retired. Gordon was a solid 6-foot tall, never weighing more than 200 pounds. He was physically fit and worked out most of his life. He had dark auburn hair, like his mother, and dark brown eyes like his father. He had a bit of an Irish temperament inasmuch as he could be very jovial or very moody. His wife could bring out these moods without much work on her part.

Rebecca Athearn was a spoiled, precocious child who grew up with the very best of everything. Even though she was spoiled she still was a hard worker. She was determined to always get the best grades all through school. She was class president, home coming queen, head cheerleader, and valedictorian graduating at age 16. She entered Boston University on a full scholarship and told her parents that she would work at the library to pay for her books if they paid her housing expenses. She graduated from Boston U with a 4.0 and a BS in Business Administration. Again, she was a valedictorian at graduation. She entered Harvard law and passed the bar at age 21-1/2 years. She returned to Tisbury and hung out her shingle with the intent of practicing business law. The Prosecuting Attorney's office in Edgartown contacted her before that shingle was hung and asked that she join their fight against crime. She was reacquainted with the handsome police officer that she had met in college, and he proceeded to court her until she finally agreed to marry him. She climbed every ladder put in front of her and at age 37 was District Attorney for Dukes County. Her career suffered a slight bump when they discovered she was pregnant. This had been nothing they had planned and frankly, nothing they had wanted. However, it was too late to do anything about it by the time it was discovered. Amanda Kay was born in December and from birth was the image of her mother-in-law. They hired a wonderful live-in nanny who subbed as a housekeeper as well. She raised Amanda to be a lovely young woman.

There! That covers the Bradley side. Now I just need to collect the Athearn side. I decided I'd work on that tomorrow evening.

I picked up the cat, much against her liking, and went upstairs. I really needed to soak in a tub of hot, bubbly water and think things through. I have a habit of looking up and down the neighborhood each evening. When I see houses are dark, I know that my neighbors are away or already in bed for the night. I'm close to my neighbors and they know that I keep an eye on them. Last week I had already done my block check and was aware that Mrs. Brice was out of town visiting the family. I had poured myself a cup of tea and just happened to look out the window and saw that a light had come on at her house. I knew it wasn't her, so I was both concerned and curious. I threw on a jacket and walked across to have a look. I knocked on her door, but nobody answered. I started to walk around to the back yard to see where exactly that the light was coming from when a man burst out of the back door and went careening across the back yard, over the fence, and out of sight. I called 911 and reported the incident and they arrived shortly thereafter to investigate. I phoned Mrs. Brice telling her what had occurred, and she came home the next day to speak with the police. After a thorough search through her home, she assured the police that she could find nothing missing. The perpetrator had broken the glass on the back door to gain entrance into the house. I called a handyman to come and repair the door for her. I had, after all, grown up across the street from her, her parents and her children. My great grandparents had built the house that I'm living in and when they died my parents moved in and raised me there. My grandparents had a house about 3 blocks south of me that remains in the family trust. When you grow up seeing these people every day you care for them as if they were your own family. Thinking that was the end of that, I put the incident in the back of my mind.

Early next morning I arrived at my office to find Dolly already there, with her pretty smile, the coffee made and my mail on the desk waiting for me. She is such a jewel. I was so very fortunate to have hired her when she was in "high demand". Dolly is 55 years old and in olden times would have been considered an "old maid". She taught school for several years until she became disenchanted with the inability to really teach children rather than just babysitting them every day while their parents played. She is very dedicated, very thorough, a wonderful administrator, and my right arm. I went through the mail, separating out the bills from the junk, and ran across one envelope that had no return address. The address was printed, all caps and marked "confidential" to me. I found that rather odd but opened it to see who had sent it. There was a single piece of white paper with red block printing that read, "Mind Your Own Business or Else!" Or else, what? My first thoughts were how bizarre this seemed, and the next thought was fear. I told Dolly that I wasn't feeling well and was going home. Dolly patted me saying, "You look terrible. Drink some tea and get better."

Rather than going home I went to the nearest police station where I asked to see my good friend, Sgt. Adler. He was aware of the break-in across the street from me and I was terrified that the letter and that occurrence were somehow related. I was told that he was off-site but if I wanted to leave a message, he would call me when he returned. I gave the desk officer my card and left. I thought about the sergeant on my way home. I met him when I was a child. His father and mine were both police officers and had worked together. He is about 10 years older than I but has always been very kind to me. He has such a pleasant demeanor. You just immediately know that he is going to help in whatever way that he can. He's a stocky built man whose probably about 5'9" tall with a thick head of cold black hair and kind brown eyes that tend to twinkle. He is truly such a nice person to call a friend.

I walked into the house, took off my shoes and headed to the kitchen for a cold glass of water. The cat (whose name is Precious, but she doesn't come to it) was curled up in her regular spot on the couch. She eyed me once and then pretended that I was invisible. She had her food and her couch, what more could she want? I poured my water and sat down at the table with my computer. I checked my messages and replied where needed. My phone rang and I saw that it was Sgt. Adler calling. I explained about the letter that I had received, and he told me he'd see me shortly. I finished my water and anxiously awaited his arrival.

About ten minutes later the doorbell rang and it was Sgt. Adler. We went into the living room, moved Precious and I showed him the letter that I had received. After scanning the contents, he asked if he could take it with him. "Of course," I told him. He was looking very sternly at me before saying anything at all. "You need to be very careful, Amanda. Whoever sent you this note knows good and well that you were the one that called the police." I started to comment, but he stopped me. "People in this neighborhood know that you watch out for everyone; you always have. If you weren't so aware of every person's coming and goings, you wouldn't have noticed a light from across the street that hadn't been there 5 minutes before." I was listening to what Sgt. Adler had to say, but at the same time I was brushing his words aside as always. Someone must watch out for their neighbors, don't they? I assured him that I would be careful and cautious. I did remind him, however, that if I hadn't seen that light that there was every chance that Mrs. Brice would have come home and discovered him there. God only knows what would have happened then! "Besides, I asked him, what was the burglar looking for? Did they have any leads on who he was or what he wanted with that sweet little old woman?" I walked Sgt. Adler to the door and bid him goodbye. I again assured him I'd be careful and would let him know if anything else happened. I made myself comfortable on the sofa, with Precious at my side, and began my search through the family albums for the Athearn side of the family.

Amanda's Maternal 2x GREAT GRANDPARENTS

ALFRED ATHEARN, farmer. He married Minerva Schmidt. Together they farmed family land. There aren't many documented records about how he came to own the land, but it is assumed that his father had quit claimed the land or inherited it from his father. He was a good Christian man who loved to read the bible to his wife and children at night around the fireplace. He loved to sing and taught many songs to the children.

Minerva's family were German immigrants. She was short in stature and rather round. Not really what you'd call pretty but had a comely appearance. She was a good and dutiful wife and she doted on her 4 children. She kept a clean home and was a good cook and baker.

Amanda's Maternal GREAT GRANDPARENTS

TENNISON ATHEARN, train conductor. He married Lucinda Smith. Tennison had a dream of traveling the world. He had been raised on a local farm the oldest of 4 children. He traveled to Boston after graduating from middle school and got a job at the train yard. He worked his way up to the conductor. Tennison lived a long life, most of which was without his beloved wife.

Lucinda was from Boston. She was a quiet girl; an only child born to older parents. She met Tennison through family friends and they began courting. He proposed marriage in the fall, and they married in the spring of the following year. She and Tennison had one son, Benjamin, born two years after they married. She was thrilled with her son! She took ill the winter following her son's 5th birthday and passed away on New Year's Day.

Amanda's Maternal GRANDPARENTS

BENJAMIN ATHEARN, lawyer, was married to Linda Stoller. Benjamin grew up with his aunt and uncle caring for him. His mother died when he was only 5 years old and his father was a conductor on the MBTA, which was a commuter train between Boston and Maine. He was gone a lot and so his relationship with his son was not good. Benjamin was very bright and did well in school. He could remember his mother reading to him day and night when he was just a small lad. He worked all through middle school and high school and saved every penny for college. He received several scholarships that helped to pay his tuition. He passed the Massachusetts Bar. He had been courting Linda Stoller and proposed marriage. After marrying they moved back to Benjamin's hometown of Tisbury where they lived until they passed away.

Amanda's PARENTS

REBECCA ATHEARN, lawyer, District Attorney was married to Gordon Bradley.

There, that should give the board what they need for my contribution to the event. I'm tired, so I believe that I'll take a bubble bath and go off to bed. It has been a less than wonderful day anyway.

Chapter 2

My alarm went off at 6am as usual. Up, shower, dress, and out the door by 7am to meet my normal busy day. I checked my daytimer while the car warmed up to see if I had any clients coming in today, but the schedule looks clear. That's good because I can get some work done. My business had stayed very busy since my return to Edgartown four years before. After graduating from high school, I had, much to my parents' objection, applied and been accepted at the University of Illinois in Chicago where I planned to get a degree in business. After graduating I spent the next two years at John Marshall Law School. My idea was to specialize in Estate Law and stay in the greater Chicago area. I hung out my shingle and spent the next 10 years doing exactly that in a city that I'd grown to love. Chicago had layers of flavors from the different ethnic groups that just captured my heart. People were born, lived, married, had children and died within a block of their entire family. It never occurred to them to move away from the warm embrace and comfort of all those who loved them. I've always been a solitude person. It isn't that I don't like to socialize; I do. It is more that my thoughts are buried in what I do and what needs to be done. I haven't dated much, not even in college. I had a boyfriend for a while in high school, but nothing serious. Then my scholarship for my college tuition was dependent upon my getting the best grades that I could. My parents offered to help with tuition and the extras, but I wanted to do as much as I could on my own. I worked part time in the library three evenings a week and I waitressed at the campus deli Saturday mornings. The rest of the time was spent studying or in class. Everything was going as planned until I received the phone call saying that my parents had both died in a car crash. Being the only child and sole heir to their estate, I packed up my business and my house and headed home to Edgartown. If you've ever visited Martha's Vineyard, you know that both Edgartown and Tisbury are the two local communities. I was born and raised there and both of my parents, their parents, and their grandparents were born and raised there also. Long story short, I wasn't very popular when I decided to move away. It wasn't that I didn't love my parents or enjoy being with them because I did. I just found that being an only child of a mother who was an over-achiever and extremely successful made it necessary for me to *prove myself.* My parents probably knew this about me even though we never spoke of it out loud. My office now is downtown Edgartown and has finally, after nearly 4 years, been accepted by the townspeople. I am now a thriving Estate Attorney with 18 regular clients that keep me very busy. My mother, the former D.A. for our county, might not have been as thrilled as I was.

Three days later there were police cars lining the street, sirens blasting, and chaos everywhere. Mrs. Brice's daughter, Lois, had come to pick her mother up for their lunch date so they could talk about her visit with her cousin Charlotte who lived in Boston. When she didn't answer the knock on the door, Lois let herself in with her key. Her mother was found in the kitchen, very dead. There were no signs of forced entry, and nothing seemed to be disturbed. The note I had received took on a whole new meaning.

Chapter 3

I spent the morning cleaning. I tend to clean and rearrange furniture when I'm stressed, and I was very stressed. About 10am I tried to call Lois to ask if there was anything I could do to help. She was very curt and simply told me that she didn't need any help from me. Hanging up the phone I felt, well, shocked. What had I done that upset her so? This puzzle was growing larger by the minute. I finished my cleaning, had a bite of lunch, and went to shower and dress. I wanted to stop by my office and see if anything was new there. I hadn't heard anything from Dolly so I thought I could just check phone messages and return any calls that I needed to.

I unlocked my office door and immediately felt uneasy. It was Saturday so Dolly would not have been in. I walked back toward my office and came to an abrupt stop. The file cabinets were on their sides and paper was strewn everywhere. Stopping only to dial 911 I then headed out the door. I locked myself in my car where I waited for the police. The patrolman arrived within minutes, and I gave them the key to enter the building. Sgt. Adler was close behind. He asked me what time I arrived, what I'd found, and what I'd done. I answered all his questions and then promptly burst into tears. I've known this man most all my life and he was happy to lend his shoulder until I regained control. It isn't always easy to be all alone, with no family or close friends. I tend to stay to myself. I always have. Just me and Precious…even though she won't allow anything close to a hug I know she loves me. "What is going on? Why would someone break into my office and go through my filing cabinets? What in the world could they possibly be looking for? And speaking of breaking in, the front door wasn't disturbed. How'd they get in?" Sgt. Adler felt it safe for me to go into the office now, so we went to review the damage. He didn't want me to touch anything until they had checked for fingerprints and photographed the room. He asked that I call Dolly and let her know what had happened and to inform her that he would be stopping by to interview her later today. I called her and the poor lady was just so very upset. She assured me that she would be there to speak with the Sergeant and if I needed anything to let her know. The Sergeant and I talked about me going back home alone. He wasn't happy about the idea but suggested that a patrolman would escort me, check the house, and position himself in front of my house round the clock. Given the way the day was going it sounded like a fine idea to me.

I didn't want to go home. I longed for the warm embrace of my parents and missed them more than even I could imagine. I wanted to run far, far away but I couldn't. I could hear my parents' voices telling me to face it squarely and find out what was going on. I followed the officer to my house and waited until he gave me an all-clear signal. He asked if I'd rather he remain in the house, but I assured him that being out front was fine. I reminded him that I have a firearm that is registered, and I'm licensed to carry on my person if I wish, and that right now, I wished. He smiled and told me if I saw or heard anything to flash the lights on and off, and he would be right there. I double checked the back-door lock, the locks on all the windows downstairs and locked the front door behind the patrolman. I went upstairs to check all the windows there and to change into comfortable clothes while I was at it. I discovered as I walked back downstairs that I was starving. I had forgotten to eat all day! I went to the kitchen to make an omelet for me and to find something for Precious.

I checked out my front window to be sure that the patrolman was still there. I went to the door and held up a mug of coffee for him. He seemed both grateful and perturbed. "Thanks for the coffee. I appreciate it. Please don't unlock your door and step outside again for any reason. If you need to leave the house, flash the lights on and off and I, or another patrolman, will respond immediately." I assured him that I would do as I was told. I went and got my coffee and a couple of cookies and went into the living room to watch a little TV. Precious laid down about an inch from me, which is her routine, and settled in to relax while I watched a program. I watched the news and then searched for a movie to take my mind off everything. I browsed through the movie station and found nothing but thrillers which I decided wasn't such a good idea this evening. I finally decided on a home remodel program. The cat and I decided to go to bed right after the 11pm news. Everything seemed ok in and around the house, so I turned off the lights downstairs and headed to bed hoping for a good night's sleep.

Chapter 4

I awoke early and went downstairs to heat the water for coffee. I checked out the front window to be sure a patrol car was still there. It was. I fixed Precious her breakfast, made me coffee and searched through the refrigerator for breakfast. I finally found yogurt and made some toast. I checked my messages while I ate breakfast and then called Dolly to see how she was doing. We visited for a while, and she seemed more relaxed than yesterday. Sgt. Adler had been to see her and assured her that they were keeping a watchful eye on me. She asked if I would be coming into the office on Monday and I admitted that I really didn't know. Nobody had told me one way or the other if I could return to my office. I told her I'd check with Sgt. Adler and get back to her.

I grabbed a quick shower, dressed and headed downstairs to flash my lights on and off for the patrolman at the curb. He came to the door right away and I told him I wanted to go downtown to speak with the Sergeant. He checked the house, upstairs and downstairs, and satisfied that everything seemed alright told me he would follow me to the station. I had called Sgt. Adler told him that I was on my way to see him. When I arrived, the Sergeant met me at the desk and walked me back to their coffee room. "My team", said the Sergeant, "has dusted for fingerprints and taken all the photographs needed and, well, found nothing. We checked the back door which was not disturbed but did find a window that was ajar, so we are assuming he/ they gained entrance through there. I would like you to accompany me to your office and go through the files to see if you can tell what might be missing. Can you do that?" "Of course," I assured him, "that is not a problem." He followed me downtown. We entered my office and I shivered noticeably. Sgt. Adler touched my elbow telling me it would be ok. I watched as he set the filing cabinets back where they belonged, and I began picking up the papers that were strewn everywhere. I started separating the paperwork by subject matter and was then able to start alphabetizing them as that's how we file them. I noted, immediately, that the Brice Family Estate paperwork was missing as was the last will they had me work up and record for them. As I continued my alphabetizing, I also discovered that the Talbott Estate paperwork was missing; Talbott was Mrs. Brice's maiden name. "I just don't get it! What is so important in these papers that would cause someone to break into my office and probably also be the person that murdered Mrs. Brice!" "I'm just so confused", Amanda said. Sgt. Adler asked if I had a copy on the computer or would Dolly have a copy. "I don't, I told him, but Dolly might". I tend to trust my hardcopy that I file but Dolly is the one that types the documents. "I'm going to ask Dolly to meet me here while you're still with me and we will see if we can download the copies from her computer".

I phoned Dolly and explained the situation and she assured me she'd be at the office within the next 20 minutes. While we waited for Dolly to arrive the sergeant and I reviewed what I knew of the family. Mrs. Brice's parents had lived across the street from my great grandparents for several years. Mrs. Brice (her name was Doris) married a boy from Tisbury and moved away for several years, returning with her son and her daughter. Lois, the daughter, lives in Edgartown, but I've not a clue what happened to the son. I remembered telling the sergeant that Lois had been very abrupt to me and told me she needed nothing from me. I found that so very odd. Mrs. Brice had come to see me about 3 months ago wanting to make some changes to her will. We recorded those changes as she directed and reviewed the estate to be sure that nothing had been sold or retired and that nothing new had been added. She assured me that the estate was correct as written. The changes that she wanted recorded were rather odd, but not a problem. She inherited the family home and estate when her parents passed on. At the time her only sibling had already passed away and to her knowledge there were no heirs. About a year ago a man came to see her claiming to be the son of her sister, Rebecca Talbott Connelly. She had listened to his story and found it reasonable. She, being the sweetie that she was, welcomed him into the family with open arms. Her two children, not so much. When she came in wanting the changes, she included him as an equal heir to her estate. He would receive one-third and the other two-thirds would be divided between her two children. The front door buzzer rang, and we went to greet Dolly. Dolly logged onto her computer, found the file in question, and downloaded the contents onto a floppy disc for the sergeant to take with him. We all walked out and locked the office together. Dolly and I decided that coffee and a donut were on the agenda. We bid Sgt. Adler goodbye and headed for the bakery.

Dolly and I sat and looked at one another over our coffee and donuts and tried to make sense of the entire situation. We cried a little and laughed a little but were still feeling in the dark about what had taken place. We decided to try and outline everything from the beginning. Being the good secretary that she is she came equipped with paper and a pen. We wanted to make the outline as simple as possible:

1. The break-in
    a. Was it related?
    b. Were there other similar incidences in the neighborhood that we were unaware of?
2. Lois finding her mother dead in the kitchen.
    a. Did she really find her dead or did she call the police after she killed her?
    b. Why was she so abrupt (she was nasty) to me when I phoned her?
3. Where is Lois' brother? I couldn't even remember his name without researching the will.
4. Where is Mrs. Brice's nephew?
5. How about the estate itself? Are there items there that are valuable that we're not seeing clearly?

We returned to our donuts and sat in silence pondering the outline. "Amanda, do you remember the scandal around Mrs. Brice's husband, Oscar? Perhaps that was while you were living in Chicago and didn't hear the scuttlebutt." I told Dolly that no, I knew nothing about this. Dolly thought for a few minutes and then started to recall the event to the best of her memories. "If I remember correctly, Dolly said, Oscar Brice paid his long-time estranged wife (they never divorced you'll recall) a visit. He wanted the bag of coins that had belonged to his father. She apparently told him that she had thrown everything that reminded her of him in the trash where it belonged. He became enraged and threatened her before stomping out of the house. She had phoned the police and reiterated the conversation to them so there should be a record of it. Perhaps Sgt. Adler could be of assistance? I also recall something about Oscar having been in prison for a couple of years, but I don't remember all the scuttlebutt about that, she said." I had to close my mouth as I'm sure it was hanging open. I knew nothing about this bizarre situation. I told Dolly that I would most definitely phone the sergeant and ask for anything he could find in this case.

I headed out to my car and noticed that my faithful patrolman was sitting at the curb waiting for me. We exchanged greetings and I got in my car to head for home. I needed to stop at the grocery store on my way as I was running low on everything. The patrolman assured me that he would wait at the entrance until I came back out. I wanted to get my shopping done and get home before it got dark outside. I must admit that I wasn't all that keen on entering a dark house given the recent events. I finished shopping, waved at the patrolman and headed to the car. After placing the groceries in the trunk and returning my cart to the cart-thing-a-my-bob I got in the car and headed home. My faithful patrolman helped unload groceries, went to the door with me, entered the house, checked upstairs and downstairs, patted the cat on the head, and bid me good night. I locked the door behind him and went upstairs to find some comfy clothes to put on before putting groceries away. I grabbed my sweats and a tee, changed and headed back downstairs. Precious sat in front of the refrigerator, in the way of course, while I put things away. I found her some special nibbles and she was content. I fixed myself a salad and sautéed some chicken and veggies to go with it. I poured myself a glass of ice-cold white wine, grabbed my plate and headed to the couch. I glanced through a magazine while eating my dinner. I finished my dinner and half of my wine and returned the dishes to the kitchen and filled my glass up while I was there. There were sirens coming from all directions! I went to the window to see if I could find out what was going on. The sirens were coming to a halt in front of my house and policemen were scattering in all directions. There was a knock and a shout at the front door that took at least 10 years off my life. It was Sgt. Adler beating on the door wanting me to open it. I opened the door for him, and he wrapped his arms around me and led me to his car. He paused long enough to say something to one of the officers and then got in and raced away. I was shaking so hard that I thought I was going to come apart. I managed to ask him what was going on! The sergeant said to just be patient and he'd explain shortly. We reached the police station, and he again sheltered me in his arms and led me to the door. Once inside we went to his office, and he went to get us some coffee. Coffee? I needed something stronger than coffee! When he returned, he closed the door and began to explain. "Amanda, the patrolman that was in front of your house saw what looked like a man moving through the bushes across the street. Rather than take any chances he radioed it into the dispatcher immediately. There were 3 squad cars, plus me, that responded to that call. The patrolmen began searching on foot. They apprehended a suspect and were getting ready to transport him downtown when I came and got you. As soon as they have read him his rights and have things in order, we will allow you to view him through the two-way glass in the interrogation room. We'll see if you recognize him. "I don't pretend to understand any of this! I'm scared to death, and I don't even know what I'm afraid of. My life is turning itself upside down and inside out, and frankly, I don't know how much more I can handle. I'm seriously considering packing up and running away; far, far away." And then, of course, I burst into tears again. Poor Sgt. Adler, he's had to comfort me way too often lately.

One of the officers came to the door and told the sergeant that they were ready. I told him that I really didn't believe that I'd have any clue who this person was. Ignoring me, we went down the hall and entered the room next to the interrogation room. I could see the man sitting at the desk. He had his head bent down so I couldn't see his features. The officer interrogating him said something and the man snapped his head upward and I gasped! It was Lois' brother (what's his name?). I hadn't seen him for years but recognized him immediately. Why? What in the world was he looking for? I told Sgt. Adler who he was, and the sergeant told me that a patrolman would see me home. No explanation. No ideas. Just an officer will take you home. As promised the patrolman showed up shortly and escorted me to his waiting squad car. I thought about asking if I could push the siren button but thought better of it. When we reached my house, he went in first, checked every room, window, door, closet, patted the cat and welcomed me in. He assured me that he would be right out front if I needed anything. Don't hesitate to flash the lights off and on and I'll come to the door. I have your extra key so I can let myself in. I thanked him, locked the door behind him, and again burst into tears. I thought about calling Dolly, but it would only upset her more than she already was. I settled myself down on the couch beside Precious and hoped it might be one of those times when she wanted to sit on my lap. Nope! So much for getting affection from my cat. I went upstairs to bed.

Chapter 5

When I awoke early the next morning, I tried to put everything back into my mental outline that Dolly and I had sketched. Was this mysterious bag of coins that important? Would Doris' husband have shared that information with her son? Why can't I remember the boy's name?? Were the father and son in touch with one another? Did Lois know what was going on? With that thought in mind I decided to give her one more call and see if I could break through. After all, we had been friends all through school. She was two years behind me, but we had always been friendly. Rather than putting it off any longer I dialed her number. No answer. I left a message and hoped that she would return the call. I fixed me an omelet and some toast and answered messages while I ate. I watched the news but wasn't really concentrating on it. My phone rang and I gasped and jumped 3-feet off the chair. After collecting my wits, I answered the call. Lois. I thanked her for returning my call and inquired how she was doing. "I've been better, she said, but I guess I'm ok". "Lois, is there anything that I can do to help with arrangements for your mother? I'm happy to do whatever I can to help." She told me that there wouldn't be any formal arrangements as there would be no funeral. As soon as the police released her mother's body, she planned on having her cremated and interned at the columbarium. I asked if her brother was helping her with these plans. "Leonard (that's his name) hasn't been here," she said. She mentioned that she hadn't seen him for years! I didn't divulge the fact that he was sitting in our local jail. I guess he either read about the events in the local paper or on the local news. I figured she'd find out soon enough. Before hanging up I asked if she was upset with me about something. There was a long pause and then she told me that it always seemed that things were good for me and bad for her and she was just tired of it. And she hung up. Well, good old Lois had always been a whiner. It was the world's fault that she was 5'-nothing and slightly round, that her ex-husband had been caught red-handed cavorting with his secretary and left her without ever looking back. Wow, what do I make of that?

I need to get out of this house! I needed to go for a run, go shopping, go to lunch, anything other than sit here and wait – for what? I called Sgt. Adler and pled my case. Reluctantly he agreed. Leonard had been released after questioning him and coming up with nothing. He had an alibi for the date of the break-in and an alibi for his mother's murder. He was aware of both, so it was curious where he was getting his information from. When I told the sergeant that Lois didn't even know he was in town he was further perplexed. "Be careful. Be watchful. If you see anything suspicious or suspect something being out of sync," said the sergeant, "I want you to call me. You have my private number, and I expect you to use it." I assured him that I would do that. I went to shower and dress for my outing. He still didn't want me going into the office so casual was appropriate. I made all the calls alerting my clients of the situation. I had received a couple of calls and courtesy messages, and everyone seemed to be alright at the time. I fed the cat, checked that I had everything, and headed out the door after flashing the lights on and off as I was directed. I noticed that the patrolman was still out front. I flashed the lights as I'd been told to do and then told the patrolman that I was leaving and would return later. He assured me that he would just follow me at a discreet distance to ensure that I was okay.

Both Edgartown and Tisbury have lots of small, locally owned shops. There are also some wonderful art galleries. Edgartown had once been a booming whaling port, so the marina still offers shops for water sports and good restaurants. I needed a couple of birthday gifts for friends so decided to try West Tisbury first. It's about 9 miles, as the crow flies, from my house. I parked near the shops that I was familiar with and set out on my shopping spree. I noticed that the patrolman was parked in the next block. I secured my purchases and put them into the car, locked it, and started out on foot for the Black Dog Tavern down by the marina. They have the best sandwiches and iced-cold beer known to man. I had gone to school with a couple of the waitstaff there so might find someone to catch up with and visit with while I ate lunch. It was a beautiful autumn day, perfect for a walk. The leaves were starting to turn, and the air smelled fresh, albeit fishy as well. When I got to the Black Dog, I saw that my friend Patty was working. I greeted her and she said she had just gotten off shift having done breakfast that morning. I asked her if she had time to have a bite with me and she happily agreed that she did. We caught up on her parents, her husband and kids, and any news that I had missed out on. I didn't feel like sharing my story. It wasn't that it was a big secret, but it was so disjointed that it would take more energy to unravel it than I have now. I truly enjoyed my visit with Patty and my wonderful lunch. I had scarfed down a bowl of Quahog Chowder and two of their delicious Crab Cakes. Patty and I bid each other goodbye, and I headed back to my car. I truly felt revived by my outing and was ready to head home. I saw that my trusty patrolman was still watching over me. I used the phone booth on the corner to call Dolly to see if anything was new on her end. She answered on the first ring and told me she was going stir-crazy. "I know, I felt the same way! I asked the sergeant to let me run free for the day and he agreed. She asked if I knew when the office would be available again, but I didn't have an answer for her. I assured her that I would find out and get back to her. I drove home, stopping for gas and a few things at the local grocer on the way. When I got home the patrolman pulled in behind me and met me in the front yard. He went to do his rounds through the house. He came back with a worried look and my cat in his arms ushered me to his patrol car and was on his radio to someone as he pulled away. When he got off the radio, he told me that the house had been ransacked, and he was taking me to the police station where the sergeant would meet me. I sat there stroking Precious, who seemed ok with it now, as the tears ran down my face. My day had been so wonderful and now it was ruined. I couldn't even go home. The sergeant met me at the curb outside the station and helped me to collect my things, the cat, and guided me to his car. He had already called his wife and was taking me to his house until we could sort through this mess.

When we arrived at the sergeant's home we were greeted by his sweet wife, Lucy. I really didn't know her very well but had been acquainted with her since my return to Edgartown. My first impression of her was that she matched the sergeant to a tee. She was barely 5-foot tall, very petite, with beautiful, shiny black hair and dancing brown eyes. Her mother, I know, was Asian and those features were just gorgeous on Lucy. I thanked her for her generosity in taking me in. I apologized saying that I must look a fright, and I was sure that my eyes were swollen and red-rimmed from crying. She welcomed me in and decided, without asking, that a cold glass of wine was preferable to coffee or tea. I gladly accepted it and apologized for bringing the cat. She assured me that they loved animals and that she had already fixed Precious a bed and a potty. I'm quite sure that Precious will be more spoiled than normal in short order. The three of us sat down in the living room and discussed the issue at hand. Nothing made any sense. What in the world could anyone be looking for, first in my office, and now, my home? While we pondered that thought we watched while Precious checked out the living room and settled on the large pillow next to the fireplace. Truly this cat is one of a kind. The sergeant, who kept trying to get me to call him David, felt strongly that Mrs. Brice's last will had something to do with this situation. When we downloaded the will and estate listing from Dolly's computer, I also copied it onto a floppy disc for me. I asked if they had a computer so that we might upload the file and look through it. The sergeant went to his office and turned on the computer and placed chairs around the desk so we could all see. I finished off my glass of wine and begged for another. Lucy smiled and refilled my glass with more wine. We all went into the office, and I uploaded the file. I was perfectly comfortable sharing this private information with Lucy Adler. Lucy is the current paralegal for the most prestigious law firm in Edgartown. She understands the need for confidentiality. I remember being grateful that I hadn't set anything down when I was waylaid by the patrolman. I had my purse, my bag of groceries, and my birthday gifts with me. We read through the opening statement and the various bequest in the will. There really wasn't anything unusual. Mrs. Brice named her two children and her nephew as equal heirs, each to get one-third of the life insurance money, anything in the checking and savings accounts, her two CDs and small investment funds that she had. Further they would equally share in either the distribution of the real property in the estate or they would jointly decide to auction the items and share in the proceeds. Mrs. Brice had a couple of small bequests; the lady that cleaned her house, her gardener, and two close friends should she precede them in death. Those bequests totaled less than $5000 combined. There was a clause in the will that bestowed $1.00 on her husband and had the language necessary to ensure that he could not contest the will. After completing the reading of the Will, we all agreed that there was nothing unusual about the contents. I, as the administrator, would be expected to contact the insurance company requesting the funds be released to the estate. Further I would contact the banks and investment firms requesting the same be done with those funds. I have thirty days in which to make these requests. I hadn't done them yet because the M.E. had not released the body and therefore, I had no death certificate to accompany my requests.

We decided to print out the estate listing and retire to the living room. I didn't need more wine, but I discovered I was starving. I had not had the opportunity to have dinner before being waylaid from my home. I'm not usually so blunt but I decided to just fess up and tell Lucy I was hungry. She laughed out loud and told me that they were probably all starving as she and the sergeant hadn't eaten either. I took the grocery sack into the kitchen and unloaded its contents for Lucy to see if something would go with whatever she had already planned. I had lots of veggies that would make a super salad which I volunteered to make. I threw together some homemade dressing for the salad and set the table. Lucy had chicken breast ready for dinner, so she cut them up and made stir fry to go with the salad. Fabulous!

My favorite dinner. We all ate hungrily and then the three of us did the dishes and put on a pot of coffee to go with the berry pie that she had made earlier in the day.

We retired to the living room, and I handed out a copy of the estate listing to each person. We went through the listing item by item. Each piece on the listing was valued. The listing began with her home, her vacation condo, her household furnishings in both residences, her personal jewelry, clothing and miscellaneous belongings. After that there was a listing of any/all artifacts, paintings, sculptures, that she had in her possession. There were three items that were underlined in double-bold lines that were to be given as bequests, separate from those in the Will. There was a painting that had hung in her living room for as many years as I could remember. That was valued at $8000, and she wanted it to go to her cousin, Doreen in Iowa. Next there was a large antique vase valued at $3500 that she wanted her sister-in-law (her husband's sister), Matilda Brice, to have. I didn't see a reference to that person's address, so I'd need to deal with that later. The third item was rather strange. It was described as a ***personal journal*** that was locked in her safe deposit box at a bank in Boston. It was to be retrieved by the Administrator (me) and delivered in person to John Sheridan, Attorney at Law, and his Boston address was listed along with a telephone number. There was no value listed for this item. BINGO! We have a winner. This must be what the perpetrator was hunting. I don't know why I had never looked through this listing before now. I usually give the client the necessary forms and ask them to list their belongings, designate any that are to be bestowed on family or friends, have the items valued by a certified firm, and return the list to me to go with their Wills. It was late and Lucy suggested that we all try to get a good night's sleep. She felt that the next couple of days were going to be busy ones. Sergeant Adler said that he would call Mr. Sheridan in the morning and make an appointment for the three of us to meet. He also said that while he did that, I would need to call the bank in Boston and advise them that I was coming in to retrieve the contents of the safety deposit box.

Lucy showed me to the guest room where she had laid out a beautiful gown and robe for me. She pointed me in the direction of the guest bath, and I found it full of everything that I would need. The sergeant asked that I give him a list of the personal items and clothing that I would need for the next couple of days and that he and a policewoman would go to my home and get those things for me. I jotted down the list and he bid me good night. Lucy hugged me and assured me that everything was going to be okay. I went in the bath and filled the tub with beautiful, fragrant scents. I soaked in the tub and tried to put things into order in my head. I'm unaccustomed to feeling totally out of control. It just isn't the way I live or work. I tried to think through this mysterious personal journal and what it might contain. I finished up my bath, towel dried my hair and headed off to that lovely, snuggly looking bed. I was asleep right after my head hit the pillow.

Chapter 6

I awoke early the next morning as usual and when I stepped outside my door there was a stack of items from my house that the sergeant had retrieved for me. I went into the shower, got dressed and headed downstairs to find a cup of coffee. The sergeant and Lucy were in the kitchen and had breakfast ready. Lucy had already fed the cat who glared at me in her normal way. We ate a lovely breakfast of scones, jam and coffee and the sergeant asked that I make the call to the bank so we could go there first. I found the number on the estate listing and called the bank. I identified myself and my position and told them that I would need access to the safe deposit box. They gave me a list of the credentials necessary for me to gain access and I thanked them and hung up. I called the M.E. and told him I needed some type of death certificate or legal looking paperwork to go with me. He told me to come by within the next 30 minutes to pick it up. The sergeant had already called the lawyer and we were to meet him at 2pm tomorrow, giving us plenty of time today at the bank and to research what we find. Lucy is going with us as this is a bit of a trip and better done in two days than one. It's about 17 miles from Edgartown to Martha's Vineyard where we board the ferry for a 45-minute trip to Wood Hole. From Wood Hole you have about another 80 miles to Boston city limits. Lucy made hotel reservations for all of us, packed us a snack for the trip, fed the cat and arranged for her neighbor to come and feed Precious tomorrow. Pretty much this wonderful lady thought of everything! We stopped at the M.E.'s office, picked up the paperwork needed, and we were off. I called Dolly and let her know that I was unavailable for the next 3 days.

Our trip was lovely. The fall colors and light wind were just perfect for traveling. The sergeant found the bank easily and we went in to find the officer I had spoken with earlier. We presented our required paperwork and Sgt. Adler presented his police shield and we were asked to wait for just a few minutes while they readied the vault for us. Lucy waited in the lobby while the sergeant and I entered the safe deposit vault. We were handed the key needed to access the box and they left, closing the door behind them. We opened the box and slid it out so we could set it on the table and review its content more comfortably. There was Mrs. Brice's passport, a copy of her Last Will & Testament that I had given her, several bank statements and bank books, and toward the bottom of all this was *the* journal. The journal was like a ledger book and quite old at first glance. "I really don't know what I was expecting," I told the sergeant. He opened it up and discovered that the first entry was over 40 years old. "Wouldn't this have been when they were first married?" asked the sergeant. "Yes, I said, I'm going to be 40 this year and Lois is two years younger than I." We gathered the contents and put them into an envelope that the sergeant had the good sense to bring with him. We put the box back into its rack, closed and locked it and returned the key to the bank officer. We collected Lucy from the lobby and headed to our hotel. We were all hungry as we hadn't had our lunch yet. We checked in, freshened up and met in the hotel café. The sergeant asked how I wanted to proceed. I considered the question and decided that we should meet in my room which had a sitting area and go through the journal together. "Would you consider ordering dinner to be delivered to our room? I asked, and we can just work through the evening without interruption." They agreed that this seemed a good idea. We relaxed and enjoyed our much-needed lunch. It was close to 3pm when we finished up. We decided that we would break until 4:30pm and then they would come to my room. I returned to my room to freshen up for our meeting. About 4:15pm I ordered a pitcher of ice water, some lemon slices, a pot of coffee and a pot of hot water for tea. The Adlers arrived promptly at 4:30pm and we situated ourselves around the table that was in my sitting room. The sergeant asked that I begin reading aloud from the journal. Before doing so I noted that the journal was kept beginning 40 years earlier and ended just two years ago. I began reading the different entries which seemed to be summaries of a happy bride's day. As it progressed there was the announcement of the coming baby, the baby's arrival (Lois) and all the advancements of that baby. Then the next important news was the announcement of another baby. What's-his-name (why can't I remember this guy's name?) arrived and there were all the entries surrounding his advance until he turned about 18 months old. The entries seemed to take on a whole new look to them. Mrs. Brice's husband was going to the bars of the evening and returning in the wee hours of the morning drunk and disheveled. Not long after that he stopped coming home at all, except to ask for money. Mrs. Brice wrote that she had talked with her parents who wanted her to pack up and come home, but she told them she wanted to try and hang in a bit longer in hopes that things would change. There seemed to be a gap in the journal and then it started up again. Mrs. Brice's husband had gotten in with a group of bad people. They knew that his in-laws lived in Edgartown and therefore assumed they had money. He started asking her a bunch of questions about her family and her neighbors and she became very suspicious of him. She wrote that her parents told her about some break-ins in their neighborhood and that valuable artwork and sculptures had been stolen. Mrs. Brice questioned her husband about this, but he swore he knew nothing about the thefts. He also threatened her if she didn't stop badgering him and getting into his personal business. One evening, about two weeks after that incidence, she wrote that a man had come to the door looking for her husband. He identified himself as Jack Sheridan. All three of us looked at one another but nobody spoke. I blurted out, "John Sheridan's what – son, brother?" I looked for where I'd left off in reading the journal. The next few entries were about the children and then about 20 or so years ago she wrote that her husband came home and had obviously been badly beaten. She had told him she'd take him to the hospital, but he refused saying *they would kill him.* He told her that he had gone with Jack and a bunch of his cronies out to Edgartown. He said that they had broken into one of the large mansions and that the owners had come home, and that Jack had shot them. I quite literally dropped the journal and abruptly stood up! What in the world? This was reading like a soap box opera. The sergeant and I both decided that it was time to break for dinner and wine was most definitely on the menu. Lucy and I scanned the menu and called down to room service. I remembered there was wine in the refrigerator in my sitting room, so we didn't have to wait for that. We all sat quietly with our own thoughts while waiting for dinner.

The young man from room service wheeled in the cart filled with beautiful goodies. We had ordered their famous prime rib which came with baked potatoes, roasted asparagus, rolls and butter. They had presented it family style so that we could each partake of whatever we wanted. There was a beautiful green salad also. We ate in silence; each with our own thoughts. After dinner we had Amaretto and poured hot coffee to go with it. There was a plate of lovely chocolates to choose from for dessert. We headed back to the journal. Lucy said she'd be happy to begin reading and give my voice a break. I had marked the spot where we left off so we could easily return to it. Lucy began reading that the next day the police were at her door looking for her husband. He was hiding in the back room, but they had a warrant and found him without much trouble. He was arrested and taken away. She wrote that she was frantic. She called her parents, and her father came the next morning to try and sort through this mess with her. Her father arrived and she told him everything she knew of the ordeal. He confirmed that the Bartletts had, indeed, been killed by intruders. Their house was directly behind Mr. and Mrs. Hunter's house. My cul-de-sac consists of 9 homes that cover 5 acres of property on both sides of the street. The Bartlett's Street was very similar in layout to our block. The house was pretty much stripped of artwork, sculptures, coins, silver, and whatever money could be found. Mrs. Brice's father, Henry Talbott, told her to dress herself and the children because they were going to the police station. She did as he asked, and they left for downtown. It was several days later before she wrote in her journal again. When she did write it was to reiterate their findings at the police station. Her husband, Jack Sheridan and two others had been arrested for breaking and entering, grand larceny, and two counts of second-degree murder. They had been arraigned the morning after they were arrested and were being held without bond. Mrs. Brice wrote that she had packed up all hers and the children's belongings, closed the door behind her, and gone home with her father. There was a gap in the journal of several months. In fact, it was Christmastime when she wrote again. She wrote that Oscar had turned state evidence against Jack Sheridan for killing the Bartletts in exchange for his freedom, and that Jack was serving his time in the State Penitentiary. The other two members of the gang were only guilty of breaking and entering and theft. Oscar was out of jail and showed up on her parents' front porch. Her father answered the door and told his son-in-law that he was to get off his property, never contact his daughter or grandchildren again. He told him that he would do him bodily harm should he trespass again. Mr. Brice turned on his heels and left. We decided to take a break from reading any more of the journal. We all felt like we needed to get some fresh air and try to relax after such a disturbing read. The hotel has a beautiful courtyard, so we decided to check it out. We ordered coffee and split a piece of carrot cake and relaxed. We talked about family and avoided anything to do with Mrs. Brice and her journal. After we had our coffee and listened to the trio that was performing in the courtyard we retired to our rooms, we planned to have breakfast in my sitting room in the morning, and finish going through the journal. That way we would be prepared for whatever Mr. John Sheridan might have to say.

Chapter 7

Early next morning the Adlers arrived followed by room service with the breakfast fare. I ordered scrambled eggs, crisp bacon, toast and marmalade. There was also coffee, tea, and orange juice to accompany it. We ate our breakfast and then immediately returned to the journal. I took charge of reading again and we found that there was a lapse in the journal of about 2 years. She wrote that her husband had called her begging to see the children. Her parents were in Europe, and she had agreed to a short meeting in a nearby park. He showed up on time and played with the children for a few minutes. He told her he had gotten a job and was trying to do the best he could. She wrote that he had told her he still loved her and wished they could start over. She had told him that it was over between them and that she could never trust him again. He had explained that he was between places to live and asked if he could just store some of his stuff in her basement or garage. Reluctantly, she agreed. She told him that it could only be for no more than one month as her parents would be returning, and her father would have a fit. She wrote that he told her he'd get his stuff together and bring it to the house the next day. The next day, as promised, he showed up with a couple of boxes to store. He thanked her and left without even a backward glance toward his children.

She wrote that she had no way to contact him. He didn't return as promised and her parents were coming home. She was frantic and angry. She had gone through the boxes and found nothing except a bag of coins that was of any value. She put the bag of coins in her bedroom bureau and took the rest of the contents to the goodwill.

She wrote in her journal, There! Good riddance to you! There were no more entries in the journal for about 10-years. She wrote that Jack Sheridan had contacted her looking for her husband. She was terrified as Jack was supposed to be in prison! She assured him that she had no idea where he was. About two weeks later she wrote that her parent's home was broken into. Their security system had alerted the police who apprehended the intruders. Jack Sheridan was arrested for breaking and entering and attempted burglary. My father was the arresting officer.

There were some newspaper articles in the journal that Jack Sheridan had been sent back to prison to complete his original sentence and an additional 10 years was added on for his current crime. She wrote that the D.A. had presented an excellent case and had asked for the maximum sentence be imposed. As we looked further there were some articles where he had been released on a Work Program about 5 or 6 years ago. There were additional newspaper clippings that showed the wreckage from my parent's automobile accident. There were no written notations after that. I ran to the bathroom and was violently ill. Lucy came to check on me, but I just couldn't respond at that moment. Someone had killed my parents. Is that what those news clippings were hinting at? For what? Why? And now they've killed Mrs. Brice? Who would be next? I really couldn't even think about that. I needed to get some fresh air and try to sort through this. I ran out of the bathroom and out of the door and headed for the elevator. Sgt. Adler was close behind me, but I stepped into the elevator and the door shut before he could stop it. I went outside and just started walking around the block trying to collect my thoughts. My whole world seemed to be spinning out of control.

After walking for a few blocks, I found that I just had to sit down and try to put all of this into order. There was a coffee shop across the street which was perfect. I went in and found a quiet corner booth and ordered coffee and a piece of lemon meringue pie. I've always tended to think better when sugar was available. I tried to recall my parents talking about a case that would have involved Jack Sheridan or Mrs. Brice's parents. They didn't usually talk about "the office" when they were at home but given the date in the journal, I'd have only been about 14 years old when all this took place. I decided the easiest way was to go to the newspaper and surf through the archives for more information. This certainly wasn't going to happen before our 2pm meeting with Mr. John Sheridan. I'm sure by now that Sgt. Adler was probably frantic looking for me. I walked back to the hotel and he was standing there, waiting for me, when I went through the doors. I took one look at him and burst into tears. Seems all I do lately is cry on his shoulder. We got in the elevator and didn't say anything until we reached my room. Lucy was waiting for us with a worried look on her face. We hugged one another and I did my best to try and explain to them what I was feeling. "When I was a young girl, I was so busy with my own life, what was important to me, that I never seemed to take the time to ask my parents how they were." I went on to explain, "I don't feel that I was selfish or spoiled, I was just oblivious to their business lives." "My father, I said, was the typical Irish cop. He was always either laughing or stomping around cussing under his breath. My mother's work was so intense that I never knew exactly what to think of it. She seemed totally devoted to her job and what it entailed. When I graduated from high school and had already received my acceptance to my college of choice, I was frankly relieved to be moving away from the whole ordeal. I loved my parents, but I simply did not want to live my life **like** my parents." I just sat there and held my breath until someone said something. At last, the sergeant just smiled and said, "I know exactly what you mean." He did? Really? I was so relieved. A person just feels so very guilty when something like this happens. The thought that someone would take their lives was just not comprehensible to me. The sergeant reminded me that we needed to get ourselves together and get to our meeting with John Sheridan.

Chapter 8

We met in the lobby and the valet brought the sergeant's car around for us. He had already mapped Mr. Sheridan's address, so we knew where we were going. I was so nervous that I kept clearing my throat until it was sore. We reached our destination and the sergeant and I took the elevator up to the 11th floor for our meeting. Lucy decided to remain in the lobby as she didn't feel that she should be present at the meeting. We entered his offices and told the receptionist who we were. She asked that we please have a seat and she'd let him know that we were here. It wasn't but a couple of minutes until a stately looking lady appeared and asked us to follow her. She introduced herself as Margaret, his secretary, and showed us to the conference room. Mr. John Sheridan entered from a side door moments later. He had a beautiful head of silver-white hair, piercing blue eyes, and a truly lovely smile. He had a mannerism that immediately put you at ease. He shook hands with us and offered his condolences to me on the passing of Doris Brice. I thanked him for his kind words. I usually can start a conversation without difficulty, but I seemed to be at a total loss for words. Mr. Sheridan, who asked that we call him John, seemed to pick up on that and began the conversation for us. John told us that he had met Doris Brice many years ago. Her husband, Oscar, and his son Jack had been involved with one another in some shady, if not illegal, deals. He wanted us to know that he was fully aware that his son was now, and had always been, a scoundrel. John said, "my wife and I have shed many tears and spent countless sleepless nights over the boy, but all for naught." "He is a criminal; a thief at best and probably more." John seemed to age just recanting that story. Doris had found his number and called him asking if they might visit. I hadn't been to Martha's Vineyard in years, so I suggested that we meet in Edgartown over lunch the following week. They met at a local café, found a corner that looked quiet and somewhat private, and she came right to the point. His son had come looking for her husband and shortly thereafter her parents' home was broken into. Jack was caught red-handed and shortly thereafter returned to prison. She had told him about her husband wanting to *store some of his belongings in her parents*. Doris had told John that she went through those boxes when he didn't return as agreed, wanting to see exactly what was in there. There didn't appear to be anything of any value except for a bag of coins. Initially she had placed the bag of coins in her bedroom bureau drawer, but she kept worrying about them being there. She had taken the bag to the backyard and dug a hole next to the doghouse and buried the bag. Feeling better knowing that it was no longer in the house she ceased worrying about it. When her parents' home was broken into and she saw that it was Jack Sheridan that had broken in, she called his father. John said, "Doris had gone out back, dug up the bag of coins, and brought them to me that day. I didn't look through the bag until I got home later that evening. Upon closer scrutiny I discovered a bizarre looking key that was in among the coins. The key was an antique key that I doubted fit anything. I didn't think about it anymore until years later when Doris called me. Doris and I stayed in touch, and she knew to call me anytime she needed to." He recalled that Jack would be released somewhere around a year or so ago. "He called me a couple of times over the years," John said, "and I learned that he was to receive an early release for good behavior. Then I learned that he was released on a Work Order a year after that and was to remain within 5 miles of the prison until February of last year. John remembered that Doris had also received a call from Oscar about that same time. Her husband was missing her, he told her. She fell for his sweet talk and met him at the park near her home. She asked him where he'd been for so long. He admitted that he'd gotten into a scrape and been sent away for 5 years. They talked about the children and current events and then he asked her if she still had that bag of coins that he'd given her to keep for her. She asked him what he meant, and he told her that he had some valuable items stored but he needed that bag of coins to get the key. She told him that she did not know where it was. He told her it was important that she remembered because there was a key in there that was very important to him. He told her that they could run away together; that they would be rich. She assured him that she had no idea of the whereabout and that it would be best if he didn't contact her again. He was very angry, and she was very frightened of what he might do. John said that she called him that evening and told him about the meeting and the conversation. I have a private detective that does work for my firm. I asked him to investigate and see what he could find. He had looked for a month or more but came up empty handed. One of the areas I asked that he investigate were the storage facilities as Oscar had told Doris that he had access to things of value and that they could be rich. There weren't that many storage facilities in the Tisbury/Edgartown area at that time. Our guess was that if that was what the key was for whoever had placed something in storage had not used their real name. Amanda and the sergeant exchanged glances and she pulled the journal out of her bag and handed it to John. She told him that they had gone through each, and every entry and had made notes. The notes were included with the journal. The last entry in the journal pointed to her parents' accident which had caused them to feel that Mrs. Brice had concerns about either Oscar or Jack being involved somehow in that accident. John listened to her and seemed to be trying to collect his thoughts before saying anything. "Amanda, after reading the journal, what do you think happened to Doris? What do you think happened to your parents?" John waited for her response which was slow in coming. Amanda told him that she felt strongly that either Oscar or Jack had broken into Mrs. Brice's home and were responsible for her death. She wasn't sure what to think about her parents' accident as she had only learned of this when reading the journal and hadn't really had a chance to digest the idea of foul play. Sgt. Adler was also slow to respond. He told them that there were no fingerprints, no signs of forced entry, nothing to help them solve Mrs. Brice's homicide. Regarding Amanda's parents' accident he was going to need time to go through the original file and try to ascertain whatever information he could. "Nobody has seen or heard from Oscar Brice", John said, "since Doris saw him last." "Does anyone know any way to get ahold of him?" "I understand that his son was picked up in Edgartown but was not charged with anything." "Might he be involved in some way?" They all agreed that there were lots of unanswered questions and that they would stay in touch with one another. John suggested that he would revisit the idea of a storage facility with his private investigator. He had some ideas on how someone might have secured the storage facility without using their real name. As we were taking our leave, the sergeant suggested to John that he take possession of the bag of coins and the key. John readily agreed.

It was too late to start for home, so we went back to the hotel for the night. Luckily, Lucy had told the front desk that we might need to keep our rooms for another night. We left the car with the valet and went to the hotel bar. We decided that a glass of wine was exactly what we all needed. The sergeant and I brought Lucy current regarding our meeting with John Sheridan. It was Lucy that spoke up saying, "we need to know exactly where both Oscar Brice and Jack Sheridan are!" She looked like she was ready to challenge the pair to fist-a-cuffs. We all agreed that another glass of wine was in order and then we would go to the restaurant and have dinner. I was only mildly familiar with the Boston area and the Adlers were not familiar with it at all so which is why we opted to use the hotel's accommodation rather than searching for another restaurant. The sergeant went to talk with the hostess to see if they could seat us in about half an hour. He came back and told us that they would be ready for us whenever we got there. The hostess seated us at a lovely corner table, and we searched through our menus. I found that I was starving (as usual) and ordered their fish special which happened to be baked Halibut with a citrus sauce. The Adlers love their beef so they both ordered steaks. The food arrived and we all ate hungrily. Lucy had remembered to call her neighbor and ask her to feed poor Precious for one more day. Her neighbor assured us that the adorable kitty was indeed precious, and she'd be happy to do that. I really wonder whose cat they were discussing.

It was still early when we finished dinner and we opted to go listen to the trio in the bar and have dessert and coffee in there. The trio was so good. They played a lot of old classic songs, and it was most enjoyable. We had decided on catching the earliest ferry from Woods Hole to Martha's Vineyard which departed promptly at noon. With an 80 plus mile drive from Boston to Woods Hole we decided on departing at 7:30am. That way if we ran into traffic or construction, we still had time to reach our destination in plenty of time. We told each other good night and headed for our rooms. I had ordered a cup of coffee to take back to my room with me. I sipped on it while I called Dolly to see if there were any messages. Dolly told me that she was worried about me and hoped that all was ok. I let her know my travel schedule and suggested that we have lunch downtown the following day and I'd catch her up. There was a short message from John Sullivan suggesting that his PI might have found the storage facility and that he'd stay in touch. He left the sergeant a message also. I finished answering messages and headed for a hot bath and a warm bed. I was tired, both physically and mentally. The last few days had been exhausting, and I still felt as if I was in a nightmare that I wanted to wake up from. I propped my pillows up and turned on the TV to see if I could catch up on the local news. There didn't seem to be much happening, so I read a few chapters from the novel that I'd been working on for, oh, about a month. I always get drowsy when I read, and tonight was no exception. I'm sure that I'll be asleep as soon as I turn the lights out.

Chapter 9

I awoke at 5:30am, showered and dressed, closed my suitcase and called for a bellman to come and assist me. He was at my door within minutes of hanging up and we headed for the lobby. I suddenly felt uncomfortable and told him to go ahead to the lobby and I'd follow in a few minutes. I'm truly paranoid about everything and everyone. I turned as the elevator closed the doors just in time to catch sight of the Adlers. The sergeant immediately asked me what was wrong. I assured him it was nothing that I was just being paranoid. The fear of getting into an elevator with a person that I didn't know was just something I couldn't do right now. He looked worried but didn't say anything. We all traveled down to the lobby and checked out. The car was waiting for us. The valet loaded the luggage, and we were off for home. It was another lovely day, and the car ride was just what I needed. The sergeant had a sun-top on his car that he had opened letting the fresh, crisp autumn air circulated through the car making us all feel exhilarated. There wasn't very much traffic that early and we didn't run into any construction, so we made Woods Hole just past 9:30am. That left us two and one-half hours before noon sailing to Martha's Vineyard. We decided to play tourist while at Woods Hole, so we set out for the Nobska Point Lighthouse. We walked all over the beautiful grounds surrounding the lighthouse. You could watch the boats come and go in the marina and see where the ferry would come in. There is a beautiful Marina and we walked all over it drinking in the sunshine and the crisp, salty sea air. The time went by way too quickly, so we headed back to the ferry landing to ensure a good space on the boat. The ferry arrived right on time, and we all boarded for

43

the sailing across to Martha's Vineyard. We decided to stop for lunch in downtown Edgartown before going home. I told them how much I loved the food at the Black Dog Saloon, so we headed there. We had a wonderful lunch and a cold beer to top it off. I paid the bill and we headed to the car. The sergeant wanted to go into the station and see what was happening so asked Lucy to drop me off. I was reminded that there would be a patrolman there to check the house before I went in. I thanked him for all he had done, gave him a quick hug, and Lucy and I headed for my house. We apparently beat the patrolman to the house, so we sat outside at the curb and waited for him. He pulled up less than 5 minutes later. He waved and went to check the house for me. He came back out and assured me that all was ok inside. He reminded me that there were still some things out of place following the break-in, but the bulk of the mess had been cleaned up. He helped me in with my luggage and waited until I locked the door securely behind him. I set the security alarm and went to observe the mess. Lucy told me that David would want to bring Precious to me after he got home and freshened up. One or the other of them would call let me know that he was on his way.

I started clearing up what mess was left and cleaning as I went. I heard my message machine pick up and heard the sergeant say he was on his way with Precious. I put a pot of coffee on to cook and waited for him to arrive. While I was waiting, I went through the mail that had arrived while we were gone. I sorted out the bills, read a couple of wedding and baby shower notices, and then found an envelope addressed to me without a return address. I hesitated to open it up as I immediately got a bad feeling about it. There was just a single sheet of paper with block printing on it that read, "You just keep meddling in people's business. This is your FINAL warning to stay out of what does not concern you." The doorbell rang. It was the sergeant.

I went to let him in. I took the cat, who allowed me to cuddle her for one minute, before jumping out of my arms and heading straight to her spot on the couch. I went and poured coffee for the sergeant and myself and handed him the letter and the envelope. He didn't say anything for a moment and then just shook his head. "Amanda," he said, "I just don't know what to make of this. It is obvious that someone knows we are working to solve this case. I'll take this to the lab and check for fingerprints but I'm relatively sure there won't be any." I told him that I was just so tired of the whole thing. He looked tired and concerned and just as confused as I felt. "You can't keep a patrolman assigned to me for the rest of my life, I said. Somewhere along the way this person or people must be caught and dealt with. John indicated in his message that he was going to try again to find out about a storage facility. I don't know if he'll have any luck with it or not. I believe that he was also going to try and find his son." The sergeant said that they were trying to locate both Jack Sheridan and Oscar Brice. The sergeant also felt like maybe he needed to revisit both Lois and Leonard Brice to see if they knew anything that could be helpful. He told me that he had made a couple of inquiries about storage facilities in the area. He found one facility that had been in business far enough back to have perhaps done business with Oscar. He was waiting to hear back. "In the short term, said Sgt. Adler, just keep the security alarm on, the doors and windows locked, and accept the fact that the patrolman is out front." I assured him that I would and thanked him again for his and Lucy's help in all of this. Precious allowed him to scratch her head as he left. Precious and I both decided we were hungry, so I poached a chicken breast for her and scrambled a couple of eggs for me. After we ate both of us retired to the living room to watch TV before calling it a very long day.

I had checked with the sergeant, and he had agreed that I should go about my business in the most normal way possible. I called Dolly and we agreed to meet at Atlantic Fish & Chop House for lunch at noon. I showered and dressed for my outing, flashed my lights on and off, and unmanned the alarm and opened the front door to greet my patrolman. I told him I was going downtown for lunch, stopping at my office, and should be back by 5pm or shortly thereafter. I arrived at the restaurant just moments before Dolly. She greeted me with her wonderful smile and a big hug. We chatted non-stop and thoroughly enjoyed our lunch and time together. I told her that I wanted to stop by the office and pick up some paperwork and she said she wanted to go with me. She followed me to the office and we both went in. It felt so good to get back to the office and a feeling of normalcy. She had a few letters and a brief that she needed to catch up on and I assured her that downloading them to a floppy disc to take with her was fine. I pulled the files that I needed, and we both left the office together. As we were locking up, I noticed Lois' car across the street. I tried to get her attention, waving and yelling hello, but she just seemed to ignore me and drove off. It was such a strange feeling. She and I had never been close pals, but we had, I thought, always been friends. When we were in junior high school and then high school it seemed that she was always a loner. She had a bit of a chip on her shoulder and a tendency to blame everyone for her misgivings. She was very young when her mother brought them back to Edgartown to live. In the beginning her dad would come regularly to see the children and then he just stopped coming around. She seemed to change about that time.

I drove home and my trusty patrolman did his walk-through and assured me all was ok. I grabbed my mail from the box on the porch and went into the kitchen to find a glass of cold white wine. I sat down at the table, browsed through my mail, entered a couple of bills, and drank my wine. My mind kept traveling back to when I was young. When did Lois really change? When did she stop being friendly with me? I kept asking myself these questions but came up with nothing. I couldn't pinpoint a specific time when she changed. I was probably a bit indifferent to her during my last couple of years at home. By then we had nothing in common and I was busy planning my life. I checked my messages and found one from John Sheridan. When I listened to the message it was from Timothy Donaldson. Mr. Donaldson said that he had taken over his father's Private Investigation firm when he retired. Further, Mr. Sheridan had contacted him hoping for assistance in locating either Mr. Oscar Brice or Mr. Jack Sheridan and/or the storage facility in question. He wrote that he would like to meet with me if that was possible in hopes that I could update him on the case. I called and left a message for David Adler and asked if he would be the middleman on my behalf. He responded immediately that he'd be happy to do so and would let me know. It was only a matter of a few minutes until the sergeant called me back saying that he and I had a meeting set up with Mr. Donaldson the next day at noon. It was agreed that I would pay for lunch…

Chapter 10

Tim Donaldson grew up in the suburbs of Boston. He was an only child born to Thomas and Lorraine Donaldson. Tim was a beautiful baby and as he grew became a truly beautiful man. He looked exactly like his father, but his personality was one hundred percent his mother's. He had blue eyes that just danced with mischief. He was very intelligent and excelled at anything he attempted. Tim loved to read, and he wrote wonderful book reports that the teachers all looked forward to reading. He was active in track and field, played basketball and baseball. The girls all pursued Tim but he had little interest. He was somewhat quiet and tended to stay to himself a lot. He had one good friend, Ronny, that was his best friend from kindergarten forward. He had goals. He wanted to be a police officer and later a police detective. His dad had been in Navy Intelligence and then opened a private investigator's service. He worked closely with Tim's mom during their marriage. Tim was just finishing up his education when he received word that his father had suffered a stroke. Without a backward glance Tim gathered up all his belongings and headed home. After his father was released from the hospital the three of them talked about the future. Tim told his dad that he was equipped and ready to take over the business if that was okay with him. His dad worried that he was robbing Tim of his dream, but Tim assured him that PI work was just like being a police detective and this would suit him perfectly. Tim's father worked hard to restore his good health and soon was back to his old self. Tim's mother had started proceedings to shut down her law firm when her husband had his stroke. It took the better part of a year, but she finally helped two of the firm's attorneys to purchase the business. Tom and Lorraine did a bit of travel but mostly they just stayed close to home.

Tim worked hard to provide the best service he could to his dad's existing clientele. It wasn't long before he picked up the four additional clients that he needed to feel financially sound. He made wise investments and was careful with his money. His parents both came from good families that were financially well-off, but he preferred to make his own way whenever possible. He hired a part-time secretary to handle phone calls and billings. Most of his clients were big law firms. John Sheridan was one of his dad's original clients and was still loyal to Tim. He didn't take any of the photos through windows or chase errant husbands. His work was mainly research for law firms who specialize in mergers and acquisitions, or major companies looking to merge or buy out another business. He was billing $550/ hour when John Sheridan asked him to meet with Amanda Bradley in Edgartown.

I awoke when my mental alarm went off but lounged for a while before getting up. Precious was curled up on the end of my bed and even let me cuddle her for a little while. I planned out what I was going to wear to our lunch meeting with Mr. Donaldson. I had been making notes since this whole event started so I would grab those to take with me to the meeting. I got up, showered and pulled a robe on and went downstairs to find coffee and make some toast. Precious was hungry so I fed her while I was at it. It was a beautiful, crisp day so I settled on a black and white coat dress and black pumps to wear to lunch. I pulled my long auburn hair up in a loose ponytail, grabbed my good gold earrings and bracelet and was ready to meet the day. I texted the sergeant (I was so happy to have this new technology) and we agreed to meet at The Grill on Main. They had good food and their booths had high backs, so they were both private and comfortable. I flashed my lights for my patrolman to know I was leaving. He met me at the door, made sure that I set the alarm and locked the door and told me to have a nice time. I told him I'd be back about 3pm or so. I drove downtown, found a good parking place close to the restaurant, checked the time, and got out to wait for the sergeant. Sgt. Adler and possibly the best-looking man I've ever seen were walking toward me. The sergeant had instructed Mr. Donaldson to meet him at the station prior to our lunch date. I greeted the sergeant, whose eyes were twinkling mischievously, and he introduced me to Mr. Donaldson. I shook hands with him and looked into the most beautiful blue eyes. His cold black hair and rather dark ruddy complexion were such a startling contrast to the blue eyes. He was very tall; about 6'3" and very well built. He was wearing a beautifully cut dark gray suit and a white linen shirt that was open at the neck. I'm quite sure that Mr. Donaldson noticed my observation of him but, let's face it, anyone that good looking has been stared at before. I came to my senses, and we all walked into the restaurant. The hostess seated us, and we ordered lemon water while we looked over the menus. The men ordered the lunch steak, and I ordered the fish of the day which was Atlantic Cod. Mr. Donaldson, who insisted I call him Tim, told me about taking over his father's PI firm about 4 years ago. I remembered to pull out the notes that I had collected regarding the case. I had made him a copy so he could review them at his leisure. Tim told us that he was based in Boston where he was born and raised. He had thought many times about relocating but didn't know where or what he'd do. He had studied in Boston and had a degree in Criminal Justice. He had initially wanted to be a police officer or work for one of the alphabet groups out of Washington DC, but his dad had other ideas. Being an only child his allegiance to his family came first. The sergeant brought me up to speed telling me that they were going to visit the storage facility that he had mentioned to me. They had a couple of other leads that they wanted to follow up on. We exchanged pleasant conversation, and the meeting came to an end. I thanked them both for their time and their help with this very upsetting situation. Tim and I shook hands and he and the sergeant walked off to wherever they were parked. I walked back to my car and drove home.

Chapter 11

I spent a leisurely afternoon cleaning the house and doing laundry. It felt wonderful to be doing something constructive rather than sitting around worrying. I had told the sergeant that I was going back into the office on a regular basis starting on Monday morning. I have clients that need my attention and I have things to do. My cell phone was ringing, and I looked at the caller and saw that it was Lucy Adler calling. I picked it up with a cheerful hello. She asked how I was doing and wondered if I would be free for dinner tomorrow evening at about 5:30pm? I told her that I was available and asked what I could bring to the table. "If you really want to bring something, she said, how about dessert?" I told her that she could count on something delicious, and I'd see her tomorrow at 5:30pm. I finished up my chores and started thinking about dinner for Precious and me. I finally settled on a piece of salmon that was one of those frozen dinners. I pulled out one of Madam Cat's chicken breasts and poached it for her. She sat, impatiently, in front of the range while it cooked. Once cooked and cooled and cut up and set before her she seemed content. The microwave was signaling that my dinner was ready as well. I poured a glass of white wine and sat down to enjoy my dinner. I love fish! I really think I could eat it every day without complaint. After I finished eating and cleaning up, I called the bakery and asked if they could prepare one of their delicious Lemon Meringue Tarts and an order of Dipped Strawberries for tomorrow night's dessert.

Today was Thursday and I had all day to get ready for my dinner engagement with the Adlers. I decided I'd stop by the market next to the bakery and pick up some fresh flowers for Lucy on my way to their home. I cleaned a couple of cupboards and did a bit of mending and just really spent my day enjoying my home. There were so many memories there. I could see my parents sitting at the breakfast nook having their morning coffee before they both headed out the door to their important jobs. In those days we had a live-in housekeeper who fed me, took me to school, picked me up, took me shopping if I needed new clothes, and showed up at all my school activities. Her name was Aunt Mamie and I truly loved her. All my best childhood memories include Aunt Mamie. I found a bunch of photographs that I hadn't tucked into a scrapbook yet. I wasn't really in the mood to do that, but I placed them in plain sight, so I'd not forget about the task. It was another beautiful Autumn Day, but I noticed there was a chill in the air, so this weather wasn't going to hold forever. I wasn't in the least little bit ready for winter. I had laid out a dark navy skirt, white blouse, and a lovely multi-colored cardigan. I was still trying to decide on flats or pumps. Lucy is so tiny, and the sergeant is about the same height as I, so I didn't want to dwarf them when I entered their home. When a girl is 5'9-1/2" in her stocking feet you consider all these choices. It was about time to go draw my bubble bath and spend time relaxing before needing to leave the house. I checked out the front window to see if the patrolman was still stationed there and he was. I flashed the lights, and he came to the porch. I asked him if he'd like a coffee or tea or a cold drink. He said he would really enjoy a cold drink if it weren't too much trouble. I assured him that it wasn't and went to get him a large Iced Tea in a plastic tumbler with a lid and straw. I picked up a couple of ginger snap cookies and a napkin while I was at it. I told him I was leaving about 4:45pm and had no idea when I would return as I had dinner plans that might run late. He said that he was on duty until 2am so he'd keep watch for my return. I locked the door behind him, manned the security alarm and went upstairs to bathe. I have always enjoyed my baths. I've always showered in the morning but there is something about an evening bath that just makes everything all better. As a rule, I would have taken a glass of wine with me, but I was going out so thought I'd skip that part of the ritual. I finished up my bath, did my hair in an upsweep with a pretty gold comb, dressed and headed downstairs. Precious was on the couch staring at me. I asked her if she was hungry again, but she simply ignored me. I checked her water bowl and gave her a fresh bowl of skim milk as she was getting a bit fluffy. I flashed my lights, and the patrolman came to escort me to the car. I drove to the bakery and picked up my order and placed it in the car's way back. I then walked over to the market and chose some lovely mixed flowers for Lucy. I checked the time and felt that I had just the right amount of time to drive to the Alders and not be too early or, God forbid, late.

Chapter 12

I parked at the curb as there were cars in the driveway that I didn't want to block. I started to get the pastries out the way-back when Tim Donaldson showed up and asked if he could help. It took me a moment to be able to speak, but finally I responded with a yes, of course, thank you. Good Lord, did anyone bother to tell me that this man was going to be here? I tried to collect my thoughts long enough to tell him it was nice seeing him again. I inquired was he spending additional time in Edgartown? "I've been nosing around, familiarizing myself with the area, and thought I'd spend the next few days", he said. By now we had gathered everything together and we were at the front door. Lucy already had the door open and was wearing a huge smile and a rather smug look. I greeted her with a big hug and thanked her again for having me. I handed her the flowers and about that time the sergeant showed up. He gave me one of his big bear hugs that I've come to love and look forward to and chauffeured me into the house. We went into their comfy den where there were both spirits and wine waiting. I settled on a gin martini and warned them that I could only have one. The sergeant mixed and served our drinks and we all settled into conversation. Lucy brought me up to speed saying that they had invited Tim to stay with them while he was in town doing research. He and the sergeant were working closely together so it made it very convenient. The sergeant told me that they had visited the storage unit that he spoke to me about. They discovered they'd had a customer since they opened their doors 20 plus years ago who pays annually. To their knowledge the customer has never visited the unit, but the money order arrives on the last day of every year pre-paying the year ahead. The sergeant said, "I asked them if they had copies of the payments and they assured me that they had seven years' worth as that was all they required to retain. They pulled last year's payment and showed it to us. There was a Boston address, but the signature said Leonard Brice." "We feel that the son and father were definitely mixed up in this whole matter," Tim said. "We aren't ready for getting warrants issued yet", said Sgt. Adler "but we are very close. We still have an APB out for both Oscar Brice and Jack Sheridan. We may find that they are all connected." "Amanda are you ok?" said Lucy. I looked at her and said, "Yes, sorry. I'm fine, just a bit stunned, I guess. It is hard to think that people you've known all your life could stoop to such a terrible act against a wonderful, sweet old lady." And, yes, that is when I broke down in tears. I managed to embarrass myself and mortify the Adlers and Tim, I'm sure. I went into the bathroom and tried to repair the damage to my tear-stained face. I opened the door to the sergeant standing there with open arms assuring me that everything would be ok. "I know it will be", I said, "but it is really starting to eat at my insides. It is just one thing compounded on top of another. To think of those people killing Mrs. Brice and perhaps being responsible for the deaths of my parents is just really weighing me down." The sergeant said he absolutely understood and that he and Tim were going to get to the bottom of this. The sergeant looked straight at me and asked, "Amanda, what do you think of Tim? Lucy and I really like him, and we are hoping that you do too." I was a bit taken back with this inquiry but assured him that I would probably grow to like him once I got the chance to know him.

We walked back to the den so I could finish my martini and try to collect myself. Lucy had a concerned look on her face as did Tim. I tried to explain to them what I was feeling, and they both told me that they understood completely. We changed the conversation to weather, current events, and old family stories which helped. Somebody decided that one more drink was a great idea with Lucy's appetizers and that either Tim or Davis would drive me home in my car and the other would follow to bring the driver back, so I need not worry. Lucy went after the beautiful tray of hors d'oeuvres while David made a second drink. David and Lucy chatted about growing up together and him pulling her pigtails all through grade school. Tim said he had grown up on the outskirts of Boston, an only child, to an Irish father and an Irish/Scottish mother. Both sets of grandparents lived within a block of their walkup. He had attended college at Northeastern in Boston and moved back home after graduation. His parents were older when he was born so his dad was ready to retire after he finished his education. He had been working for or with his dad until he retired permanently. He told us that while it makes him a decent living it isn't at all what he wants to do. He had always dreamed of being a police officer and it was still very much in the back of his mind. The sergeant listened to him and just smiled. Tim asked me about my family, and I brought him up to speed. Lucy had excused herself to go put the finishing touches on dinner and she promised to let me know when she was ready for my help. The sergeant and Tim and I continued with our friendly banter until Lucy called my name. I excused myself and went to help. She had a beautiful roast beef with all the lovely vegetables to serve family style along with a salad and some homemade bread and butter. I started putting things on the table and she gave me the wine to pour for everyone. She called for Tim and David to come and join us, and we sat down to enjoy her beautiful dinner. There is simply nothing that compares to a New England Beef Pot Roast dinner. It is so warm and satisfying and just the scent alone is intoxicating. She had chosen a lovely Pinot Noir to pair with the beef, and it was perfect. We all ate hungrily tossing out compliments to the chef between bites. After making a serious dent in her dinner we decided to wait for dessert. Tim and I volunteered to clear the table and do dishes so that David and Lucy could go relax. Tim was no stranger in the kitchen, and we seemed well matched on getting our tasks done. We even put on a pot of coffee to go with dessert! We were pulling our aprons off when he asked if we might get together again while he was in town. "How so?" I asked. "Well,", he said, "I thought we might have dinner together tomorrow evening." I looked up at him (glad that I'd decided on wearing flats) and saw what I believed to be a truly good man. I told him that I would be happy to have dinner with him tomorrow night. He had a rather mischievous look on his face and told me that we had reservations at l 'etoile downtown at 7pm. He said that he knew I had a soft spot for lobster, and he had heard that theirs was superior. I assured him that it was and that the prices were as well. He squeezed my elbow and told me, "Only the best for you, Amanda". We went back to the den carrying trays of coffee and dessert and joined David and Lucy. We visited for a little bit after dessert and then I begged for someone to drive me home. Two drinks and two glasses of wine were having an effect and I needed to get to bed. The sergeant said he'd drive me home and Tim could follow. I hugged precious Lucy and thanked her for a wonderful evening and delicious meal. I told her that the next meal would be at my house. I love to cook so it would be something to look forward to.

The sergeant and I didn't talk a lot on the way to my house. He knew I was tired, and I had a feeling that he already knew that Tim had asked me out. He walked me to the door and waited for me to unlock it. He went in first, checked everything upstairs and downstairs, and told me all was good. I hugged him good night and he waited on the porch until the door was locked and the security alarm was manned. Precious was waiting up for me so we cuddled on the couch while I watched the news. I was tired so the two of us headed to bed.

I awoke the next morning feeling excited to greet the day. I had a small breakfast, fed the cat, flashed the lights and was out the door headed to town before 9am. I wanted to find a new dress to wear to dinner tonight and I knew just the perfect boutique. ***Lily Pulitze*** r on Main Street was a dress boutique that offered one-of-a-kind dresses which was exactly what I was wanting. I parked the car and walked about a block to the shop. I hadn't gotten 5-feet in the door until I saw "the dress". It was a black cocktail length dress with cap sleeves. It had a scalloped neckline that was just daring enough while remaining modest. I tried it on and swore it had been made for me. I found a lovely black lace mantilla to wear over it as a cover up that I could just allow to slide off my head and fall around my shoulders. I planned to wear my shoulder-length auburn hair down tonight for something different. I had the perfect pair of 3-inch pumps in black patent that would put me more "eye level" with my companion of the evening. I was feeling giddy when I left the shop. I called Dolly to see if she had eaten lunch already and she hadn't, so she met me at the bakery for lunch. We had a wonderful visit and I caught her up as much as I could without going into a lot of details. We finished lunch and I told her I'd see her Monday morning at 9am sharp. I stopped at the market and picked up some fresh veggies and chicken for Precious and then headed home. My patrolman helped me with my packages and checked out the house. He declared it safe and sound and bid me a pleasant afternoon. I told him that I was expecting company a little before 7pm so he wouldn't try apprehending Tim at the curb.

I fixed Precious some chicken and then took all my packages upstairs to start getting ready. I drew my bath while I cut off tags and laid everything out on the bed. I wanted to spend at least 30 minutes in my bath relaxing. When I finished bathing, I did my hair and my makeup and then donned that beautiful little black dress. I felt like a princess. I slipped on my shoes and grabbed my mantilla and headed downstairs to wait for my "date" to arrive. Tim rang the doorbell exactly 20 minutes before 7pm. I unlocked the door and greeted him. He petted the cat while I put on my mantilla and got my purse. He looked at me for a moment and then said, "Amanda, you are stunning. You are more beautiful tonight than I'd even imagined possible. I love your hair down. You should wear it that way more often." I blushed and thanked him and told him that he didn't look half-bad himself. I'm not sure if the clothes make the man or if the man makes the clothes. Either way it was a glorious thing. We locked up the house and thanked the patrolman. We let him know that we'd be back later that evening. We got to the restaurant and parked the car with the valet. Tim held my elbow as we walked in to be greeted by the host. He showed us to our table which was sitting close to the fireplace. There was music playing softly in the lounge area. Our waiter brought our menus and Tim asked me if it would be okay if he ordered for us. I assured him that I would love that. He ordered Chilled Katama Bay Spear Point Oysters; 2 ways for our appetizer to share. He told the waiter to bring us a Salad of Roasted Red and Golden Beets, Watermelon, and Sheep

Feta with Crispy Prosciutto to share afterwards. He ordered both of us the Etuve'e of 1-1/2-pound Menemsha Lobster for our entrée. I just stared at him. Where was I going to put all this food? Our appetizer arrived, along with a beautiful Pinot Grigio to go with it. The oysters were succulent and delicious. We fought for our own portion of the fabulous salad that they set before us. The beets were slightly crisp and juicy and so delicious. When our lobster arrived, paired with a Cabernet Sauvignon, I just stared at it. Where to start? I did everything short of licking the plate. We talked non-stop throughout the entire meal. You'd never have guessed that we'd only just met. When we finished our entrée, we agreed to order dessert and take it back to my house to share with a pot of coffee and an Amaretto. Tim ordered the Black Cherry-Vanilla Bean Crème Brule to go. I excused myself to go to the ladies' room and then met Tim in the foyer. He had already called for the car, so we were on our way. We were quiet on our drive back to my house. My trusty patrolman met us as we drove up and excused himself to go and do the walk-through to insure all was okay. The patrolman came back out and announced that all was well. He reminded me that he was on duty until 2am and to flash the light when my gentleman friend was ready to depart. I assured him that I would. When I looked at Tim his eyes were twinkling with that wry sense of humor that I'd already started to get acquainted with. I excused myself to go put on coffee and asked Tim to pour the Amaretto that was sitting on the bar. He poured the liqueur and then opened the dessert box just as I walked in with the small plates, forks and a cup of coffee for each of us. My fireplace is gas, so I threw the switch for a little ambience. We seated ourselves in the living room on either side of Precious. She had eyeballed the dessert but apparently decided it wasn't for her. The dessert was delicious, rich, but very decadent. The Amaretto paired perfectly with it. Tim and I talked about my home and family, and I gave him a little history about it. My paternal great grandfather had been the designer of the home and took part in the erection of a part of it. He had started building the home shortly after he and my great grandmother had married. He finished the project in time for my grandfather's birth a year and one-half later. My great grandparents had wanted a large family and set out to have one. My grandfather was the eldest son but there were 5 more boys and 2 girls that followed. There were ten years between the oldest and the youngest child. My great grandfather was the mayor of Edgartown for eighteen years. He was an attorney but only practiced from the time he graduated for about 5 years. He really loved politics, so the role of mayor was a good one for him. My great grandparents met in school and married so very young; they were only 21 and 22 when my grandfather was born. My grandfather grew up helping to take care of all his siblings and to help his mother around the house. He went away to school, but it didn't agree with him, so he returned home and joined the local police force where he worked until he died. My grandmother was a local girl and she and my grandfather had attended school together. She was a year younger than him. They had reconnected when he came home from school, and they married soon thereafter. My father was an only child and they doted on him. My parents went all through school together. They were so very ambitious and full of expectations for the way their lives should go. I'm sure I came as a surprise to them! Dad was 45 and mother was 43 when I arrived. My parents moved into this house when my grandparents passed away. When I was 2 years old my granddad was killed in the line of duty. So that pretty much sums up my home and family. You already know about my parents' passing, so I needn't go into that. The rest is, as they say, history. Tim didn't say anything for a few minutes and then kind of shook his head. "My God, Amanda, you are like a historical part of this community! I can't wait to hear about the other side of the family. Let's save that for our next date. It's late and I need to take my leave before your patrolman comes in to escort me out," he teased. I helped him on with his overcoat and thanked him for one of the best meals I had ever eaten. He looked at me for just a moment and then kissed me on the cheek and flashed the lights for the patrolman. I started to shut the door, but he turned and said, "I'll call you tomorrow so we can make a plan." I shut the door, locked it, manned the alarm, and leaned against the door frame. I missed him already.

Chapter 13

I awoke feeling grumpy which was so very unusual for me. I crawled out of my cocoon and shuffled down the stairs to find coffee. I tripped on the top stair, scaring myself half to death before recovering my balance. "Get it together, Amanda!" I muttered to myself. Precious was standing at the bottom of the staircase looking at me with contempt on her face. It really is a good thing that she can't talk because chances are, she'd have been out on the street the first year. I turned the pot on for coffee, fed Precious her yum-yums, stuck a piece of bread in the toaster and searched in the refrigerator for something to go with it. I found some yogurt that had expired and settled on soft boiling a couple of eggs. I checked my messages and found one from Tim that was sent at 5:30am. An early riser! I read that he was planning an outing for Saturday and hoped that I would enjoy a car ride. My gloomy mood all but disappeared! I wrote right back that I would love a car ride and asked if there was anything that I should bring. The sun was shining, and I felt wonderful! I ate my eggs and toast, drank my coffee, petted Precious on the head, and headed upstairs to shower and dress. I found a pair of comfy jeans and a sweater to wear, pulled my hair into a ponytail, put on a dab of lip gloss and headed downstairs. I flashed my lights, and my trusty patrolman came to the door. I told him that I was going shopping and would be back later in the afternoon.

I headed for my car, humming, and smiling at what a beautiful day it was. I knew from Tim's email message that we were going for a drive, and the dress was to be casual. I decided it was the perfect excuse for a cute late Fall outfit. I don't usually splurge on a lot of clothing, but I hadn't really bought anything, other than my dress, for quite some time. I found a parking place close to my favorite boutique and went in to see if they had what I wanted. I found a cute pair of dark red skinny jeans, a floral top and red jacket to match the jeans. Perfect! I have a pair of cream color deck shoes that will go perfect with the outfit. I don't usually wear red, but this was darker red rather than the orange shade, so I felt like it looked good on me. I called a girlfriend to see if she was free for lunch as I was right around the corner from her office. She said that I caught her just as she was leaving but if I could wait about half-hour, she would meet me at the Dock Street Coffee Shop. I told her that was perfect and went to put my purchases in my car. Marty and I had been friends since grade school. Her folks and my folks were fast friends that got together at least monthly to play cards and share potluck. Marty is divorced now with two children and owns the local insurance agency. She had dreams of working on Wall Street when she graduated from college and did for 5 years. After the 5th year she started feeling like something in her life was missing. All she did was go to work, come home with work to do, and go to bed, alone, and dream of work. She met Robert through friends in New York and they dated for about a year before they married. Robert was a banker and Marty worked in banking investments in another branch in New York's suburbs. About 4 years later they decided to pack up and move back to Edgartown. Robert found work in the local bank with no problem and Marty bought the local insurance agency. Everything was going great until Marty got pregnant with Robin. Robert didn't really want to be saddled with a family as he was ambitious, and kids got in the way. When Marty became pregnant with Jenny just 18 months later it was pretty much the end of their marriage. Robert left town with one of the bank tellers and Marty filed for divorce. I got to **The Dock Street** and got us a table. The waitress took my order for lemon water and Marty walked in. Pretty as ever. She's always been such a pretty girl. I think it is because no matter what life throws at her she smiles. We hugged and both started talking at the same time. We laughed and agreed to go one at a time. I asked her to catch me up on the children and her business. "The kids are great," she said, "Robin is 4 going on

30 and Jenny is 2-1/2 years old." They are such great kids and I'm glad that Robert takes an interest in them, so they don't feel the pain of our being apart." I reassured her that I knew she and her parents were doing a great job to ensure that the children felt loved and happy. "The business, she told me, is darned near too much for me alone. I'm thinking of hiring someone at least part time." "That's wonderful! That speaks volumes on how you are impacting the community." I told her that I would ask Dolly if she knew of anyone looking for work. She asked how I was doing. She knew about my neighbor, Mrs. Brice, and was sure that it had been very hard on me. "You have always doted on those neighbors of yours. I hope they all know how lucky they are to have you." I tried to bring her up to speed without really divulging anything confidential. I told her that a private investigator from Boston was looking into the matter. She looked me straight in the eye and said, "What's going on? You're positively beaming!" I tried to laugh it off but finally confided that I had met someone. She knows me well enough to know that I don't go off half-cocked and would take any relationship slowly. I did have to confess though that I really liked him. She asked if I was going to see him again and I told her I had a date with him on Friday. She just smiled and squeezed my hand across the table. We ordered our lunch and continued to talk non-stop as we always have. We finished up and promised to keep in closer touch with each other. She reminded me that Jenny has a 3rd birthday approaching and that I'd be getting an invitation. I assured her I would be there with bells on. It was still early in the afternoon, so I decided to stop and visit the sergeant if he was in.

Chapter 14

Sergeant Adler was in, but busy interrogating Leonard Brice. I asked the desk sergeant if I could wait in his office, and he escorted me back there and then found me a cup of tea. The sergeant came into his office about 20 minutes later. He looked upset. "I'm glad you're here, Amanda," he said, I've just finished talking with Leonard Brice about the storage unit. Leonard had sworn that he didn't have a clue what the sergeant was talking about. That he knew nothing about any storage unit or key or coins or anything else to do with his father. I tend to believe him, Amanda, said the sergeant, how about you?" I thought for a moment and told him, "Sgt. Adler, I really feel that he is probably telling the truth. I have a terrible feeling that Lois is involved in this mess somehow. Have you heard if the M.E. has released Mrs. Brice's body yet? If he has, I need the death certificate so I can finish up and then administer the will. The way it's looking right now that could be interesting." "Yes, said the sergeant, he released the body yesterday and it's my understanding that Lois and the funeral home took possession." "Can you take care of the loose ends on Monday morning and then make arrangements to administer the will the following week?" I assured him that I could do that. I would instruct the insurance company and the investment companies to forward the funds overnight mail and charge me accordingly. I started to leave, and he asked me if I was looking forward to my date tomorrow. "Are you checking up on me? I teased. Yes, I am very much looking forward to my date with Tim tomorrow." He smiled and said, "You know, he's really a nice guy. Both Lucy and I like him a lot." "Well, I said, if things work out maybe you can keep him!" We both laughed and I hugged

64

him goodbye. I got about 5 steps out the door and turned saying, "I almost forgot. Would you and Lucy be free for dinner on Tuesday evening? I'm cooking." The sergeant said, I'll check with Lucy and one of them would get back to me but as of this second, it sounds great." I entered what I needed to do into my day timer and called Dolly asking that she be in the office early Monday morning so we could get everything done. I believe she squealed with joy at the thought!

I stopped at the market and picked up a few things and then headed for home. I pulled into my driveway and started to walk toward the door to meet the patrolman when I heard Lois yelling my name from across the street. I turned and waved at her letting her know that I'd heard her. She was waving me over to her mother's house, but my instincts warned against that. I walked over to the patrolman and asked if he would accompany me? He agreed and we both walked over. Lois was obviously perturbed that I'd brought the patrolman with me, but I assured her that I was simply following police instructions for all my comings and goings. I asked her how she was doing and what I could help her with. She said that she had claimed her mother's body yesterday, had her cremated, and was wondering when the will would be read. "Well, as it turns out, I told her, I was going to phone you, your brother and your cousin next week and make an appointment. I was only just able to obtain the death certificate necessary for completion of the paperwork for getting funds released. How is everything else going? Can I be of assistance with any arrangements?" "I don't need anything from you, Amanda, except my part of the will," she said. And with that she turned and stormed off. The patrolman and I looked at each other, shrugged our shoulders, and went back to get me safely ensconced in my house. He did his walk through and then stepped aside to let me in. He went after the groceries, locked my car and returned to the porch. My trusty patrolman is a jewel. I thanked him, locked up, set the alarm, and went to put groceries and my other purchases away. Precious was sitting in front of the fridge singing her favorite song. She has an annoying habit of meowing continually until she gets what she wants. We call it singing so as not to hurt her feelings. I assured her that I would get her supper very soon. She just continued to sing. I finished up and then got her chicken hearts and gizzards out that I'd prepared for her earlier in the week. She likes them warm, so I stuck them in the microwave for 1 minute. I set her dinner before her majesty and poured her a little skim milk to go with it. I walked upstairs to put my purchases away and changed into some sweats and a tee. I went back downstairs to put a load of laundry in and to decide what to have for my dinner. After surfing through the refrigerator, I ended up with a chicken sausage and a salad. I poured myself a glass of wine and waited for the sausage to heat through. I filled my plate and headed for the couch before Precious could beat me to it. I ate my dinner and skimmed through a magazine that had been in the mail. I checked my messages after I finished eating and there were three messages. I had a basket of candy for any trick-or-treater that might come to the door. These days most of the children attend parties and stay off the dark streets. Tim wrote to let me know that he'd pick me up at 10am tomorrow morning. Lucy wrote saying she and David would love to come to dinner on Tuesday evening and that she would bring a pie for our dessert. I ate some of the candy before putting it away. As usual there weren't any callers and I'm guessing that the police car out front may have been partially responsible for that. The last message was from Mrs. Brice's nephew, Duncan Ford. He was wondering if we had a date for distributing the will and would appreciate my getting back to him at my earliest convenience. As has been my habit of late, I forwarded that message to David Adler. I watched the news and then decided to head upstairs to read for a while and get a good night's sleep. I was excited for my outing with Tim tomorrow and wanted to feel fresh and ready to go.

Chapter 15

I awoke before my alarm went off and went downstairs to get my coffee going. I scrambled a couple of eggs and shared them with Precious. I cleaned up and then went upstairs to start getting ready. I showered and dried my hair debating on whether to let it down or not. There was an Autumn wind blowing so I opted for pulling it back with combs and leaving it long in the back. I did my makeup, donned my new outfit and went downstairs to wait for Tim who was due to arrive any moment. It was only a few minutes before the patrolman, with Tim in tow, were on my porch. I opened the door, thanked the patrolman, grabbed my jacket and purse and headed out the door with Tim. He opened the car door for me, gave my elbow a squeeze, grinned and went around to get in the car. We were off on our adventure! Tim told me we were headed for the Morning Glory Farm where we would fill our empty picnic basket with goodies and then we were headed for Mytoi to relax, walk and enjoy the beautiful gardens, and eat our lunch. He told me that if I wasn't too tired after that we could go to Bad Martha Farmer's Brewery and sample their offerings. "Before we go there," he said, I'd really love to stop by the Old Whaling Church. I understand it's beautiful and I've never seen it before." I told him that I thought he had planned the perfect day. He went on to tell me that he hadn't made any dinner reservations but thought we might just go to the Seafood Shanty and pig out on seafood. I laughed at the thought and told him it was one of my favorite past times. We chatted non-stop which has become our norm. I blurted out, "I almost forgot! Are you free for dinner at my house on Tuesday evening? I invited the Adlers, who have already accepted,

67

and obviously I just assumed you'd say yes!" I blushed as I blurted all this information. I'm sure it clashed with my outfit. Tim just laughed, and said, "I was wondering if you were ever going to invite me! Yes, I would love to come to dinner. Better yet, if you're game, I'd like to come early and help make dinner. I'm very handy in the kitchen." I told him that would be wonderful. We agreed for him to come to my house about 2pm on Tuesday ready to go to work. We arrived at the Morning Glory and went exploring to see what we could find to fill the picnic basket with. They had both Genoa and Toscano Salami, so we took a 2" slice of each, some Manchego cheese, a loaf of Italian bread, a beautiful mustard that they make locally, some figs, two pears, and a bottle of Champagne and Orange Juice to share. The basket had plates, silverware, napkins, and glasses so we had all we needed. We filled our basket and headed back to the car to drive to the ferry to Chappaquiddick in route to Mytoi Gardens which is about 3 miles from the ferry landing. There is a beautiful walking path that winds through the gardens. I hadn't been for years, and Tim had never been there. We arrived just as the ferry was landing. We were loaded onto the ferry and ready to go within 15 minutes of our arrival. The ferry to Chappy, as the locals refer to it runs, "as needed". There is no set crossing time as it depends on how choppy the water is. It is necessary to plan your visit to include *returning* so you don't miss an opportunity to catch a ferry going back to Martha's Vineyard. We had a map that we'd got in Edgartown, so we knew our route to the Mytoi Gardens. We parked the car, grabbed our blanket and picnic basket and went on our search for the path. The gardens were beautiful in this late Autumn weather. The colors weren't as brilliant as they would have been in Spring or Summer but lots of reds, orange, and purples blending in with the greenery. We walked for about 15 minutes before finding a beautiful setting to have our picnic lunch. We spread our blanket out and started unloading the basket. Neither Tim nor I are shy about eating. We seem to bask in the smells and taste of all kinds of food. I cut the bread and salami while he got our Mimosa ready. We used a knife to break off chunks of cheese. We were both eyeballing the figs and pears hungrily, so we decided to just cut into one and share it. It wasn't long before we had empty bags and dishes. Now the big decision was to pack up everything, take it back to the car, and go exploring until our designated time of departure, or take a nap. We decided that we'd best go exploring. The gardens are 14 acres of lush greenery and floral offerings. Hugh Jones, the creator of the gardens, titled it My Toy and decided on the spelling MYTOI. He bought the land and began his project in the early 1950s. You can pump ice cold water the old-fashioned way and it was delicious. I remembered that from my childhood and was able to share that with Tim. I also recalled that we were lucky to find a parking place. If it were prime season for tourists, we might have had difficulty as the garden parking lot only holds 15 cars. If you are the 16th car you are turned away having to either come later or visit another day. It was time to head back to the ferry landing for our trip back to Edgartown. We had spent such a wonderful time together and were so comfortable with each other. While waiting for the ferry Tim told me that he had really been remiss in telling me how beautiful I looked today. "You always look so pretty, Amanda," he said, but you seem radiant today. Perhaps it is your beautiful red outfit?" I blushed and thanked him. "I really like your hair down, he went on to say, but this suits you to a tee!" He was enjoying laughing at me as I had pulled my hair back with combs to let it blow in the wind. Blow it did! All over everywhere. It was a blessing that Tim was inept at pulling my hair up and shoving it into a scrunchie! I had forgotten all about it and dreaded looking in the mirror.

We arrived back on the outskirts of town, and I asked Tim if he might consider foregoing the brewery in lieu of scrambled eggs, bacon and toast at my house. He readily agreed. We were both tired from our outing and not hungry enough to face a big seafood dinner. I went on to say that tomorrow was a big day as I had to try and connect with all the banks and investors to get the funds for administering Mrs. Brice's will. I hadn't told the sergeant yet but told Tim about my encounter with Lois. He was glad that the patrolman had accompanied me across the street. He felt that given our last meeting she was being anything but friendly to me. I also told him about Duncan Ford's message, and he said that the sergeant had apprised him of that when I forwarded it to him. "Have you gotten any closer to being able to access the storage unit?" I asked. He told me that the interview with Leonard had fallen short and that he and David were considering a warrant so they could open it up. Tim said, "we really want to be able to find all the players, solve the murder, and access the contents of the storage unit as well." I confided that I was so tired of seeing a police vehicle in front of my house and someone knowing my every coming and going. It's gone on long enough I told him. I looked across the car at him and felt myself tear up. He seemed to feel it and reached out and took my hand in his. "What's wrong, Amanda? He asked. Is it something I said?" "Oh no, Tim, it isn't that at all. I took a deep breath, and said, I guess I just know that before long you're going to have to head back to Boston. You have a life and a business there. I must admit I will miss you when that time comes." Tim pulled over to the side of the road. "Amanda, you're right, I will have to go back eventually," he said; however, I'll only be a couple of hours away. I have no intention of letting you go. I'm falling in love with you. I'm sure you know that, and I believe you feel the same way." I looked at him and decided there was no way that I could, or wanted to, deny how I felt about him. I felt that he was the other half of me that made me whole. I didn't realize that I'd spoken that out loud until he pulled me into his arms and kissed me, finally, for the first time. It was absolutely as I had imagined it would be. Perfect. "Amanda, I can't explain it. I've never felt this way before, he said, but I'm basking in the glorious feeling." We didn't say anything else, and Tim pulled back onto the street to continue the journey. We got to my house, parked, and waited for the patrolman to greet us. He went in and did his check declaring all was ok. I told him that we would flash the lights when Tim was ready to leave later that evening. We locked the door, manned the alarm, and went into the kitchen. Precious was wandering through Tim's feet wanting attention. I asked if he wanted coffee, tea, or wine. He opted for coffee, so I put the pot on. Both of us were slightly wind-burned from our walk. I went to the bathroom and found some sunscreen and we both applied it to our faces and necks. He would tan… I would be red as a lobster. I poured our coffee, and we went to the living room to curl up on the couch in front of the fireplace. We sat curled up together like an old married couple. What a thought! I can't believe that I said that even just to myself! Tim started laughing at me and said, "You look like you're ready to punch someone." "I am, I said, myself!" "Care to share?" He asked. I told him I thought it was best to leave it where it was.

We finished off the pot of coffee and decided it was cocktail hour. I don't usually drink spirits, but I felt like something different. Tim fixed us both a Gin and Tonic which was perfect. I cut a couple of slices of cheese and grabbed some crackers to go with it. Tim told me that he wanted to make a definite plan with me on us seeing one another when he had to go back to Boston. He felt that as time goes by, we could perhaps trade off weekends. One weekend I'd come to Boston and one weekend he'd come here. I told him I thought that would work. I did stress though that winter was upon us and that driving that far in the snow and ice wasn't my idea of fun nor did I look forward to staring out the window until his car pulled up at my house. I put my arms around him and hugged him tightly. "It'll be fine, Tim. We're going to figure this out because I've no intention of letting go of you, I said." He hugged me back and told me he agreed completely. We finished our drinks and went to start supper. Tim put the bacon in the oven and scrambled the eggs while I fixed the toast and set the table. He and I both love our white wine, so I poured a glass each to go with dinner. We ate our meal, each with our own thoughts, in relative silence. After we were through eating, we gathered up the dishes and went into put things away and cleaned up. We decided on another glass of wine and a movie if we could find one. He surfed through the channels and found an old John Wayne western. By the time the movie was over we were both half-asleep and yawning. Tim hugged me to him and whispered in my hair, "it'll be ok, Amanda. I love you." With that he donned his coat, flashed the lights and let himself out of the house. I locked the door, manned the alarm, picked up the cat and went upstairs to cry myself to sleep.

Chapter 16

I lounged in bed longer than usual and finally crawled out about 7:30am. Precious was already hollering for her breakfast. I went downstairs and started my coffee while I found Miss Precious some food. I decided on scrambled eggs and a muffin for myself. I ate a leisurely breakfast, checked my messages and answered as needed. Tim had texted that he was working on some leads but if I wanted to have dinner with him, he'd be more than happy for my company. I texted him back that I had a birthday party to attend this afternoon but could meet him about 5pm at the Black Dog if he didn't mind eating early. He wrote right back that the hour was perfect, and he'd see me there. Cassandra was a friend from high school and her daughter was turning 10 years old today. I had already gotten her gift and promised her mother that I would be there to help chaperone 10 young ladies. I watched the news and a couple of home remodeling shows and then went upstairs to shower and start getting ready for the party and dinner. I dried my hair, leaving it down for a change, and found a cute A-shape dress that was perfect for the cool weather. I decided on wearing flat shoes in case I had to chase any of the 10 young ladies. I grabbed a coat sweater and my purse and flashed my lights for my trust patrolman. He escorted me to my car, and I reminded him that it would be at least 7pm before I got home. I drove to Cassandra's house, grabbed her daughter's gift, and headed for the door. She and I have always had such a great relationship with one another. No matter how much time lapses between visits, we always just started where we'd left off the last time. The house was decorated with ribbons and balloons everywhere and there were 10 adorable girls all gathered in the living room. Cassandra introduced me to each of them and Sheila, her daughter, gave me a huge hug and thanked me for coming. We had a list of games for the girls to play and while they did that Cassandra, and I made their lunch buffet. Everything was prepared already and just needed to be placed on the endless stacks of plates that were on the sideboard. Cassandra had made little English tea sandwiches of tuna, chicken salad, bologna and cheese. There were vegetable sticks and dips, chips, pickles and olives. She had made a beautiful assortment of cupcakes. It was truly a beautiful sight to behold. The girls raved about all the goodies and started filling their plates. Cassandra just beamed as she realized that she'd had a successful party for her beautiful daughter. After lunch she and I cleaned up while the girls watched a Disney movie. Cassandra and I caught up on what was new in our lives, and she was truly thrilled that I had met **the** man. I checked my watch and told her that I needed to leave to meet Tim on time. We hugged and promised to get together soon. The girls all hugged me goodbye, and Sheila thanked me again for coming to her 2-digit party.

I parked right outside the restaurant and Tim was standing by the door waiting for my arrival. He came around and helped me out of the car. He gave me a hug and kiss and told me I was beautiful as always. I looked him up and down and told him he wasn't too bad himself. We had a wonderful meal. Their entrée salads are stuffed with all kinds of seafood, and I thoroughly enjoyed mine along with an ice-cold beer. Tim had a burger the size of his head! I've never seen a hamburger that big, and he ate every last morsel of it. He told me that he wasn't coming in, but he was following me home to be sure I arrived safely and unscathed. I told him I very much appreciated the attention. We parked in my driveway, and he walked me to the door while the patrolman went in to check things out. When he came back, he bid us goodnight and Tim gave me a hug, told me he loved me, and headed for his car. I seem to be alone again except for the cat.

I awoke before my alarm went off, grabbed a shower, dressed, did my hair and makeup and went downstairs to get a cup of coffee and a slice of toast. I fed Precious who chose to ignore me. Most likely because I picked her up last night without asking first. I grabbed my briefcase, purse, coat, and keys, flashed the lights and waited for my patrolman. He greeted me and made sure that I locked everything up tight. I told him I was headed to my office. I got to the office about 15 minutes ahead of Dolly. I already had the lights on, the heat turned up, and the coffee was brewing when she arrived. I gave her a list of things that I needed her to do, and I went to work on my list. I phoned the bank directly, gave them the head's up on what I needed and obtained a name and address for forwarding the written request and copy of the death certificate. They agreed to send everything to me via next day air which meant I'd have it on Wednesday. I then placed the call to the investment firms and was finally connected with the person I needed to deal with. I gave them my information and they explained that the request had to be in the form of a letter, signed and dated, and presented in triplicates. I got the address where to next day air that information and told Dolly what she needed to prepare. I dictated the letters to the heirs asking if the following Thursday afternoon at 2pm was good for them. If they were not able to make that meeting time to please let me know at their earliest convenience so we can reschedule. Dolly came in with all her projects in hand and we sat down at the conference table to be sure we had everything. As is our practice, Dolly will read the will aloud to me thereby giving me an opportunity to critique it if necessary. There are blank sheets ready for adding or deleting anything from the estate listing that the heirs want to bid on or change. We made the copied sets necessary and put them into binders. I had already done a spreadsheet on the valuation of the larger estate items and all the expenses that the administration of the will had incurred to date. I had captured the fair market value of the houses, the cars, the household furnishings, the bank accounts, the investment accounts, and the artwork. This would give the heirs a ballpark figure on what they could expect to receive when all is done. Dolly took everything that needed to be mailed to the post office and UPS picked up the next-day-air for the investment firm. I had another will to administer the end of the month but that could wait to another day. I decided that I needed to talk with Sgt. Adler.

Chapter 17

I phoned ahead to ask if he had time to see me. We decided that we would eat ice cream cones in the park and visit there. We found a bench that was secluded so we could talk privately. I asked him what his plans were regarding the storage facility. I also asked if he was any closer to finding a suspect for poor Mrs. Brice's murder? I told him that I fully realized that this was his job and that he knew what he was doing but I had some major concerns here. I have a cop living in my front yard that I really want to get rid of! And then I burst into tears! Poor, poor Sgt. Adler. This is all I ever do when I'm around this man. He must think that I'm in need of hormone shots or something. "Amanda, he asked, what is really going on?" I blurted out, "I don't want Tim to leave! Ever!" "I know, he said, neither do we. The thing is he's going to need to return to the mainland and figure out what he wants to do with the rest of his life. He's confided in us that he told you he loved you. We sorted of already suspected that from the moment he saw you walk down the street. He wants to be a police officer and I'm working on that. He's nervous about the changes in his life, as he should be, but I believe we'll come up with a good plan in the end." He thought for a few moments and then said, "Amanda, I don't want to bust into that storage facility and lose all hope of finding out who was behind this from the beginning. Boston has called us with a possible John Doe that may turn out to be Oscar Brice. Tim is going to follow through on that when he gets back to Boston. We are turning over every rock trying to find Jack Sherman. I don't trust Leonard Brice. I don't trust Lois Brice. Something isn't right there, and we need to get to the bottom of it." I told him that I had sent out all the letters readying myself for administering the will a week from Thursday. "I'm a little nervous, I said, about meeting with these people without you there but I can't find any logical way for you to be present. I do plan on Dolly sitting in on the meeting so at least I have someone to back me up. I don't know Duncan Ford at all and I'm still unsure where he really fits in. "Amanda, would it be possible, the sergeant asked, for Dolly to keep a cell phone on speaker during the entire meeting? Nobody would know. I could close myself into a room where there isn't a chance of anyone entering or speaking. Wouldn't it be best to hit "record" like you would for a video? Would the cell phone work for the length of the meeting?" Amanda thought for a moment and then told him, "I've got a better idea. We have a tape recorder that we used before cell phone and all the other electronic gadgets. We can place it on the shelf where nobody will be the wiser and it can record the entire meeting." We felt that we had a plan that would work and so we bid each other goodbye until tomorrow evening's dinner time. I wanted to stop and shop for dinner, so I headed to the market. I had made a menu in my head but hadn't laid it down on paper yet. When I got to the market, I pulled out my notepad and started writing down my menu and then made my shopping list. I love lamb and had planned to make it with a Moroccan dipping sauce. I thought that Israeli Couscous, fresh steamed asparagus, and roasted tomatoes would be the perfect dinner. We could start with a salad of fresh, crisp greens, orange slices, slivered almonds, and avocado with a vinaigrette. Lucy was bringing a pie, and we would have coffee and a liqueur for dessert. I put my list together and headed inside to get my groceries. What felt like 40 sacks of groceries later I was on my way home. My trusty patrolman met me at the car and told me to wait while he checked inside and then he'd help me with the groceries. While he was doing his rounds, I felt the hairs on the back of my neck stand up. It felt as if someone was watching me. Truth be told, I've felt this before but chose to ignore it. I looked across to Mrs. Brice's house but didn't see a car. My first inclination was that my watcher was Lois. The patrolman returned saying all was good and started helping me into the house with my groceries. When we were inside the house, I told him that I felt someone was watching us outside. He said he would discreetly research this when he goes back outside. "Miss Bradley be sure that you lock the door and man the security alarm after I shut the door. If you feel frightened or are disturbed about anything just flash the lights and I'll come, running." I assured him I would and thanked him for his thoughtfulness. I told him I was sure it was nothing and thanks for not laughing at me. "It is certainly nothing to laugh about" he said. I locked the door and manned the alarm and went to put my groceries away. Precious sat on the kitchen chair and watched me. I'm sure she was looking for specific items that belonged to her. I had gotten her a piece of liver to go with her chicken breast for a little later. After getting the groceries put away, I started pulling the serving dishes that we would need for tomorrow night. I had asked the butcher to French the baby lamb chops, so they were ready to go. I always fix them in the oven, so I got the big baking sheet out that had about a one-inch lip on it. This would work perfectly and prevent any grease getting in my oven. Cleaning the oven was not my favorite chore. Which made me think, just when did I clean the oven last?? I looked and decided that turning on the auto-clean was my chore for the evening. I have a large steaming basket that fits over a skillet that would work perfectly for the asparagus. The Israeli Couscous would be cooked in a saucepan so that was easy. I have a recipe for a dipping sauce that is made from balsamic vinegar, garlic, sesame oil and red chili flakes. It is delicious and pairs perfectly with the lamb. I checked my wine collection and chose a Pinot Gris to accompany the salad and a Syrah for the main course. I got the wine glasses down and hand washed and dried them, so they'd be ready. I put the glasses for the white wine in the refrigerator to get cold. I had a nice chunk of Parmesan Reggiano to grate over the couscous. I had purchased a variety of cherry tomatoes to roast in the oven. I sliced garlic and shallot to roast with them. I drizzle a balsamic reduction over them before serving. I had my plans all laid out and it would be easy for Tim and myself to get the job done. I had a variety of cheeses and crackers to munch on for an appetizer. They could all decide for themselves what they wanted to drink. My bar was full of the basics. That done I peeled the shrimp for my dinner and put the water on to boil for pasta. I sliced some garlic and a jalapeno to cook with shrimp and put the fettucine into the boiling water. I warmed up Precious' dinner and she and I ate with gusto. I took another glass of white wine in the living room with me and turned on the TV to see what the news had to say. The breaking news of this evening was that the unidentified body found in the landfill last week on the outskirts of Boston had been identified as Oscar Brice of Tisbury. The apparent hole in his forehead suggested foul play. I know that the sergeant had said this was a possibility, but it is always a shock when you see it. I wasn't exactly sure what this meant to the case, but chances are it's relevant. It was too late to call the sergeant and I didn't want to bother him during his free time anyway. This could wait. Perhaps tomorrow night we could limit this discussion to one hour during our cocktail time and then go on to more enjoyable topics. There was a movie coming on that Precious and I wanted to see, so we curled up together to watch and enjoy. Perhaps me more than she. After the movie was over, I went in to get a cup of tea and a cookie. I still had the eerie feeling that I was being watched. I had pulled the blinds tight when I came home but I rechecked them to make sure. I was just being silly. Probably due to the news about Mr. Brice. I took my tea and cookie back into the living room and started to sit down but noticed that Precious was staring at the door. I started to walk over to the window to look out but froze out of fear as my doorknob was being twisted from outside. I got my phone and dialed 911. I told them that someone was on my porch trying to get in my front door. They told me to step away from the area and if I had a weapon, I might want to get it. They told me that help was on the way. I was not able to collect my thoughts because all I could think about was where was my trusty patrolman? I got my gun, undid the safety, and dialed the sergeant's number at the same time. He answered immediately and then said he was on his way. The doorknob shook a couple more times and then stopped. Because I'm confident that unusual things scare people, I began flashing my porch light off and on, off and on. I heard someone running down the stairs and felt they had run away. I looked out my window and could hear sirens approaching from two different directions and one of them had stopped midway down the street and the officers were out of their car and approaching something or someone. About that same time the sergeant texted me to open the door for him, which I did. He came in asking if I was alright and I assured him I was other than being scared to death. I told him that Precious had just become a hero as she had stared at that door knowing something was amiss. I asked him about the patrolman out front. He said that the EMTs were on the way to see to him. He had been hit with something heavy and sharp while smoking a cigarette outside his patrol car. "The other patrolmen, the sergeant said, have apprehended someone so we'll know more about that soon. Are you sure you're alright? I need to go downtown to interrogate whoever this is, but I don't want to leave you if you're still upset." "I'm ok, I told him, just nervous and worked up. Is Tim with you?" The sergeant said "that Tim was outside talking with the patrolman and staying with my trusty patrolman until his help arrives. I asked him to stay outside until I'd seen to you. You may be involved with Tim, but you are still my special charge and my very special friend." I hugged him and told him that I understood completely. "Amanda, if you're ok, I'd really like Tim to go with me to the station. I feel that he needs to be involved in this if we're ever going to get to the end of it. One or the other of us will call or text you and let you know what we find out. It may be morning though, so get some sleep. I want you to be alert when you're preparing my dinner. Also, I'm positioning a non-smoking patrolman out front." She walked him to the door, locked it and manned the alarm again. She doubted that she'd be able to sleep so she went to make some coffee. I looked out the window and saw the EMTs caring for my poor trusty patrolman. I'll bet he never smokes another cigarette. I looked for the sergeant and Tim but didn't see the car. They had apparently already headed downtown.

About 12:15am the sergeant called and said he and Tim were outside if I had any coffee made. I laughed and told them to come in. I waited until I knew they were on the porch, checked through the window blinds, and then unmanned the alarm and opened the door. They both hugged me and asked how I was doing. I told them I was ok and that the coffee and cookies were in the kitchen. We sat at the peninsula, and they started by telling me that they were sure the news of Oscar Brice's death had been a bit of a shock even if I had suspected it would be the case. The patrolman, my trusty patrolman, was going to be ok. He'd probably have a headache from the blow to his head and a butt ache from the kick in the rear that he'd gotten for his stupidity. It could have been a bullet instead of a boulder, which they found, covered in his blood. The other patrolman apprehended the perpetrator and he's in our jail. We have questioned him trying to get to the root of his actions, but we are certain this isn't the person that was trying to get into your house. He had a dog leash in his hands when he was arrested and swore that he was calling his dog that had run off. We tend to believe his story as he lives 3 doors from you. We are at a loss to know who was trying to break into your house but if we had to guess we would say Jack Sheridan. If he's looking for the bag of coins and the key, why would he imagine that you have them? We finished our coffee and cookies and the sergeant announced that he was going home, and that Tim was going to sleep on my couch. With that news he gave me a hug and headed for the door. I unmanned the alarm and unlocked the door, thanked him for everything, and waited until he was in his car before closing the door and securing the house. My new patrolman was at the curb and Tim was standing behind me grinning. I asked him what was so funny. He said, "well, this certainly wasn't the way I daydreamed about spending the night, but I guess it will have to do." I told him I was going after blankets and a pillow and would be back shortly. I found a couple of blankets and a pillow and threw them down the stairs saying, "Here you go. Sleep tight." I could hear him laughing from the landing. I was so tired and now I knew I could rest easy.

Chapter 18

I awoke when I heard my alarm go off. I started to run downstairs to start the water for coffee but then I remembered that Tim was downstairs. I decided to head for the shower instead. I showered, dried my hair, put on some lip gloss, pulled my hair into a ponytail, and threw on some sweats and a tee shirt. I headed downstairs to see what Tim was up to. He had already showered, put his clothes from last night back on, and was making our breakfast. I greeted him with a hug and a kiss and asked what I could do to help. He told me that he'd already fed Precious, who was laying in front of him with her head on his shoe, and to get me some coffee and he'd have my breakfast shortly. I told him I'd already shopped for tonight's dinner. He told me he'd noticed all the pretty dishes and wine glasses were out, so he knew I had been getting ready. He asked if he could borrow my car to run to the Adlers and put on fresh clothes and then be back to help with dinner. I told him that was fine. "How about we go through the menu and grocery list before you leave," I said, to be sure I didn't forget anything. Do you know what kind of pie Lucy was making? Does it require ice cream?" He told me he wasn't sure but would find out and yes, let's be sure we have everything before I go. We ate the lovely breakfast of avocado toast with a poached egg and then he was ready to go through the list. I read him off the menu and he was drooling. The only problem he had was the addition of oranges to a salad. "Fruit doesn't belong in a salad," he said. I assured him he was wrong, and we went on from there. I then read the grocery list so he'd know what I had gotten, or not gotten as the case might be. He decided that I had everything and was now starving for dinner. He kissed me and told me he'd be back in an hour. "I love you, he said, but I'm guessing you know that." I followed him to the door, started to turn off the alarm and unlock the door, but instead I turned and wrapped my arms around his neck and looked him square in the eye and told him that I loved him more. He squeezed me and said, "we'll see." I flashed the lights for the patrolman to know he was coming out, handed him my car keys, and watched him walk down the stairs. What a lovely sight that was.

I cleaned the downstairs bathroom, vacuumed, dusted, and had just started washing the kitchen floor when Tim texted that he was rounding the corner. I went to the front and flashed my lights for the officer and waited for him and Tim. The officer greeted Tim and escorted him to the door. I thanked him and asked if he'd like coffee or a cold drink. He thanked me but said he was fine. Tim secured the door and the alarm and came in to see what I was up to. I asked that he not walk on the kitchen floor until it was dry. He offered to dust, and I threw him a rag and the spray. I started setting out the dishes on the dining room table and lifted the silverware box out of the buffet. The dinnerware had been my maternal grandma's and the silver had belonged to my maternal great grandma. I remembered that Tim had asked me to bring him up to speed on my mom's side of the family and we hadn't done that yet. I'll have to save that for another time. I needed to clean the silver. I should have thought about that yesterday but forgot. I took all the pieces into the kitchen, which was now ok to walk on and started cleaning them. I grabbed the salt and pepper shakers for the table while I was at it. I set out the silverware and went after the red wine glasses. The napkins and napkin rings were in the buffet, so I got those to set out also. I went back to the table and set out everything just the way I like it. I wouldn't take out the white wine glasses until we were ready to pour the wine. Tim was finished with his dusting and waiting for his next job. I told him I was ready for a sandwich and a glass of milk if he was game. He wanted to know what kind of sandwich. I'm going to have trouble with this one, I can just tell.

After lunch we started laying out a plan for the preparation of dinner. Tim told me he thought the table looked beautiful. I was very pleased that he took notice of things like that because the items carry lots of wonderful memories and mean a great deal to me. I finished vacuuming the living room and did a double take that all was clean and tidy. Tim was getting the lamb out to come to room temperature before cooking it. I got the pots ready for the couscous and the asparagus and started getting the vegetables out to prepare the salad. Tim made the dipping sauce and got the tomatoes, garlic and shallots ready to roast. "I think we're pretty much all set", I said. Tim agreed. He asked if I planned on rearranging my hair before the Adlers arrived. "No, I think I'll just stay in my sweats and tee. "Yes, I said, I need to go get showered and changed. Did you bring a clean shirt?" Tim assured me that he had his toiletry bag and clean shirt all set. "I'd like to use the upstairs bathroom when you're finished, if that's ok? he said. I told him to give me 20 minutes and it would be all his. With that I raced upstairs to get ready. I took a quick rinse off, brushed my teeth and freed up the bathroom for Tim. I hollered down the stairs for him to use one of the other bedrooms to change clothes. There are two bedrooms that share the 2nd floor bathroom. My parents, after they moved in, had the back bedrooms made into one large master suite with a bathroom. I've always used the room that I grew up in. For some reason I just couldn't face taking my parent's room. Perhaps what I need to do down the road is remodel the house so that it will become my house rather than my parent's house. I found a cute, comfy dress and flats that were perfect for the evening. I pulled my hair up into a loose ponytail, put on my good gold earrings and some lip gloss and called it good. The shower was already running when I went downstairs. I poured both of us a glass of cold white wine to sip on while we finished everything. I always keep a bottle in the fridge that has a very low alcohol content, so it makes me feel like I'm having a treat but isn't at all intoxicating. We had about 40 minutes before the Adlers were to arrive. Tim came downstairs looking handsome as always. He had a beautiful light cream color short sleeve shirt that went beautifully with his dark coloring. The shirt was tapered and showed off his physique. He is such a beautiful man. I have a hard time not staring at him.

I met his eyes as I was thinking all of this, and they were twinkling like always. I swear he knows exactly what I'm thinking all the time. It is quite exasperating. We sipped on our wine and checked on all the dishes. The oven was red hot for the tomatoes and the lamb. The tomatoes would take 15 minutes longer than the lamb, so we agreed on a time to put them in. I made the salad and set it in the fridge to stay cold. The vinaigrette was already made. I pulled out the various pieces of cheese that I had and sliced some and put them on a tray with some crackers for munchies. Tim had already put the highball glasses in the freezer to get iced cold and had the ice bucket waiting for the ice. I think we're ready!

The sergeant called saying that they were parking outside. Tim and I went to the door to greet them. Lucy was toting a beautiful apple pie for dessert and looking as adorable as always. The sergeant spoke with the patrolman on duty and then joined us. We're all in the habit now of locking the door and manning the alarm. The sergeant took care of that when he came in. A very strange thing for your guest to be accustomed to doing. Tim and the sergeant went to the bar to get drinks while Lucy and I caught up on the local gossip. Someone had decided that we were all drinking Old Fashions tonight so that is what the guys did. We talked non-stop and nibbled on the cheese and crackers and enjoyed our drinks. I excused myself to go get the salads set out on the table for the first course. Tim excused himself and put the tomatoes into roast. Everyone came to the table to enjoy our salad. Tim poured the cold white wine to go with the salad. Lucy and the sergeant both raved about the delicious salad. Lucy said that she never would have thought about adding the orange slices and that they were delicious. It was time to boil the stock for the couscous and put the asparagus on to steam and get the lamb into the oven. I asked Tim to keep the Adlers company while I put on the final touches. "Let me know when you're ready to serve, he said, and I'll come and help." I stirred the couscous into the hot stock and fluffed it with a fork. I shaved Parmesan over the top. The asparagus was perfect, so I drained it. The lamb smelled delicious! I had already pulled the tomatoes out so that they would cool slightly before serving. I started taking everything up on individual dinner plates and called for Tim to come and help. "Please drizzle the balsamic over the tomatoes, I said, and don't forget the individual cups of dipping sauce for the lamb." "Aye, Aye Captain, he said,' and then walked away." I heard him laughing as he joined David and Lucy at the table. I followed him in with the other two plates and sat down to the wonderful smells and equally wonderful comments from my guests. Everyone seemed to eat with gusto and enjoy every mouthful. When the last bite was devoured David and Tim started clearing the table and Tim said he would put on coffee to go with the pie. Lucy said, "he seems very comfortable in your home." "Yes, he does, doesn't he?" I responded. We both started giggling as it was every girl's dream to have a man be comfortable in your home, your life. We could hear them talking and laughing and it was wonderful to see the way they got along. The sergeant seemed more relaxed than I'd ever known him to be. Tim came out asking if we wanted our pie yet. Both of us said that we'd like to wait a bit. The sergeant carried in coffee and Tim poured Amaretto to go with the coffee. The sergeant said that he had a bit of news that he wanted to share if we were up to it. We all agreed that we were all ears. "Well, he said, it would appear that I've been promoted." Lucy jumped out of her chair to hug him! "You didn't say a word, she said, not one word." "I know, he said, I wanted it to be a surprise. The rest of my news is that we have an open position in the squad. I've spoken with my captain, and he would be interested in receiving an application from Tim if he's interested." Tim looked positively shocked. "I don't know what to say. Do I have to go through an academy or the likes to be considered? He asked. "No," said the sergeant, because your 15 years of private investigation credentials will be sufficient. If you're interested you only must make application, meet with the captain, and it is pretty much a done deal." Tim's brow was furrowed as he tried to collect his thoughts and his words. This was a big decision. This was what he wanted, had always wanted, but didn't imagine it possible. He turned to Amanda, and asked, "What do you think? Does this work in our plans? Into our lives? Can you tolerate me being a cop? You don't have to answer immediately, of course, but it is important to me to know how you feel about this." Amanda looked at the sergeant, and then at Lucy whose mouth was hanging open. She looked back at Tim and said, "If this is what you want, then it is what I want." Tim turned to the sergeant and said, "please tell the captain that I will call him tomorrow morning for an appointment. And, David, thank you so very much for your confidence in me and my abilities. It means more than you'll ever know."

We all sat around the table staring at one another, smiling and laughing, and then Tim got up from the table and came around and kind of lifted me out of my chair and into his arms. "We are going to make it, you and I," he said. I just hugged him back. The sergeant broke the mood by demanding his pie and ice cream! Lucy and I went after pie and ice cream and poured more coffee. I really didn't know what to think. There were so many things going on all at once that my head was spinning. We were eating our dessert and the sergeant asked if anyone would mind talking business for just a few minutes. We all agreed that it would be ok. The sergeant asked me if I'd heard from anyone regarding the Thursday meeting next week. I told him that I'd not heard from anyone yet and that I was going on the premise that the meeting was good as scheduled. He said that his patrolman had scoured the area and, had talked with neighbors to see if anyone had seen the person who tried to break in. Nobody seemed to know anything. There were some shoe tracks on the stairs and the walkway, and they had captured those. He said he was still just so perplexed over what the person or people were looking for and why they thought Amanda would have it. "I know," said the sergeant, that Tim needs to return to Boston, but I am hoping this can wait until after you administer the will next week. "That's no problem, Tim assured him, I don't want to leave Amanda until this guy is in jail. Which brings me to another thought, I don't want you staying here alone until this guy is caught. I don't want to ruin your good reputation by continuing to stay here but I'm at a loss on what to do or how to handle this." Amanda was looking at him with a strange expression. The sergeant finally asked her if she was ok, and she didn't really answer him. Finally, she looked around the table and said, "I cannot hide in my house. I have clients to take care of and a job to do. I have a life to live and whoever this person is, they haven't the right to infringe on that. And as for my neighbors, they all know me. They've known me their entire life. They know that I don't have men come and go through my door as if it is revolving. They know that terrible things are going on in my life right now and that my friends are trying to protect and help me. And, if they choose to have nasty thoughts about me, so be it. I guess with that said, I can only add that I hope you can continue to sleep on my couch or in the spare room until the sergeant finds this horrible person." The sergeant and Lucy assured her that they agreed entirely. Tim said that he had planned on asking to stay, either on the couch or on the porch. This got the look from Amanda and then a smile. "Thank you, she said." It was getting late, and everyone had work tomorrow so the Adlers began making their way to the front door. The sergeant told Tim to walk with him to the car that he had his suitcase with him. He looked back at Amanda and grinned. Amanda and Lucy hugged one another and promised to see each other soon. The sergeant came back and thanked her and hugged her before taking his leave. Tim went to the patrolman and explained that he was staying so he wouldn't be expecting him to leave soon. Amanda told Tim that she had a meeting early in the morning and was going to go to bed. She hugged him and kissed him goodnight and headed up the stairs. "Amanda, Tim said, are you ok? "I am, she said, more than ok. Take the spare room. Sleep tight. I love you."

Chapter 19

Amanda was up at usual early hour. She listened but didn't hear any activity out of Tim. She showered and readied herself for her day at the office. She went downstairs to find coffee and a scone and jam sitting waiting for her. There was a note from Tim that he had alerted the patrolman that he was going for his morning run and that you should be getting up soon. He told her he'd be back in an hour. He also alerted her that he had already fed Precious so that she wouldn't be begging for seconds. The cat was becoming more and more spoiled by him. They both were. He had left about 20 minutes ago according to the note so she very well might miss seeing him this morning. Funny, the very thought of that made her so very sad inside. She needed to talk with him tonight about some private stuff. She wasn't necessarily looking forward to it, but it needed to be done. She ate her breakfast, checked messages, grabbed her briefcase and headed for the door. She flashed the lights, and the patrolman came to escort her to the car. She locked up and asked the patrolman to please let Mr. Donaldson know that she had left for the office, and he could reach her on her cell. She reached the office, parked, grabbed her things and went in to meet what she hoped to be a productive day. Dolly was already hard at work and had the coffee going. We hugged and said it was so good to get back to a regular routine. She gave me two messages that needed answering and I went into my office to get organized. I looked at the messages. One was a client needing to make an appointment which I gave back to Dolly to handle, and the other was from the investment firm saying that they had overnighted my check and paperwork and that I should have it later today. Well, it is Edgartown after all, so it'll be tomorrow. I started readying my paperwork for the other will that I was administering later in the month. I copied Dolly on those items and let her know what else was needed and how many copies would be necessary for the meeting. I started going through some other messages that needed to be responded to or printed and dealt with. There was one from a prospective new client that I needed to have Dolly answer by snail mail which would include our flyer with services and pricing. I started sorting through mail that seemed to be a larger stack than normal. There were the normal bills to be paid, tax periodicals to review, estate law seminars that were going to be in my area and a plain white envelope with no return address and the addressee was handwritten. I put the letter aside and texted the sergeant. I didn't want to open the letter without him there. I also texted Tim and let him know that I had received this and that I had already texted the sergeant. Oh boy, here we go again.

The sergeant showed up at the office about 15 minutes later with Tim hot on his heels. They all went into Amanda's office and closed the door for privacy. Amanda handed the sergeant the envelope, and said, "it may just be an overactive imagination, but I didn't want to take any chances." The sergeant assured her that she had done exactly the right thing. Tim looked worried as the sergeant opened the envelope. He had put gloves on as a preventive measure, but it was probably in vain. The letter had come through the U.S. mail so had been handled by who knew how many people before reaching Amanda. The sergeant pulled the letter open so they could all see the contents. It was block printed, by hand, on white notebook filler paper, and read:

> *You keep sticking your nose in things that don't concern you. You keep involving the police in business that is none of yours or theirs. You are pointing fingers at the wrong person for crimes being committed. You need to be very careful as sometimes accidents happen when you least expect them.*

We all just looked at one another trying to absorb the contents of this letter. Finally, I asked, "what wrong person have we pointed our fingers at? So far as I know we haven't been able to successfully tie any one person to a murder, possibly two murders, and a couple of break-ins." Tim started to speak, but the sergeant stopped him saying, "Tim, I have an idea. Amanda, will you be ok for the rest of the afternoon? I'm taking Tim with me, but we'll be back before your office closes at 5pm." "Yes, of course, I told him, do whatever you need to do." Tim hugged and kissed me goodbye and the pair or them were off to do who knows what. I tried to bring Dolly up to speed without frightening her any more than she already was. She and I both had plenty to do today so we needed to get started. It was almost lunch time, so I suggested that we call for something to be delivered. Dolly said she'd take care of it.

Chapter 20

Tim and the sergeant headed toward Tisbury in his unmarked squad car. Tim inquired if the sergeant had some specific destination in mind. Sgt. Adler said, "you know, we've combed the area in and around Edgartown trying to locate Jack Sheridan. So far, we've come up empty handed. His buddy, Oscar Brice, was from West Tisbury. As I recall from sifting through paperwork on this case, Oscar had a sister and a cousin who both lived in West Tisbury. What say we go pay them a little visit and see if we can sift out a rat?" The sergeant radioed the precinct for the two addresses he needed. They put them into the GPS, so they'd know how to find them without difficulty. They decided to start with Oscar's sister. They found her house, parked and walked up to the front door. They rang the doorbell but there was no answer. The sergeant was sure he heard voices, so they went around the side toward the back yard. Sure enough, an older lady and a middle-aged man were talking in the backyard. The sergeant identified himself and said that he was looking for Mabel Brice Jones. The lady said that she was Mrs. Jones and what did the Edgartown police want with her? "We'd like to speak with you privately, if you don't mind," said Sgt. Adler. The man said he'd take his leave if she wanted him to. The sergeant advanced a couple of steps and said, "she wants you to." The man left in a huff, and she pointed toward lawn chairs that she had on the patio. "Mrs. Jones, the sergeant began, we don't mean you any harm or discomfort. We wanted to extend our condolences to you and your family on your brother's demise. We are here, specifically, looking for one of his old cronies, Jack Sheridan." Mrs. Jones' eyebrows shot up at the mention of Jack Sheridan. "I got no use for that criminal," she said. "He's most likely the one that killed my dear brother and left his body to rot in some landfill. I ain't seen him for years and I don't want to 'less it's in a courtroom that says they are going to kill him once and for all." The sergeant told her that he couldn't really disagree with her given all the information he had about Sheridan. The sergeant gave her his card and asked that she please notify him should she have any contact with Jack Sheridan. Tim and the sergeant went back to their squad car and as they were getting in, Tim asked the sergeant if he felt like someone was watching them? "Yes, they were watching when we first arrived here," he said. The sergeant radioed the Tisbury PD, identified himself, gave them Mrs. Jones' address and asked for a patrolman to drive by periodically.

Tim brought up the cousin's address in the GPS and they decided their route to his house. As they were driving away from Mrs. Jones' house, they saw the patrol car in their side mirrors. That ought to deter anyone from bothering her. They arrived at Henry Brice's shack. The screen door was hanging half-off, the place hadn't been painted in 20 years, and there weren't any signs of a car in the yard. They went up to the front porch and attempted to knock on what was left of the door. A voice yelled from inside wanting to know who it was and what did they want. The sergeant held up his badge in the front window and identified himself. The door opened slightly, and the person asked what the cops wanted with him? The sergeant told him that they needed to talk to him face to face and to please either open the door and allow them inside or come out on the porch to talk. Henry Brice opened the door and told them to come in. He was a small man, perhaps 5'2" tall and 100 pounds. He was in his late 70s but looked older. He also looked like someone had used him for a punching bag. The sergeant asked him what had happened to him, and he told them he slipped and fell. "You know, Mr. Brice, I don't believe that for a minute. Let me guess, did Jack Sheridan pay you a visit? What exactly was he looking for? Mr. Brice tried to deny it, but finally said, "if he finds out I talked to you, he'll kill me next time rather than just beating me up." The sergeant told him that they were going to position a police car in front of his place which should deter Jack Sheridan from coming around. Also, both the Tisbury and Edgartown police departments were going to pursue finding Sheridan so nobody else had to be bothered by him. Mr. Brice told them that Jack kept asking where Oscar put that bag of coins? I told him that I didn't have a clue what the hell he was talking about and that is when he started punching me. He's nuts. Really nuts.

The sergeant and Tim pulled out of the driveway after he phoned the Tisbury PD again requesting that they add this address to their surveillance route. The sergeant said that he had a suspicion on where they might find Jack Sheridan. They drove a couple of blocks and sure enough, the sergeant spotted a car that seemed to be tailing them. The car was a couple of blocks back so they couldn't get a good look at it for a description or plate number. The sergeant turned left and then quickly down an alley to see if the car showed up. There it was! The sergeant pulled out and was in pursuit. He radioed the Tisbury PD for backup. About four blocks in front of them the Tisbury PD was staged across the road in front and on both sides. The car in front of them wasn't going any further. The officers approached the vehicle, with weapons drawn, telling the driver to exit the car with his hands on his head. The sergeant asked Tim to stay put and flanked the car as the driver stepped out. The sergeant had him on the ground and was cuffing him in a matter of seconds. Jack Sheridan was finally in custody. Jack had a handgun in the glove box and that would help to keep him in jail. The sergeant spoke with the lieutenant at the Tisbury PD to take possession of Jack Sheridan and transport him back to Edgartown. The lieutenant said he was glad to be rid of the likes of him. Sgt. Adler suggested that someone go to Mr. Brice's house and get him to lodge a formal complaint against Jack. The sergeant and another patrolman led Sheridan outside and placed him in the sergeant's squad car. Tim and the sergeant rode back to Edgartown in silence. Tim told the sergeant that he was going to call Amanda and see if she could pick him up and they'd talk later. Sgt. Adler agreed that this was the best idea. Tim used his cell to phone Amanda who said she'd be there in 10 minutes.

Amanda pulled up and Tim got in. He looked positively exhausted but had good news. Jack Sheridan was in jail! They decided to wait until they were home to talk about the situation. Tim told her that they were out of white wine, chicken breast for Precious, and something for dinner unless she had laid something out that morning. She looked over at him and then burst out laughing. "You're just so darned cute," she said. Tim smiled and chose to say nothing. They stopped at the store and ran into get the chicken and wine and decide what sounded good for dinner. "Do you like Pizza, Tim?" she asked. "Yes, of course, doesn't everyone" he responded. They got the ingredients to make the dough and the toppings, paid the bill and headed home. They greeted their new trusty patrolman and asked how Patrolman James was doing. "He is suffering with headaches, but they said that was normal considering the blow he took," said the officer. He helped with groceries, checked the house, and said all was ok for them to enter. They thanked him, closed and locked the door, manned the alarm and headed for the kitchen. Precious was sitting in front of the fridge glaring at them. As soon as they set the groceries down, she began singing her song. Tim hadn't heard her beautiful singing voice yet, so he was in for a real treat. Meowwwwww, meowwwww, meowwww she said. He laughed so hard that he had tears pouring from his eyes. He thinks she's adorable. She thinks he should feed her, which of course he did.

We decided on having a Gin & Tonic and talking in the living room before worrying about fixing dinner. Tim fixed our drinks, and I got us some cheese and crackers to go with them. He filled me in on the capture of Jack Sheridan. Unbelievable. This guy is a real piece of work. Poor Mr. Henry Brice. That must have been terrifying for him. Tim told me that he was absolutely in awe of the way the sergeant approaches everything. He's so detailed, so precise, and so very capable. And then when he came up behind Sheridan and just slammed him to the ground, cuffed him and brought him back to his feet by the scruff of the neck. Well, it was something to see. David is a good six inches shorter than I am and probably 20 pounds lighter and I'm betting could put me on the ground in nothing flat. I told Tim that I knew the sergeant, and should we be saying the lieutenant, is extremely capable at his job. My father was always so impressed with him as a young man and continued to praise him when he entered the force. So, now that we have Jack Sheridan in jail and we're home alone, I have something to talk with you about. Tim looked puzzled but said, "sure, anything you want to discuss is good with me." "Okay, well here's the thing, said Amanda, what is your middle name? When is your birthday? How old are you? I didn't know you were a runner. Is that something you do daily? What is your favorite food? What's your favorite movie?" "Whoa, said Tim, one thing at a time woman." He leaned over and took her hands in his and started trying to remember each of the question she had just thrown at him."

Ryan. My middle name is Ryan. My father's father dropped the O' before Donaldson when he came to the United States back in the 30s. My mother is Lorraine Evanston Donaldson. My father is Thomas James Donaldson. They are both in their 70s and live in the suburbs of Boston and have for my entire life.
Let me try to give you a little background on my parents and family.

THOMAS JAMES AND LORRAINE (EVANSTON) DONALDSON

Tom received a BS in Criminal Justice from U of Mass. Tom joined the Navy following his graduation. He applied to Naval Intelligence and was accepted and served for almost 20 years. He opened a PI biz and worked until he suffered a stroke and was forced to retire.

Lorraine attended U of Mass and received a BS in Biz Admin. She studied Law at Harvard and achieved her master's degree in business/Corporate Law. She passed the Mass bar on her first try. She opened a law firm specializing in Mergers/Acquisition Law. She had 6 other lawyers and 3 paralegals in her firm. She met Tom at U of Mass and kept in touch. They married when

Tom was 24 and she was 22. They had one son – Timothy born almost 40 years ago when they were 36 and 34 years old. My birthday is January 12th and I'll be 40 years old. I realize that you're too old for me, but we'll manage somehow. I glared at him, and he just laughed. I'm a runner. I run every morning and sometimes after dinner of an evening. I have a membership with a local gym, and I like to play racquetball, lift weights, or run track. I'm a swimmer. I played basketball all through school and college but was just mediocre. My favorite food is whatever the woman I love is fixing to feed me. My favorite movie is whatever I'm watching at the time. I'm not much for TV. I love to read, and I usually have at least one, if not two, books that I'm enjoying. I'll take you to the movie if you want to go and I'll most likely enjoy it. Now, I'm going to fix us one more drink and then it's my turn to ask questions. Ok?" She nodded and waited for him to return with the drinks. "Have you had a lot of girlfriends, Tim?" she asked. He cocked his head at her and said, "I wouldn't say a lot. I had a girlfriend through my junior and senior year in high school. We were sure that we were in love and would always be together. I went to college, and she married her next-door neighbor. I dated some in college but nothing I'd call serious. When I finished my education and took over my dad's PI practice, I was way too busy to consider dating at all. I've had my share of clients that have made gestures that I've not been at all interested in. I guess that about covers it. I've always known what I wanted, how to achieve it, and how to hold on to it. I knew that the woman for me was out there, and I just needed to be patient until she showed up. I'm a Catholic, Amanda. I was raised in the church and went to parochial school. My faith is very important to me. I had hoped that you were a church goer and that we could attend together. Are you? Do you have a church that you belong to?" Amanda told him that she had been brought up Episcopalian and that up until her parents died and she moved home she had always attended church. When she came home, she was so full of questions and loneliness that she avoided attending. "I don't know if that makes sense to you, or not, but that is how I felt, she said." Tim told her that he understood completely. He asked if she might consider attending a local mass with him while he was there. She told him she'd love to and thanked him for thinking of it and asking her. "Okay, he said, my turn for questions. How come someone as beautiful and wonderful as you are hasn't been snatched up by some local fellow? I told him that I had dated a boy in high school and that we had thought it was serious, but it turned out to not be. Then in college I worked and tried to pay my way through without asking my parents, so I was very busy. I also had a scholarship that had to be met with good grades so that added to my busy schedule. I dated a few men in Chicago but never anything serious. They all seemed to have the same idea in mind that if we went out twice, I was supposed to sleep with them. I had and still have a very bad feeling about someone thinking I owe them a pound of flesh for an evening's entertainment. And I'm not referring to you Mr. Donaldson, as I know better, but I wanted to tell you the truth about how I felt. Amanda thought for a minute and then looked at him, and said, "Tim, I've never slept with anyone other than my teddy bear and Precious." I could feel my face burning with embarrassment but there it was, out in the open. I will admit that Tim looked almost shocked, but he recovered very nicely. He was quiet for a moment and then announced he was starving and that we should go fix dinner. I'm sure I gasped but decided to just let it go for the moment. We had a pizza to make.

Chapter 21

Tim made the pizza crust like a pro. I warmed the sauce, grated the cheese, took out the pepperoni and separated them, sliced the mushrooms to sauté with some red onion and garlic before putting it on the pizza. Tim put everything together and placed the pie in the oven to bake. We poured chilled glasses of white wine and set the bar to eat in the kitchen. While we were waiting for the pizza to bake Tim told me that he hoped I knew that he would never infringe on my morals. "The only thing I expect out of you is love, he said, and I hope respect. I promise to always earn that from you. When it comes time for you to walk down that aisle, probably on the lieutenant's arm, I hope you'll be ready to share the physical side of our lives together. I know already that we're going to be wonderful together. I know that because we are the two halves that make a whole person. Now if you'll move your little posterior, I'll get my pizza out of the oven so we can eat." We finished our dinner, cleaned up the kitchen and made coffee to take in the living room. Now that I know that Tim has no interest in watching TV I went through my library and found a book that I had been wanting to read. We settled in like a couple of old married folks. Truth be told that was a very warming thought. Tim mentioned that he had an appointment with the captain in the morning at 10am and would like to do a load of laundry if that was ok. I told him I'd be happy to do it for him, but he refused saying, "I'm quite adept at laundry, ironing, housework, cooking, and other things that you'll just have to wait to find out." With that he trotted off to get his dirty clothes. I yelled after him, saying "you want my laundry too?" Hmm, no answer.

Tim came back into the living room after he'd completed all his chores. I asked him if he was nervous about his meeting with the captain. "Yes, of course, he said, but excited as well. I'm really looking forward to the opportunity to finally do what I've always dreamed of doing. After you administer the will next Thursday to these strange people, I want to make plans for us to go to Boston, well, technically Somerville, so you can meet my parents. Can we do that?" Amanda looked shocked but managed to tell him that yes, that would be fine. "Tim, she said, are your parents going to freak out when I show up?" He laughed and said, "No silly. They already know that you exist. They already know that I'm head over heels, finally, with the girl of my dreams. My mother is over the moon wanting to help plan the wedding. My father wants to pull you under his wing and never let you go. I think it fair to say that they love you already. I know I haven't officially asked you to be my wife yet, but I will as soon as I get home and can get my grandma's ring sized for you. You do want to marry me, don't you?" I looked into those beautiful eyes, in that gorgeous face, and thought myself the luckiest woman I the world. This man loves me, and I love him back. How is it that I got so lucky? "Yes, Tim. I most certainly want to marry you," I said. I thought for another moment and said, "Tim, I'm really looking forward to meeting your family. It will be wonderful to see where you grew up. Thank you for asking me." He hugged her and assured her that everything was going to be wonderful. "I know, he said, that I may be moving fast. I hope not too fast for you, but Amanda, I don't want to be separated from you ever again." "No, she said, I feel the same way, Tim. I think I get nervous because, well, I'm totally alone. I have no family. I've been alone for so long that it is quite new to me to have someone caring for and about me. Does that make sense?" "yes, totally, he said. We need to get this other stuff out of the way, the cop out of your driveway, and our lives. I think you'll relax then and feel more excited about us making our plans." She totally agreed with him and said so. Tim finished up his laundry chores and laid his clothes out for morning. He really was quite self-sufficient. Precious followed him upstairs and then followed him back downstairs. The cat is obsessed with Tim. So much for her being my cat. Tim brought us both a cookie and asked if I wanted more coffee which I declined. He said he was turning in, gave me a kiss, told me he loved me and he and Precious headed upstairs. Ok, well fine, I'll watch the news.

<h1 align="center">Chapter 22</h1>

I was up at my regular hour and out of the house headed for the office while Tim was out running. I left him a note wishing him good luck and asked that he call me later and let me know how it went. I parked my car and went to open the office. I was running a little ahead of Dolly it seemed. I got the coffee going and turned the heat up a bit. It appeared that fall was leaving, and winter was arriving. I answered messages and finished a couple of estates that I had been working on for later in the year. I looked online to hunt a baby shower gift that I needed and took care of that. I still had a shower gift to consider and would do that before the end of the day. Dolly arrived and came into greet me. She had a couple of letters for me to review and sign so she could get them mailed out later today. Next week at this time we'll get this will read and hopefully put that to rest along with poor Mrs. Brice. I decided to call a block party for my neighbors. I really wanted to try to bring them up to speed on what was happening in my life. I phoned Mrs. Taylor who lived next door to me, and she said she'd love to come and would bring cookies. I phoned Mr. Winchell and he said he'd be there with bells on. I phoned Mr. and Mrs. Hunter who live directly across the street from me, and they also readily accepted the invitation. I left a phone message for Mr. Crawford and for Miss Weatherby also. I was finally able to reach the Johnsons by phone and Miss Lawford said she would be there. I had arranged for them to come to my house on Saturday morning at 10am. I was hopeful that Tim would be able to attend the meeting so he could be properly introduced to everyone. I texted the lieutenant and told him of my plan and replied saying that he thought that a good idea. He was sure that his patrolmen had probably frightened all of them with their questions. Miss Weatherby returned my call saying she had a terrible cold and didn't think she'd be able to attend. She said that she had called Mrs. Taylor and asked her to take notes for her. Very typical of my wonderful neighbors.

I told Dolly that I was running errands during lunch and asked if I could bring her back something. She thanked me and told me she had brought a salad. I hadn't heard from Tim yet and it was already 11:30am. I thought his meeting would be over by now, but I apparently was wrong. I didn't want to chance texting him if he hadn't turned his phone off. I started walking down the street just as my phone went off. It was Tim asking if I was free for lunch? I had to laugh. Great minds working together. I texted him back that I was headed for the Seafood Shack, and I'd treat him to lunch. We both arrived about the same time. He hugged me and had a huge smile on his beautiful face. He had the job. The captain and he had hit it off immediately. The captain was pleased that Tim had a master's in criminal justice, and an AA in business law. He felt that Tim was going to be a great asset to the department and would fit into the lieutenant's squad perfectly. We found a table and ordered chowder and a side salad. While we were waiting on our food, he told me that he would be taking several aptitude tests, would take a defensive driving course, and would both drive a squad car and be shot gun in a squad car all within the first 90 days of employment. Tim was concerned that the pay would be considerably lower than he was accustomed to but that he had an IRA, some stocks and bonds, and a savings account so we wouldn't have to worry. I reminded him that I make good money and pretty much live off the dividends from my grandparents and parent's estates. He looked at me with a furrowed brow and said, "Amanda, I know you're self-sufficient and capable, but I want to feel that I'm supporting our family. I want you to be able to do whatever you wish to do with your funds and live on what I make. Does that make sense to you? Are you ok with that?" I thought about it for a moment and kept silent until the waitress had delivered our food. "Tim, what I have is ours as well. When we marry, I will change my will to make you the sole heir to all I have, which is considerable." "Oh My God, he said, I'm engaged to an heiress!" "Not yet, you're not. I haven't a ring on my finger yet," I teased. We finished our lunch talking and laughing and I told him of my "coffee group" coming on Saturday morning. "Do you want me there?" he asked. "If you're comfortable with it, yes, I responded. My neighbors are lovely people that I've known my entire life. I want them to know that I am ok as I'm quite sure they are all worried. Also, if it is ok with you, I want to tell them that we are engaged and that we'll expect all of them at our wedding. I will also assure them that you've been standing guard over me but from another bedroom. They would never ask but they will wonder. I told David about the meeting, and he felt it was a good idea. And now, Mr. Donaldson, I must return to my office. I still have work to do but plan to leave work about 3:30pm and head for home. Will you be home or what?" Tim said that he had some leads to follow up on but expected to be home by 3pm. If he was going to be any later, he would text me. He walked me back to my office, waved and threw kisses to Dolly and took his leave. He hugged and kissed me and told me to have a good afternoon. I went into the office to a grinning Dolly. "He's such a nice man, she said. You're a lucky woman." I told her I knew that, and that she was correct because he is a very nice man. I went into my office to get some work done.

Chapter 23

I cleared up my desk and readied myself to leave about 3pm. I was just getting ready to walk out when Dolly called my intercom and announced that Duncan Ford was hoping to see me before I left. I told her to get her pad and pencil and to accompany Mr. Ford into the conference room. I walked into the conference room and Mr. Ford stood up to shake hands and greet me. He thanked me for making time to visit with him before the will was administered. I asked him how I could help him. He said, "I was hoping to speak with you privately." I assured him that this was as private as our conversation was going to be. He frowned but shrugged and said that was fine. "Well, he said, as you know Doris Brice's sister was my mother. My mother passed away when I was just a baby and my father, Charles Connelly raised me until he grew tired of the chore and gave me to the orphanage when I was 5 years old. I only had a couple of photographs and a baby book that gave me any clue to my heritage. I found a passage in my baby book that said that my Aunt Doris had given me a beautiful layette when I was born. That was the only reference I had to having any family. I arrived on my aunt's doorstep, told her what I knew, and she welcomed me into her family. Her children want nothing to do with me and I don't blame them. I heard that you'd been broken into and then another attempt at your home. Wow! I wonder what they're looking for. I mean, someone must want something bad to think the lawyer has it. Right? I looked at him very closely before answering him. "I'm not sure where you're getting your information, Mr. Ford, I said, but I don't think you should concern yourself with it. I will expect to see you here next Thursday. I will administer the will and read the contents of the estate and decisions can be reached at that time by all heirs involved. Whether Mrs. Brice's children like or dislike you are of no concern to me. I can't help but wonder though, why did it take you more than 20 years to contact your aunt? I mean, you must be what, about 40-45 years old?" He looked upset by my comment but kept his counsel. "Miss Bradley, I'm not sure what you're hinting at, he said, but I can assure you that I looked up my aunt as soon as I had things figured out. Now, if you'll excuse me, I'll take my leave. Thank you again for your time today." Dolly walked him to the door and then locked the door and put the closed sign out. She came back to see if I was ok. She also put a plastic bag over his water glass and told me she had bagged the vase that he had handled while in the foyer. "He's a very strange man, Amanda, she said, and I don't think he's very likable." "No, he isn't, is he? I replied. Dolly, did you have the feeling that there was much more to his story than what he told us?" She agreed that he hadn't been very clear and certainly was unclear about what it was he wanted today. I thanked her for her candid response and told her I was grabbing my purse and briefcase so we could walk out together. I would alert the lieutenant that I had lab material for him.

I didn't hear from Tim so assumed he'd be at the house when I arrived. My new trusty patrolman told me that Mr. Donaldson was already inside and told me to have a safe and enjoyable evening. I started to text Tim, but he was already opening the door for me. We went inside and I headed straight for the refrigerator. Tim asked me, "what's wrong? Something is up because your coloring is off. Are you ok?" I told him the entire story about Duncan Ford's visit. I told him that he was a very strange character to say the least. "I haven't said anything to David yet, but I need to contact him because I have a vase and a water glass with his fingerprints all over them, I said." Tim just grinned. I asked him if he'd gotten anything for dinner tonight and he informed me that it was already marinating, and I was going to love it. I asked him for details, and he simply said, "Thai." Yum, my favorite. I ran upstairs to change into comfy clothes and hollered down that wine was in order. I heard laughter from downstairs. I changed into my normal sweats and tee, ran a brush through my mop of hair and pulled it back into a scrunchie and headed downstairs. Tim had already poured our wine and had ice cold prawns and cocktail sauce for an appetizer. Precious was showing real interest in the shrimp but Tim told her she'd have to wait. He downed a couple of prawns and some of his wine and then went to the fridge to get her baby shrimp and skim milk. I'm telling you that this cat is becoming so spoiled that she is in jeopardy of becoming an outdoor kitty. And she's fat, to boot! I told Tim that I needed to call the lieutenant and bring him up to speed. Tim agreed and handed me my cell phone. The lieutenant answered on the second ring, listened to my findings, and asked if we could meet him at my office so he could take possession of those items. I assured him we could, and we would. "We'll meet you in 10 minutes, I said." I told Tim that he wanted those items right away. Can we go now and eat when we get back? "You bet, he said." We flashed the lights, told the patrolman where we were off to and would be back inside 30 minutes. We parked right outside the office and David was already there. We went in and he grinned when he saw that Dolly had them all bagged for him. "She watches too much TV, he said with a grin." "Before I completely forget, she said to the lieutenant, do you know anything about Oscar having been imprisoned for about 5-years or so? I know I'm probably just groping at straws but I'm beginning to think all these scoundrels may be related in some way." David told her that he had seen where Oscar was in prison for stealing a car and writing bad checks. He would check into it further and see what he could come up with. We hugged each other and headed back home. I just realized that I went outside, downtown, and hugged a cop in my sweats and a tee with little or nothing else on. What was happening to me?

We went home and Tim asked me to make rice to go with the chicken that he had marinating. I told him I'd be happy to and asked if he wanted me to sauté the spinach while I was at it. "Yes, please, he said, that sounds delicious." We finished preparing dinner and decided to eat at the dining room table. I set the table and Tim got a fresh bottle of iced cold white wine out for us to share. Dinner was delicious. I was really getting used to being waited on with such excellence. We finished eating and just sat and enjoyed each other's company while we finished our wine. I had an apple turnover in the freezer that we could bake later to go with coffee if we felt like dessert. I was so pleasantly full that I couldn't imagine wanting anything else to eat before tomorrow.

Chapter 24

I try my best to take Fridays off so I can get laundry done, beds changed, the house cleaned, and take anything to the cleaner that needed to go. I also try to do my basic grocery shopping on that day as well. I looked around the house and discovered that it was clean already. The laundry had already been done by someone and both beds had been made up fresh. Apparently, I have an angel maid that I was not made aware of. I had asked Tim if he had Friday plans and he said he was playing something called squash with a couple of the patrolmen that he'd become friendly with. I told him to have fun and I was off to do my errands. I flashed my lights and my trusty patrolman showed up at the door. It was patrolman James! I didn't even hesitate but gave him a big hug telling him how happy I was to see him back on the job! He just smiled and told me he was glad to be back. I told him that Tim would be in and out and that I'd be back later in the afternoon. I had called an old friend, Suzy, to see if she could have a bite of lunch. She was getting married in a couple of months and I hadn't seen her for quite some time. She was thrilled that I had called, and we planned to meet at the Black Dog about 1pm. I dropped everything at the cleaners and picked up some items that I had totally forgotten about. I went by the local pharmacy and stocked up on my vitamins. While I was there, I looked through their cards and picked out a few for baby showers, bridal showers, birthdays, and who knows what else. It was just about time to meet Suzy, so I headed for the Black Dog. Suzy and I had gone all through junior and senior high school together. She and I had both been cheer leaders in high school and had shared a couple of other classes together. She had married her high school sweetheart shortly after graduation, but it had ended in divorce about ten years later. She is a sought-after CPA in Edgartown and had stayed busy after the divorce. Somewhere along the way she met a delightful man named James something-or-other, and they were being married the day after Christmas. I waited in the foyer for her to arrive. She came through the door with a huge smile and her usual boisterous way of screeching my name. She always makes me laugh out loud the way she does that. We hugged and the hostess asked if we were ready for our table. We locked arms and followed her to a lovely booth at the back of the restaurant. We were guessing that they were afraid we would disturb the other guests! We both talked at once, catching up on all the news since our last meeting. She and James were going to have a quiet ceremony that she was hoping I would attend. I assured her that Tim and I would be there. She stopped cold! Tim? Tim who? Tell me everything she insisted. I laughed and gave her a run-down on the man in my life. She got tears in her eyes telling me that she was so happy for me that she could hardly stand it. She's such a sweet person. She asked if there was a chance that the four of us could get together before the wedding? Amanda, she said, why can't we celebrate our birthdays together? Mine is on the 12th of December and yours is the 10th. It would be perfect! I told her I'd check with Tim and see what his schedule looked like and then give her a call. We enjoyed our lunch of delicious tuna salad sandwiches and chips and a cold beer. We parted promising to stay in touch. I walked back to my car and headed for the grocery store. I had my list all ready so it should flow quickly. Several bags later I was headed home. Tim was already there so he came out to help with groceries. I thanked Patrolman James and told him again how happy I was to see him. We got the groceries into the kitchen and Tim said, "Amanda, we need to head for the PD. David is waiting for our arrival." "Why, I asked, what is going on now?" "I'm not exactly sure, he said, but he didn't waste words. He just said to come to the precinct as quickly as possible."

We arrived at the precinct and asked to see Lt. Adler; that he was expecting us. David came out and walked us back to his nice office. He asked if we wanted coffee or water or anything. We said water would be wonderful, so he spun around in his chair, opened his mini fridge and grabbed 3 bottles. He started telling us that he had put a rush on fingerprints and possible DNA from the water glass that Duncan Ford had used. He also told us that he had researched further regarding Oscar having been incarcerated. It turned out that Duncan Ford's real name was Scott Schwartz. He was originally from New York and had been a small-town criminal since his teenage years. He had been Oscar's cell mate for almost 5-years. "I believe, he said, that this is all beginning to come to a head. I'm sure that Oscar must have educated him about his wife's family and somehow got him to pretend to be her nephew. That would have gotten someone into the house and into her life to try and find what Oscar wanted all along which was the bag of coins with the key in it. Now the question is, who killed Oscar? Was it Jack Sheridan who hated him and had done time while he ran free? Or was it this Scott Schwartz character who decided he didn't want to share with Oscar. The thing is we are going to have to move toward this Schwartz person before the will can be administered on Thursday. What do we have to do, Amanda, to remove him from the will? Amanda said she would need to advise both Leonard and Lois Brice of this situation and they would have to formally contest his inheriting anything from their mother. I can draw up the papers, have them sign them, and get them to the judge to sign off on. The thing is that we don't want Duncan or Schwartz running off before we can deal with him. Lt. Adler told her that he could issue a warrant and arrest Schwartz for Criminal Impersonation. That would give her time to get with the Brice heirs. Amanda said that she would call Dolly to help her put all the paperwork together and she would present it to the judge in the morning. Lt. Adler told her that was perfect. Tim and Amanda said their goodbyes to the lieutenant and headed home. We had groceries to put away. It was a quiet ride home and when we got into the house we just seemed to work as a silent team putting things away, getting the cat fed and preparing dinner. Tim finally broke the silence as he presented me with a hand-shaken margarita. "Amanda, this is like being on a roller coaster that we don't seem to be able to stop" he said. "I know, I told him, and the thing is I've always led a rather quiet life, so this is really starting to take its' toll on me. "I have dark circles under my eyes from lack of sleep!" Tim thought for a few minutes and drank part of his margarita before saying anything out loud. Finally, he said, "If the bullet they found in Oscar's head matches up with the gun that they took out of Jack's truck that will pretty much complete that issue. Would it be too much of a stretch to hope that the same gun was used to kill the Bartletts? We now know for a certainty that Duncan or Scott or whatever his name is knew Oscar Brice. Oscar must have told him about double-crossing Jack and the others and then putting the stolen goods away for safe keeping. What I can't figure out is did Oscar suggests that Schwartz impersonate Doris' nephew, or did he think that up on his own. I'm guessing that Oscar had to have schooled him on the information needed for him to successfully convince her that he was her nephew." Yes, said Amanda, Oscar would most certainly have had to educate him about all the family information. He must have promised him a percentage of the stolen goods when they were able to sell them." Tim said, "I wish we had that bag of coins and that key so we could examine them closer." Amanda told him that she didn't think that was a problem as David hadn't put them into lock-up as they technically were not tied directly to any case that he was involved in. He's got the bag at his house. "I think I'll call David and asked if we can borrow them, Tim said." Tim called David's home number and asked if that would be possible. "Certainly, he said. If you want it tonight, I could run it over or you could pick it up in the morning, the lieutenant said." Tim told him he'd pick them up tomorrow after the block meeting; probably about noon if that's ok. David assured him that would be fine. It seemed that for the rest of the evening that both Tim and Amanda were in deep thoughts wondering what tomorrow would bring. Later in the evening Amanda phoned Dolly and told her what they needed to do. "I would like to meet at the office at 7am, Amanda asked, if you can do that? Then we can walk the paperwork over to the judge and get him to sign off on it. If that goes as planned, I can then drop off copies to the lieutenant." Dolly said that sounded great and she would see her at 7am. Amanda told Tim that she would leave about 6:30 and be back in plenty of time to greet guest before 10am. He asked if she wanted him to accompany her, but she said that was silly. She'd be fine. "Tim, she said, which room are you sleeping in?" He looked at her rather strangely and said the small room just beyond your closed door. "Why, he asked?" "I just wondered. I thought perhaps you'd taken my parent's room as it is larger and has its own bath. You are welcome to do that if you want to. I've just never been able to make myself go in there with the idea of staying. What do you think about having the house remodeled and making it more our own?" Tim responded immediately saying, "Yes! I love that idea. I have a couple of ideas to share with you about enlarging the kitchen while we're at it." She just smiled and said they'd sit down and look at that soon. "I'm off to bed, Tim. I'm tired and tomorrow will arrive early." She kissed him and he pulled her onto his lap for a few more hugs and kisses. "I don't want to let you go, he said." "Nor do I want you to, she responded."

Chapter 25

Amanda was up, showered, dressed, had her coffee and a scone and was out the door at 6:40am. She arrived at the office on the heels of Dotty. Together they gathered everything together that was needed, got it all documented and ready for the judge. She thanked Dolly for all her help and headed for the courthouse. The sitting judge was most always in his office early. Amanda remembered him from when her mom was the D.A. She would stop by to say hello to Uncle Judge Henry, and he would give her a bright colored sucker. So many memories. She knocked on his door and he yelled, "enter". When he saw her, he beamed and came around his desk to give her a big hug. The judge stood back staring at her, and said, "Amanda Bradley, it is just wonderful to see you!" She told him that she was thrilled to get to see him that it had been way too long. He poured coffee for them and wanted to catch up. She quickly related what she could about the Brice fiasco. She told him that this was what had brought her to the courthouse today. "I need some papers signed, she told him, if that's possible." Lt. Adler is holding both Jack Sheridan and Scott Schwartz (aka Duncan Ford) in the city jail. The judge looked over the paperwork and signed off without question. Hopefully this will suffice for you advising the heirs of this situation and removing his name from the will and the estate reading. "Yes, I think it will be fine now, she said. I'm so glad that I got to visit with you today even for just a short while. There are some changes coming in my life and I would like you and Aunt Lorna to come to dinner soon. I will phone her, and we will make a plan." He hugged and kissed my cheek and told me he'd look forward to that dinner. I stopped by the police station and dropped

David off a copy of the paperwork and then headed home. I didn't want to be late for my block meeting.

Amanda greeted Tim with a hug and kiss and told him all was good. She had gotten the judge to sign off on the paperwork and she would contact heirs on Monday morning. In the short term, let's put on the buffet pot for coffee, the electric kettle for tea and put out teacups and saucers, mugs, cream, sugar, honey, and spoons. There is a 12-pack of bottled water in the fridge on the back sunporch for those that don't want coffee or tea. Mrs. Taylor will bring cookies and trust me, there will be plenty because all the neighbors have talked with each other. I went to freshen my makeup and hair and came back down just in time to greet my first guest, Miss Lawford. She is a little tiny petite lady in her late 80s or early 90s. She never married but I'm sure she had lots of suitors. Tim came and extended his hand and introduced himself. He showed her to a seat and asked if she'd care for a beverage. She ordered tea with lemon, oh good grief I forgot to slice the lemons, and he went to take care of that order. At about that same time Mr. and Mrs. Johnson arrived with Mr. Winchell hot on their heels. They all came in, hugged me and told me how wonderful to see me. Tim introduced himself and started taking drink orders. They found their own way to where they wanted to sit. The Johnsons are probably the youngest in the neighborhood. Laverne Johnson is in her late 60s or early 70s and Peter Johnson is about 75 now. They had married young and had their family soon afterwards. I had gone to school with both of their boys. Mr. Winchell is a short, round little man with sparkly eyes and a teasing sense of humor. He was a schoolteacher from the time he got his teaching certificate until he retired about 15 years ago. Mrs. Taylor let herself in and my trusty Patrolman James was toting her cookie tray. So much for police protection. I thanked the patrolman and told him that the Hunters were the only other couple to arrive shortly. I greeted Mrs. Taylor and thanked her for the beautiful array of homemade cookies. She had owned and operated the downtown bakery for over 40 years. When her husband passed away, about 10 years ago, she just seemed to lose interest in working. She sold the business and has been a real homebody ever since. I heard Patrolman James greeting the Hunters on the front porch, so I went to the door to let them in. I thanked the patrolman and told him I would flash the lights when the meeting breaks up so he'd know that everyone would be exiting. Tim had everything and everybody in control. Tea, coffee, and water was distributed, and everyone had taken at least two cookies to munch on. I walked over to stand by Tim and addressed the group in my living room. "I'm sure by now you're all very curious, and probably a bit concerned, about what in the world is going on in my life. I know that Tim has introduced himself, but I want to formally do so now. Everyone, please allow me to introduce my fiancé, Mr. Timothy Donaldson. There were oohs and aahs from the entire group and I swear I saw a couple of people dabbing at their eyes. As you are all aware there has been a police squad car parked in front of my home for some time now. Shortly before Mrs. Brice's demise, I received a threatening letter telling me to mind my own business. I didn't know what to make of it but after Mrs. Brice was murdered it took on a whole new meaning. As you know, I'm closely acquainted with Lt. and Mrs. David Adler. The lieutenant worked for my father for a short time before his passing and my dad had also worked with Lt. Adler's father. He has been instrumental in ensuring that I'm watched over to prevent any harm coming to me. Tim is a licensed private investigator out of Boston. He came here to investigate Mrs. Brice's death and we met and fell in love. Because of an attempted break-in here in my home, on the heels of a break-in and theft at my office, Tim has moved in with me. Let me assure each of you that Tim is a gentleman and very honorable. Our living arrangements are strictly above board. I could never deface my parent's memory by having it any other way. There have been a lot of different actions going on since Mrs. Brice passed away. Tim, the lieutenant, a lawyer in Boston, and myself are all working hard to solve this puzzle and put the guilty people behind bars where they belong. At this time, I would ask each of you to search your memories. If you've seen anything suspicious around my house, I'd appreciate you reporting it either to Tim, the lieutenant or me. We've always been a close neighborhood and we rely on each other. You all mean the world to me. I can look at your faces today and a flood of memories come to mind. Before I forget, I'm sure you're all wondering about Mrs. Brice's children. I'm uncertain about Leonard's coming and goings, but I know that there has been a serious change in Lois' attitude toward me. Why? I have no idea. "Mrs. Taylor, I said, I know that Miss Weatherby asked that you take notes today for her. I'd appreciate it if you did not do that. I don't want anything passed along and misinterpreted by anyone. I will phone Miss Weatherby directly to see how she is feeling, and I will bring her current with all this news. Is that ok with you?" "Absolutely, she said, I agree completely. We all hugged and said our goodbyes and I assured them all that they would get invitations to the wedding. All of the ladies thought Tim was dreamy and I quite agree. I started to close the door, but Mr. and Mrs. Hunter had walked back up on the porch with Patrolman James close on their heels. I assured him it was fine and let them in. They both looked rather upset and told me that they didn't want to say anything in front of the others but needed to speak with me privately. I assured them that it was fine but that I wanted Tim included in this conversation. "Of course, of course, they said, we didn't mean to exclude him." I asked them if I could get them anything, but they refused. "Amanda, Mrs. Hunter said, we are almost certain that we saw and could identify the person who tried to break into your house." I stared at her as if I'd seen a ghost. I asked her if she'd said anything to the police and she said they were afraid to. "Mrs. Hunter, this is a very important thing you're saying. You're saying that you saw the person who broke into my backdoor? You're saying you really believe that you saw the person who hit Patrolman James over the head and tried to break into my front door????" "Yes, sweetheart, she said, we're pretty sure we did." "Did you recognize them? Do you know them? She thought for a moment and then said, "No, we didn't really know them. But we've seen his picture on the news and in the paper over the years. His name is Jack Sheridan." "Well, that's certainly an interesting piece of news, I said." I told the Hunters that I would have to inform the lieutenant of this and that he would come to take their statement. "Are we going to get arrested, she asked?" "No, of course not, I said, he'll just probably scold you though for not letting him know sooner." We hugged the Hunters and thanked them for telling us. Tim was already dialing

David's direct number. I went upstairs, started drawing a tub of water and threw about half a box of bubble bath into the water. I needed to think. Tim left to go after the bag of coins from David so we would sort through that this afternoon. I finished up my bubble bath, dressed in comfy sweats and a tee, pulled my hair into a ponytail and went downstairs to feed Precious and find something for lunch for Tim and me. About 15 minutes later Tim walked in and sat down at the kitchen bar. We visited for a few minutes about how the morning had panned out and he asked if he could help make lunch. I told him that tomato soup from a can and crackers from a box were just about ready, but thanks for offering. We ate and then cleaned up the kitchen, fixed coffee and headed for the dining room table where we could empty the contents of the bag out. I put down some butcher paper to keep everything contained on the table. We sorted through the coins and Tim recognized several as being valuable. "I'll look them up on the internet later, he said, and see if we can find the current value." The key was indeed a strange looking object. It reminded me of a pirate for some reason but I've no clue why. It was a long slender key, probably 5" in length with a fat round tip. There were 6 numbers stamped into the backside of the key. Tim studied it for a moment and said, "Amanda, I think we need to break into the storage unit!" "Why, I asked?" "Because, he said, I think there is something in the storage unit that has to do with these 6 numbers. They don't appear to have been a part of the original key. The numbers look to have been engraved after the fact." I told him I thought he should follow his instincts, call David, and decide to enter the storage facility.

Chapter 26

Even though it was Sunday morning I wanted to go into the office and prepare the letters for the Brice heirs. I called Dolly and asked if there was a chance, she could come in Monday morning about 7-7:30am so she could type the letters, make the copies, and prepare the certified mailing labels for taking to the post office when they opened at 9am. She assured me she would be there and that it would be handled, and in the mail shortly after 9am. I showered, dressed, left a note for Tim who was out running, and left for the office. Patrolman James assured me that he would alert Mr. Donaldson of my whereabouts should he ask. I inquired how his head was doing and he told me that it was still tender, but he was feeling good. I drove to the office, parked and went in. I locked the door and set the alarm before turning the lights on. I'm still squeamish about entering the office by myself but I need to get past this if I'm ever to get over it. I went into my office and dictated the letters for Dolly to type. I put copies of the judge's order in the folder for Dolly to include with the letters. I took a few minutes to reflect on everything that has been happening since Mrs. Brice's home was broken into. How could people hold grudges for all these years? It has been some 36 years since this whole mess began. According to the journal that Mrs. Brice maintained her husband and Jack were breaking into homes, stealing artifacts and whatever. Why had Oscar never entered the storage unit and taken whatever it was that he thought he could sell to be rich (according to what he had told his wife)? What was really the significance of the bag of coins and the mysterious key? While sitting there pondering all of this I thought I heard a knock on the door. I can see who is at the door or in the foyer without them seeing me. I looked and saw Lois Brice standing there. My gut instinct told me to NOT open the door to her. I was shaking like a leaf as I called David and Tim. David answered immediately and said he was on his way. She kept pounding on the door and then started yelling my name to open the damned door. The lieutenant drove up as she was screaming at me and took control of the situation. He cuffed her and helped her into his squad car, and it pulled away. I felt violently ill. I was shaking like a leaf, and I started retching as I headed for the bathroom. I stayed in there shaking, throwing up, crying, until I heard my cell telling me that Tim was calling. I got control of myself and went into call him back. He knew David had already been to the office and he was standing on the sidewalk outside. "Would I please let him in, he said?" I went and unmanned the alarm, opened the door, and fell into his arms. I was crying so hard that I couldn't talk; couldn't think. Tim was trying to console me best he could. "Amanda, sweetheart, are you ok, he kept saying?" Finally, I calmed down and collected myself so I could talk to him. "Tim, it's so horrible, I told him. Mrs. Brice was murdered. Mr. and Mrs. Bartlett were murdered. My parents were murdered. My office and my home have been broken into and for what? And now someone I've considered a friend for 40 years has been arrested for pounding on my office door, screaming profanities at me." And then I started crying again.

Lois was just held over until Monday morning. She wasn't arrested as David decided to let her play all her cards. She was out of control due to thinking that the reading and distribution of the will would be held up due to Scott aka Duncan being arrested. David had asked her specifically how she came to know about that. She had told him that Leonard and Duncan were friendly, and she had heard it from Leonard. The lieutenant planned to follow through with that piece of news. When Lois was released, she called me and left a message apologizing for her behavior and hoped that I would forgive her. The letters would be received by her and Leonard either later in the day or early Tuesday morning. The meeting for the administering of the will was still scheduled for 2pm on Thursday.

I was still feeling very emotional and not at all like me. I needed to try and get my focus back so I could take control of my life once again. I had told Tim last night that I would really like to begin attending the Catholic church here in Edgartown with him. That way when he goes back to Boston to settle everything, I'll be comfortable in continuing by myself. It was important to Tim, and most likely his entire family, that I convert to Catholicism. He confessed that he had already visited with the local priest and that he was looking forward to our attendance. He's a capable man, my Tim.

Chapter 27

Dolly and I had several estates that were in the works and a new client to schedule and get set up. I asked if she would please call them and make an appointment for the following week if that worked for them. Tim had requested that we go to Boston following the Brice will being settled. I thought that we were getting so close to Thanksgiving that we might want to try and schedule our visit around the holiday. I hadn't talked with him about that yet, but I would try tonight while we were preparing dinner. Dolly had managed to reach the Hollingers, and they agreed to Tuesday morning of the following week. I put it on my calendar and went back to working on the estate that still needed to be settled later in the year. Dolly and I shared a pizza for lunch and then finished up letters and filing and decided to call it a day. I stopped and got gas for the car and then stopped to pick up a couple of steaks for dinner. It was a lovely day with just a slight breeze so I thought perhaps we would grill the steaks and I'd make a salad to go with them. I got to the house to find Lt. Adler visiting with Patrolman James. I parked and got out to greet him. I picked up my briefcase, purse and groceries so we could go into the house. Patrolman James went in and did his rounds and came back saying all was okay for us to go in. I fixed a glass of iced tea for David and myself and asked how he and Lucy were doing. We visited about non-police stuff before he finally came to the specific reason for his stopping by. "Amanda, he said, I visited with Leonard Brice today about several different issues. I asked him specifically if he had become friendly with Scott Schwartz aka Duncan Ford and if he had told his sister about Schwartz being arrested. Leonard said that he hadn't spoken a word to his sister for a long time. As for Schwartz, he hadn't even met the man! His mother had told him about a man showing up at her home claiming to be her nephew. He had warned her then that he doubted this was the case. Lt. Adler thought for a moment and said, "I tend to believe this man. He seems very upfront with me, answers all my questions directly, and has been available anytime I've called him. I really don't believe anything that Lois is telling me and certainly don't believe Schwartz about anything. I've been trying to figure out if they are tied together in some way but haven't yet reached a conclusion. I do know that I plan to attend the reading of the will if you have no objection." I told him that I was relieved that he would be there with me. I explained that I'd been very emotional and upset over this entire ordeal and that he knew firsthand that it wasn't my normal attitude toward things. He just hugged me and smiled. I do love him so.

Tim got home about an hour after David left. I tend to never ask what he does all day. I guess I figure he'll either tell me or it isn't any of my concern. Perhaps I need to start quizzing him when he comes through the door! I smiled at the very thought of that. Tim came in and picked up Precious on his way which he seems to do daily. The cat and I tend to glare at each other often. He kissed me and asked how my day was while he was setting the cat down and looking in the fridge for something to fix her for her dinner. I am pretty sure that Precious has become somewhat fluffier since Tim arrived. I told him about David's visit, and he said he was already aware of that. I couldn't stand it another minute, so I asked, "what do you do all day?" He started laughing and hugged me saying, "Oh, I run after pretty women and drink beer most of the day. Silly girl, while you're working, I'm taking the classes that I need to attend and flanking some of the beat cops, so I'll know what to expect when I start my new job. I've already been officially hired so it seemed smart to take the written courses that were mandatory, and I started my defensive driving course today." I looked at him for a long time and finally managed to tell him how proud I was of him. "Tim, you're just such an organized, responsible human being. How will I ever measure up to you!"

Tim got the steaks ready and started grilling. I fixed us a Gin and Tonic and started in on the salad and some steamed asparagus for our supper. Tim had already fed the chunky kitty so that was handled. I set the table in the dining room and found us a lovely bottle of Syrah to go with our steaks. Tim sipped on his drink while the steaks were cooking and sniffed around to see what I was making. He went back out to collect the steaks from the grill and I took up the asparagus and put the bowl of salad on the table. I was pouring the wine when he came in with the steaks after they had rested for a couple of minutes. I had some soft music playing in the background while we enjoyed our lovely dinner. I asked him what his thoughts were about going to his parents around Thanksgiving. "Well, that might work out perfectly, he said. My mom loves to fix big holiday dinners for everyone. My dad has a brother who is a widower who will join us, and my mom's sister and her husband will attend as well. The entire family usually attends mass either early on Thanksgiving morning or after supper. Would you be able to take the entire week off? I know you have a couple of estates to settle so perhaps that would be too much time?" "No, I told him, I think that will work fine. I need to be back the first week of December to administer one of the estates. The heirs were out of the country, so we had to postpone until their return. The other estate is just to get with the client and be sure that everything is accounted for, logged and valued so that can be done any time during December.

Tim and I checked the calendar finding that Thanksgiving was Thursday, November 28th. That left us just over two weeks to get the Brice estate settled, try to resolve the loose ends with the murder(s), go through the storage locker, and ready ourselves for the trip to his parents. He felt that we should arrive on the Monday before Thanksgiving which was exactly two weeks from today. He said that way I could be back in Edgartown and at work on Monday, December 2nd. We agreed that we had a good plan. I asked him for his parent's phone number as I wanted to call his mother, introduce myself, and ask if there was something that I could bring for the holiday dinner. Tim stared at me like I had two heads. I asked him what was wrong. "Amanda, he said, nobody is that courteous. My mother will be shocked but thrilled."

"Timothy, let me remind you, I said, I was brought up in a civilized household of well to do people who helped write the book of etiquette. I don't take this stuff lightly. It is inbred in my system!" He laughed and hugged me saying, "I think it's adorable".

Tim told me that he and David were planning on entering the storage locker tomorrow morning. "Do you want to come with us, he asked?" I told him I didn't but thanks for asking. "I still have quite a bit of paperwork to sort through so Dolly can start making the appropriate number of copies, and then I need to get them filed with the City, County and State offices. Perhaps you two could stop by the office tomorrow when you return and let me know what you find?" Tim said that sounded like a good idea and they would plan on it. It was late and I needed to take a bubble bath and go to bed. I kissed Tim goodnight and headed upstairs. Precious, of course, was staying with her knight in shining armor.

I got to the office right after Dolly and we turned up heat, made coffee, and readied the office together. I gave her the papers that needed to be copied and filed with the different agencies and she went to work. I phoned Mrs. Donaldson to introduce myself. She answered on the 2nd ring and sounded just like Tim had described her. "Mrs. Donaldson, my name is Amanda Bradley. I wanted to introduce myself before your son delivers me to your front door." She laughed and asked that I call her Lorraine, so she didn't have to call me Miss Bradley. I assured her that was a fine idea. We talked about who would be attending the holiday dinner and what I might expect. She assured me that my staying there was of no inconvenience and that the guest room was already done up and waiting for me. I asked if there was something that I could bring for the holiday dinner. She thought for a moment and said, "Tim tells me that you make a table into a work of art. Would you mind taking command of that chore and any other decorations that you want to add? I could have everything ready for you and we can get anything else that you want to add." I was just thrilled at the thought and told her so. "Lorraine, I said, it's been such a long time since I've spent a holiday with anyone. You just can't possibly know what this means to me. Thank you so very much for your warm generosity." Lorraine told me that she and Tom were thrilled that their son had finally found *the girl*. We knew he was dead serious when he called and talked to us because he just doesn't do this lightly. "He's a wonderful man, Amanda, she said, but I know you already know that." "I do, I said, and I count myself fortunate to have met such a wonderful man. I'm looking forward to meeting you and Tom. Thank you again for the invitation." I hung up feeling like I'd been given a real blessing. Tim's mom was so warm and genuine; so very different from my district attorney mother who never hugged; never said I love you.

Tim and David arrived at my office about 2:30pm. We went into the conference room where I fixed tea and coffee for us. David was unusually quiet, and Tim's pallor had taken on a gray hue. I was immediately frightened. Tim started to speak but David cut him off. "Amanda, we would have been here several hours ago, but we had to work the crime scene before I could leave." "Somebody please explain what happened, I cried." The lieutenant said that he and Tim arrived at the storage facility about the time they would open. They tried the door, and it was locked. They could see a car parked in what would seem to be the place employees would park. The car was locked, and the hood was cold, so the car hadn't been parked recently. The lieutenant said, "I just had a bad feeling when the place was locked up and nobody responded. We tried calling the number and received the answering service. I phoned for backup and a squad car was onsite within 5 minutes. We broke the front door and entered the building. The person that we know to be the on-duty manager was found dead behind the counter. We found the maintenance worker out back by the storage units; also deceased. Two of the units had been broken into with what appeared to be a crowbar. There were several paintings that looked as if they'd been thrown against the wall in anger. A couple of other items looked as if they'd been kicked out of the way. The second unit was pretty much empty except for a safe. The safe is one of those antique safes that weigh about 2500 pounds. If I had to guess I'd say that whoever broke in was very angry, couldn't move the safe and couldn't open the safe and that they took their anger out on the manager and the maintenance man. Tim here believes that he may possess the combination to the safe, but we were reluctant to open it without you there. Care to take a ride?" I stood there with my mouth open, my heart beating like a trip hammer, wishing with all my heart that I could disappear. "Sure, I said." We went to the storage facility which had yellow tape surrounding the building, and there were still quite a few police onsite. We walked back to the lockup where the safe was sitting. Tim had the key that we'd pulled from the bag of coins. He had a hunch that the 6 numbers were the safe combination. He cleared the wheel and input the first 2 numbers to the left, then the next 2 numbers to the right, and the last 2 numbers back to the left. Nothing. He cleared the wheel again and put the numbers in beginning right rather than left. When he put the last 2 numbers in the wheel clicked. He looked up at us and then took hold of the wheel and opened the door. There was a second door inside that needed a key inserted! David suggested that he close the door and turn the wheel to lock the safe and that we find a tow truck capable of moving the safe to the precinct. We all agreed that this was the best idea. He called for two patrolmen to cover the lockup. One patrolman to watch the safe and the other patrolman to watch the safe and the other patrolman. He explained that someone's butt would be sore if that safe moved out of their sight for any reason. He made a couple of calls and had a tow truck that works exclusively for the police department to come and relocate the safe.

Chapter 28

Tim and I drove home in silence. My car was still at the office so Tim would have to take me to work in the morning. We took out a bottle of chilled white wine and settled ourselves in the living room. After a few minutes I asked, "What do you make of this? Obviously, whoever broke in, killed those poor people and ransacked the lockups didn't care about anything but the contents of that safe. Were they so stupid that they thought they'd be able to come back and get it before the police discovered their actions?" "I don't know what to think, he said, but I know that they've come to a dead end. They wanted the contents of that safe which is now and forever unavailable to them. I'm going to research the maker of the safe and see what can be done to open the second door. There's considerable value in what's left in the lockup as far as paintings and other artifacts go. It was stupid of them to ruin what they did as that would have been additional money in their pockets."

"Tim, Amanda said, I'm not hungry but we need something to eat. Can we just do a grilled cheese and a glass of milk?" He agreed and they went to prepare it. Precious was sitting in front of the refrigerator preparing to sing her song but thankfully Tim noticed and began fixing her dinner. I told Tim about the phone call with his mother. He was so happy that we had connected as we had. "I just know you're going to love her, he said." Amanda confessed that she hadn't ever experienced that kind of warmth from anyone except Aunt Mamie. She also told him she was excited about doing the table and the decorating. She asked him if he knew of a florist near them that she could communicate with. He said that he did and would get her the number. They ate in the kitchen and then cleaned up and decided that they were both worn out. "Are you going to read for a few minutes? she asked. If you are, I think I'll go soak in the tub before turning in." Tim told her to go ahead, and he'd see her in the morning. She poured a glass of wine to take with her and headed upstairs. The bubbles and fragrance were working their magic as she laid there enjoying the peace and solitude. It is so difficult sometimes to take a person who has been raised with such order and silence and toss them into such chaos. She had specifically chosen estate law because it lacked the arguments and anger that criminal law invites. She finished up her wine, toweled off and donned a fluffy terry robe. She started for her room but realized that she hadn't kissed Tim goodnight. His light was on under his door, so she went and knocked softly. Tim answered immediately worried that something was wrong. She explained that she wanted a hug and a kiss and to tell him goodnight. "It doesn't seem right anymore if I don't do this, she said." He hugged her to him and kissed her, perhaps a bit longer than usual. She looked up into that gorgeous face and kissed him back. Tim warned her that this wasn't a good idea, but she wasn't listening. She held on tight, kissing him back, and discovering feelings that she didn't know existed. Tim warned another time, making sure that she knew what was happening. Amanda stepped back, looked directly into those beautiful eyes, and kicked the door shut.

Amanda awoke before the alarm. She stretched and yawned and started to roll over but discovered that she was still in Tim's bed! She could hear that he was already downstairs fixing breakfast and talking to the cat. Her first instinct was embarrassment and then realized that she didn't want to feel that way. She was finally whole! She was officially, at just short of 40 years old, a woman! A woman that was in love with the most glorious creature she'd ever imagined. She laid there thinking about the night before. It was dawn before either of them had slept. She recalled looking at Tim and admiring the most beautiful body she'd ever seen. He had adored her from head to foot. She couldn't help smiling and she thought, "there's no going back now!" She jumped out of bed, headed for the shower humming. She finished up quickly, threw a pair of slacks and a sweater on, pulled on a pair of ballet slippers, brushed her hair out and then pulled it into a scrunchie. There! She was ready to go to work! She hurried down the steps and into the kitchen. She was smiling broadly as she wrapped her arms around Tim's neck. Go back? I think not! "I love you, Timothy Donaldson!" "Well, a darned good thing, my girl! he said." Tim told her that her breakfast was ready and that she looked adorable. She told him that she thought this might very well be her new uniform of choice. They both laughed and sat down at the kitchen bar to eat breakfast. Precious was glaring at Amanda so she just glared back at her. The cat fluffed her tail at her and went into the other room.

They didn't speak about last night's encounter but every time they came in close contact with one another they would reach for each other's hands. Amanda kept thinking to herself that being in love was the most wonderful, profiling feeling in the world. Judging from Tim's face he felt the same. She wondered if this would change their entire relationship going forward. Typical of Amanda, she started to panic! Would he still want to marry her? Would he still love her? Would he think less of her for having succumbed to her passion? These thoughts were flowing through her head at a great rate of speed. She stopped long enough to notice that Tim was staring at her with a smirk on his face. "Amanda Kay, he said, I love you! I can't wait until we're married and all this crapola is behind us. I think you're the most beautiful woman I've ever met, both inside and out. I'm quite relieved to discover that you could no longer ward off my charm as I was really beginning to worry that I'd lost it completely." She shook her finger at him, and said, "You know, you're not all that funny. You need to take me to work." With that she hugged him, grabbed her coat and briefcase, scratched the cat on the head and went to flash her lights at the cop in her front yard.

Chapter 29

Amanda and Dolly spent a busy day preparing for tomorrow's meeting. She called the lieutenant to be sure he'd be at the office prior to meeting time. He assured her that he would be there. Amanda went through her mail, answered a couple of letters for new client inquiries, answered her messages and brought her calendar up to date. She checked the schedule to see about her and Tim leaving on Sunday the 24th. Everything looked good for that entire week to be away, and she had Dolly revisit the following week's schedule insuring that they hadn't forgotten anything. Amanda called Suzy to see if she and her fiancé were free for dinner the first week of December. Suzy checked her calendar saying those dates were open. Amanda told her that they would come up with a date and time when she returned from Boston. Dolly went out shortly before noon and came back with fish and chips for the two of them to share with a cup of tea. Dolly told Amanda that she was going to her sister's house in Louisville, Kentucky for the Thanksgiving holiday. She mentioned that she hadn't traveled that far in a long time so was really looking forward to the holiday with family. Amanda made a mental note to put together Dolly's review, raise, and bonus before she left for Boston. They finished up their day, tidied the office bathroom and vacuumed prior to turning out the lights and going home. Dolly walked with Amanda to her car as she wasn't comfortable that it had sat on the street overnight. All was good and Amanda hugged and thanked Dolly for her thoughtfulness. She called Tim to see if she needed to stop for anything before heading home. He called her back immediately saying he was already home, and the booze was cold! He really does think that he's funny she said to herself with a smile. The patrolman out front wasn't James, but he assured her that all was fine. James had taken the day off and would return tomorrow. He walked her to the already open door and Tim waiting for her. She thanked him and went inside. Like always, and out of habit now, they manned the alarm and locked the door before heading for the kitchen. Tim had ice cold Margaritas in a pitcher and some cold prawns and red cocktail sauce for a snack. Heaven on a plate! They sat at the kitchen bar enjoying their happy hour refreshments while the simmering seafood stew cooked away. It smelled so good she felt like she could consume the entire pot full. Tim had something on his mind, but she was unsure what it was. She asked him, "Tim, what's up? I know you're concerned about something." Tim looked directly at her and said, "Amanda, what happened last night was in my mind the most wonderful thing in the world. We love each other. We expressed that in every way possible. But I'm concerned about you. You're going to be 40 years old next month. I'm assuming you're still capable of conceiving. I would be thrilled if that happened but never at the risk of your health. We've not talked about this as we're both pushing the envelope age-wise, but we need to be realistic. Are you taking any birth control medications? Am I off base here with these questions? I consider myself a grown up but right now I feel like a stupid child." Amanda thought for a moment and then kind of started giggling which is very much foreign to her personality. "Tim, I hadn't even thought about that! Good grief, I'm the stupid child not you. Wow! I guess I should pay a visit to my doctor and talk with her about all of this. This is what happens when you seduce a 40-year-old! Oh, wait, I guess I did the seducing. Never mind." And then she laughed out loud. "No, she said, I'm not taking anything because there was not any need. I'm very healthy and very regular so I would say there's a strong chance that we could produce a child." Tim hugged her and told her that nothing would make him happier if she was okay with this. She smiled and told him that she would be more than okay with it. "The thing is, she said, are we changing up our entire living arrangement now? If we are, I'd like to book the remodel to begin as soon as we return from your parents. My bed is a queen size and very comfortable, but probably a bit girly as it has always been my room.

Your room is dingy at best as I've not touched it in all these years. I am not prepared to move into my parent's room until the remodel is completed. Can you handle a girly room?" "I'll take my chances, he said, and with that ran upstairs and started moving his stuff into her room!" "Take your time, she said, I will just sit here and finish my pitcher of Margaritas."

They ate dinner, cleaned the kitchen, read until about 10pm and headed upstairs. Amanda wanted to be in the office by 7am to make sure everything was perfect for the meeting. Tim slipped in behind her and hugged her to him, whispered good night, and they went to sleep. Precious sat on the foot of the bed glaring at them.

Chapter 30

Tim was already up and had breakfast started when Amanda awoke. She headed for the shower dreading the meeting this afternoon. She showered, dried her hair and pulled it into a loose ponytail, applied minimal makeup and went to don a dark suit, white blouse and black pumps. She eyed herself in the mirror and decided the look was perfect for the day. She went downstairs and stopped at the bottom landing to pet the cat. Precious purred and seemed fine with the attention. Tim had scrambled eggs and bacon ready to go in the kitchen. He handed her a cup of coffee, gave her a kiss and a swap on the backside. "You look very lawyer today, Miss Bradley, he said. Is this your armor for getting through this meeting?" "Yes, it is, she replied. I'm so relieved that David is going to be with me. I must admit that even though Lois is trying to apologize for her actions I'm just not buying it. I don't know what is really going on with her, but I don't trust her at all. Tim agreed completely. He told her that he had received a response from the makers of the safe and that they weren't very encouraging. He and David were going to get together and try to come up with another solution. Amanda hugged him goodbye and headed for the door. "I'll see you about 5-5:30 when I finish up, she said. Do you want to meet for appetizers or dinner?" "I'll call you later, he said, after I find out what the day holds." Amanda flashed the lights and waited for the patrolman to come to the porch. She greeted Patrolman James and told him she was glad to see him back on the job. He walked her to her car and told her to have a good day. She parked right outside the office door and noticed that Dolly's car was already there. She knocked on the door rather than unlocking it and letting herself in so she wouldn't scare Dolly. Funny how things you've always done now cause you fear because some person has infringed on your safety. Dolly let her in and relocked the door. No reason for it to be open until after 9am. Dolly got a cup of coffee for Amanda and then went to the conference room to start laying out the copies of the will and the estate list. She also made sure that the paperwork that had to be signed, witnessed and notarized were included in the stack for each heir. Dolly had decided that recording the meeting was still a good idea and told Amanda that she had that all set up. Amanda agreed that this was a good idea. They went about their normal routine answering phone messages, letters, phone calls, etc. The day was moving very rapidly it seemed. Dolly called for take out to be delivered and about noon the truck arrived out front and then driver brought in lovely chef salads and toast for the two of them. She paid for the meal out of petty cash, thanked him, and then locked the door behind him so they could eat their lunch without interruption. They ate their salads, drank a cup of tea and cleaned up the kitchen area. Dolly made a new pitcher of iced tea, prepared the pot for those that wanted coffee and set out a bucket with ice and bottles of water. Amanda went into the ladies' room to freshen up and came back out just in time to get a phone message from Tim. He had made a reservation at the Atlantic Fish & Chop House and would see her there at about 5:15pm. She called him back saying that this sounded perfect. She heard Dolly greeting Lt. Adler and she went out to the lobby to make him welcome. They went into the conference room and Amanda told him that Dolly had the recorder set up to record the meeting. About ten minutes later Dolly buzzed the intercom announcing the arrival of both Leonard and Lois Brice. I walked out to the lobby and greeted them and asked that they follow me into the conference room. Dolly offered to take their coats and asked if they'd like a beverage. Both asked for coffee which she served them and then went to the bookcase and turned on the recorder. I thanked them for coming today and told them that I was sure they both knew Lt. Adler. They agreed that they did. I asked them if they had any questions before I began reading the will. Neither of them had any questions and with that I began the process. "Today, I said, I am charged with administering the Last Will & Testament of

Doris Elizabeth Talbott Brice. At this time, I would like to convey my personal condolences on the passing of your mother. She was a dear friend and a wonderful neighbor. That said I continued with the where-with and what-for until I reached the distribution of the estate. Doris Elizabeth Talbott Brice stated that her entire estate, both real and property, should be divided equally among her children, Lois Diane Brice and Leonard William Brice, less the sum of $1.00 (One Dollar and no cents) to her husband, Oscar William Brice, should she proceed him in death. I looked at the children and again stated my condolences on the loss of their father. Neither child showed any emotion whatsoever. There are a few bequests that will be made at your mother's direction. There is a notation that if for any reason one or both of you are unable to accept your inheritance that I am, as attorney in fact, authorized to dispose of the funds as I see fit, which would include other next of kin and so on. Our office has compiled a final income tax return as is required by both state and federal law enabling you to see the taxes due on the estate. There have been other charges incurred that are detailed in my bill. These costs will be deducted from the estate prior to distribution. Your mother inherited from both your grandparents. There were trusts in place from both sets of great grandparents as well. Lois, you have been receiving dividends from your mother's inheritance from her parents for the past ten-years. That money is to be deducted from your share of the net estate." At this news, Lois jumped up and started yelling at me that her mother would never have done such a thing to her! Red faced and screaming she pounded on the conference table that her mother had stolen everything from her. First her father and now her inheritance. The lieutenant went around the table to confront and try to control Lois' behavior. Leonard got up and moved to the other side of the room. Lt. Adler told her that she would either conduct herself like a civil human being or this meeting would be adjourned. Which was it to be? Lois ran out of the room toward the restroom. We all just held our breath until she returned about 5 minutes later. Lois came in and apologized for her behavior and assured us it would not be repeated. She asked that I please continue. I completed the rest of a very lengthy will and then picked up the estate listing. I read off each of the bequests that were to be pulled out of the net estate. I read each of the items listed and their value. When that was completed, I looked at the heirs and asked once again if there were any questions. They both said that they had no objections or questions. I then started to list the parts of the inheritance that they were to receive. Both heirs would receive fifty percent of Two Million Dollars ($2,000,000.00) life insurance money. That money will be distributed into whatever bank account that you direct us to. There is to be an immediate disbursement of Three Hundred Fifty Thousand ($350,000.00) to each of you from your mother's savings account. That money will be deposited into the bank of your choice. You are to share equally in the trust funds from your paternal great grandparents which will be disbursed monthly in the sum of Fifteen Thousand Dollars ($15,000.00). That monthly disbursement will continue for another twenty-three years. You are to share equally in monthly disbursements of Four Thousand Five Hundred ($4,500.00) from the trust funds left by your maternal great grandparents. That disbursement will continue monthly for another nine years. The trusts from your Talbott grandparents will be disbursed as a monthly dividend as those funds are all tied up in stocks and bonds. The portfolio is presently at $4.3 million. Your mother received a cash settlement and the house with all its' furnishings when your grandparents passed away. There were no funds left from the Moser estate at the time of your mother's passing. There are no funds that we are aware of from any Brice ancestors. The Talbott home and your mother's vacation home are to be sold and the money shared by you equally. She left a provision that stated if either of you care to purchase either of those homes that you must state so with 48-hours of the reading of the will. If you wish to purchase one of the homes, I am to have the house listed with a local realtor and monitor the sale through to its conclusion. The homes have already been valued and such is listed on the estate listing. Are either of you interested in purchasing either property? Leonard responded that he had no interest in either property. Lois said that she felt Leonard should relinquish his interest in the Edgartown house and allow her to live out her life in it. Leonard told her she could go to hell. With that little bit of news, Lois wanted to know when the checks would be ready. Again, I reminded her of the way that the will reads, that the funds were to be deposited into a bank account designated by them rather than a check being issued to either of them. Lois said, "Well, I don't have a bank account anywhere. My mother always gave me cash." Amanda looked directly at her and said, "I think it may be time for you to remedy that situation. Let me know when you have any account number. Also, I need the key to both houses as they are now officially out of both of your control. If there is nothing else, then Dolly will see you out. I'll expect to receive those account numbers soon. Thank you for coming in." Leonard shook hands with me and thanked me for my time today. He had his signed copies and said he'd give Dolly the account information. Lois threw the keys at Amanda, said nothing and walked out. I turned to David, and he just stared at the door. I walked over and turned off the recorder and closed the conference room door. "What do you make of her? I asked." "Be darned if I know Amanda, he said. She is really a piece of work." Amanda thought for another moment, and then said, "They are both going to be extremely wealthy people."

Chapter 31

Amanda and David bid good night to Dolly and headed out the door. Tim had called a few minutes before, saying he'd had to cancel their reservation and asked if they might meet him at the house. David told Amanda he'd follow her. They parked in the driveway and Patrolman James came to greet Amanda and spoke to the lieutenant. He told them that he had done his walk through when Mr. Donaldson arrived home, so the house was okay for them to enter. They thanked him and Tim was there to open the door when they walked up onto the porch. Tim had a pitcher of iced tea for them to drink while he filled them in on his findings. "I received word back from the safe manufacturer. The first people told me I was pretty much out of luck as there aren't any skeleton keys that are available to open the second door. The people that I spoke with today said that they would need a formal request from a judge, and they would be able to provide us with the skeleton key. We'll need to give them the serial numbers and they've told me where to locate those. Do you think you have a judge that will assist us?" Amanda told him that Uncle Judge Henry would be glad to help them. "I have another thought I'd like to run by both of you, Tim said. I keep thinking about the mysterious bag of coins and the key that we found in there. Oscar would have known that the key had the combination engraved on it; Jack Sheridan would have also. Oscar and Jack would both have known that they needed the second key. Oscar didn't give it up to Jack and ended up dead. We now know for a certainty that Jack killed Oscar. Jack went to Oscar's sister looking for Oscar. Maybe he was also looking for that second key. He also went to Oscar's cousin's house, and we know physically attacked him. I'm starting to think that there must be a connection between Oscar's sister or cousin and Lois Brice." "If you'd have heard her today, Amanda said, you'd have been positive about that. She was screaming about her mother having sent her father away. I remember that they were close when she was a little girl. I would bet that they remained close throughout the years." David intervened and said, "You know, we need to find a way to see just how connected she might be to her dear relatives. After listening to the will be administered today Lois is going to be a very rich woman. If she has had a relationship over the years with Oscar's family, they may very well be looking to cash in on some of that money. I am going to order surveillance on her comings and goings and see what we can find out. In the short term, Amanda, will you talk with the judge and see if he can get the paper that Tim needs to procure that skeleton key? Tim, if you'll come by the station in the morning, you can guide me through locating the serial number." He hugged me goodbye, shook hands with Tim, and we walked him to the door. "David, I said, please give Lucy a hug and tell her I miss her. Let's plan to get together after Thanksgiving so we can catch up." He assured her he would do just that. Amanda and Tim locked up the house, manned the alarm and looked like they wanted to collapse for the evening. Amanda suggested breakfast for dinner and Tim agreed that the idea was perfect. "You want bacon or sausage, she asked?" He said sausage and she went to put the patties in the oven. Tim got the eggs ready to poach and put bread in the toaster. He mashed up an avocado and added salt, pepper and hot sauce to it to spread on the toast. Glorious! Best dinner ever. They ate with gusto, washed it down with cold milk and made a pot of tea to take to the living room. Precious had turkey sausage and a scrambled egg with some skim milk so she was also very content. They both read for a while and then called it a night.

Amanda awoke early and found Tim still sleeping soundly. She tiptoed out of the room and pulled the door shut so he could continue to rest. She went downstairs and fixed coffee and laid out the makings of pancakes and bacon for breakfast. She fed Precious and she let her hold and pet her for a change. This cat is really changing her habits since Tim arrived on the scene. Amanda checked messages to see if anything was new. There were a couple of messages to answer which she handled and then went into the living room to watch the morning news. There wasn't anything of interest in the news, so I switched it off. It was then that I heard Tim walking around upstairs. He came down with his usual grin and bright disposition. He's just always happy or so it would seem. He patted me on the backside as I walked toward the kitchen and reminded me to call and make that doctor appointment. I promised I would. "Tim, I asked while he was preparing the pancake batter, is your family home fancy or cozy or what? How do people dress for the holiday dinner? Do we walk or drive to church?" Tim told her that he would consider his family home as modest, cozy, and very comfortable. My father, as you know, is retired from his private investigation business. My Mother was a professional woman for many years but retired when my dad had his stroke and has been a home body ever since. They own their home outright and I believe they would be considered middle class. My father will wear slacks, shirt with the cuffs rolled back, probably a vest of some sort. My mother will wear a lovely dress which will be protected by a frilly apron. Everyone tends to dress up a bit and we do walk to church, and it will be very, very cold. Snow and wind are normally on the weather agenda for Boston at Thanksgiving time. Whatever you choose to wear you will be perfect as you always are. You're equally beautiful in a cocktail dress as you are in sweats and a tee. More accessible in sweats and tee however." Amanda threw the dish towel at him, stuck her nose in the air and walked off to set the dining room table for breakfast. "Timothy Ryan Donaldson, I'm ready for my breakfast, she said." He was laughing as he set her plate in front of her.

They visited about the coming trip, started at opposite ends of the house and met in the middle when all was cleaned and tidy. They decided they would go grocery shopping together and then perhaps get lunch before coming back home. Tim was starved to death for Veal Shanks, so they set about making a menu and grocery list, so they'd have all the ingredients necessary for Osso Bucco.

It would be fun to work together making this complicated dish for dinner. Amanda had phoned her doctor earlier and made an appointment for next Tuesday at 9am. She called Dolly to note the appointment and that she would arrive at the office late that day. They went upstairs to get showers and get ready to leave the house. Amanda switched the lights off and on and the patrolman on duty came and greeted them as they stepped out on the porch. Tim told the patrolman that they would return late afternoon. They headed to the Stop n Shop which has a lot of specialty foods and delicious meat. Tim knew exactly what he wanted and was hoping they would have it available. The butcher was very helpful and had two shanks that he cut in half to make 4 shanks, so they'd have two meals out of this beautiful meat. They were planning on serving the Osso Bucco on creamy polenta, so they got the needed ingredients for that. Amanda's wine collection was well stocked so there was no problem in finding a good Italian red to go with this beautiful dinner. They finished up their shopping and headed to the Wolf's Den Pizza to share a pizza and a pitcher of cold beer. They found a quiet corner and ordered the Meat Lover's twelve-inch pie and sipped on their beer until their order arrived. The smell was intoxicating. Sausage, Chorizo, Pepperoni, and the works. They had three slices left over to munch on tomorrow for lunch with a salad. Pleasantly full and happy they headed home. When they rounded the corner of their street, they were greeted with fire engines, emergency vehicles and police cars who were all attending to the inferno that had once been Mrs. Brice's house. Amanda simply could not fathom what she was seeing. What in the world had set off this horrible fire? They parked in their driveway and the Patrolman James escorted them to the door, went in and checked on things, and came back to allow them inside. He cautioned them that it was perhaps best to stay inside as they didn't yet know what they were dealing with. It seemed hours later before they finally got the fire contained. They had saved a portion of the back of the house but the rest of it appeared to be a total loss. Tim and Amanda just seemed to be stunned over this matter. It was like the last straw in a series of terrible events. Tim had asked Amanda what her role in this property loss would be.

"I'm not totally sure, she said. I'll have to speak with the insurance company and get their advice on the next step. One thing for sure, it won't move quickly as they never do." They decided to read for a while and then call it a night.

Chapter 32

Tim was already up and had gone for his run when Amanda crawled out of her cocoon. She went downstairs to find coffee, scones and jam waiting for her. She smiled to herself over his thoughtfulness. She just couldn't get over how lucky she was to have found this wonderful man. She asked Precious if she'd eaten yet and was rewarded with a fluff of her tail as she walked away. Tim had apparently already tended to the cat. Her phone started ringing and she tried to locate it. She found it stuffed under a sofa pillow and saw that she'd missed David Adler's call. She called him back and he answered immediately. "Amanda, can you and Tim come down to the station sometime this morning?" "Of course, she said. Tim is on his run, but I'll get ready and we should be there within an hour." She ran upstairs to shower and dress so that the bathroom would be available when Tim returned. She was drying her hair when she heard him come in so she yelled downstairs that he needed to get showered so they could go meet David. He yelled good morning from the upstairs landing as he went to get his clothes ready. She finished up and he headed for the shower. Within 15 minutes they were ready to go. "Do you have any idea why David wants to see us, she asked?" "No, not a clue, he said." They flashed the lights, greeted Patrolman James, and headed into town. Lt. Adler met them in the lobby of the precinct, and they walked back to his office. "It would appear, he said, that Scott Schwartz (aka Duncan Ford) wants to talk. He specifically asked that Amanda be present during this meeting with him. If you are both willing, I can have him escorted to an interrogation room immediately." "Why would he want me to be present, she asked?" "I'm not sure, the lieutenant responded, but

perhaps he feels that you're the person in control of the Brice heirs."
Tim asked if he could accompany Amanda to this meeting and David
told him that this was why he was there. "Let's get this over with,
Amanda said." The lieutenant called down to lock up and asked that
they escort Schwartz to Interrogation Room Number 3. "Let's go, he
said." The three of them walked down the hall and entered the room
just ahead of the officer escorting Schwartz. The lieutenant told the
officer to handcuff Schwartz to the table and then to please stand guard
outside the door. Lt. Adler told Schwartz that this was his meeting,
and they were ready to listen. Scott Schwartz looked at each of them
and thanked them for the opportunity to speak with them and then
he began:

> "I've been in and out of trouble since I was a teenager. I had
> gotten arrested for burglary and was sent to prison. While I
> was there my roommate, as I'm sure you're now aware, was
> Oscar Brice. Besides being stupid and uncouth he was also
> very talkative. He bragged about what he and his cousin
> and his cousin's son had done while they were teamed up
> with Jack Sheridan. He bragged about how he turned state's
> evidence against Jack for killing those poor people and that
> he got his sentence reduced to breaking and entering only.
> He had served his time for that and was ready to lay claim to
> all the goods that they had stolen together and stashed in a
> storage locker when he got arrested again and ended back up
> in prison. He figured that I was a smart guy and because my
> time was almost finished that I would be a great asset in his
> attempts to get certain goods and information from his lovely
> wife. He started schooling me in the family names and events
> and decided that I should pass myself off as his wife's dead
> sister's son. As you know, that's exactly what I did. Doris was
> a truly lovely woman and welcomed me into her family just
> like Oscar said she would. Oscar's cousin and his kid were, if
> possible, even more ignorant and uncouth than Oscar was.
> They knew that Doris was the last person to have the bag of
> coins and that the key they needed for the safe was in there.

They all bragged about how we'd all be rich as soon as we got the damned thing opened. Oscar had stayed in touch with his daughter over the years and she thought of herself as Daddy's little girl. He could maneuver her comings and goings like a puppeteer. Oscar's son was probably the most intelligent one in the group and in absence of his father was doing a great job of leading the troops. A great many years passed due to someone always being in jail. Oscar was finally free and he and Leonard and the cousins, who had escaped involvement in any of the escapades, were ready to move in on the storage facility and take what was theirs. Only cog in that wheel was that Jack Sheridan was also out of jail and was hunting Oscar. It didn't take him long to find him and we all know how that played out. Jack was hellbent on finding that bag of coins. He turned Miss Bradley's office upside down and her home as well but came up empty handed. He went to the cousins and came up empty handed there as well. So now you've got Jack in jail, you've found me out and I'm in jail. Oscar is dead. There were bodies found at the storage unit, but so far, no arrest made in that crime. And, as you know, news travels quickly in a jail, I understand that the Brice home is burnt to the ground. You might be ready for my help now in bringing all these puzzle pieces together and finalizing this dreadful situation."

He sat there with a rather smug look on his face and the lieutenant asked him what he hoped to gain from all this interesting information. "A reduced sentence would be nice, he answered. I impersonated a man to gain financially but I've not had anything to do with the rest of these things. I know what I've been told and what I've heard and I'm willing to share all of that with you. Initially I was promised $25000 to impersonate Doris' nephew and help Oscar gain access to that bag and the key. There's another key, as I'm sure you're aware of, and I might be able to help you out with that as well. It is quite apparent that I'm not going to get my money, but I don't feel that I should take the fall for things that I had nothing to do with." The lieutenant told

Schwartz that he would be returned to his cell while we all have time to digest this information. "We will get back to you, he said."

Amanda, David and Tim just stared at each other when he was escorted out. The lieutenant said that he wasn't necessarily surprised by this as right now Schwartz was pretty much the fall guy for everything. He did express, however, that he was surprised to hear of Leonard's involvement. "All along, he said, I was sure it was Lois and that Leonard was in the clear." Amanda asked, "What happens now?" The lieutenant told her that he needed to speak with his superiors and was pretty sure his butt was going to be in a sling. "We can't take someone's word for all this, he responded, we have to prove it. That said, it may be easier to start tying people together. I'm thinking that after I speak with the captain that perhaps I need to make a trip to the cousin's place and bring them in for questioning." Tim and Amanda took their leave, thanking David for his time, and headed for car. Once safely inside the car Tim just kind of had a meltdown. "I cannot fathom what the hell all these people are doing! They've run all over the place, killing people, upsetting people's lives, swindling, cheating, lying, and for what?" "I know, I said, I feel the same way. It's like you want to run away from your own life but you can't. I certainly hope that David gains some leverage talking with the Brice relatives. They kind of scare me." By law I had up to 6 weeks to distribute the funds to the heirs. I felt that waiting was not a bad idea to see what David would find out about the Brice relatives.

Chapter 33

We heard from David later that afternoon advising us that they had picked up Oscar's cousin, his son, his sister, Leonard and Lois. They were all being held for questioning. The lieutenant, along with his captain, had pieced together a time frame and the involved parties that appeared to be working quite well. The lieutenant was feeling confident that the cousins would start singing loudly as soon as the charges were all mentioned. They could now be tied to the Bartlett's murder, Doris Brice's murder, and the two homicides at the storage facility. That would either put them away for the rest of their lives or get them a cell on death row. They were his two first choices to begin questioning. The lieutenant had the older Brice cousin brought into the interrogation room first. He laid out what they knew, going back to the break in at the Bartlett's home and their subsequent death. He told them that they had the evidence necessary to place him at the scene of that crime. The cousin, at first, refused to say anything and then after being given a few minutes to think it over he sang a different tune. He and his son had gone along with Oscar and Jack to rob the house, but they had nothing to do with those people being killed. That was all Jack and Oscar's doing. Then Oscar turned state evidence against Jack, and they were all able to walk away from that mess. "I never heard nothing else from any of them until Oscar showed up at my place in when he got out looking for some damned-fool key or something, he said. I didn't have no idea what he was talking about. I didn't have no damned bag of coins or no key either. Then just lately Jack shows up and almost kilt me asking the same damned questions. I told him the same thing that I didn't have no idea what he was talking about." The lieutenant asked him about his relationship with Leonard. "Well, he said, Leonard has been needing some help moving some goods that he owns from place to place. We try to help him out anytime he asked." The lieutenant told him that the goods held at the storage place had gotten moved out. What could he tell him about that? "Let me think, he said, I don't remember much about any storage place. Maybe my boy helped him out there." After a few more questions the lieutenant decided to trade George Brice for his son, Barney. Lt. Adler told George that he'd be held for a while longer in case there were any more questions. The officer took George out and brought Barney in. Barney sat down as he was told and, if possible, looked more stupid than the father had. Lt. Adler got right to the point telling Barney that he was implicated in several murders, burglaries, and movement of stolen goods. The son had an attitude and was set on displaying it. He told the lieutenant where he could shove his questions and his threats. He hadn't done anything wrong and even if he had, they didn't have any proof against him. The lieutenant explained to him that his father had just implicated him in the Bartlett's house invasion, burglary, and death. That he had implicated him in assisting his cousin, Leonard, in breaking into and removing the goods from two storage units and then killing the two employees. Barney Brice stared at the lieutenant and then burst out laughing. "My old man wouldn't have said any such thing, he said. I was only 17 years old when they broke into the Bartlett's house and kilt those poor folks. I didn't have nothing to do with the stuff they took. Oscar and Jack moved all that shit somewhere. I didn't have anything to do with it. As for the storage unit, Leonard asked me to drive the truck for him and he paid me damned good for doing that. Me and my old man helped him unlock those two units and loaded the truck up. I don't know nothing about anybody getting themselves kilt except what I read in the newspaper. Leonard and Lois have been at each other's throats for years trying to do whatever their old man told them to do. And I don't know nothing about any fire either. That was probably Leonard or Lois." The lieutenant looked at Barney and he immediately realized the error he had just made in mentioning the Brice house fire. The lieutenant thanked Barney for his time and told him that he would be held for a while longer in case they had more questions. The officer led Barney out and brought Lois in. David's first impression of Lois Brice was that she was the most belligerent person he'd met in a long while. She faced every situation with anger and resentment. The lieutenant began by mentioning the cousin's implications in several murders, burglaries, and movement of stolen goods. She just stared at him. He asked her when the last time she saw or spoke with her father was. She glared at him and said, "before he died." The lieutenant explained that he knew that Oscar and she kept in close contact over the years and that he was sure she would help her dad out with whatever he asked. David asked, "were you and your mother close, Lois? Did you do a lot together? I know she helped you out financially for most of your life. You never worked, did you? Your mom always paid your bills and made sure you had whatever you needed. Am I right? Lois just glared at him. "Would it be safe to assume, David said, that you were closer to your mom than your dad? He was always either in jail or in prison and didn't seem to ever be there to help you during your growing up years. Did he ever come to any event you were involved in? Did he ever come to a recital or a game or anything that you did?" Lois screamed at him, "You don't know anything! My father loved me! That hateful bitch sent him away when I was a little tiny girl. I hated her!" The lieutenant never wasted a second before asking, "did you kill her?" She looked like she'd been struck. The lieutenant told her he was done questioning her, but she'd be held for a while longer in case there were any more questions. The lieutenant told the officer to release her in about one hour saying they would let her know if they had more questions for her. The officer took a screaming, crying Lois out and brought in Leonard Brice. Lt. Adler was immediately aware of the intelligence and confidence that emitted from Leonard. He seemed to be in total control of the situation. I wanted to mention at this time that none of these players were aware that the others were at the precinct. That would be a little surprise that the lieutenant would supply later. Leonard shook hands with the lieutenant and asked him how he might be of help to him. Lt. Adler told him that they had made some recent discoveries in the storage unit murders and burglary. He told Leonard that today's technology was so much more sophisticated that say twenty years ago. "Today, he said, we conduct a sweep of the crime scene and then patiently wait to see what shows up. Your mother was a very organized woman. She was keen on technology and was fascinated with ancestry as I'm sure you are aware. She worked diligently to tie her DNA to her ancestors. I'm sure she did this to protect you and your sister from any harm. With the reading of her will it was apparent that she came from wealth and had made sure that the wealth was protected for you and your sister. DNA is such an interesting thing. We had found two hairs at the storage unit crime scene. One on the body of the manager and one near the entrance to the second storage unit. Those hairs were carefully collected and tested, and you'll be pleased to know that we have a 95% positive match on the owners of those hairs. Do you want to venture a guess as to who they belong Leonard?" Leonard Brice stared at the lieutenant and said, "I believe what I want, Lt. Adler, is my lawyer." Lt. Adler told him he would be happy to summon that person for him. "In the short term did he wish to make any kind of a statement?" Leonard told him that he thought it best that he speaks with his attorney first. "As you wish, said Lt. Adler, and you are under arrest. The nice officer behind you will read you your rights and then escort you to a holding cell.

David went to get a cup of coffee and tried to choke down a sandwich before continuing. He couldn't quite decide which way to proceed. They were all up to their necks in this mess. While eating the sandwich he decided that Barney Brice was probably his best bet on implicating the rest of the players. He went back to the interrogation room and the officer brought Barney back in. Lt. Adler told him that Leonard Brice had just been arrested for the burglary and murders at the storage facility. You and your father were accessories to those crimes, and I want to advise you now that you are being placed under arrest for those crimes mentioned. Barney started yelling about him and his old man not having nothing to do with those killings. "That was all Leonard, he said. All we did was load the truck and drive it where he told us to go." The lieutenant told him that they had requested and been given a search warrant for both his house and his father's house. "After conducting that search, he said, we found several empty cans of gasoline. We also found a note in the garbage can where you stupidly wrote down the Brice house address. It appears that we now have enough circumstantial evidence to tie you to torching the Brice house. Between the Bartlett's home invasion, burglary, and murder, the storage unit burglary and murders, and now the Brice home arson there is enough to put you and your father away for the rest of your lives. Even if you didn't pull the trigger, you are guilty of accessory in those multiple deaths. Do you have anything to say? Do you wish to make a statement?" Barney thought for a moment and said, "I guess I need me a lawyer. As for making a statement, I would just like to say, I didn't mean for nobody to get hurt. I just done what my old man told me to do." The officer read Barney his rights and removed him to a holding cell. David went through the same thing with George. When Lt. Adler asked him if he wanted to make a statement he said, "You know, I guess you got me dead to right on this shit, but you've still got a lot of loose ends that you ain't figured out. You let me know if you want my help with any of that."

The lieutenant stood alone in the interrogation room trying to work through all that had just happened. He now had Jack in jail for the Bartlett's murder and for Oscar's murder. He had George and Barney Brice as accomplices to the Bartlett case, for the storage unit case, and now closure on the arson case. He had Leonard Brice guilty of the murders at the storage unit and probably an accomplice to the arson of his family home. What he didn't have was who had killed Doris Brice, who had broken into the office and home of Amanda Bradley, and who had the second key. It appeared that his job was not quite complete yet. He would take George Brice up on his offer to help him out but not before tomorrow. He was hungry, he was tired, and he wanted to go home to Lucy.

Chapter 34

Lt. David Adler got to the precinct early and asked them to bring George Brice upstairs to the interrogation room. He had thought long and hard about how he was going to approach this. He was pretty sure that George only cared about himself. He wasn't going to go out on any limb to save his son or his cousin's son. Just his own slimy hide. When George came in the lieutenant made it very clear that the conversation was being recorded and that anything he said could and would be used against him. George just waived his hand and asked him what he wanted to know. The lieutenant told him, "That's simple. Everything." David asked him about the key to the safe. George said, "I knew there was a bag with old coins and an ugly old key. Oscar gave that bag to Doris for safe keeping but the old woman either lost it or tossed it. There was some other key that Oscar gave to Lois years later, but I don't know if she still has that or not. Not sure what it was for." The lieutenant asked him who had killed Doris. George said that he really had no idea about that one. "Could have been either one of them far as I know, he said." David told him that was all for now and the officer returned him to his cell. Leonard, George and Barney would all be arraigned before the circuit judge on Monday morning. David couldn't help feeling curious about Jack Sheridan. He decided that he'd like to have a talk with him. Jack had been transferred back to the State prison. David gave Tim a call to see if he wanted to go with him on Monday.

Tim's received a phone call while he and Amanda were doing laundry. He answered and talked with David and told him he'd talk with Amanda and call him back. Tim told Amanda that David wanted him to go with him tomorrow to the State prison to speak with Jack Sheridan. Will you be ok, he asked, if I'm away possibly overnight? The prison is in Shirley which is northwest of Boston proper. I'm guessing it's about 4-5 hours give or take traffic and such." Amanda told him that of course she'd be okay even though she was thinking just the opposite. Tim called David back and David asked if it was ok for him to stop by a bit later that he wanted to share some news with them. Tim assured him that they'd be home, and it was fine for him to stop. "I can throw some ribs on the BBQ, Tim said, if you can grab Lucy and both come over." David told him he'd call him back shortly. It wasn't but about 5 minutes until David called and asked, "what time?" Amanda and Tim looked through things just to verify that they had everything they needed. She had put a pot of pinto beans on earlier and added some crisp bacon and onions to them while they simmered away. She told Tim she'd throw together a potato salad and like magic, dinner. They set about their individual chores, straightened the living room, and decided to set the kitchen bar for a casual dinner. Tim knew that Amanda was more silent than usual and that she was probably terrified at the idea of being alone overnight or even for the entire day as far as that was concerned. Hopefully David would help to ease this uncomfortable feeling. They got everything finished up and made a pitcher of margaritas just before the Adler's rang the doorbell. Amanda was truly glad to see them and had especially been missing Lucy. They all hugged and talked at once as they headed for the kitchen to get drinks. Tim poured the margaritas and Amanda set out some cheese and crackers to nibble on until dinner. They all got settled and David explained that Leonard, George Brice and Barney Brice had all been formally arrested for various crimes and were in lockup. They would be arraigned on Monday and the captain would be present at that arraignment. There were a couple of snags that still needed to be worked out and he felt like Jack Sheridan might be able to clear up those questions which is why he had asked if Tim wanted to go to Shirley with him. David told Amanda, "I'm sure you're concerned about being alone and I'm aware of that. Lois is still running free and is still a potential problem. I believe you've met Detective Carla Simmons, and she would like to be with you tomorrow morning until our return. We may very well get back tomorrow evening without a problem, but I just can't guarantee it." Amanda told him that she didn't want to be a burden to still another police officer. David assured her that was not the case. "Amanda, he said, until we have the rest of the pieces worked out, I believe that Lois Brice is a threat to you, and I don't know how many others. Do I have your permission to assign the Detective to you? If you're unhappy with that I can put you in central lockup to ensure your safety." He was grinning at her, and she was threatening tossing her napkin at him. "Fine, she said, I just love camping out with cops." They all enjoyed a delicious dinner together and David explained that they had an early morning and he felt they should break away early. They drank a pot of coffee and had some delicious chocolate chip cookies that Amanda had picked up from the bakery. David and Tim agreed on a departure time and the Adlers took their leave. After they locked up, they decided to have a nightcap and just try to play catch up before heading off to bed. Amanda grabbed a stack of those cookies while Tim poured the coffee. Precious was curled up on the end of the sofa but never offered any complaint when Tim picked her up and put her onto his lap. Traitorous cat. Amanda asked Tim if they were going to try with his parents if they couldn't get back from Boston tomorrow night. He admitted that he hadn't even thought about it but that was a really good idea. He knew that she was sad about him being gone but with Detective Simmons with her he wouldn't worry. Tim asked, "Are you going to try to go into the office tomorrow or are you just going to hang around here?" "I don't know, she answered, I hadn't even thought about it. I have a lot to do so I'm thinking I'll go into the office. You and David have an ETD of 6:00am so I'm sure that the detective will most likely show up at the same time. She can either stay here or follow me to the office I suppose. The way all of this has come about we haven't even had a chance to make our Osso Bucco. I think we should plan to make it Tuesday evening. Does that work for you?" Tim thought that was perfect. They cleaned up the kitchen and then headed to bed. Tim packed an overnight bag just in case they couldn't get back tomorrow night.

Chapter 35

Tim was up and getting ready at 4:30am. He went for a short run and then came back, showered, dressed and was all set to leave when David drove up. The detective was directly behind David, so he brought her in to introduce her to both Amanda and Tim. Amanda explained that she'd like to go into the office about 9am and hoped that would work for her. Detective Simmons assured her that whatever her schedule that it would work for her just fine. Tim and David both hugged and kissed Amanda goodbye and were off on their trip. Amanda was feeling sad but knew it would pass as soon as she got busy doing something. She locked up, fed the cat, asked the detective if she would like to share breakfast with her. The detective said that sounded wonderful and what could she do to help. Together they made breakfast and were fast friends by the end of the meal. The detective insisted she call her Carla. She had been a police officer for over 15 years. She had made Detective 1st grade last year. Very pretty and very capable. Amanda excused herself to go get ready and was back downstairs, ready to go, in about 25 minutes. They flashed the lights and waited for Patrolman James to come and escort them. They locked up and went to their separate vehicles. Amanda noticed that Lois' car was parked at the burnt remains of her mother's home. She let both the patrolman and the detective know that this was the case. Detective Simmons asked Amanda to wait a moment while she walked across the street. Amanda could see that the detective was identifying herself to Lois and obviously had told her to leave as it was still a working crime scene. There were obvious signs of arson and the fire chief had labeled it a crime scene and the police had yellow tape strung around the parameter of the property. Lois was screaming obscenities at the detective as she got in her car and raced away with tires squealing. The two ladies exchanged looks and got into their cars and drove downtown. The detective escorted Amanda into the office and staged herself in the lobby where she planned to stay until Amanda was done for the day. She suggested they lock the door and only open it for pre-planned appointments. Dolly and Amanda agreed. They set about their normal routine. Amanda wanted to get everything she could completed prior to leaving for Boston over Thanksgiving week. She had a few minutes to spare and started compiling her notes for Dolly's bonus. She had the review pretty much completed as she tended to work on it all year long so as not to forget any good or bad parts. She brought it up on her computer screen and completed the balance of the review. She tended to grade on a 1-5 basis: 1 being the most unsuccessful and 5 being above standard. The review was calculated, and Dolly came out at 4.5 points. This score left room only for continued education or on-the-job training in paralegal work. Dolly would expect that on her review and would not feel badly that she hadn't scored a full 5 points. Amanda had made Dolly a salaried employee about 2 years prior. She calculated a 3% cost of living increase, 4.5% for her merit increase and a bonus of $1000. She compiled the paycheck and called Dolly into her office. They had about 20 minutes before the lunch hour so that would be the perfect amount of time. Dolly came into the office immediately and Amanda asked that she close the door. Amanda poured them both a cup of tea from her hot pot and gave Dolly a copy of the review. They read through the review together and discussed each of the points of the review. Dolly was very pleased with her overall review as it showed the progress that she had worked to accomplish this past year. She asked Amanda if it would be okay for her to sign up online with DeVry College to take some paralegal courses. Amanda told her that would be wonderful and that she would be reimbursed for tuition, parking, and books. She handed the paycheck to Dolly who immediately started to cry. She was just thrilled with her new pay scale and the bonus. It made me feel so wonderful to know that something delightful had happened today! I went and asked the detective what she'd like for lunch and suggested that we were going to order delivery. We all decided what we wanted, and Dolly called and ordered for us. After the delivery boy left, we all retired to the conference room to enjoy our lunch together. We talked about our families and lives, in general, and enjoyed our sandwiches and sodas. After lunch I finished up a bit of paperwork and told Dolly that I was calling it a day. I hadn't heard anything from the guys so figured they were deep into the investigation.

Tim and David arrived at the prison shortly after noon. David had already made the necessary arrangements to be able to interview Jack Sheridan. The guards had David remove his weapon and they showed them to a conference area where Jack was brought into shortly thereafter. Sheridan eyed David and said, "What do I owe this visit to Lt. Adler?" The lieutenant told him that he wanted to go over a few things with him and was sure that he would be able to set the list straight. Sheridan told him that he would listen to the list and let him know if he was wanting to discuss any of it with him. The lieutenant reminded Jack that he was going to be there for the rest of his life so he might as well do something useful with the time he had left. Jack just raised an eyebrow. He did, however, turn to Tim and asked, "Just who might you be?" Tim identified himself as being a PI from the greater Boston area. "Oh, said Jack, one of my old man's puppets? But wait, you look familiar. I'm sure I've seen you out in Edgartown." Tim assured him that he hadn't. David suggested that they get to the list and see what kind of progress, if any, that they could make. He asked, "Can you name your associates that were part of the home invasion, subsequent murder, and robbery at the Bartlett's home in 1983?" Jack thought for a moment and said, "Well, let's see. There was Oscar Brice, his stupid cousin George, George's oldest boy, Barney the idiot, and one more that I can't remember. Does that help?" David asked, "Did you have anything to do with the murder of Doris Brice?" Jack responded with a laugh, "Me? Hell no. She was a nice old lady even if she did hook up with a no-good like Oscar. You might check with Oscar." David eyed him and reminded him that he was in prison for the murder of Oscar Brice so that wasn't going to happen.

"Oh yeah, he said, I plumb forgot about that. Well, that leaves his dumbass son, Leonard or the lard ass Lois. Either one of them could have done it. They both hated the old lady." The lieutenant asked if he thought the cousins might have been involved in that." "No," he said. They were both stupid cowards; scared of their own shadows. They did what Oscar told them to do and then later they took their orders from Leonard. They couldn't have put 2+2 together and come up with any reason to have done away with Doris." Lt. Adler asked Jack straight, "Did you break into Amanda Bradley's office and then later on into her home?" Jack thought for a moment, looked at Tim and said, "Now I remember where I saw you! You and that pretty lawyer have a thing going. Well, I'll tell you Lieutenant, I believe I did. I was hunting high and low for an object that belonged to me that my slimy friend Oscar stole from me. He stole it about the same time as he lied, and they put me away. I had hunted for that object but came up empty handed. Did you ever find it Lt. Adler?" David ignored him and asked, "Do you have any idea why anyone would burn down Doris Brice's home?" This time Jack really did look genuinely surprised. "No idea at all, he said. That's kind of stupid, isn't it? I mean she had two kids who would get everything with her dead. Why burn down that much money? Doesn't make a damned bit of sense to me." The lieutenant told him that he appreciated his candor. He thanked him for his answers and would report to the warden that he had been pleasant and helpful. He hoped that it would get him a favor along the way. Tim and David took their leave. When they reached the parking lot David asked Tim what he thought of the interview. He said, "Actually, Jack was far more intelligent and pleasant then I would have imagined. He's a lifelong criminal after all." David agreed. "I guess, he said, that when you've built up that many crimes that you finally figure out that you're never getting out of there so you might as well just accept it. Do you want to try for the last ferry and get home tonight or do you want to go to your folks?" Tim looked at his watch. It's 2:30pm, he said, we can be at the ferry for the 5pm crossing and be home in time to take the girls to dinner. Let's hit the road, David!" Tim called Amanda and asked her to call Lucy and they'd meet them at the Seafood Shack between 6:15 and 6:30pm.

Amanda phoned Lucy and both ladies were glad that their men were on the way home. Amanda told the detective what the plans were, and she was going to follow Amanda to the restaurant and wait until the lieutenant arrived and officially took her off duty.

Chapter 36

Lucy and Amanda arrived about the same time and walked into the restaurant together. They both knew the manager and he found them a quiet table where they'd all be able to visit when the men arrived. It wasn't more than 10 minutes and the guys walked in to join them. After hugs and hellos to everyone the men detailed their interview with Jack Sheridan. The ladies seemed surprised that he was as amiable as he was. David pointed out that he felt like Sheridan had nothing to lose; nothing to gain so there was really no reason to try and withhold information. Amanda related the story about Lois being at the ruined remains of her family home and her horrible response to the detective asking that she stay clear of the crime scene. David just shook his head and said, "She is really a mystery to me. I can't decide if she is grief stricken or up to her neck in guilt. Sheridan seemed certain that either Lois or Leonard was the responsible party for their mother's death. Also, the arson, if it turns out to be that, apparently wasn't the idea of the cousins. Sheridan indicated that they didn't know how to put any plan together without instruction so we're leaning toward Leonard." They all enjoyed a wonderful meal and good conversation and promised to get together between the holidays. David and Lucy were going to have a night cap together before leaving. Tim and Amanda were ready to call it a night. Tim drove Amanda's car home. The patrolman met them at the foot of the stairs, and he went into check everything out before they entered. The patrolman came back and assured them that all was good except the cat was screaming. Tim and Amanda just laughed and said they were on their way to feed the feisty animal. Poor Precious was sitting in front of the refrigerator singing her sad song. Tim went into rescue her and find her dinner for her. Amanda went upstairs to put on comfy clothes. She remembered that she had a doctor appointment in the morning. She wondered how that would pan out. She headed back downstairs in time to find a cup of tea and a pile of cookies in the living room where Tim was now sitting. He was checking messages and pulled her close to him when she sat down. She snuggled into him and breathed in the wonderful scent that is part of him. They sat snuggled up for quite a while before they discovered they were sleepy. "What time is your appointment? Tim asked." Amanda told him 9am. "Do you want me to go with you, he asked. Or would that be a bad idea?" She thought for a moment and decided that it would be a nice idea for her doctor to meet him and they could all exchange information or ask questions that they might have. "I think it is a fine idea, Mr. Donaldson, she said. Let's go to bed before I spend my night here on the couch." They headed upstairs and were asleep when their heads hit the pillows.

Both Tim and Amanda were up early and had their breakfast and showers out of the way. Amanda needed to go get dressed for her appointment, so she was taking her time drinking her coffee. Tim had already gone for his run, showered and was dressed ready to go. She finished her coffee, petted the cat for a moment and then headed upstairs to dress. She decided on a brown wood A-line dress that looked good with her coloring and was warm on these chilly mornings. She decided on brown pumps and grabbed her beige wool coat, scarf, and mittens and headed downstairs. Tim had his coat on and was ready to go. They flashed their lights, waited on the patrolman, locked up and headed for the car. There was a cold, icy dribble going on that wasn't quite rain but was threatening none the less. They arrived downtown at the clinic, parked and went into the reception area. Marty, the receptionist for her doctor, greeted her and she introduced Tim to her. Marty told her the doctor would see her shortly. They were both quiet and a little nervous. A pair of jittery 40-year-old people. Karen, Dr. Andrew's nurse, came out and greeted Amanda. Amanda introduced Tim and said he would be accompanying her to visit with Dr. Andrews. They were seated in the doctor's office and told she'd be with them shortly. The doctor stepped through the doorway moments later and greeted Amanda. Amanda introduced Tim to Dr. Andrews, and she congratulated them on their engagement. Amanda was terribly nervous but set out to ask her questions and get armed with the best information possible. "As you know, she said, I'll be 40 years old next month. Up until this month I've never been sexually active." Tim coughed, the doctor hid her smile behind her hand, and poor Amanda tried to continue the best she could. "We want, she continued, to be responsible about our actions. We haven't set a definite date yet for our marriage as we are just going to be visiting his family at Thanksgiving time. As you're aware my family are all deceased so I'm very much on my own. I have no idea whether I am physically capable of having children as it has never come up in any conversation that I've ever been involved in." By this time poor Amanda's face was glowing a lovely shade of scarlet. Tim took hold of her hand and told the doctor that if they could have children, they both certainly wanted them. Did she have an opinion on this matter? Dr. Andrews looked at and said, "As I'm sure you know there are certain risks involved in pregnancies occurring in later life. 40 isn't exactly considered later life. Amanda, you've always been very healthy, I don't recall any problems that you've had during your menstrual cycle, or any difficulties with anything to do with your health. Your weight has been the same since you were 16 years old. Yes, Mr. Donaldson, I've known her for that long and longer. I delivered Amanda, so I know her quite well. She had a huge smile on her face now and was obviously enjoying herself. Amanda, have you had a period since you and Mr. Donaldson became intimate?" Amanda shook her head no. "Amanda, are you okay? Are you feeling alright? Are you comfortable having relations with Mr. Donaldson?" "Yes, of course, she answered. It's just that, well, you know how I was brought up. We just never talked about anything of a personal nature. My mother would have gotten up and walked out of the room if I'd have said anything about having a period." "I know, said Dr. Andrews, but times have changed. You have changed. From what I'm seeing you have found pretty much the best specimen of manhood that I've seen for a while. I congratulate you on your find." Tim loved the fact that the doctor's eyes were twinkling and that she was smiling from ear to ear. "Tim, are you healthy? Is there anything that we should know about your present health or family health for that matter?" Tim thought for a moment and replied, "I'm healthy and to my knowledge my parents are. My dad had a stroke about 15-16 years ago but totally recovered from it. He's never had any other problems that I'm aware of. Like Amanda, I'm an only child. My mother and father both have siblings, and they are still living. I've not heard about any disease or problems regarding any of them. Amanda will be meeting my parents at Thanksgiving. They are already over the moon about her. I would like our wedding to take place by the end of January or first part of February if Amanda can get everything together by then. I know that her family is gone, but she has a host of friends that will all want to be included in the festivities." The doctor absolutely agreed. "Amanda, she said, I would like to get you weighed, your height, and do some blood work. Karen will take care of this while Tim and I get better acquainted. Amanda looked from one to the other but went with Karen to have the test done. The doctor got right to the point. "Tim, I just want to be very sure that you are aware of how vulnerable Amanda is. Your relationship is new and fragile and with all that she's going through in this community right now it must be weighing her down terribly. I hope you don't feel I'm speaking out of turn. She means a lot to me, and I would be remiss if I said nothing. I'm counting on you to take very good care of our girl. She loves you. I can see that clearly on her beautiful face and I believe you feel the same about her. I'm going to suggest when she comes back in that she uses a contraceptive at least until after the wedding. At that time if you both are sure you'd like to start a family than I'm here to help you accomplish that. Does that sound like a good plan to you?" Tim never hesitated but answered, "Absolutely Dr. Andrews. I love her more than life. I've waited almost 40 years to find her and now I feel whole and complete. I think that having a family would be awesome, but we can also consider adoption. There are a lot of children out there that need a loving home. I'm good either way. It really is ultimately her decision. The only question I have is whether there is already a chance that she is pregnant and if so, will the contraceptives cause any problem? "We will wait, she said, until her next period before starting any drugs. If she is already pregnant, we'll know soon. She has always been very regular, and without problems, so I have no doubt that she will continue to follow that pattern." Amanda knocked softly on the door and then came back in. The doctor gave her a prescription to start following her next regular cycle. If, on the chance that you don't start your period when it is due, please call me. We want to stay on top of this. And, Amanda, you are going to be fine. Tim is a wonderful man and I have a feeling that you're going to gain a wonderful family to go with him." Amanda hugged Dr. Andrews and thanked her for her time and her wisdom. Tim and Amanda left the office and walked out toward the car. The bakery was only about 2 blocks and Amanda suggested they grab a coffee and a pastry and sit for a minute. Tim thought that was a great idea. They walked to the bakery and found a quiet booth. Tim went up to the counter and got them coffee and a Persian pastry. Amanda was stirring her coffee even though she drinks it black. He asked if she was okay. "I feel like such a child, Tim, she said. There are so many things that I've been sheltered from or purposely avoided throughout my life. It's a good thing you're a good teacher or we'd be in a heck of a fix." And then the tears. Tim moved over to sit next to her and comfort her. "Honey, he said, it's ok. Don't cry. You have every right to feel confused and even angry. I took advantage of you without even considering that we didn't use any protection. That was thoughtless of me, and I beg your forgiveness. It'll all be okay. We'll figure it all out together. I love you, Amanda. Please don't cry." Amanda looked up at him with red blotchy eyes and smiled. "I love you too, she said, and then started crying again." Tim went and got her some cold water and hoped that it would help. He was really stumped. She didn't appear to be the crying type but lately that's all she's done. All these crimes and murders and all had really taken its toll on her. She drank the water he brought and apologized again. "Tim, I just feel out of control, she said, but I have no damned idea why! You're everything I've ever dreamed of or wanted and here I am driving you away with my blubbering." You couldn't get rid of me, he said, if you cried all day and all night. I love you and I'm not going anywhere." She hugged him and told him thank you for his kind words and understanding. "I'm feeling better, she said. I really don't understand what's going on.

I'm not a crybaby and I'm a strong, capable woman." And then more tears. "Tim, I'm ready to go home. I don't want to go into the office today. I feel emotionally drained, and home seems like the perfect place." "How about instead of home we take a drive, he said." "Oh, that would be wonderful! Can we walk by the water or something? She asked." "Absolutely, he said. Your wish is my command." They walked back to the car and Tim put on some soft music and they headed out for a long, leisurely drive. Amanda loved nothing more than to hum along with the radio or a CD, drive along the water with the breeze blowing through her hair. It was exhilarating and relaxing all at the same time. It was so thoughtful of Tim to think of this, and she was feeling better already. Tim found a place where they could get out and walk along the boardwalk and maybe grab a cold drink or a cup of coffee. They walked along, not talking, just holding hands and enjoying each other. Amanda said, "Tim, thanks so much for understanding and for helping me to work through this. I don't know what's wrong with me, but I really feel it is just a lot that is happening and I kind of had a meltdown. It wasn't the doctor's visit today as I was prepared for her reaction as well as her advice. I love her dearly and I know she cares about me both as a patient and a person. And, Tim, if I were to find out I was pregnant I would be thrilled. Granted, I'd prefer that we be married first, but it isn't a big deal one way or the other. Speaking of which, what would you think about just going through the classes at the local church so I can convert and then just a small ceremony with a big party? See there, I'm just full of questions!" Tim told her that he felt the same way. "Why don't we go by the church and talk to the priest today about starting the classes? He said." She agreed and they drove back toward town to see if he could meet with them.

Chapter 37

They arrived at St. Elizabeth and found Father James in his study. "Good afternoon, Father, Tim said, we wondered if you might have a few moments to talk with us?" Father James assured them he had plenty of time for them. Tim explained that they were getting married, and that Amanda wanted to convert to Catholicism before the ceremony so he would be able to officiate. The father told them that he was very happy indeed to be a part of their lives together. Father James asked Amanda if she was active in any church. "I'm a native of Edgartown, Father, and I was dedicated and baptized in the Episcopalian church here locally. I've been an active member at St. Andrews for 40 years next month." Father James smiled and asked, "Are you ok with changing your church, Amanda?" "Yes, I am, she said. Tim and I have discussed it and I know how important his faith is to him. I admit that he's been far more faithful about his attendance than I have been. I'm hoping that by making this choice together that I will be more actively involved. I have a business in town that keeps me busy, but I want to volunteer and help where and when I can." "Oh, I'm well aware that you have a busy practice in town, Amanda." Your reputation in Edgartown is quite impressive as was your parents, grandparents and great grandparents, he said. So, let me see what my calendar has in store. Could you do 4 sessions alone on Monday evenings at 7pm and then 2 sessions together on Thursdays at the same time? Amanda consulted her calendar and told him except for Thanksgiving week that those times would work for her. "I must warn you, though, that I may come with a police escort. I seem to still be in the middle of a police investigation." The father assured her that the police were more than welcome in his parish. The father gave Amanda some paperwork to review, and they agreed to seeing each other on December 2nd at 7pm. They thanked him for his time and left. When they got to the car Amanda and Tim looked at each other and started reviewing their calendar. If she has her 4 sessions on December 2, 9, 16, and 23 and they have their 2 sessions together on Thursday December 27 and January 3rd they could be married any time after that. Tim asked her if she had a date in mind. "I do, she said, how about Saturday afternoon on the 12th of January?" Tim cocked his eyebrow at her and said, "Really? My 40th birthday? Oh, wait, I get it. That way I can never forget our anniversary. You're a very wise woman, Amanda Kay. I think that sounds like a wonderful idea. Will you be able to get your dress by then? Flowers, Maid of Honor, and all the rest? Who will you ask to walk you down the aisle? I have a best friend in Boston that I've known since kindergarten, and I will ask him to stand up with me." Amanda thought for a moment and said, "Well, I was going to ask David to walk me down and give me to you. I was going to ask my best friend Suzy to stand up with me, but I need to check to see when she's honeymooning. Flowers? No problem. I've known the owner of the Black Dog all my life and he would be thrilled to cater for a small group. How many people are you thinking on your side? Tim thought and said, "I haven't a clue. I need my mama." She smiled and told him all would be ok. "As for a dress, she said, I was thinking of wearing my grandmother's. We are just about the same size so there wouldn't be a big alteration involved. It's very delicate, lacy, beautiful bead work, and it's what I've always seen in my dreams. Are you ok with that?" "Huh, he answered, it hasn't a thing to do with me." "It's your wedding, Timothy." "Should we go back in and ask Father James to book the afternoon of January 12th?" "Yes, she answered, we must!" They ran back into the church and found Father James. Tim asked him to check his calendar and see if 2:00pm on Saturday the 12th of January would be open for their ceremony. The father smiled and asked that they wait for just a moment while he looked. "I believe, he said, that we can squeeze you in that day. Will you be having a reception to follow here or elsewhere?" Amanda told him that she was going to ask Darci and Hank Smith at the Black Dog if they could either cater or handle the group there. We are thinking, she added, that we want a small ceremony so perhaps 50 people in your chapel rather than the sanctuary?" Father James thought that was a perfect idea. "We will be in touch with you before long, but please mark us down in ink for now." "I will my dear, he said, it'll be a blessed day." "Tim, he said, before I forget, have you spoken with your parish priest? Will he be ok with me officiating? If he has any reservations, he is more than welcome to conduct the ceremony here and I can assist. Just let me know." Tim was sure there'd be no hard feelings. He said, "I'm planning on taking Amanda to meet Father McMurry while we're visiting my parents over Thanksgiving time. He will understand that she is deeply rooted in Edgartown and needs to be married here among her friends." They bid him goodbye again and this time headed for home.

They arrived home and Patrolman James greeted them. He did a walk through and came back to let them know all was ok. "Miss Bradley, he said, Lois Brice came by here earlier looking for you. I told her she needed to call your office and make an appointment or call and leave you a message. She wasn't very happy. I hope that was alright?" "Yes, thanks so much, she said." They went into the house and Amanda asked Tim what he thought she should do. "I think you should let David know that she was here, he said. I certainly don't trust her to be anywhere near you alone." Amanda agreed. She called David and advised him of the visit and asked for his advice. He told her to leave it be and see if she calls the office tomorrow. "Be sure, he said, that you and Dolly leave your office door locked at all times." Amanda told him she would do as he directed and thanked him. "Oh", she said, are you and Lucy busy on Saturday, January 12th about 2pm? If you're free I'd like you to give me away." David let a yell out and was shouting to Lucy that they had set the date! "Amanda, really? I would be honored to escort you down that aisle. Thank you so much for entrusting me with this honor. I'm just so very happy for both of you." Amanda had tears in her eyes as she bid them goodbye and hung up. Tim looked at her and hugged her, feeling the same way. Everything, finally, was coming together for good. Now all they had to do was get rid of that Lois Brice and her nasty disposition.

Amanda arrived at the office right after Dolly. She locked the door and told Dolly that the lieutenant had suggested they keep it locked until all these problems were resolved or behind bars. Dolly told her that she would make sure it was always locked. Amanda went into her office and started working on some paperwork for upcoming estates. Dolly buzzed her a few minutes later that Lois was on the telephone. She thanked Dolly and picked up the phone. She greeted Lois as she always had and asked how she could help. "I want to know when I'm getting my money, Lois asked." Amanda reminded her that she had yet to receive a bank and account number information for the deposit(s) to be made. Lois told her that she didn't want to deal with some bank stealing her money. Amanda repeated that the only way the money would be distributed would be when that information was received. "Also, Amanda added, with your brother in jail and all that up in the air I don't want to distribute the funds until we know how that is going to be settled. I have 6 weeks in which to distribute the estate funds. If you need some money, Lois, just let me know and I'll be happy to advance you the funds. Would that help you?" Lois thought for a minute and told Amanda she needed $5000 but she wanted it in cash. "Can you do that, she asked?" "Yes, of course Lois, she said. Give me a couple of hours to obtain the funds. Where will you be so I can call you?" "What do you mean, Lois asked, why do you want to know where I'll be?" Amanda told her that she noticed that Lois had called from her apartment landline and wondered if that would be where to reach her when she had the money. "Oh, said Lois, yeah, that's fine. Call me and I'll come and get it." Amanda hung up and called David Adler. Amanda asked him, "What would you have me do? I don't want her here without police protection. She scares me to death." David told her to get the funds and he'd come to her office and verify the transaction. Amanda phoned the bank manager and told him what she needed and that she would prefer a courier deliver it to her office if he didn't mind. He assured her he would get right on it and she should have the funds in her hands within the hour. Amanda let Dolly know that a courier would be coming to the door and to let her know when he arrived, and that Lt. Adler would be there about the same time. She called David back and left him a message, so he'd know when to arrive. She called Lois back and told her what time to arrive to pick up the money. She pulled out the form necessary to be signed by both she and Lois prior to handing her the funds. It was simply beyond Amanda's wildest imagination as to why someone would want to walk around with $5000 cash on them. She continued with her paperwork until the courier arrived. Dolly buzzed her and she went out to greet him. He held up his shield and the paperwork from the bank and she unlocked the door. He had her sign the form and thanked her for her time. She noticed immediately that Lois' car was across the street. Why? What was she up to? David got there 15 minutes before Lois was to arrive. He saw Lois' car and mentioned it to Amanda. Amanda told him it had been there since before the courier arrived. David waited in the lobby until Lois showed up at the door. He unlocked the door, and she came in. She was huffing and puffing and wanted to know why he was there. "Well, he said, as long as you continue to conduct yourself in the manner in which you've acted since your mother's death I'll continue to be here." She told Dolly to "Get Amanda. I want my money." Dolly glared at her and buzzed me. I came out and greeted Lois. "I heard you speaking rudely to my assistant, Amanda said, and I want you to know that I will not tolerate such abusive language out of you again. The balance of your mother's estate will be distributed exactly 6 weeks from the reading of the will and not a day earlier. If you need anything further, you will need to obtain a court order. Until such time as the funds are distributed you will stay clear of me and clear of my office. Do we understand one another, Lois? I will not tolerate your rude behavior. I don't know what your problem is, but you need to solve it. Now, sign this paper, take this money and get out of my office." Lois started to open her mouth and then thought better of it. She signed the form, threw it at Amanda, took the money from Dolly and stormed out of the office. David looked at me and said, "Remind me to never piss you off." With that, he turned and left, and I locked the door behind him. I simply don't remember ever being so angry. Poor Dolly just sat there staring at me. I finally went and hugged her and told her, "Nobody is going to be mean to you while I'm around." Amanda left the office about 3pm and headed home. Nothing was going to stop her and Tim from making their Osso Bucco for dinner! He was already in preparation-mode when she walked in. The house was already smelling wonderful. She walked into the kitchen to hug and kiss Tim and to give Precious a pat before running upstairs to change. She opted for Jeans and a tee rather than sweats. They were having a lovely dinner after all. She ran back downstairs to see what the chef wanted her to do. He asked that she make the polenta and then set the dining room table. He had already opened a bottle of Chianti so it could breathe while they finished up. Amanda had the polenta done and on top of a double boiler to stay warm, so they decided to have a cocktail while the meat finished up. Tim made drinks and they sat at the kitchen bar to enjoy them. Amanda caught him up on the day's activities and Tim told her about the class that he finished up today. Tim asked Amanda if she had researched what would happen to the inheritance with one of the Brice heirs already in jail and Lois acting the way she was. She told him that she had done her research, and it was mind-boggling. There weren't any secondary beneficiaries name by Doris. Following the trial, if Leonard were found guilty, his part of the inheritance would transfer to Lois. The only exception to that law would be if the court placed a judgement on a portion of his inheritance to 1) make restitution to the family or families of the victim of the crime or crimes, and/or a portion to the prison system to offset the cost of his/her incarceration, or 2) the funds could transfer directly to a next of kin. In Leonard's case he, to my knowledge, has never married. There has never been any evidence of an illegitimate child from any relationship that he had. It can and probably will get very complicated before it is over. The estate attorney is named automatically as trustee for the estate so this will all fall to me to handle. "Wow, Tim said, what a mess. It looks like the dinner is done so let's pour the wine and eat this wonderful faire." Amanda poured the wine and dished up the polenta into the shallow bowls she had chosen. Tim placed the meat, veggies and gravy atop the polenta and rained a bit of Parmesan over the top. He carried the bowls into the table, and they sat down to breathe in the aromas. There is simply nothing remotely close to the fragrance of veal shanks cooked in this manner. At first Amanda had looked at all the food in the bowl and figured she'd never be able to consume it all. Wrong! She was the first one done! Magnificent! Tim went back and got a little bit more as he had so enjoyed this dinner. They drank their bottle of Chianti in silence. It had been a meal they had dreamed of and longed for, and they were both so happy with the outcome. They cleared the table, cleaned up the dishes and made a pot of coffee to take into the living room. Against her better judgement, Amanda had given Precious a few bites of the veal shank minus the gravy. Precious brushed up against her purring with gratitude. They were all snuggled up on the couch when Amanda's phone rang. She didn't recognize the number so didn't answer. She tended to let it go to voice mail and she'd decide from there how to handle the call. About 5 minutes later the cell dinged that there was a voice mail waiting for her. She read through it and then handed it to Tim. Oscar's sister, Mabel Brice Jones, had left a message asking Amanda to return the call at her earliest convenience. Tim said that he would listen in with her and that he thought she should return the call. Amanda dialed the call back number and Mrs. Jones answered immediately. Amanda identified herself and asked how she might be of service. Mrs. Jones told her that she had talked with her niece, Lois, and learned that her sister, Matilda Brice, had been a beneficiary in Doris' will. "That's correct, Amanda said. Mrs. Brice had several friends and relatives that she made bequest to." "Well, said Mrs. Jones, funny she didn't leave me a damned dime. I catered to her every whim for more than 30 years and for what? Every time she had a feather up her chimney, she'd call me wanting advice or help. My darling niece waited on her hand and foot her whole life and now all she gets is insults and police harassing her." Amanda carefully worded her response saying, "Mrs. Jones, I'm very sorry to hear that you feel you've been overlooked but I can do nothing about that. Mrs. Brice was very clear on her bequest and how her estate was to be distributed. As for Lois, I'm truly sorry that she is having a difficult time, but she has made some bad decisions of late. I'm sorry I can't be of assistance to you, and she hung up." Amanda asked Tim what he made of that. Tim brushed it off by telling her that they were truly a greedy group of people. Amanda told him that she thought, just to be on the safe side, that she might call Matilda Brice tomorrow while at the office. Perhaps just to let her know that her relatives aren't happy with her gift from Mrs. Brice.

Chapter 38

Amanda got to the office about 10am. Dolly had been hard at work and had a pile of papers for Amanda to review and sign off on. She got right to work on reading through the documents and signing as needed. She was about halfway through the pile when Dolly buzzed her saying that Matilda Brice was on the phone for her. "Wow, she thought, how's that for mental telepathy? Amanda picked up the phone and greeted Miss Brice. She had met her several times over the years. She was a lovely lady and Amanda knew that Doris Brice was very fond of her. Miss Brice told Amanda that she had received a phone call from her sister last evening ranting and raving about her being remembered in the will when nobody else was. "I told her, said Miss Brice, that I hadn't expected anything from Doris. I reminded her that Doris and I had been close friends throughout all the years and that they hadn't ever gotten on." Amanda told her that her sister had phoned her last evening in about the same state of mind. "I'm so sorry that you had to be talked to in that way, Amanda told her, but I guess just try to shrug it off." "Well, she said, that's the reason I'm phoning you my dear. I can't shrug it off as she and Lois threatened me bodily harm. Mabel told me that I should sell that vase and give her the money if I knew what was good for me. Lois was verbally abusive, terrible language and totally out of control. I am considering calling the police and taking out a restraining order against them. I wanted your advice though, dear, before doing so. I'm happy to pay you of course." Amanda assured her that she wasn't concerned about payment but was concerned about her well-being. Unfortunately, it could come down to your word against theirs. "No, dear, I don't think so. You see, I am

174

a very old-fashioned lady and I have one of those contraptions that takes messages. You know, it records and then I play it back. I have the entire conversation on tape." Amanda couldn't contain herself; she laughed out loud! "I'm sorry, Miss Brice, that was very unprofessional of me, but given the circumstances, I couldn't help myself. Please accept my apology." Miss Brice told her that she understood completely and so what should she do? Amanda told her that a lovely man named Lt. Adler was going to be calling her shortly. Amanda hung up and called David. She related the story to him and provided him with Miss Brice's address and phone number in Boston. It was lunch time and Amanda decided she and Dolly should go out to lunch. She called the Black Sheep to see if they would save her a table for two. She went and told Dolly to get her coat that she was taking her to lunch. The Black Sheep makes the best grilled flatbread with veggies she'd ever tasted. They locked up and decided to walk to lunch. It would take them about 15 minutes but that would be perfect timing. While they were walking Amanda related the telephone conversation from Miss Brice. "Holy cow, said Dolly, where will it all end?" "I don't know, Amanda told her, I just don't know." They got to the restaurant and put in their order. Flatbread with artichokes, mushrooms, tomatoes, leeks, and Fontina cheese. Their lunch came and they devoured it! They both sat back and tried to relax while sipping their iced tea. Stuffed! It had been exactly what they both needed. Dolly thanked Amanda for thinking of this special treat today. Amanda told her it had been her pleasure. They walked back to the office and finished up the paperwork for the day. Amanda helped Dolly sort through everything to be sure nothing was missed. They had copies to mail out to clients, copies to take to the courthouse for recording and copies for their files. They found they had equal stacks, and all were signed so they were good to go. Dolly told Amanda that she would stop at the courthouse on her way home. Amanda thanked her and headed for her car. She had that same uncomfortable feeling of being watched but didn't see anyone. She shrugged it off as being just slightly paranoid. She drove home and was greeted by Patrolman James. He told her that Mr. Donaldson was already home and to have a nice evening. She thanked him and asked if he wanted a cold drink or coffee. He told her thanks, but he was fine. Tim was waiting at the front door for her. He hugged and kissed her, and they locked up behind her and set the alarm. Tim had drinks waiting for her and told her to hurry and change clothes. She went upstairs and changed into her evening uniform and came back downstairs to join him. She wandered into the kitchen to see what he was doing. He had brauts and sauerkraut already to go. He had made a pitcher of margaritas that looked delicious, and she had her glass ready for him to pour the drink into. She told him about her lunch with Dolly and that she was glad she'd been able to fit that in today as the holiday was upon us. Tim agreed and said what a sweetheart that she was. He told her that he'd gotten his scores and had passed everything, so the new position was good to go starting the first week of January. He told her that this might very well give them an opportunity to get all the wedding arrangements finalized and perhaps be able to sneak away for a few days around Christmas time. "I know my mother is going to want us to come there for Christmas, Tim said, and I'm ok with that unless you'd rather do something just the two of us." Amanda never hesitated and said, "Tim, I can't think of anything more fun than having Christmas with a family! I love to Christmas shop and will have a wonderful time preparing for the holiday. Please don't forget that when we come back from Boston, we are going to meet my best friend Suzy and her fiancé. She and James are being married the day after Christmas in a very small ceremony. Suzy's sister will stand up for her and James' brother is standing up with him, so it'll be just the immediate families at the ceremony. It's her second marriage and she didn't want to have a big affair. They are planning a big party the end of January which will work perfectly for our wedding. Tim said he would look forward to meeting her and her fiancé after they get back from Boston. Amanda told him that she and Suzy had discussed meeting around the 10th or 12th of December so they could celebrate their 40th birthdays together. Tim told her that perhaps he needed to meet James before that date so they could compare notes on birthday bashes. She just laughed. They ate their brauts and sauerkraut on delicious grilled hoagie buns and had another Margarita to go with it. There was potato salad from the deli that went perfectly with the sandwich.

Chapter 39

It was officially Amanda's weekend, so she told Tim that while he read or whatever she was going to find a movie that she'd been wanting to watch. He told her that he had some studying to do and would read for a while and enjoy her movie. She got the movie into her VCR player and got her coffee and a stack of cookies to munch through while watching the movie. After the movie was over, she turned the news on. She watched the breaking news bulletins, the weather and decided to call it a night. The cat had already disappeared and was probably upstairs asleep with Tim. She checked all the windows and doors as was her habit and then went upstairs to join them.

Amanda's phone was ringing off the hook at 7am. She looked and saw that it was David Adler calling her. She got up, brushed her teeth and headed downstairs to call him back. Why would he be calling so early? She called him back and he answered right away telling her he was sorry to have disturbed her at such an early hour. "It's fine, David, she said, what's going on?" "A couple of things, Amanda. May I come by in about 15 minutes?" She told him of course and then raced upstairs to throw some clothes on and brush her hair. She donned her tee and sweats and pulled her hair up in a ponytail just in time to hear the doorbell ring. She went back downstairs and let David in. "Apparently Tim is out on a run, she said." She and David went into the kitchen, and she got them a cup of coffee. David told her that he had phoned Miss Brice and had made a quick trip to Boston to interview her. He had obtained a copy of the tape and he and his captain had already decided that it was a very threatening conversation. He and a patrolman were going to be visiting both Lois and Mabel Brice and inform them that a restraining order had been placed against them. "Amanda, this thing is spiraling out of control. Lois is a loose cannon and I'm not sure what or where she is going to land. I want you and Tim to be always on your guard. Check your rearview mirrors, always lock your cars, always park in a well-lit, busy area. I don't mean to frighten you, but I do mean to protect you." "I know David, she said, it is just so hard to comprehend anyone acting in this manner." David looked at her and told her, "Amanda, I've got reports back from the fire. It was arson. There were signs of the back door being broken down and an incinerate being disbursed on all floors of the house. We found a couple of shoe prints when we first investigated the fire, and we have a shoe size and style on file for that. We have a match to that shoeprint that belonged to Barney Brice, so we have them where we want them. Barney says that Leonard paid them to set the fire. We found a ten-thousand-dollar cash withdrawal from Leonard's bank that matches the dates, so we believe we've tied that up. So, the only loose end is Doris Brice's murderer. I have my suspicions on that and just need to be able to either prove it or get her to confess." "David, you think it's Lois, don't you?" "Yes, I do, he said, and that is why I'm worried about you. We are going to change the patrolman out front. James has done this too long and he's starting to recognize everyone as the nice neighbors. We'll put a new patrol car out front with two officers. We are also assigning someone to follow you to and from work. They will escort you into your office and you will call their direct cell number when you're ready to leave the office. This goes for Dolly, too. I really feel with this last outburst by her in your office that she is getting ready to explode or implode. I'm just unsure which." Amanda thanked him for his candor and his concern and assured him she would follow his instructions to the letter. "I'll call Dolly after you leave and alert her of the circumstances." "Good idea. Thanks Amanda." Tim came in about the same time as David was leaving. She told him she'd fill him in. She summarized what David had said and what she was advised to do. "I need to call Dolly and give her an update, she said." Tim agreed. He told her he would shower quickly and have breakfast for them shortly. Amanda phoned

Dolly but she didn't answer. She left her a voice mail asking that she call her back at her earliest convenience. Tim was out of the shower and Amanda went to get the coffee going and help with breakfast. Precious was hungry so Amanda fixed her breakfast before she decided to break out in song. Tim joined her in the kitchen and asked if an omelet sounded good to her. She told him that it sounded delicious. The phone rang while she was pouring the coffee. She saw that it was Dolly calling her back. She was smiling as she answered with a cheerful, "hello there." There was a slight pause before Dolly told her that it looked like they might have a problem. Amanda started to ask what she meant, but a screaming Lois was on the phone. Amanda braced herself as she held the phone out for Tim to hear too. Lois told her that she had paid her little assistant a visit and she would be staying with her until her money, all of it, was delivered in cash. Amanda interrupted her trying to say that this was an impossible task to accomplish. Lois told her that she wasn't listening to anymore of her crap. You get me my money, all of it, by 6pm tonight or you can plan your little assistant's funeral. Amanda sucked in her breath and again tried to make Lois understand that obtaining that amount of money in cash was impossible. Lois told her that she wanted her half of the life insurance money and her share of her mother's saving's account which adds to $1,350,000.00. You get me that, now, and I don't give a rat's ass about the rest of it. Do we understand one another? If I don't have that money by 6pm tonight your assistant is dead. And, Amanda, if that happens then your pretty boyfriend will be next. I know where you all are all the time and I'm not playing anymore games. If you call your cop buddy, she dies. I'll call you at 5:30pm and give you the address where to drop the money. You'll come alone or she dies. My mother made a mistake in misjudging what I could and couldn't do and you know where that got her. And the phone went dead. I was shaking so hard that I couldn't breathe or think straight. What was I going to do? Where would I get that kind of money, in cash, by bank closing time? Tim was already on the phone to David. I started to object but I knew that he was right in calling him. Lois, or one of her family members, were probably watching our every move so we needed to be very careful. Tim hung up from talking with David and came to hold me telling me it would all be okay. But would it? How many more innocent people would suffer at the hands of this horrible family? Tim told me that David wouldn't come to the house as that would alert them that we had talked. He was dispatching undercover units to stake out Dolly's house so they could maybe see what they were up against. I called the bank manager and explained the circumstances to him. Did he have that much money in cash that he could release to me? He told me no, he didn't but could work with one of the other branches and gather it together if that was what I really wanted him to do. I told him we had no choice in the matter and asked what time I could expect a courier to deliver the money to my house? He told me he'd call me back.

David called Tim back and updated him on what they'd found. One of the undercover officers was able to see through a side window into Dolly's house. He was able to make out Lois and at least one other person, a man, in that area. Dolly was not visible from that window which was frustrating as they wanted to know exactly where she was being held. David asked whether I'd be successful in obtaining the funds and Tim told him it seemed a strong possibility and that we'd know more when the manager calls back. Tim gave the phone to Amanda, and she asked, "Do you honestly think they'll hurt Dolly? Lois pretty much confessed to me that she had killed her mother. I'm terrified thinking that I must hand this money to her." David told her to keep working on her plans as if the drop was really going to occur. "My people, he said, will continue to survey Dolly's house to find out exactly where they are holding her. If we know that we can move forward without fear of her being harmed." I didn't ask for specifics as I had a pretty good idea what that meant. Tim and I tried to eat breakfast, but it felt like lead going down our throats. I didn't know what to do or where to turn. Amanda's phone rang about 30 minutes later and the bank manager told her that the funds would be delivered to her by 4pm today. She thanked him for acting so quickly and for his help. He told her that he hoped that everything would work out ok. She reminded him that he was to say nothing to anyone about what was transpiring, and he assured her that he would not say a word. Tim called David back advising that the money would be delivered. So now they wait.

Chapter 40

Amanda's phone rang about 1:30pm. It was Lois wanting to know what was going on. Amanda told her that the funds would be delivered to her by 4pm and she just needed to know where to bring her money to her. "Don't be in a such a rush, Amanda. I'll let you know when I'm damned good and ready." And with that, she hung up. Amanda and Tim just sat at the kitchen bar unable to talk, or think, or anything. This just couldn't be happening. Everything in Amanda's life, up until her parent's death, had been quiet and orderly. Nobody yelled. Nobody got angry or smart-mouthed anyone else. Everyone was polite and appreciative of one another. How could a wonderful little community like Edgartown breed such horrible people? They moved into the living room with hopes of being able to read or something.

The phone rang about an hour later and he saw that it was David. He answered and David told him to call the bank and cancel the money delivery, and to grab Amanda and come to the police station. Amanda did as David directed, and they got their coats on and flashed their lights for the on-duty patrolman to come and escort them to the car. He waited while they locked up the house and then walked them to the car. They drove downtown dreading what was awaiting them. When they got to the precinct David was waiting for them in the lobby. He took them into his office and closed the door. "First of all, Dolly is fine. She is quite shaken and is in the hospital for observation. Mabel Brice Olson's son is dead. Lois Brice is dead. We had a sharpshooter surveying the premises and as soon as we located Dolly in the house they acted as directed. It's over." Amanda just stared at him and then passed out cold. They got her revived and were encouraging her to drink some water. "I want to see Dolly, she said. I want to see her right now." David got his coat and told her to grab an arm. The three of them headed for the hospital. Dolly had been admitted and was resting. They had given her a mild sedative to try and relax her as she was very frightened and the ultimate end to her captivity had been extremely upsetting. Amanda went into her room and sat beside her bed weeping quietly. It wasn't long before a hand reached out to rub her shoulder. Amanda stood up and engulfed Dolly in a huge hug, while they both cried. What a horrible ordeal this had been. Amanda kept telling Dolly how very sorry she was that this had happened. Could she ever forgive her? Dolly told her that it certainly wasn't her fault. "These people were just bad to the bone. Not a one of them was worth a plugged nickel, she said. Now Amanda, I want you to go home, have a nice drink, and let me get some needed rest. Those horrible people broke into my house before sun-up, so I've missed out on some of my beauty sleep." Amanda hugged and kissed her on the cheek and told her to call her immediately if she needed anything. When you're released tomorrow, Tim, and I will come and pick you up. Perhaps you should stay with me until you're ready to head out on your vacation. Dolly told her that she thought if they picked her up that they could wait for just a few minutes while she threw some things in a suitcase and then drop her at the airport. "I'm thinking I'll just leave a bit early for that vacation."

Amanda and Tim and David all headed back to the station. David told them that they needed to talk about some things, but it could wait until tomorrow. They all agreed that tomorrow was the perfect time. They got in their car and headed home. The trusty patrolman had already been pulled from what he probably thought was his permanent duty station. Everyone that was involved in the entire scheme was either dead or in jail. They went in and turned on the TV to see if the local news had picked up on this event. When the TV came on it was all over the news! The police had tried to negotiate with the kidnappers without success. A man had come out the front door holding the hostage in front of him telling the police that he'd kill her if they didn't back off and let him pass. The hostage brought her foot up and kicked backwards connecting with her captor's shin resulting in him letting go long enough for the sharpshooter to fire. The other kidnapper came to the door with both hands in the air saying that she "gave up" and then opened fire on the police. The sharpshooter fired again successfully ending the hostage situation. "Oh My God! Amanda's mouth was hanging open and she was crying and laughing and was genuinely hysterical. Did you see her? Amanda was shaking Tim's arm and crying. She simply could not believe what she had just witnessed. Dolly hadn't said a word about how courageously she had conducted herself. Oh My God!" Tim was holding Amanda trying to comfort her or at least get her to settle down. He was afraid she was going to keel over again. "Amanda are you ok, he asked. Shall I get you some water or something?" "No, I'm fine Tim, really. I cannot believe what she did. Have you ever seen such a brave act before? I would have been shaking in my boots, but Dolly? No, she kicks the son of a bitch and gives the police a good shot. I'm just numb. She never uttered a word about her bravery. My God, Tim, how will I ever thank her for ending this horrible situation?" Tim had gone and poured her a straight shot of whiskey and made her drink it. He figured she'd either throw up or feel better. So far, she was keeping it down. He remembered that neither of them had eaten a bite of food all day and that he'd best get something down her. He ran into the kitchen and got some bread in the toaster and found some good homemade raspberry jam to put on it. He got the peanut butter out of the pantry thinking that would be the protein they'd both need to tide them over. Amanda started to dismiss the sandwich and then thought better of it. Her head was swimming from the ordeal as well as the whiskey. She took one bite and then devoured it and asked for more. Tim gave her his sandwich and went to fix himself another. She hollered and asked for milk too. He came back with a glass of milk and his half-eaten sandwich. "Are you feeling better, he asked." "Yes, much. Thanks, she said. I just find that I'm having a terrible time processing this entire event. Lois is dead. My friend for 36 of my 40 years is dead. Why? Because of greed. She killed her mother Tim. Can you fathom that? How does someone commit such evil on the person that has loved and adored them all their lives? I can see her as a little girl. She was never a beauty, but she used to have a pretty smile. I've thought about it long and hard and find that I can't recall her smiling much when her father stopped coming around. She obviously grieved for him all her life. I can't help feeling badly about how this turned out for her. Someone was ringing the doorbell. Tim went to investigate but not without caution. It's been so long since we had anyone come to the door other than policeman that we'd forgotten how it felt. Tim saw that it was my neighbors! He opened the door and greeted them best he could remember. Mrs. Taylor was the first in the door, followed closely by Mr. and Mrs. Hunter, Mr. Winchell and Miss Weatherby. Coming up the driveway was Mr. Crawford and Miss Lawford. They all came in and were hugging Amanda and they were all crying together. They were all so very upset over the tragic ending to this situation but glad that Amanda and her assistant and that good-looking Tim were all okay. Amanda fixed coffee and tea and Tim got out cookies and other pastries and set on the table. Everyone was talking at once so Amanda finally interrupted and told them what she knew. She assured them that even though it was a tragic ending at least now they could all relax and not be afraid anymore. Mr. Crawford asked Amanda about a funeral for Lois Brice. Amanda assured them that there would certainly be a service. "We all loved Mrs. Brice, she said, and that is the least we can do for her." They drank their beverages and ate their pastries and one by one took their leave. Mrs. Taylor was the last one to leave and turned to Amanda saying, "I just want you to know how proud we are of you. You've handled this mess like a real trooper Amanda and your folks would have been very proud of you. The entire neighborhood shares my feelings in saying that we know you look out for us, and we love you for it." Amanda hugged her and thanked her for her warm words. She told her that she would be getting a wedding invitation in the mail soon and that she hoped she'd be able to attend. Mrs. Taylor assured her that they would all be there with bells on!

Chapter 41

Amanda turned to Tim and told him that she couldn't recall ever being so very tired. She felt like she could sleep for a week. Tim told her that perhaps a nap was in the immediate future. They raced upstairs and were sound asleep immediately. They woke a little after 8pm and were starving. They went downstairs to be greeted by a very mad kitty cat. Precious had missed two meals and was barely able to stand. She glared at them hoping that she was instilling much guilt in her humans. Tim found her some dinner and Amanda warmed up her skim milk. She swished her tail at them but seemed to be enjoying her meal. Tim decided that scrambled eggs and toast would possibly hold them over until morning. They ate 3 scrambled eggs each and 2 slices of toast. Tim made a pot of coffee and they just sat at the kitchen counter staring at one another. "Is it really over, she asked." "Well, I don't know if I'd say it's over or not, he said. We still have a funeral and at least two trials to go through. And you have a ton of work to do to figure out how you're going to distribute Mrs. Brice's estate." "I know, she said, I have thought it over and I believe that I may have a solution for that part. Do you think Leonard knows or even cares about his sister?" Tim told her that people in jail and prison knew more about current events than anyone else. "It's like they have a direct line to the news station, he said." Amanda told him that regardless of how Lois and her cousin's lives ended today that there were people that were going to feel badly about their passing. Oscar's sister, Mabel is a horrible woman but I'm betting she loved her son. I don't know if David will deal directly with her or not. I also don't remember if Mr. Jones is still living. It seems to me that he passed a few years back.

She may still be a problem. If I recall correctly the Jones' didn't have two nickels to rub together. I'm sure that is why she was so angry with her sister, Matilda who was always well off. Perhaps we can provide a small bequest to her that would help her to see there is still good in the world." Tim told her that she was one of the few good people in the world.

Tim and Amanda spent a quiet evening in the living room. Several times Tim caught Amanda looking toward the front window. He was sure she was seeing her friend in happier days. He understood how sad she felt and was unable to say or do anything to help ease her pain.

Amanda was up by 5am and impatiently waited until 6am to call David Adler. She paced while she drank her coffee and waited for Tim to get up. She heard him stirring around upstairs and waited until he came downstairs to see if he wanted coffee or was off on his run. He asked her if she was ok, and she assured him she was but had things that needed to get done before she left for Boston. He headed out the door on his run and she automatically locked the door and set the alarm. A habit that would be hard to break. She phoned David and apologized if she woke him. "No, it's fine, he said. I'm up and headed to the station. What's going on?" She told him that she was going to be at the hospital at 9am to await Dolly's release. She would then take Dolly to her house to help her pack for her vacation and then take her to the airport. "Are you going to need any kind of statement from her any time soon? I would like her to take a full month, perhaps returning after the first of the year." David told her that Dolly had already made her statement and was free to leave without any worries from them. "Ok, she said, next on my list of things. The release of Lois Brice's body. I want to arrange a small service and burial for her. I know that sounds strange, but it is something I must do." It's fine, Amanda, he said, I understand perfectly. Both bodies are at the city morgue, but the M.E. has already signed off on everything. I would imagine that she could be moved by a funeral home at your direction. I will alert the M.E. that either you or the funeral home will be contacting him later today. Are you ok? Is there anything that I can do to help ease your pain?" She told him she was fine but that she had loose ends to tie up before going off on a holiday. "I'll get back to you before we leave, David. Thank you for everything." She hung up the phone and sat staring at the wall. Her heart was heavy and her mind full of memories. She couldn't help the tears from flowing. Precious came and sat with her as if she knew that her human was hurting. Amanda pulled herself together and called John Gleason at the Chapman, Cole & Gleason Funeral Home. She asked him, since she was Executor for the Brice will, if she could arrange for a small, closed casket service for Lois Brice tomorrow. He told her that this would be a bit of a rush, but yes, he could arrange that. She told him she also wanted to have her buried in the local cemetery. "I'll handle all of the cost so please just bill my office, she said." He told her that he would arrange pickup, and they could plan on a 2pm service tomorrow in their chapel. Amanda thanked him and hung up. She then phoned Mabel Brice Jones. Mabel picked up on the first ring and seemed genuinely shocked to hear Amanda's voice. Amanda told her that she was having a service for Lois tomorrow and asked if she'd made arrangement for her son's internment. Mabel started to be her normal nasty self but then simply said, "No. I can't afford no burial, Amanda. I guess he'll get put into a pauper's grave." Mabel was softly crying, and Amanda's heart went out to her. "Mabel, she said, I don't know you very well and we obviously haven't had any kind words with one another recently, but I cannot allow you to suffer like this. I will arrange with John Gleason to pick up your son's body and then handle an internment in the Tisbury Cemetery. He will phone you directly and arrange a time so you and whomever can arrange a graveside service." Mabel told me that she was so sorry for this whole horrible ordeal. She thanked her for her thoughtfulness and Amanda reminded her that it was a wonderful lady, her sister-in-law, that was footing the bill for all this. She was simply the messenger. She hung up and called John Gleason back and told him about the phone call. She gave him Mabel's telephone number, and he said he would handle it and yes, he would send her the bill. Tim came back from his run and Amanda brought him current on what she had arranged. "I'm going to phone the neighbors, well, a couple of them and then they'll phone each other, and tell them about the service for Lois. I feel they will all want to be there. Tim went to shower and said he'd get breakfast going for them while she made her calls. She suggested that he make breakfast, and they could shower together in a little while. He cocked his head at her, winked, and went off to make breakfast. How could he pass up that invitation?

I spoke directly with two of the neighbors and asked that they contact the rest of the block. They were happy that there would be a service for that poor lost soul. I phoned the pastor at the Episcopalian church and asked if he would just say a few words and offer a prayer at the service tomorrow. He told me he'd be happy to officiate. Well, at least that is taken care of for now. Tim and I spent a quiet day together cleaning, grocery shopping, and lounging. We had decided that we would be packed and ready to leave for Boston following the service tomorrow. After we put groceries away, we both went upstairs to stage our packing. Our plan was to be gone an entire week so a minimum of 8 days of casual/comfy clothes, a dress for Thanksgiving and possibly one more dress in case we decided to go out. It was turning cold, and the snow was threatening so I packed three wool A-line dresses to be on the safe side, 8 pairs of jeans, 8 tees, 4 sweaters, 4 cardigans, shoes, scarves, unmentionables, sleepwear, etc. Tim just shook his head as he tried his best to close 2 large suitcases containing my stuff. He packed 4 pairs of jeans, 4 shirts, sweats and tennis shoes and said he had more stuff at his folk's house. It dawned on me that I didn't have a clue if he still lived at home or had a place of his own. I decided I'd asked him while we were driving to Boston. Well, except for toiletries we are all packed. We went back downstairs to decide what to fix for dinner. Precious was hungry and ready to start her song if we didn't attend to her needs very soon. Precious? Oh, my goodness, what was I to do with Precious? I called Lucy Adler and asked if she would consider a houseguest for a week. She was thrilled to say the least. She fell in love with Precious and I knew they'd be okay together. I told her about Lois' service tomorrow and asked if David would mind picking her up as he still has my house key. She told me they would come together and be happy to do so. She reminded me that we were to get together after our return and start making wedding plans. "I have my calendar right here. Why don't we decide on a date and you guys come over to dinner? How about Friday, December 6th about 5pm?" Lucy checked her calendar and decided that sounded perfect. I went back into the kitchen to see what Tim was fixing. "I decided on spaghetti with a Marinara sauce. Is that ok with you?" "Sounds divine, I told him." I made a salad and set the kitchen bar and opened a bottle of red wine to go with the pasta. Dinner was delicious and just what we needed. After we finished, I started clearing up the bar and loading the dishwasher. Tim noticed that I was quiet and asked if everything was ok. "I'm fine, I told him, but I'm sad. I can't remember ever having so many sad things happen in my life. I guess now that I'm going to be 40 years old, I'll have to accept the fact that bad things happen." Tim hugged me to him and told me that life wasn't always going to be rosy, but he would try his best to always bring me as much happiness as he was able to. "This is just one of the many reasons why I love you, Tim." We finished cleaning up and clearing up and decided to read for a while and then go to bed early. My mind and my body are both exhausted.

Chapter 42

Tim and I awoke early, and decided against running as it was so cold out. Not exactly perfect weather for burying someone. We fixed pancakes and sausages for breakfast, and I set about fixing a week's worth of food and snacks for Precious. I put together an envelope with information about her vet, snacks and so on. I put some cash in the envelope to offset the cost of her skim milk and anything else that was needed. I cooked some white fish and some chicken breast for her. I also cooked a nice piece of calves' liver that she loved. I was sure she'd be fine with the Adlers. Tim called his mom and reminded her that we would be there, but it might be early evening so not to wait dinner on them. We didn't want to try to explain all the stuff that had been going on. Chances were that she'd seen some of it on the TV news and put two and two together. Tim felt that it was an imposition to have David come after the cat, so we decided to get everything together and take her ourselves before the service. Tim called David to let him know the change in plans. I wanted to get to the funeral home a little early to see if John Gleason needed anything signed before the service. I also wanted to greet the pastor that was officiating at the service. Pastor Thomas had been ill, and I wasn't sure I'd ever met Pastor Robert. I went upstairs after breakfast and laid out my clothes. I wasn't crazy about traveling in my black suit but didn't really see that I had a choice. I asked Tim if he needed anything pressed but he had already taken care of it and was shining his shoes when I hollered downstairs. I showered and washed my hair. I usually try to towel dry it, but it was so cold outside that I decided to use the hair dryer. This was perhaps not my best idea. I was looking quite fluffy! I started brushing it trying to get it to settle down. I finally just pulled it together and put it in a loose ponytail. There! I look about 12. I did my makeup and then went and got dressed. I had chosen a beautiful ecru lace blouse to wear with my black suit. I chose a pair of low heel black pumps and got out my heavy winter coat. I looked through my dresser drawer and finally settled on a pretty wool scarf and matching gloves. I went into my parent's room and found my mom's black pillbox hat which would be perfect for the service. I gathered everything together and went downstairs. Tim had already showered and shaved and was dressed to the nines. Man, oh man, does my man clean up nice! He had his dark gray suit on that he'd worn when I first met him. He had chosen a cream color linen shirt and black/cream striped tie. He looked gorgeous! His beautiful eyes were dancing as he checked me out. He went and loaded the suitcases into the car and then came back to get Precious and her bed. He wrapped a blanket around her so she wouldn't take cold on the ride over to the Adlers. He came back and offered me his arm, set the alarm and locked the door. We were officially on our way.

We arrived at the Adler house and delivered Precious to Lucy. I gave her the box with food and instructions and told her how much I appreciated her watching our precious kitty cat. We both just smiled over that comment. We know good and well that our Precious has a slight attitude problem. They hugged us and bid us farewell on our journey. David commented that it was a typical "Amanda thing" to do for Lois and he knew that her mother was looking down and appreciating it. Given all the circumstances it just felt the right thing to do for my lifelong friend. We headed to the funeral home to set about completing this task at hand. We went in and found John Gleason and I thanked him again for his speedy response to my needs. He assured me that it was fine, and he was happy to be of service. Pastor Robert introduced himself and I thanked him for coming. I had typed up a bio on Lois and gave to him to review. I asked John if I might step into the chapel for just a few moments before the service. He escorted me in to where Lois' casket was and then took his leave. I stood there staring at this box that would house her body for all eternity. I started to quietly weep as I remembered us playing outside, riding our bikes, celebrating birthdays together and all the other things that children do with their neighbors. I thought of her wonderful mother and what a lovely person she had always been. I then, and only then, was able to focus on the terrible deed that Lois had done to her mother and then her outrageous behavior that ultimately took her life. I prayed that God would deal with her as He saw fit and that He would help me to recover from this terrible ordeal. I felt Tim touch my shoulder and I gladly went into his arms to just be held and loved for a moment. "The neighbors are arriving, Amanda, he said, so you need to greet them." I thanked him and we walked out to the foyer. All the neighbors were there, and to my surprise, so were both Matilda and Mabel Brice. I thanked everyone for coming and John Gleason led the way into the chapel. Pastor Robert had pretty much memorized what I gave him and spoke as if he'd always known her. He asked if anyone wanted to speak but nobody moved. He offered a prayer, and the service was concluded. All in all, about 20 minutes. So very sad. I walked out with all the neighbors and thanked them for coming. The aunts told me that what I had done for Lois was above the call of duty. I assured them that I had acted on behalf of my client, Mrs. Brice. "It is so nice to see you ladies together, I said." Matilda Brice said, "You know, right after all this happened my sister called me and told me how sorry she was for being so greedy and mean to me. I told her that I loved her regardless and that everything was ok. We've decided to sell that beautiful vase and share the money. We are thinking of taking a cruise together." I just smiled and told them that it sounded like a wonderful idea. I hugged them both and then Tim and I walked out to the car. "Well, that's over, I said. It is such a strange feeling. At first, I was so very sad and then standing there looking at that cold black box all I could think of was how angry I was at her greed and stupidity. I believe that feeling will help me to get past this who ordeal."

Chapter 43

The car ride to the ferry was uneventful. We got onto the ferry within 5 minutes of our arrival. The ferry ride itself was beautiful. The sky was a bright blue, lots of fluffy white clouds and the wind was crisp and smelled delicious. We disembarked and decided to stop about halfway to Tim's parents so I could freshen up. I felt that we looked rather austere in our dark suits, but we would explain once we could talk with them face to face. We found a lovely café just off the highway and stopped to grab a cup of coffee and share a pastry. We were making great time and so Tim called his mom and let her know to set two extra seats for dinner. I'll bet she was just thrilled to get that phone call…not. "I really think we should order a pizza or something to be delivered, don't you?" "Nah, he said, she has a mission at hand now. She'll be fine." I just shook my head at him. I went into the ladies' room and freshened my hair, brushed my teeth and applied fresh makeup. "There, I said, you look reasonably presentable!" I walked back out to the café area and saw that Tim was paying the bill, so we were ready to finish off this journey. We were driving along, and I told Tim that I had a couple of questions and didn't want to forget them. "Fire away, he said." "Well, first of all, do you live with your parents?" "No, I live with you, he said in his normal cocky tone." "You know what I mean. When you were not living with me were you living with your parents?" "Sometimes, he said." Okay, this is going to be a long trip. "Timothy, do you have an apartment or house of your own when you're not living with your parents?" "Yes, he said." "Tim!" "Okay, don't get grumpy, he said. Yes, I have a condo that I bought several years ago. I also have an office that I used to work out of. My plan is that while we're visiting my parents, we'll take a full day to shut down the office and then call my best friend who is a realtor to put my condo on the market. Unless you'd like to think of it as an in-town home?" "I'd like to see it first, I said, before deciding. I rather like the idea of being able to visit Boston and not stay in a hotel. Is it paid for? If not, we need to pay off the mortgage." "It's paid for so that is already handled. It has 2 master suites and a rooftop entertaining area. It's in a good area and I'm ok whichever way you choose; keep it or sell it. Your call. My parents are in Somerville and my condo and office are in Brookline. What else, my lady?" "I want to call John Sheridan, I said, and ask him if his son had left any personal belongings at their house. Or you could ask. I'm thinking that Jack's mother may have had softer feelings for Jack than his father did. Perhaps Jack left the key with his mother. We've sort of put all of that off to the side with the Lois disaster, but I'd like to see about finalizing things. I need to figure out what to do with the estate as soon as we get back to Edgartown." Tim said, "Good idea, Amanda. I hadn't really forgotten about the safe, but it seemed unimportant compared to Lois' demise." "I agree. Also, I need to go to the florist that I spoke with. I'd like to go tomorrow if possible so I can select the wreath, centerpiece, and floral arrangements. I wanted to walk through your parent's home before finalizing those purchases." "Amanda, if you will, Tim said, I'd appreciate your helping me to close my P.I. business. I have a couple of clients that I've worked closely with for years, so I want to refer them to another investigator. And we also need to call my best friend, Ronny, and try to get together with him while in Boston. This is going to be a jam-packed week." We just passed the sign for the turn off to Somerville, so we were apparently very close to Tim's home. I admit I was nervous but also very excited. I liked his mother over the phone and was sure I was going to love her in person. I had not more than thought about that and Tim was pulling up to a curb in front of a very charming home. All the lights were on, and you could just tell that this was a house that was stuffed full of love.

We were getting out of the car and started to grab a couple of bags to start with when both of Tim's parents magically appeared on the sidewalk. They were both hugging us and telling us how glad they were to see us. You'd have thought they'd known me always rather than my being a total stranger to them. Lorraine, Tim's mother, just didn't seem to want to let go of me. She was so beautiful and smelled so wonderful. I felt like I could stay there forever. Tom, Tim's father, was just as loving. He was obviously so glad to see his son that he just couldn't contain himself. They helped grab bags and ushered up the stairs and into the house. The home was a beautiful Tudor style. The foyer was not grand but rather just welcoming. There was a lovely staircase leading up to the second floor off to the right of the entrance. There were ancestral photographs that lined both sides of the foyer and showed that they were both very proud of who they were and where they came from. They set down the suitcases and miscellaneous bags and walked us into the den where there was a fire going. The room was stuffed full of comfy chairs and sofas. The room was traditional with its board-and-batten wall paneling in a dark stain. The massive fireplace's hearth was beautiful brick to the ceiling. Some chairs were positioned by the fireplace while others were off in corners making wonderful reading nooks. There was a pot of coffee and cups on the sidebar and a fully lined bar was beckoning. Tim and I both opted for gin and tonics and his parents had their "usual" martini. Lorraine suggested that when I finished my drink that she would take me on a tour, so I'd know where everything was. They inquired about our trip and how everything else was going. Tom said that he had caught the news and knew that the entire mess had pretty much come to an end. We explained about the service for Lois which further explained us being in dark dress suits. Lorraine said if I was ready, we'd take that tour and then we'd see about some food. She grabbed one suitcase and I the other and we climbed that beautiful staircase. There were six doors that I quickly counted when we reached the landing. She ushered me toward the first door on the right. "This is your room dear, she said. Your bath is attached, and I hope you'll find everything you need there. If you don't, you just let me know and we will see to it that we get it for you." "It's lovely, I told her. Thank you so much. Oh, my, it's very pretty and the bath is luxurious. That tub just cries out for use." We set everything down in the corner and then went back out to the landing so she could explain the rest of the doors. As you can see, the landing is kind of a horseshoe. The first door on the left is Tom's and my room. The next door on the left is a guest room that doesn't have an in-suite bath, the door on the left corner is a bathroom, next on the right corner is Tim's room when he's here, and the door beyond you on the right is another guest room. That guest room and Tim's bedroom share a Jack-n-Jill bath that isn't accessible from the hallway. I hung a small wreath, you may have noticed, on your door so you'd know where you were. Let's go back downstairs so I can show off the rest of this mansion." I noticed when she was teasing or making a joke that her blue eyes danced and twinkled just like Tim's did. He looked exactly like his father but was 100%, his mother. From the staircase landing we walked through the foyer into the massive formal dining room. There was a lovely bay window that overlooked the backyard and the gardens. Off to the right was the kitchen which had obviously been remodeled over the years. It was set up for a gourmet chef complete with double ovens, a 6-burner range, and a massive refrigerator. There was a breakfast nook with a smaller bay window and a beautiful view of the gardens. The bar ran most of the width of the kitchen and had 6 bar stools. Tom's office was off the kitchen area and was typical of that era of homes complete with dark paneling, lined with bookshelves, and a huge roll-top desk. The small hall that led from the formal dining room took you to the formal living room which was just exquisite. Beautiful Queen Ann chairs and settees mixed with some Louis XVI chairs and occasional tables. Lovely artwork and sculptures completed the room. While it didn't offer the coziness of the sitting room it was truly a magnificent room. We walked into the den and joined the guys for another adult beverage before sitting down to dinner. Lorraine brought me up to speed on what to expect for Thanksgiving dinner. She explained that she'd already shopped, and the order would be delivered early Wednesday morning. Tim and I assured her that we were happy to either help with the cooking or do the cooking, whichever she wanted us to do. "Well, if I know my son, and I do, she said, he'll be nosing around my kitchen anyway so he might as well just take the lead." We both laughed and told her we were happy to do whatever she wished. We finished our drinks and went into the kitchen to eat at the breakfast nook. I loved the cozy table and warmth of the room. It was perfect. Lorraine had made a huge beef stew, homemade biscuits with whipped butter and raspberry jam and big glasses of ice-cold milk. She served and Tim brought the plates to the table. We all ate with gusto and each of us returned for a second helping and more of those delicious biscuits. Tim explained to his mother that there was nothing shy about my appetite. I threw my napkin at him, and he just laughed. Tim and I cleared up the table and loaded the dishwasher while Lorraine made coffee to take to the den. She had several different kinds of cookies that she'd made, and she filled a basket with them for us to munch on.

Tom asked us about what had gone on back home. Between us we filled them in on all the sordid affairs. Lorraine had asked a couple of specific questions about how the estate would be handled with one heir dead and the other imprisoned. Her questions were so well phrased that I found myself looking at her with curiosity. "Lorraine, I said, forgive me for asking, but have you always been a homemaker, or did you work outside the home?" Lorraine smiled and said, "Well I've been retired now for about 15 years. I closed my practice when Tom had his stroke. I practiced law since before Tim was born. I had my own firm and employed 6 attorneys and 3 paralegals." I couldn't help jumping up and hugging her! "I just knew that we'd be best of friends, I said." She was laughing that same contagious laugh as Tim. Tim and Tom just sat there grinning. "Did my son tell you nothing, she asked?" "Well, I said, it isn't all that easy to pry information out of him. He's a very close-mouth individual." Tim grabbed the basket of cookies and started picking out the ones he wanted and ignored us as if he couldn't hear us. We visited for a bit longer and then all of us decided to call it a night. Tim wanted to call Ronny tomorrow and I wanted to call John Sheridan. Before I could start upstairs Tim stopped me and asked me to come back to the den with him. We walked back there, and that beautiful man got down on one knee and formally asked me to marry him and then presented the most exquisite ring I've ever seen. It had a beautiful 3.0 carat tanzanite in the center and was surrounded with diamonds. He slipped the ring on my finger, and it was warm and fit perfectly. I was crying and laughing all at the same time. His mom and dad stood over by the door, but I could tell they were emotional and enjoying the scene. "Well, will you marry me, he asked?" "Well, since there isn't any way that I'm giving you this ring back I guess I'm stuck with you. Yes, you wonderful man, I'll marry you!"

Chapter 44

The house was very quiet, so I tried not to disturb anyone by getting up and showering. I showered, did my hair and dressed in what I hoped was appropriate apparel for meeting Ronny and going to the florist. I had chosen a lovely pair of black wool slacks, a plain crème color blouse and a black cardigan. I could wear black flats and be comfortable. There! You look ok ole' girl! I had pulled my mop of hair back and fastened it with a big barrette in the back and left it long. My coat was downstairs, so I'd grab it on our way out. I went downstairs to find every single person up, dressed, and breakfast ready! I give up! I apologized if I was late coming down and they all, simultaneously, looked at their watches and said, "It's just now 6:30am so you're good!" I was speechless. I just rolled my eyes and asked how I could help. Lorraine handed me a cup of delicious smelling coffee and told me to sit down and enjoy it. "Breakfast is about 10 minutes from done, she said." Tim came over and hugged me and kissed me good morning and just stood there smiling at me. "What is your problem, Timothy, I asked." "I have no problems, my girl, he said. I have the perfect woman in my life. What more could I possibly need?" Tim told me that he'd already talked to Ronny and that he and Peg would meet us at 5pm for drinks and that they were buying dinner. I called John Sheridan, left a message, and he has already replied. He said that he would check with his wife and that it was highly possible that she was storing some of Jack's belongings. He'll call us back. He knows we're in Boston and that we'd like to tie this up while we're here. The florist opens at 8am," Tim said. "I figured we could have breakfast, watch my dad do the dishes, walk down to the florist and talk with them. Then we can walk back and get the car. I want to show you everything. We need to go over to my condo so you can decide what you want to do with it. I want to go by my office so you can help me decide about shutting that down. I want to show you where I went to school, where our church is, and then if there is time before our dinner engagement, I'll bring you back so you can don a dress for dinner. How's that for a busy schedule?" Tom was laughing until he cried, Lorraine was laughing as she finished breakfast and I just sat there staring at him. "Really, I asked? Was that the best you could do by 6:30am?" Truth be told, my head was spinning. These people are funny. Further, they are all just alike. I'm going to have to buck up and bring on my A-game if I'm to be part of this family. Lorraine set breakfast on the table, and I just sat there devouring it with my eyes. She had made the most beautiful eggs benedict that I'd ever seen. There were fat sausages and crisp bacon and a stack of what looked like homemade bread for toast. Fantastic! "This is, second to none, the most beautiful breakfast I've ever seen, I told her." Lorraine just beamed and told us to dig in. While we were eating breakfast the phone rang, and he checked to see who was calling. He excused himself and mouthed John Sheridan to me. He took the call in the hallway so as not to disturb anyone. He came back and everyone was waiting to hear what had transpired. "Seems that Mrs. Sheridan has several boxes of Jack's belongings in the basement that her husband wasn't aware of. John has gone through everything and has found a key that may be what we're looking for. I asked him if he was going to be in the office tomorrow and he said, no, but to come by the house. I, of course, know where he lives as I've been his P.I. for the last 15 years. I told him we'd come over in the afternoon and would call first." I didn't say anything as I tried to digest this news. Perhaps we really would be able to bring this entire mess to a head and finalize it once and for all.

After breakfast we helped clear up and clean up before walking down to the florist. I had taken my notes and knew exactly what I was looking for. I asked Lorraine if it'd be alright to have the things delivered Wednesday morning. "Absolutely my dear, she said, whatever you wish to do is fine with me." We hugged Lorraine and Tom goodbye and set out on our walk to the florist. It was a beautiful morning. Crisp and clear and all the shrubs and trees smelled wonderful. We arrived at the florist, and I introduced myself to the manager. We had already covered most of my needs over the phone, so I just needed to select my wreath, centerpiece for the table and sign off on the rest of the floral decorations. I asked that she deliver the items Wednesday morning to the Donaldson house. She assured me that she already had the address and that the order would be handled timely. I thanked her and we walked back to get the car. "Where do you want to go first? Condo or office?" I told him the condo first. Tim told me that Somerville is north of the city and that Brookline lays just south of the city. "It's about 6 miles as the crow flies but unfortunately it is a slow drive due to the traffic." The drive was lovely. He skirted the downtown Boston area to get to Brookline. The condo was located on a quiet residential tree-lined street. It sat on a corner and was a grey brick building. We parked in his spot in the back and walked in through the mudroom. The backyard was small but pleasant with a fire pit and small deck. The mudroom was beautifully tiled, and the washer and dryer were housed in there. From the mudroom you entered a glassed-in sunroom that was beautifully furnished. The kitchen was a nice size, well equipped and had a corner table with wrap-around bench that could be used for casual meals. From the kitchen there was a hallway that led to the guest bath. The hallway was lined with cabinets. There was a formal dining room and living room all beautifully furnished. The living room had a huge bay window with cushioned seating that just cried out for readers and a cat! We walked upstairs where there were two master suites. The one that Tim used was furnished with a massive king-size 4-poster bed that matched the dresser, chest of drawers, two side tables, 2 comfy chairs and a small table between them. The bathroom was made for a king! I wanted to jump into that tub and never leave! There was a huge master closet with windows and a bureau in the center to house all kinds of stuff. I walked to the other bedroom and saw that it was just as large, just as grand and furnished totally different. The furniture was very modern, bright colors, a happy place to be! So far, during this tour, I'd not said a word. I finally looked at him and said,

"Don't even think about selling this place! I love it!" Tim laughed and said, "I thought you might feel that way. It is kind of cool, don't you think?" "Cool? I think it is incredible! I'm going home and calling the contractors. I want to redo my house! Let's go see your office."

Tim and Amanda arrived at his office, which was only a few blocks from the condo. It was a modern looking building on a corner lot. There were 4 parking places to the side of the building. He unlocked the door and they entered. It was beautifully set up. Light gray walls, modern silver furniture and lamps, vertical blinds at the windows. They went down the hall which had two doors next to each other, marked Gentlemen and Ladies, and then a beautiful conference room. The table was a huge slab of wood that had been shined to a high gloss. The seating was dark brown high back leather chairs. At the far end of the building was Tim's office. It was lined with bookcases and housed a huge walnut desk. Again, I just looked at him as though seeing him for the first time. "Tim, this is simply scrumptious! Can you redo my office for me, or did you hire a professional to do this?" "No, this is all me. I think I have a hidden desire to be an interior decorator. I would pursue that career but I'm so cute people would get the wrong idea." I glared at him and said, "You're just so terribly funny, you know. Seriously, do you own this building or lease it? How much do you bill? Do you still have a secretary or what?" "My oh my, he said, aren't we just full of questions. Yes, I own the building. Why would I want to lease it? Isn't that just throwing good money out the door? I was billing $550/hour when I met up with you. The price has gone up since then. No, I turned my secretary loose when I moved in with you. It just didn't seem fair to keep her wondering." I glared at him before I threw a piece of wadded up paper at him. He can be so annoying. "$550/hour? Are you kidding me, Tim? I only bill $425/hour and I'm lots smarter than you are!" Tim was laughing out loud, and she couldn't help joining in. "Seriously, I should raise my rates and you should decorate my office. What do you think?" He laughed until he had tears but finally told her he'd be happy to assist her with her needs. "Which reminds me, I said, I miss waking up next to you. We need to go home soon." And she walked out. Tim locked up and followed her out to the car. He told her that they'd head back toward Somerville and go by the school and the church. He wanted to stop by the church to see if his priest was in. I asked him if I was dressed okay to go into the church or should he drop me off first. "You're fine, Amanda. You look beautiful no matter how much or how little you're wearing." I just stared at him. Tim drove by the elementary school and then the middle/high school that he had attended. I didn't realize until that moment that he had attended parochial school for all 13 years. The church was huge! It just kind of loomed up in front of you. Tim said that the Patronage of St. Joseph Parish was built in 1869. He knew that at least 3 generations before him had attended mass there, been baptized there, been married there and been buried out of there. I asked him how he could even consider our being married in a different church? "Well, he said, I want to talk with Father McMurry today about that. Would it be ok if after our wedding in Edgartown if we had a second ceremony in the chapel at St. Jo's?" "Absolutely Tim. I think that would be perfect for all your family and friends here. In saying that, would you have some idea how big that guest list might be?" Tim thought for a while and said, "I wouldn't think it would be more than 400-500 tops." "What! Are you serious, Tim?" "Well, you can talk with my mom about this, but I think it would be easier to have a second wedding here for family, friends and business associates than to try and get them all to Martha's Vineyard. Don't you? Also, the parish at St. Elizabeth's is rather small. I doubt it would hold more than 250-300 people." "I'm going to need two wedding dresses, my darling. I'll not be wearing the same old gown for a second wedding." Tim came around and opened my door and pulled me into his arms. "I know this is kind of sudden, but don't you think it sounds like fun?" "Yes, fun, I said."

We walked into St. Jo's, and it took your breath away. It was so huge and grand that it was beyond words. Fr. McMurry was just walking down the aisle when we entered, and he broke into a beautiful smile as he greeted Tim. Tim introduced me and he was just as gracious to me. He was just a dear man. Tim asked him if he had a calendar handy and he just laughed. "Come on into my office and let's see what we can find, he said." Tim told him that we were getting married in Edgartown in the afternoon of Saturday, January 12th. "We are hoping that you might have space on your calendar for a second ceremony here on say the 17th, 18th, 24th or 25th." Fr. McMurry looked at those dates and told us, "the 18th of January is clear and available. Are you thinking to fill the sanctuary or the chapel?" Tim said, "the sanctuary for sure". "I think we will go home and talk with my parents this evening and then my mom will be able to coordinate with you. Will you please ink us in for say 2pm on Saturday the 18th of January?" Father McMurry assured us that we were inked in on his calendar and he'd be happy to work closely with Lorraine to pull this event together. "I'm sure, he said, that you'll want a reception following the mass. And then will you have a reception in our hall or elsewhere?" "I'd like to have it here if that's ok. It'll be winter and cold, possibly snowy, so people won't have to drive any more than is necessary. Thank you so very much, Father, for making the church available to us. Amanda and I are most appreciative. She is taking her classes at St. Elizabeth's and will be confirmed prior to our wedding ceremony. She's not very happy with me right now, but she's very pretty when she isn't boiling over." The father just laughed out loud and gave Amanda a hug. We took our leave and headed for his parents to get ready for our dinner engagement. I didn't feel like talking to Tim right now. I wasn't mad or upset, just a tad nervous. Two weddings?! What in the world had I gotten myself into?

Chapter 45

We were driving back to the house when Tim asked if I was ok. "I'm fine, Timothy, just fine." He glanced over at me and apparently decided to stop asking questions. I asked him, "what are your intentions regarding the office building." "I figured we'd sell it. We don't need it, do we?" "No, I said, but I do need the furniture. I'll arrange for a moving van to pick it up and deliver it to Edgartown. Have you done all your final billings?" "No, my mom will do that after my dad, and I split the list up and call people to give them referrals." "You start your new job the day after New Year's, right?" "Yes. I want to try and get all of this finalized before that, he said." We arrived at the house and his folks were waiting for us in the foyer. His mother had that look on her face that Tim gets on his when he knows he's in trouble. "Lorraine, it's fine. We've spoken with Fr. McMurry, arranged for a date to remarry with 500 of your favorite people cheering us on. I've already told him that I need a second dress. I refuse to be married in an old hand-me-down." She was just grinning ear to ear and hugged me. "Thank you, Amanda. I know it's a bit much, but we're so imbedded in Boston that we couldn't imagine doing this any other way. You're not upset?" "Upset, well I'd be lying if I didn't say that I was a bit taken back by the whole idea. I never dreamed of a second wedding. Good grief I'll be 40 years plus when I say my vows as it is. For now, though I'd best go upstairs and change before my man tells me that he can't be seen with a frumpy woman." With that I turned on my heels and headed upstairs to change clothes. I took a quick shower, did my hair in an upsweep, donned one of my wool dresses, matching scarf, heels and purse and headed back downstairs.

I got to the bottom of the stairs in time to see my handsome escort come out of the den. He still just takes my breath away. We hugged his parents and headed out to meet Ronny and Peg for dinner. It was starting to snow as we got into the car. Winter was upon us. We arrived at the restaurant which was right in the middle of downtown Boston. The valet took possession of the car and we headed for the bar to look for them. Ronny spotted Tim before we saw them and came galloping over to grab Tim in a big bear hug. Ronny was the exact opposite of what I'd expected of Tim's best friend. He was about 5'10" tall, overweight by no less than 30 pounds, had sandy blonde hair and a smile that took up his whole face! I loved him on sight! He turned to me and I started to put out my hand, but I was too late. A bear hug for sure. Peg walked over and introduced herself to me, told Ronny to settle down and gave Tim a kiss and a hug. She was just beautiful. A natural blonde, petite, bright green eyes and a figure to kill for. We all walked over to the table that Ronny and Peg already had taken. Tim and Ronny were chatting away a mile a minute and Peg and I tried to get acquainted best we could. Finally, things started to slow down enough for the four of us to have a conversation. Ronny told me that Tim had pretty much brought him up to speed on all that had been and was going to happen. He was ever so happy for the pair of us, and he could tell that we were perfect for each other. "Tim has waited for his whole life to meet the perfect girl, he said, and well, there you were in Edgartown!" We all laughed. Tim told them about the second ceremony here in Boston. Ronny looked at me and said, "Poor girl. You're going to marry this oaf twice!" "I know, I said, but you know how persuasive he can be. We spoke with the priest yesterday and I know that Tim's parents are very relieved by this decision." We drank our drinks, and the maître d' came to escort us to our table. The dining room was beautiful. Twinkling lights in artificial trees and large urns with beautiful floral arrangements. The waiter took our drink orders and Ronny ordered both red and white wine to go with our dinners. We all ordered salad to start with. I found orange roughie on the menu and ordered it as it is a delicacy that is hard to find, and I love it. The men both ordered prime rib and Peg ordered the shrimp scampi. Everyone's food looked delicious, and we all ate with gusto. We ordered one dessert and 4 spoons and had fun sharing. Ronny assured us that he and Peg would be in Edgartown on the 10th and ready for the ceremony on the 12th. I gave them the information on the bed and breakfast that I had reserved for family and friends that were coming from out of town. We had a second cup of coffee and then decided to call it a night. We all walked to the front door and waited while the valet got our cars. The snow had stopped, thank God, and the roads were a lot better than when we arrived.

Tim's parents were in the den watching TV when we came in. They came to greet us and asked if we'd had a nice evening. Lorraine wanted to know if we wanted ice cream, but we passed as we were stuffed from the delicious meal we'd just eaten. Tim and his dad got into a conversation, so I followed Lorraine into the kitchen. I reminded her that the florist would arrive early on Wednesday and that I would be downstairs ready to greet them. She thanked me again for taking over the chore as it was one that she was neither good at nor fond of. We talked about who would be attending Thanksgiving dinner. Lorraine told me that Tom had one brother, Jim, who was a widower. His wife, Alice, had passed away several years ago from Cancer. She was the love of his life and he's never considered looking for anyone else. My sister, Teresa, and her husband George will join us as well. "Jim and Alice never had children, she said. Teresa and George made up for that as they had 9! Their kids and grandkids all live somewhere between California and Florida, so holiday visits are out. It is too expensive for them to think of traveling during holiday time. George was a good provider, but they always lived modestly. My cousin Janey and her partner, Terrance, will also join us. She is my mother's cousin but closer in age to me than my mom. They will all arrive by 11am on Thanksgiving Day. We usually try to eat around 3-3:30pm and then we walk to the church for the 6pm service. I know the young people usually try to do this Friday after Thanksgiving shopping thing, but it is not something that interest me. Does it you?" "No, not at all, I said. I love to shop for gifts, and we have some wonderful boutiques and children's shops on Martha's

Vineyard, so I usually spend at least one full day going from shop to shop in search of Christmas goodies. Tim and I talked about starting the prep work right after breakfast on Thursday. Where can we send you and Tom, so you'll do something fun?" Lorraine told me that if I didn't mind that right after breakfast, they were going to go to the family cemetery and take flowers for everyone. "You're welcome to join us if you wish, she said." I told her that we'd do that another time and I was just happy that they'd be able to take the time to do that. "Speaking of Christmas, I said, would you and Tom like to come to Edgartown and spend it with us?" Lorraine never hesitated. She grabbed me and hugged me saying, yes, yes, yes! I laughed and told her that we would be enduring a total house remodel but that the bed and breakfast that my friends own is just delightful and very close to the house. I hope that will suffice for you guys?" "Absolutely, Lorraine said, that will suit us perfectly. I'm so excited! It will be such fun to share in the holidays with you and Tim. Should we plan to stay on until the wedding or plan to return for the *dress rehearsal* so to speak?" I laughed and told her if she could stay until the 12th that would be great, however, I need to work every day, and Tim is starting his new job so you may be on your own a lot of the time. "Ok, she said, let me ponder that and get back to you." "So, I said, we've talked about tomorrow and Thursday but what about Friday?" "What did you have in mind, she asked?" "Well, it won't take the entire day, but if you're up to it I'd like to discuss ancestors. We are having our 380th celebration of Edgartown in January and I have my paternal and maternal ancestry in order, but I'd like to add Tim's if you're okay with that?" "Oh my, she said, that sounds wonderful! Let's plan on starting right after breakfast and I can find additional stuff in the attic if needed." "It's a date, I said."

I walked in to give Tim a kiss and hug and headed upstairs to bed. I had a busy day tomorrow and wanted to be ready for it. I asked Lorraine if she minded my taking a bubble bath and she told me to go and soak and relax and hugged me goodnight. I went upstairs and walked right in to prepare my bath. "Bubbles, I love them!" I had grabbed a cold glass of white wine on my way through the kitchen and was planning on enjoying every drop. I had a wonderful soak in the tub and was ready to call it a night about 30 minutes later. Tim obviously heard me walking around and knocked on the door for one last hug and kiss. He felt so good as he pulled me to him that it took all my restraint not to pull him in through the door. His parents would be mortified! Or not!

I was up bright and early and headed into the kitchen. "What time are we going to John Sheridan's house? I asked." Tim told me that he'd call in an hour or so and see if he was available. We helped make breakfast and then I told him that I needed to go to a couple of stores downtown and could he drop me off near them and then perhaps meet for lunch? "Where do you need to go, he asked?" "To a store, I said. Or would it be better if I called a cab?" Tim looked shocked at my response, stuck out a pouty lip and told me to be ready in 45 minutes or he'd leave without me. His parents just shook their heads at this exchange of conversation and went on about their business. I finished my breakfast, loaded the dishwasher and ran upstairs to get my coat. I had addresses of the two stores that I wanted to go to so Tim would know where to drop me off. The addresses looked like they were relatively close to each other. Tim was waiting at the base of the stairs when I came down, helped me with my coat, told me to put my collar up, scarf on and prepare to freeze. We headed for the car, and I found that he wasn't kidding! My God, it was freezing outside! When we got in the car, he said we'd give it a few minutes to warm up and while it was doing that he wondered if I was mad at him about something? "Why would I be mad at you, Tim?" "Well, because you were short with me and in front of my parents." "First of all, I'm never short. I'm 5'9" tall for Pete's sake. Second, I didn't want your mother to know where I was going as it is a surprise." "Oh, he said, what kind of a surprise?" "If I tell you, it won't be a surprise, will it? Please drop me downtown at Faneuil Hall Marketplace. Could we please meet for lunch at 1pm at Zuma Tex-Mex Grill? It sounds very interesting." "Yes, of course, he said. Amanda, does this mean you're going shopping and I'm going to go to John's house alone?" "Yes, I think that would be best." He still looked rather perplexed, but he'll be okay. He found a corner that looked okay to drop her off. She kissed him goodbye, told him she loved him, and jumped out of the car and was on her way. Tim stared after her for a few minutes before driving off.

Chapter 46

I entered the mall and walked over to the directory. I found what I thought might be the perfect store for what I was looking for. I had noticed that Lorraine had several beautiful pieces of Staffordshire Blue Willow dishes. I wanted to see if I could find something special to fit in with those pieces as a thank you gift. I browsed through two shops before I found what I was looking for. It was a beautiful 16" platter in mint condition that I knew would be a great addition to her collection. They gift wrapped it for me and I told them I'd pick it up on my way out of the mall. I found an interesting looking boutique on my walk through and went in to see what they had. Hanging on one of the fitting room doors was the most beautiful dress I'd ever seen. It was street length with bell sleeves and a brocade top. The colors went from pumpkin to shades of gold to brown. It was perfect for Thanksgiving dinner! I tried it on, and it fit like it had been made for me. I had brought brown pumps with me which would be perfect. They had a lovely pair of thick gold loops that I bought to finish the ensemble. I paid for my purchase and again asked that I pick it up on my way out of the mall. It was close to lunch time, so I headed that way toward the restaurant.

I found the restaurant without difficulty and Tim came through the door about 5 minutes later. We were shown to a corner table and ordered margaritas to start with. The place was enchanting. The tables and chairs were bright colors with birds and flowers painted on them and there was a guitar playing softly in the background. We both love Mexican food, and we were hungry (as always). Tim ordered the Chili

Verde, and I ordered the Chili Colorado. We figured that way we'd both get to sample the red and the green sauces. Our food was delicious! We'll be returning here! We visited for a while over a cup of coffee and then went to retrieve my packages. Tim was thrilled that I'd found a new dress. "You don't treat yourself often enough, he said." "Well, I couldn't pass this up. It's just a beautiful addition to my wardrobe." We walked to the other store and took possession of the beautifully giftwrapped box. Tim was curious, I could tell, but didn't say a word. We took the elevator to the parking garage and easily located the car. We headed back to his parent's house and on the way, he filled me in about his visit with John Sheridan. Mrs. Sheridan went through all the boxes that their son had left there and found 3 different keys that they gave to Tim. "John was very quiet while I was there, Tim said, and it worries me that there is something else going on that I'm unaware of." "Well, I said, give him a call in a week or so and see how he's doing. Perhaps he was having a bad day."

We arrived at his folks and took my packages in. I went upstairs to hang my dress up. When I came back down Lorraine asked how my shopping had gone. "I had a wonderful shopping spree and got lunch bought too!" I asked her if she had any coffee made and she told me she did. We all four went into the kitchen and she fixed each of us a cup and a couple of cookies to go with it. I told her that I had something for her and handed her the beautiful box. She genuinely looked shocked! She had tears in her eyes as she asked, "what in the world?" I told her it was just a thank you for her hospitality. She opened the box and I thought she was going to faint! "Oh, my land, Amanda, this is the most beautiful piece I've ever seen! Tom, look at this! Oh, my goodness, it is just gorgeous!" Lorraine grabbed me and hugged me and kept exclaiming over how beautiful it was. "Amanda, I love it but it's too much. You shouldn't have been so generous. Never mind, I'm keeping it, I love it and I love you!" Tim looked like he might cry over how happy his mom was. "I thought it would fit perfectly with the rest of your collection. Now that I know you have those pieces; I'll be able to add to them for special occasions." Lorraine just looked at me and hugged me some more. "I've always used the other pieces for our Thanksgiving and Christmas table, Amanda, so now I'll be able to display my beautiful platter with the sliced turkey on it. It's perfect and I do thank you so very much, she said." We finished our coffee and cookies and then I went upstairs to try and organize my thoughts for tomorrow morning.

I came back downstairs about an hour later to find everyone in the den. Tim came to hug me and walked with me over to the couch. "We were just discussing how very cold it is, said Tim. Usually, we walk to the church for the evening service, but it's so cold I don't think it is good for any of us. I was just about to call a limousine service and see if they could arrange 3 cars to drop us and then collect us again after the service." "That's a wonderful idea, Tim. This cold weather can be very dangerous." Tim went to order the service and Tom made Lorraine and me a drink. We sat chatting and enjoying our drinks when Tim returned to let us know it was all set up. Tim asked, "What's for dinner, ma?" "Well sonny boy, I'll tell you. We are having fish and chips and you're cooking it!" I started laughing and Tim just looked awe struck. He asked if he could drink his drink first or should he shuffle right off to the kitchen. We all just laughed at him. "I'll make a coleslaw, Tim, and fix the tartar sauce. Are you going to do a dry coating or a beer coating?" "Any more questions, little lass, and you'll be doing this on your own." With that he walked off toward the kitchen. I rolled my eyes and told them I'd best follow his majesty to be sure I do my part. I got to the kitchen and started to get the ingredients I needed when suddenly Tim grabbed me and hugged me and then kissed me…like he meant it. I looked up at him and we both knew that we needed to go home soon! I made my tartar sauce and fixed the coleslaw while Tim was mixing up the beer batter. Lorraine had purchased some beautiful Atlantic Sole which was going to be delicious deep fried. I looked in the freezer for French fries and didn't see any, so I set about peeling potatoes, cutting them in wedges and put them in the oven with salt, pepper, and garlic salt on them. I set the table and Tim asked if I knew I was humming. "I was? No, I had no clue. I didn't know that I ever hummed." He smiled at me and said, "You know, I think my girl is just very happy in the bosom of her new family." "Oh, well, you could be right. I love your parents and I can't wait to meet the rest of them." I checked the oven and turned each of the wedges and seasoned that side while they continued to cook. Tom brought us in another drink, and we sipped on it while we did our chores. Tom told me I needed to go look at the buffet in the dining room. Tim and I both walked in there and found that she had given the platter center stage among her other pieces. I smiled and told Tom that I was so glad she was happy with her gift. "Amanda, he said, you have no idea how much this meant to her; how much you mean to her. She's always wanted a daughter to offset the brat of a son she got and now she has one." He was smiling to himself as he left the room. We went back into the kitchen and Tim asked me to yell for his parents to come to dinner. I opened the kitchen door and hollered, "supper is served in the outer dining room."

Dinner was delicious. The fish was crispy on the outside and moist and delicious on the inside. My potato wedges were a hit. Tom and Lorraine opted to clean up and Tim and I went into the study to continue forming a plan to shut down his business. "I've called 75% of the client list so far and made recommendations for each of them. The remaining 25% are mostly one-time clients and I'm not sure I should bother with them. My receivables are current, bank statements are reconciled, my secretary is paid off, and I believe that about handles it. My mom has my power of attorney and dad is on my checking, savings, and investment accounts as a secondary contact. We'll put the office on the market tomorrow afternoon and my parents will monitor possible sales and so on from here. Hopefully it will be sold by the time they come to Edgartown for Christmas. "Will you miss it, Tim?" "Nope. I've waited all this time to do and be what I believe I was meant to be. I'm going to be a good rookie cop and I plan to move into detective status within 3 years. That will give us the annual salary we need to match where I am now. Speaking of which, we need to decide what we're going to do about banking, etc. Do you have any thoughts?" "Yes, I've already drawn up all my documents necessary for adding you to my corporation, bank accounts, investments and trusts, and I have a new will prepared that we'll ask Lucy to notarize for us. As a paralegal she is eligible for doing that. I think we should leave my business account separate and join our personal accounts together. Is that what you were thinking?" "Yes, he said, pretty much right on with my thoughts. Can you redo my will and health care instructions, or do I need to find another attorney? Also, are you able to do what's necessary to add yourself as beneficiary to my investments and such?" "I don't feel it would be appropriate for me to do the new will, but I have colleagues that I work with on other things that will be happy to assist us. And, yes, I think I can do the editing on investments and banking without conflict. We probably need to do this soon, right?" "Well, he said, there is the question of name changes. Are you changing your name or what? Have you even thought about it?" "I'm going to keep Bradley, she said, as a middle name and add Donaldson. I need to notify social security for the name change and can then use that document for getting the rest of it handled. Is that ok with you?" "It is more than ok, he said. It is perfect. I love you so much Amanda. I'll be so glad when the official crap is behind us. Which reminds me, where are you going to look for a second dress? Were you serious about that?" "No matter, my darling, I've already got it taken care of. Your mom and I are meeting in the foyer early Friday morning and collecting data on ancestors. And then we are going shopping!" "That's wonderful. I'm so glad you and my mom have hit it off. I knew you would though. Invitations? Who is going to handle that?" "Your mom is. She did up a draft and I approved it and she ordered 500 to be overnighted. She had the list on her computer so she can print off address labels. I've given her $2500 out of my business account to pay for the invitations and the postage. I will talk with the florist tomorrow when she arrives and see if she can help beautify the already gorgeous church. You'll need to either buy a tux, which is probably a good idea, or rent one. Do you already own one? Never mind, it would not do. You need a new one. I would appreciate you and your attendants being in black tux, white French shirts, and gray cummerbunds. How many attendants will you have? Just Ronny? You need a minimum of 2 ushers. We can use my girlfriend's son and daughter for ring bearer and flower girl. I've asked Suzy to stand up with me…again. I'll ask Lucy and

Peg if they'll consider being bride's maids. There! We've planned the entire wedding in 15 minutes!" And then came the tears! "Amanda, what is wrong? Amanda, please stop crying. Are you okay? What is it?" All I could do was sob on his shoulder. Finally, I got myself under control and told him I had started my period that morning and there would be no baby this time. And then came more tears. "I'm so sorry Tim. I must not be able to have children because I'm so old." "Yes, I'm sure that's the problem, he said. Or perhaps the good Lord above wanted us to wait until January to start our family." I felt better after Tim said that. "I don't want to start the meds she suggested. I want to try and start our family. Is that okay with you?" "It is perfectly fine, he said. I love you. We will either make a baby or we will adopt a baby. Either way, Amanda, we will have our little family. Only two, though, okay?" "Yes, two it is. Two boys that look just like you would be perfect." We both just hugged and held on to one another and felt better afterwards. We went into the den to find Tom and Lorraine having coffee. "Amanda, are you ok, she asked?" "Yes, I'm fine. Just a little weepy, but otherwise fine." Tim assured his folks that all was good, and they were satisfied that we had it under control. We had coffee with them and then I said I was going to take a bubble bath and get a good night's sleep. I hugged Tom and Lorraine and Tim walked me to the stair landing. "It'll be okay, honey, I promise. Please know that I have all the faith in the world that our lives will come together exactly as we hope for. We were meant to be together and that is all that matters. Now, go get that bath." I headed up the stairs but turned to tell him again that I loved him. His smile was, as always, enough.

Chapter 47

I awoke early, grabbed my shower, towel dried my hair and pulled it up in a loose ponytail, threw on jeans, a tee, and a cardigan and headed downstairs. I appeared to be the first one up. I got the coffee going, set the table for breakfast and set about juicing the oranges. Lorraine arrived a few minutes later, followed closely by Tim. We were all busy getting breakfast when Tom arrived. I was starved for Tim's scrambled eggs so while he made those, I did the toast. He popped fat little sausages into a pan to go with the eggs. Everything smelled delicious and I was starved. We all chatted during our meal and then Lorraine said that she had some office work to do. Tom offered to do dishes, but we told him we had it handled. I loaded the dishwasher while Tim cleaned counters and the stove. There! A shiny kitchen. It was only a few minutes until the front doorbell rang and I went to greet the florist. Kathy, the owner, came in carrying the wreath. She explained that her two assistants were unloading the truck and would follow shortly. They brought in several boxes and one of them went out to get a ladder. Kathy and I discussed where I wanted things to go, and I showed her each room. I told her that Lorraine was busy in the study and Tom was in the backyard. Tim was leaving shortly, and I would be there to help in any way she needed. "Kathy, I said, before you get started, I wanted to ask you something." "Of course, Amanda, what is it?" "Do you think you could assist me in having flowers for our marriage ceremony on January 18th at 2pm? We are being married in my hometown of Edgartown, but Tim and his family want another ceremony at St. Jo's. We wouldn't need anything terribly elaborate as the church itself is quite ornate. I will have 3 attendants, as will Tim, a flower girl which I would love to have toss wildflowers as she comes down the aisle. Possibly 2 urns on either side of the altar, chiffon draped from pew to pew with a bouquet at the end of each pew. We are having the reception in the conference hall of the church so the urns could be moved to the main table area and then low-profile arrangements on each of the tables. We are guessing a maximum of 500 attending so with 8 at each table approximately 63 tables. Oh, yes, and my bouquet which would need to be long stemmed yellow roses. Does that sound like something you could do? I realize it is very short notice, but I don't know how to fix that at this moment." "Good grief, Amanda, breathe. I really don't know how you do what you do. I'm exhausted just listening to your list. Yes, of course we can do it. I don't care what else is going on in my life, I'm doing this wedding for you! I've come to love you already and I hope my husband and I can be added to that already enormous list of guests!" I hugged her and thanked her for being there for me and told her that of course they were invited. "Amanda, we'll put a list together and I will present it to you by the end of the year along with the available flowers. That way you can select the flowers and match them to the appropriate placement/usage." "That's perfect, Kathy. That just took a huge burden off me."

Kathy's assistants had most of the decorations placed. She and I were going to work on the staircase railing. We set the ladder up in the foyer so we could help hang the arrangement from around the chandelier. I went up to the top of the staircase and started winding the fall garland the way I had envisioned it. Kathy approved the placement and between the 4 of us we had the railing completely draped in less than half-an-hour. She and I went through each room that had decoration and she critiqued a couple of the placements. Beautiful. The entire house was aglow with soft color and a fragrance that couldn't be described as anything other than wonderful. I had already paid Kathy when I was in the shop. I had two one-hundred-dollar bills that I gave to her assistants. They seemed thrilled with my offering. I had already made out a check for what I felt was a reasonable deposit on the wedding flowers in hopes that Kathy would agree to help us. I handed her the check, and she was genuinely surprised. "Thank you, Amanda, I'm sure there won't be much of a bill left over after I apply this generous deposit. Thank you again for selecting my shop and I wish you and yours a happy Thanksgiving and a blessed Christmastime. We will talk soon." She hugged me and kissed me on the cheek, and they were out the door. I turned around and looked at the house and couldn't wait for the family to see it! I knocked on the study door and Lorraine yelled, "Enter!" I told her I didn't want to disturb her, but did she have time to walk through the house with me? "I certainly do, she said, but first will you go get Tom? I want us to see it together. I'll wait for you right here." I went to the back door and asked Tom if he could join us. "You bet, he said." The three of us walked the back hall so we could enter the foyer first. I thought they were going to faint! Both just gasped and then started talking at the same time saying it was the most beautiful thing they'd ever seen. I opened the front door so they could behold the beautiful wreath. From there we went into the den which was just dressed to perfection. The formal living room had been adorned with fall garland on the mantle and two beautiful tall urns on either side of the fireplace. There was a beautiful wreath in the window. The dining room was left for last. Lorraine started crying as she walked in to see each of the 16 chairs adorned with a drape of fall colors. The center piece was a low-profile that stretched the entire length of the table. It was truly a beautiful room. Tom grabbed me and said, "Amanda, you are unbelievable. How did my son ever win the heart of someone like you? I'm truly overwhelmed with what you have done to our home." Lorraine just stood there silently weeping. I tried to get her to stop but she seemed happy in her tears. Finally, she told me that I was everything she had ever dreamed of plus about 500% more. I looked at them and told them it was such an honor to be able to help in some way but more important than that was the way they had accepted me into their family. "I've never really enjoyed the warmth of family. Don't get me wrong. My parents were wonderful people, but I don't think I was really part of their plan. Your son has taught me to love and be loved. He has taught me that physical contact is okay; it's more than okay. It's wonderful! I can't recall my parents ever hugging me or telling me they loved me. I know they did but they never said so. It feels so wonderful to be able to touch you, love you. You will never know what this means to me." They both just encircled me in their arms for a wonderful group hug. Tim walked in just in time to see this. Rather than saying anything he just joined into the hug. Tim kept hold of me but stepped back to check out the dining room. "Man, oh man, Amanda, this house looks incredible. I was blown away when I saw the staircase. Have you thought about giving up your day job and doing this?" "No, because my husband to be is going to enhance my billing and I'll be able to retire a bit earlier than I planned." We went to get coffee while I told them all the news of Kathy being able to take care of the flowers. Lorraine said, "Tom will stop by and give her a check for a deposit." "Well, I said, I've already given her that. Technically my parents should be paying for all of this, so I've taken on that expense out of my trust fund." Tom asked, "What can we pay for, Amanda? I know you're planning on a reception to follow the ceremony at St. Jo's. Can we have that catered for you?" Tim and I looked at each other and told them that would be wonderful. "With the ceremony being at 2pm and being high mass, I would imagine everyone would be hungry for either appetizers or an early dinner. What are you thinking, Dad?" "Well, Tom said, the ceremony will take at least one-hour which puts us at 3 or 3:15pm. Let's say an open bar and appetizers from 3:15-5pm and dinner at 5pm with cake to follow. What do you think, Lorraine, will that work okay?" "Yes, she said, I think that is perfect. Let me make a couple of calls and get the ball rolling. Amanda dear, we can call back and forth with selections and hopefully have a committed menu before Christmas." "This is so very generous, I said. I think whatever you come up with works fine for us. Lorraine, are you still good to go shopping with me this afternoon? "Yes, of course, she said. I'm ready whenever you are. What are you boys going to do?" "We are coming with you, Tim said. We will drop you girls wherever you say and then dad and I are going tux shopping. Let's figure out where to meet about 4-4:30 for drinks and dad will buy you girls dinner." Tom laughed and said that sounded good to him. "This way, Tim said, the house stays spotless for tomorrow." I went upstairs to change telling Lorraine I'd just be 30 minutes. I brushed my hair out, leaving it long, did my makeup and pulled on my navy wool dress and navy pumps. I pulled the sides of my hair back with combs, put on my gold earrings, grabbed a coat, and was ready to go. The boys dropped us at L'elite and we agreed to meet at Basile's for dinner at 4:30pm.

Chapter 48

Lorraine and I were greeted by the manager, and I told her we had an appointment with Paula. She asked if we wanted coffee, tea, water or champagne while we were waiting. We opted for nothing. Paula came right out to greet us. I told her that I had looked online and found two dresses that I especially liked and hoped that she still had it. I had verified that all the L'elite dresses were a one of kind creation. Both dresses I had chosen were Gemy Malouf creations, and I gave her the number associated with the photo I had seen. She excused herself to check and came back with one of the dresses I had selected and another from Bliss Monique Lhuillier's line. I went into the dressing room to try the dresses on. I stepped out of the room when I had the first dress on to see what Lorraine thought. She gasped and then started to cry. "Amanda, it is incredible!" I laughed and told her to just wait until she sees the next dress. I went back in the dressing room and Paula helped me into the second dress. Unbelievable that both dresses would fit like they'd been made for me. I stepped back out so again Lorraine could see the dress. Again, she gasped and commented on the beautiful gown. "Ok, I said, it is up to you Mother-in-Law to be." "Oh Amanda, she said, I can't take that responsibility. They are both gorgeous." "Well, I said, you must pick. Which one will it be?" Lorraine thought for a few moments and then said, "The one you have on!" "Yes, ma'am, I quite agree, I said. The Bliss creation is the winner!" I went to change clothes and asked Paula if she felt there were any alterations at all that were needed. "No, she said, incredibly the dress fits like you had been the model for it." "Wonderful, I'll take it. Now, I asked, can you help me to select three bridesmaid dresses. I'd like my maid of honor to be in a steel gray gown and the other two in dove gray. My maid of honor and one bridesmaid's dresses will need to be shipped to the bridal shop in Edgartown. I've already spoken with the owner, who is an old friend, and she will also take care of the dress for my flower girl (Sheila age 10 years) and my ring bearer (Robin aged 4). The other attendant will be able to come in for fittings. My maid of honor is a tall size 6 and my other attendant is a very petite size 3. Paula began looking through her catalogue and we found the perfect dresses. I had already phoned Peg and asked her if she would stand up with me and she seemed thrilled to do so. I had phoned Suzy and checked to be sure on her size and then called Lucy and asked her to stand up with me as well. She also seemed very happy at the invitation and told me her size. Paula assured me that the dress order would be taken care of. "After the two ladies in Edgartown are fitted and any alterations handled, I'd like the dresses to be shipped back to you for delivery to St. Jo's. Will you be able to take care of that?" Paula assured me that she could and would. "Now, I said, I have one more favor. Can you please drag my MIL into here and find her a beautiful gown for my wedding?" Paula smiled and said, "Yes, I certainly can." I went out to sit down while Lorraine was shown the catalog of possibilities. She settled on a beautiful midi-length suit with matching jacket in a medium gray with a jeweled collar. "You look spectacular! I said." I gave her my credit card and the bridal shop's address in Edgartown to Paula. We checked our watches and agreed that we had perfect timing for the boys to buy us dinner. Paula called us a cab and we were off for a wonderful evening.

The cab dropped us at the restaurant, and we found the boys in the bar. Tim went to tell the host that we were ready for our table in about 30 minutes. We ordered drinks and joined Tim and Tom at their table. Tim asked if it were a successful mission. "I believe it was, I said." My eyes were twinkling with excitement as Tim said, "It looks like it might have been very successful." "Tim, my dress is extraordinary! The attendant's dresses are chosen and the arrangements in place for them. Your mother's dress is spectacular!" Tom said, "Well, we were also successful. We met up with Ronny, John and Donald and we all were fitted for our tuxedos. At Tim's suggestion, he and I purchased ours and the rest of the party rented theirs." "Oh my gosh, I said, Tim, have you called David and told him what to get?" "Yes, my girl, he said, I've already done that. David knows the exact color of the cummerbund and the brand of dress shirt and he's on it." "Whew, I said, that just about checks off everything on the list. We've got invitations, flowers, apparel, church, priest, and Tom is taking care of the caterer. Did I mention that the ring bearer and flower girl's clothing are being done in Edgartown and will be shipped to Boston with the rest of the order. Who are John and Donald? Is there anything missing?" "Well, Tim said, John and Donald are old friends, and you'll meet them at the wedding and, well, the music perhaps." "Oh, my goodness, I said, I hadn't even thought about that. What should we do?" "Well, lucky for you, Tim said, my dad and I have it all taken care of and it will be a surprise that you don't have to worry about." "Why am I already suspicious, I asked?" Lorraine said, "It'll be fine, dear, really it will be." I looked at each of them with a suspicious eye but decided they had it under control. The host came to take us to our table for dinner. The restaurant was just lovely. Very cozy and a romantic atmosphere. There is something about the aroma of garlic and olive oil that just sets my heart aflutter. Tom and Lorraine were familiar with the restaurant and ordered the Veal Marsala as it was their favorite. Tim had been to the restaurant previously but didn't really have a favorite dish to select. He and I discussed sharing Insalata Mesta, a bowl of clams and mussels with crunchy garlic bread and leaving room for dessert. We decided that was perfect. We ordered a bottle of white wine to accompany our salads and red wine for our entrees. Our salad arrived at the table and were just beautiful. Tim and I eagerly attacked our salad from a shared plate. The waiter had said he'd bring separate plates, but we assured him we'd be just fine sharing. We laughed as we fought for our fair share of the salad and drank our white wine. Our entrees were served and the fragrance of the garlic and tomatoes in the broth that our clams and mussels were cooked in was intoxicating. Tom and Lorraine's dinner looked delicious and Lorraine served me a sample on a small plate. Delicious! We all finished up our entrees and red wine and looked at the dessert menu. Tiramisu was high on my list but not on Tim's.

Tim and Tom both wanted the dark chocolate gelato, so Lorraine and I agreed to share the tiramisu.

We all ordered coffee and ouzo and sat and relaxed and talked about tomorrow's holiday dinner. Tim told his folks that he and I are a well-oiled machine and would take care of everything. He told his mother that there were flowers to pick up at the rear entrance of the florist tomorrow morning on their way to the cemetery. She has covered them with a plastic tarp and has my name on it. I appreciate your taking care of it for me. I didn't say anything or asked as I hoped he might share with me later. He had reached out and squeezed my hand while he was talking to his parents, so I knew he felt my concern. We finished up, Tom paid the bill, and we went to have our car brought up front. We arrived home in record time and Tom and Lorraine said they were tired and going to head on upstairs and they'd see us in the morning. Tom was taking Lorraine to breakfast and then they had two cemeteries to go to with flowers. Tim asked me if I wanted a glass of white wine and sit and relax for a few and I agreed that it was a great idea. I went after the wine and he pulled up the chairs in front of the fireplace. I kicked off my shoes and curled up in the chair enjoying the wine and Tim's company. I truly missed our cuddling and couldn't wait to get home. We talked about the dresses, the plans for alterations and such, and I mentioned that we needed to make hotel arrangements for David & Lucy, Marty and her children, Suzy and Cassandra and her daughter. Tim said he'd call on Friday to a place he knew of and see if he could secure reservations for all of them at the same place. "I don't think it will be a problem, he said. It's a lovely inn that I believe has about 15 rooms." "That's perfect, I told him." Now Amanda, he said, I want to talk with you about the flowers that my mom is picking up for me. I'm sure you'll recall that I told you that I dated a girl in high school and that we had thought we were in love. You'll remember that I told you she married the boy next door? Well, they have been married for all these many years and had 3 terrific kids that were all in junior and senior high school. Sheila and I stayed friends throughout the years and always, at the very least, exchanged holiday cards. This past spring, Sheila and 2 of her 3 children were in a fatal car crash. It was horrible for all of us that knew her as she was a really special girl; a terrific wife and mother." Amanda just sat quietly crying as she listened to Tim tell this terrible story. I got up and went and sat down on his lap and wrapped my arms around him. "Tim, I'm so very sorry for your loss. What a terrible thing to happen to a young family." Tim said, "I know. I always felt like she was exactly where she was supposed to be. Her husband, John, was just a peach of a guy and really loved her; Actually, he'd always loved her. Growing up next door to her he just watched her from afar. I'm sure when she and I were getting serious that his heart was breaking. Now that this terrible thing has happened, the only way I am able to do to feel better is to be sure that flowers are there for her and her two sons. John doesn't object and understands that it was out of love and respect for his entire family." "I think it is an honorable thing to do and I'm sure he appreciates it." We sat snuggled up together in front of the fireplace until we both drifted off to sleep. About 3am Tim woke me up and we both went upstairs to try and get some more sleep. "I love you, Tim. I love you more than you'll ever be able to imagine." "I feel the same, Amanda, he said. You're the other half of my heart. Sleep well my girl."

Chapter 49

Tim and I met on the landing at just after 6am and headed downstairs. Tom and Lorraine were having coffee. Tom said, "I came downstairs to be sure you two were ok and found you sound asleep. I just didn't have the heart to wake you even though I was sure you were both going to have sore necks. Are you both okay? I know that Tim told you about Sheila and the boys and I'm sure it was a difficult story for him to tell and you to hear." "It was, I said. It does, however, just add to the list of goodness that I know to be your son." Lorraine said that they were going to finish their coffee and then head for breakfast. They were meeting some friends to share the meal with before going to the cemeteries. Tim and I decided we'd settle for toast and jam and a cup of coffee and then get started with the holiday meal. The fresh turkey was a handsome bird, and I was guessing he was going to be delicious. Lorraine left me notes on which dinnerware and silverware to use and where they were stored. I sat down with my coffee and Tim, and I set about reviewing our menu. We had already shopped for everything and just wanted to start prepping so that we too could enjoy the holiday. My side of the list of duties included cooking and preparing the sweet potatoes, making the cranberry sauce, mixing the ingredients together for the bread stuffing and the cornbread dressing, prepping the Brussel sprouts, setting the table, selecting the wines to pair with each course, and heating up the store-bought rolls. Tim's duties included the turkey, he had already cooked the giblets for the gravy, peeling the white potatoes, and cooking the bacon for the Brussel sprouts. We would both get the green salads prepared and Tim had made his grandmother's Crab Bisque to start the meal with.

I prepped the sweet potatoes and got them in a big pot of water and told Tim to turn the heat down when they came to a boil. I cleaned the sprouts and cut them in half and put them in water to boil. I told Tim "Ditto on the sprouts". Lorraine had made the cornbread when she made the pies so that was ready to use. I chopped onions and celery, parsley and thyme and mixed in with the cornbread cubes. I cooked some breakfast sausage for the dressing. I had a huge bowl with the cornbread, vegetables and herbs that I added the sausage to. I dropped in a couple of beaten eggs and added a bit of chicken broth to help bring it all together. I had a big casserole all buttered and ready. I put foil paper over the casserole and set it in the refrigerator until it was time to bake it. I used the other half of the chopped onions and celery, sage and a pinch of red pepper flakes to go with the store-bought bread cubes. I added the beaten eggs and chicken stock and put that into the other buttered casserole dish. After covering it with foil paper I put it into the refrigerator beside the other dish. I use my grandmother's cranberry sauce recipe which I think is delicious. I cooked the whole fresh cranberries with some sugar and a cinnamon stick and then added mandarin orange segments and orange juice to the cooked berries. I covered this dish with saran wrap and placed it in the refrigerator. Tim told me that my bacon was cooked, drained and cooled so I grabbed my sprouts. I chopped a shallot and mixed it all together and put into a small baking dish, wrapped it with foil and into the fridge it went. "When the sweet potatoes are done will you please turn the heat off and just set them aside. I'm going to go find the dinnerware and then start looking for the perfect wines." "Give me a kiss, Tim said, and I'll be happy to oblige." I did as he asked and went about my chores. Tom had already pulled the extra chairs, so the table was ready for 9 place settings. He had placed the extra chair on the side, but I moved it so there were 2 places at the end closest to the kitchen. Tim and I would sit there. I found the placemats, napkins, the dishes and silverware without any problems. We had already placed the runner down the center prior to setting the centerpiece on the table. Each person had a place setting that included a placemat, napkin, a charger, a dinner plate, a salad plate and a soup bowl. The silverware was all set up to match each course and there was a small fork laid horizontal to each plate for the fresh oysters that we had gotten for an appetizer. I set out water glasses, white wine and red wine glasses and put cordial glasses on a glass tray on the buffet for those that desired after dinner liqueurs. I went into the study to look for wine. I pulled the Prosecco to go with the oysters. There was a lovely Pinot Grigio that was perfect for the salad and soup course. A selected a Sauvignon Blanc and a Zinfandel to accompany the main course. I was going to just take a couple of bottles at a time to avoid disaster. I took the Prosecco and whites into chill and put the red on the buffet. I stood back and looked at the dining room and decided it looked fabulous. There were 6 low-profile candles in the centerpiece to be lit before dinner.

I went back into the kitchen to check on Tim and my sweet potatoes. He handed me my pot of potatoes with a kiss on the cheek and I went to work mashing them. I added butter and brown sugar and pomegranate and then put them into a buttered casserole dish. I started mentally counting casseroles and found corresponding wooden warmer stands for the setting on the table or sideboard. I took them back to the dining room and set them up on the sideboard leaving room for the turkey platter, mashed potatoes, gravy boat and rolls. I found small salt & pepper sets for each place setting in the buffet drawer and set those out. Butter? I need to set small bowls of butter balls at each end of the table. I went back to see if Tim needed help with anything. He asked me how I was at making gravy. "Not bad if you can open the package up for me." I don't believe he found humor in that response. "It truly isn't my strong suit, I told him." "Okay then, he responded, how about you mash the potatoes and put the pot into a larger pot of hot water to keep them warm." "Yessir, I can do that, I said." I mashed the potatoes adding lots of heavy cream and sweet butter. I had a large pot of water coming to a boil which I would turn down to simmer when I set the potato pot into it. I started marking off our "to do list" and checked the time. The turkey was roasting beautifully. I had about an hour to go before putting the casserole dishes into bake. "Tim, we're serving oysters mignonette at the table. Should we have some cheese and crackers or something to put out in the den? Or does your mom use the formal dining room for holiday dinners?" Tim wrinkled his brow in thought and said, "They will all want coffee or tea when they first get here. There are some scones and croissants in the bread cupboard. How about we cut those into bite sizes and put a bowl of mom's jam in the center? That will give them something to munch on without filling them up too much. And I think the den is fine. It's family after all." "Ok, I said, I will get those things together and then check the den to be sure all is in order there." I cut up the goodies into bite size pieces and set a beautiful bowl of Lorraine's jam in the center of the platter. I grabbed paper napkins and set cups and saucers on the tray to carry into the den. I came back to the kitchen to make the big urn of coffee and filled the reservoir on the family-size tea kettle. I grabbed teabags, sugar packets, and creamer to take back to the den with me. I fluffed pillows and made sure that there was adequate seating for all the family. They were older folks and so I made sure that seating was close together in case one or more didn't hear as well as they used to. Again, I checked the time. Tom and Lorraine should be returning within 30 minutes or so. The family would start arriving about 30-45 minutes after that. I need to go get ready! I went back to the kitchen to check on Tim. "I'm going to go get dressed before everyone arrives to find me in jeans and a tee shirt!" He laughed and told me to "Go". I looked through each room again on my way upstairs. The house looked warm and elegant just as I had imagined it would. I jogged up the stairs to my room and laid out my clothes. I went in and washed my face and hands, brushed my teeth and started applying my makeup. I pulled my hair up into a loose ponytail and went to get dressed. My new dress that I'd found for the occasion was just beautiful. It felt like it was floating as I pulled it on. I pulled on my brown pumps and found the big hoop earrings that I'd bought to go with the dress. There! You look darned good for 40! I went back downstairs and walked into the kitchen to show Tim. I twirled around and he pulled me into his arms telling me how beautiful I looked.

I heard the front door open and went to greet Tom and Lorraine. They ooh'd and ahh'd over how pretty I looked. I hugged them both and inquired how their trip and breakfast had gone. Lorraine said that breakfast was not only delightful company but really good food. "We should take you there when you're here next," she said. We found all the graves, delivered all the flowers, said prayers for each and maybe shed a tear or two along the way. All in all, it went well and we're good until Christmas when we'll do it all over again." "Well, we're just glad you're home. Can I get you a coffee while you wait on your guest?" "I don't think so, Lorraine responded, I think I'm going to go lay down for 20 minutes and then I'll freshen up to greet the family. Are you coming along, Tom?" He smiled and followed her upstairs. I went back in the kitchen and asked Tim, "does your mom usually lay down after going to cemetery or a similar outing? Is she okay?" "Did she look okay, he asked?" "Yes, I think so, I was just surprised when she said she was going to lay down for 15 minutes and then she'd get back up for company." "I'm sure it's fine, honey. If we don't hear them moving about in 15 or 20 minutes, I'll go check on them." I told him thanks and went about the rest of my chores.

Chapter 50

We heard them moving about and figured all was ok. When they came down Tim told his mom that I was concerned and was she okay? "Yes, dear, I'm fine, she said. Just a little tired. I must admit that sometimes visiting with our parents and grandparents, siblings, and more that it gets a bit overwhelming. You can't help but think that someday it will be you visiting us on holidays." With that bit of news, I burst into tears and threw myself into Lorraine's arms. "Please don't even think such a thing, I said, you're in wonderful shape and you'll live to be 100!" Lorraine told me to go powder my nose and all would be fine. She wasn't going anywhere just yet. I went upstairs and repaired the smudges. It hit me all at once that I was going to be part of this amazing family and that I already loved them all. I couldn't bear the thought of ever losing any of them.

I went back down to the kitchen and Tom gave me one of his special hugs and assured me all would be fine. "It's simply part of growing old, I guess. Don't worry another minute about it." Tim gave me a hug and he and I returned to our duties at hand. I heard the doorbell ring and assumed the family was arriving. Tim took off his apron and walked me to the foyer to make introductions. Tom's brother, Jim, was first to arrive. He was a shorter version of Tom, but you could sure tell they were brothers. He gave me a big hug telling me that he already felt like we were old friends. We hadn't even moved from the foyer when the doorbell rang again, and it was both Teresa and George and Janey and Terrance. Tim made the introductions and again everyone hugged me like we were old friends. They all were remarking on how beautiful the foyer and staircase looked. Lorraine told them it was all her daughter-in-law to-be's handywork. "Just wait until you see the rest of the house, she said." Tom and Tim took coats and ushered everyone toward the den. I went to get the teapot of hot water and Tim brought the coffee urn. We excused ourselves and returned to the kitchen to see what needed to be done next. "I believe I'll start the salad and heat up the soup if you can get the oysters and the vinaigrette ready for those?" "Yes ma'am, I'm on it, Tim said." The soup was warming slowly. I checked the oven, and the dressings and veggies were doing fine. I got the rolls ready to put in when everything else came out. We didn't want to rush the clock. We still had about an hour before we wanted to start the appetizer course. Tim suggested that I go back into the den to get acquainted with everyone after I prepped my salad. I agreed that I should probably do just that.

I went back into the den and sat down on the fireplace hearth. Teresa and George seemed like lovely people. They were chatting about their children and grandchildren and wishing that they didn't all live so far away. "It's hard, Teresa said, yet you bring them up to be independent people and you should expect that this can happen. Luckily, they've married well, and they do come to visit each year. The thing is though, the children grow so quickly, and they don't remember you after a full year. I guess we're going to have to start saving so we can visit them in between time." Everyone agreed that it sounded the best plan. Everyone inquired about my life and family in Edgartown and said that they were looking forward to our wedding here in Boston. "If any of you would like to attend the practice ceremony in Edgartown on the 12th, you're most welcome, I said." They all laughed at the thought of it being a practice ceremony. I went on to explain that my family ties were deeply imbedded in Edgartown which is why we had chosen originally to be married there. "The Boston wedding was a bit of a surprise but now that Lorraine and I pretty much have everything under control I'm thinking it's going to be lovely. Did you all get coffee or tea? May I get anything for any of you before I return to the kitchen?" Nobody needed anything so I went back to see what I could do to finish helping Tim. "Should I pull the small plates for the appetizer, I asked?" "Yes, please. And why don't you grab the soup bowls and put on the sideboard next to where we'll set the tureen. If you want, you could build your salads in here and we can just pull them from the fridge when you're ready." "Yes, I said, all masterful ideas. What in the world would I do without you?" "I hope, he said, that you never want to find out. I love you, sweet girl." I went back into the dining room and gathered up the appetizer plates for taking back to the kitchen. I moved the soup bowls over by the trivet that would hold the tureen. I picked up the salad plates and grabbed the appetizer plates before heading back to the kitchen. I set up the appetizer plates and started putting the oysters and vinaigrette on them. I filled the tureen with the lovely crab bisque and carried it into the dining room and set on the trivet. I was so glad that the trivets that Lorraine had in her buffet were the extra-large heavy-duty type that would essentially hold anything! I went back into the kitchen and started building my salad plates. I got all the prepped veggies out of the fridge and started in. I laid the bib lettuce leaves first, heirloom tomato slices, avocado slices, orange segments, and thinly sliced radishes. I decided not to dress them until I came to serve them. Tim turned to me and said, "I believe we are ready, my lady. Are you?" "Yes, my lord, I believe I am ready." We walked out to the den and announced that dinner was served. Tim offered his arm to his mother, and I offered mine to Tom. We showed everyone to their seats and Tim made sure to pull chairs out for all the ladies. In his most commanding voice, Tim said, "Amanda and I will be seated at the end of this beautiful table as we are the chefs du jour. We will do our very best to serve you if my father would be so good as to ask God's blessings on this holiday bounty." Tom stood and said grace as he does before every meal eaten in or out of his home. I'm becoming accustomed to the practice and will miss it should we not continue it in our home. I squeezed Tim's hand as the prayer was ending. Everyone joined in with a heartfelt "Amen". We excused ourselves and went to fetch the oysters. We loaded up the serving tray and went back to the dining room. Tim held the tray while I served the appetizer. Tim poured the Prosecco for each person. We set the tray down at the side of the buffet, so we could rejoin the family. The oysters were succulent. Ice cold and perfect. The entire family seemed to really enjoy this offering. I cleared away the plates while Tim began ladling soup into bowls. I got back just in time to begin serving the soup to each person. Tim started pouring the white wine in each glass while I delivered the soup bowls. We sat down together to enjoy our soup with the rest of the family.

Chapter 51

Tim asked for everyone's attention as he had something to share with the family. "First, I'd like to take this opportunity to publicly thank Amanda for gracing my life and joining our family. She is not only smart and beautiful, but genuinely one of the nicest, most thoughtful human beings that I've ever met. Her heart is huge and filled with love for everyone that she meets. Her neighbors all adore her as do each of her lifelong friends. My parents are testimony to how she can fill your life with joy. They like me, I'm told, but they love her dearly." There was laughter and hear, hear heard from around the table. Tim said, before we begin our next course, I have something I'd like to tell all of you. I will begin by advising you that this beautiful woman next to me can make fire shoot out from her eyes when she so desires. If this occurs in the next few minutes, please know that it will be okay soon. Amanda, unlike most women, does not like surprises. She enjoys being in the driver's seat and taking command of any journey she chooses to travel. Recently, as you know, I applied to and was hired by the Edgartown Police Department. I was supposed to start my new job on January 1st but with all that has been happening I've asked for the start date to be moved forward to March 1st. Amanda and I are hoping to begin a restoration of her home. She has graciously said that it is *our* home and I look forward to sharing it with her for as long as the good Lord leaves me here on this earth. As you all are very much aware, I'm a mama's boy, well I'm a daddy's boy too, but mainly a mama's boy. I love my parents dearly and it has been hard being away from them. Now that I know that they love Amanda and that she has come to love them as well, I've made a huge decision without consulting my love. Tim turned to Amanda and said, I hope that you can forgive me for not consulting with you earlier, but I've had to move quickly to get things to come together for both of us." I told Tim that it was fine. "I'm sure, I said, that whatever you've done was done for both of our good." "That's great, he said, because I bought a house about two blocks from our home in Edgartown." "You what?!!" I couldn't help that it came out so fierce or so loud, but well, it was quite a shock! "Timothy, my dear man, what house have you bought and why, pray tell?" "See what I mean everyone? See the fire shooting from those beautiful brown eyes? Ok, well, here is the story in a nutshell. My parents don't want to give up their family home, but they don't want to be this far away from us either. If the good Lord decides to bless us with a family my folks want to be close at hand. So, I bought your grandparent's house." "Timothy Ryan Donaldson, you're telling me that you purchased an entire house! For what? Your parents are welcome to stay with us. They don't need an entire house." "Actually, they do. They are going to turn the house into a B&B. My parents are going to house friends and relatives when they want to stay over but other than that six-months each year they will operate it like a B&B. What do you think?" I turned to the table full of people staring at me with open mouths and tried to assure them that it would all be okay. "I'm going to kill Tim, but it will all be ok, I said. What do I think? I'll tell you what I think. I think that buying my grandparent's home is the best gift ever. Had you bothered to consult me you would have learned that you will be part owner as it is held in the trust. However, since you didn't do that, I will assume that you have already decided that you will never, ever do something like this without talking with me first ever again. Am I right?" "Yes dear, Tim said quietly. I am sorry Amanda, but I had to move quickly. My parents are going to wait until Spring to do any restorations or changes necessary before they open on May 1st. They will operate from May through October and then return home for the lovely winter months." "I'm thrilled that your parents will be close to us. That way when I'm not speaking to you, you will have somewhere to go. Seriously though, the house does not need restoration. It is in perfect condition. Did you see it prior to purchasing it?" "Well, he said, I saw some lovely photographs." "Well, my lad, I'll tell you this. The house is a Greek Colonial Revival home built by my grandfather. The home has 2 master suites and 4 more guest rooms, 6 bathrooms, a huge kitchen and butler pantry, maid's quarters off the kitchen, a huge living room, a music room, a den/study, and an office. There is a carriage house that houses 4 automobiles. We left my grandparent's furnishings there when they passed away. My parents would check on things weekly and we've always had maid service to keep the home spotless. And, while we are on the subject, Timothy, from whom did you make this purchase because the house still belongs to my family's trust." "Yes, I discovered that. Your realtor told me that I should make the check out to the trust account or you, personally, whichever you wished me to do. Amanda, are you angry with me?" "Let's just suffice to say that my salad is getting cold, my wine glass is empty, and I think we should continue this conversation later. I will, however, offer this to my future in-laws. I love you both dearly and I couldn't be happier that six months out of every year going forward we will be neighbors. Also, Lorraine, should God bless us with a family I'm going to need your expertise to keep my law practice going. Now, Timothy, let's get the salad." We left the table in silence and headed for the kitchen. I didn't say anything to him. Part of me was over the moon thrilled and the other part was ready to slice his head off with a dull knife. He grabbed hold of me and pulled me to him and well, the mad part was instantly gone – like always. "Tim, the house was a part of the trust. If you'd told me what you wanted to do you could have avoided spending all that money. Besides which, I'm a bit miffed at my banker who didn't even bother to call and asked if I agreed or not." "Well, Tim said, in his defense, I asked that it be a surprise. I transferred the money to the trust account last night. I didn't want the trust to suffer financially for any reason. We'll have to wait until it goes through escrow but that shouldn't take long. The title is being set up in both of our names and I've made up a lease for my parents to sign. They will be paid a salary and a percentage of paying guests annually. I hope that is alright?" "Yes, Tim, it's all fine. Is there anything else? Do you have any other surprises for me before salad?" "No, that's all I've got, he said." "Tim, I said, to satisfy my curiosity, what did my trust fund charge you for my grandparent's home?" "I transferred $1.5 which he said was fair market value for the house." With that, he gathered up a trayful of salad and was gone. I followed him into the dining room and helped to serve the salads and pour fresh wine. I thought about just drinking mine from the bottle. I had glanced over at Lorraine who mouthed, are you okay? I assured her I was and added a wink, so she'd know most of this was for show and to keep her son in line. We ate our salad and as we were taking up the empty dishes, we advised everyone that if they cared to stretch, smoke, or whatever that it would be about 15-20 minutes for the main course to be served.

Chapter 52

Everyone scattered in different directions with that bit of news. Lorraine and Tom followed Tim and me into the kitchen to be sure all was ok. Tom said, "Amanda, we warned this blockhead that he should talk to you first, but he decided living on the edge sounded like fun. We hope you're ok with all of this." "Tom, I'm fine. Tim knows that, and I believe your wife does also. I was a bit taken back as I'm sure you can imagine, but not at Tim's actions but rather at my bank not communicating with me. As the trust officer I believe he should have, and I will be reminding him of that when we get home. As for the house and the thought of a B&B I am thrilled. I so look forward to your both being close and us being able to spend lots and lots of time together. Tim and I are hoping that we'll be blessed with a family. I may be too long in tooth to expect such a miracle, but I'm still hopeful. It would be a blessing to have you there with us. I was also a bit surprised at Tim's announcement about postponing his start date, but as it turns out, I think it was wise. We need to remodel our house and I've not got time to do that. I have four estates coming up in January and a couple of weddings also so I'm going to be plenty busy. You are still coming for Christmas, aren't you?" "Yes, of course, Lorraine said. We're looking forward to it and to sharing in both of your weddings." Tim gathered me into his arms and told his parents that he had found the best woman in the world. "Yes, Tim, his dad said, I believe you have at that." Tom and Lorraine went to check on the rest of the guests and we put the final touches on the main course. Tim had been busy checking things while we were talking with his parents and was now busy slicing the bird. I started taking casseroles out of the oven and removing the foil getting them ready for the sideboard. I put the rolls in the oven and got the cranberry sauce from the fridge. I also grabbed the pitcher of water on my way. I filled water glasses, set the cranberries down and went after the other casseroles. I had to take them all separately as they were heavy and very warm. The mashed potatoes were in a beautiful bowl, and I had put dollops of butter on the top. I set the potatoes on the buffet about the same time as Tim came with the bread stuffing. I went back after the cornbread dressing, and he picked up the Brussel sprouts. He went back after the gravy boat while I went to fetch the family. I asked each person if they wanted red or white wine and started filling glasses. Tim announced that they should form a line and fill their dinner plates with whatever they wanted. Everyone got their plates filled and returned to their place at the table. Tim and I filled our plates and joined them as well. Everything smelled delicious. The family all commented on how delicious every morsel of food was. The turkey was a showstopper. It was moist and tender and delicious. Terrance and Jim both went back for seconds, and Lorraine even got a second helping of turkey and gravy. Tim and I looked at each other and decided we'd done a pretty good job. "Next year, I said, you are all invited to Edgartown for Thanksgiving. There will be plenty of room for everyone to stay in one or the other of our houses." There was laughter throughout the room.

We decided that dessert would be in about an hour, and everyone headed for the den. We had put out liqueurs, fresh coffee and such for those that wanted it. Everyone settled into a comfy chair or sofa, and some looked as if they were dozing off. Tim and I went upstairs to my room to talk. He apologized for surprising me in front of family but was worried that time was running out. I told him that I understood that and wasn't upset with him but that I was upset with the bank manager. "He works for me, I said, and he should never take someone else's word for what I want and don't want. I haven't added your name to the trust or my other accounts yet as I must wait until we are legally married to do so. That is really my only problem with this entire issue." "I understand, he said, I hadn't even considered that. He seemed to know who I was and accepted my word for it. I can see clearly that we both acted very foolishly and without thinking about consequences should there be any." "There won't be any, Tim, I said, because I will call him on Monday when we are back and set him straight. If he wants to continue to handle my affairs, and later our affairs, he will act with propriety or not at all." "I understand, he said. Now that we have that out of the way, does everything else meet with your approval? I want to call the restoration people on Monday and get started with our house remodel. I have a plan drawn up if you'd like to see it?" "Yes, is it here, I asked." "Yes, I'll just run and get it. I've had to have something to do with you sleeping away from me, so I've worked on the remodel." He left to go to his room and was back in a flash with a rolled-up tube of paper. "Here are my drawings, he said. If you have changes, we'll initiate them and be able to give these to the person chosen to do the remodel/restoration. I say restoration Amanda because even though we're adding to the house and remodeling it there is some restoration in need of being done. The house dates back, I believe to the late 1880s and could use a facelift." "I absolutely agree. These plans look wonderful, Tim. You're really a man of many talents. Do you have any thoughts on how much money I'll need to move from the trust to cover these repairs?" "None, my girl. That is the rest of my surprise. I had a phone call from an associate who not only wants to buy the office but the business name also. He offered $2.25M and I accepted. We need to reinvest those funds which was one of the reasons for purchasing your grandparents' house. We will need the house purchase and the remodel to offset the capital gains, won't we?" "Yes, I can see that, Tim. That is a wise move financially, but it is unacceptable from my perspective. You'll be able to use the house purchase and the business sale on your personal income tax for this year, as a single man. We won't be able to claim the remodel until next year; after we're married. It might have been a good thing to have asked your business purchaser to wait until January 1st and asked the bank to accept your transferred funds using that same date. I'm surprised your mother didn't suggest this to you." "She might have, he said, had I had the brains to have asked her or you before going off half-cocked. Will we be able to resolve this?" "I believe so. Let's worry about it next week. Have you received a transfer of funds from your buyer yet?" "No, I used personal funds for the purchase of the house." Well, on Monday let us see if we can't bring all these loose ends together. I really like the plans for the remodel, Tim. Really well done. I want to walk through the house and look at these as I go to see if I find anything missing." "That sounds like a good plan, Amanda. Again, I'm sorry, Tim said, for not having been a smarter husband-to-be." He pulled her to him and hugged and kissed her. She looked up at him again, as always, thinking how lucky she was to have found this man. I told him we needed to go back downstairs before they came looking for us!

Chapter 53

We walked back downstairs and joined the family who were all in different conversations. We joined his parents and asked if they were ready for dessert. Lorraine checked her watch and told everyone to return to the dining room for dessert and coffee. Tim and I went to get his mom's beautiful pies, whipped cream, and coffee urn. We carried the pies back in and everyone had their forks ready! We laughed and Tim asked, "pumpkin or apple or peach?" He cut the requested pieces of pie, and I piled on the whipped cream. I was pretty sure they'd want seconds on dessert! The pies were delicious, and we all made room for just one small piece of the other pie. Tim and I went to clean up the kitchen. We had already cleaned a lot as we went so there really wasn't that much to do. We washed up the pots and pans, got them dried and put away in quick order. I went to freshen up before going to mass. I went upstairs and washed my face, reapplied my makeup, straightened my hair and decided I looked okay. I walked back downstairs, and everyone was starting to get coats on and ready themselves for our ride to St. Josephs. Tim helped me on with my coat, pulled my scarf snugly around my neck and gave me a kiss. We all got into the limos, and reached St. Jos in record time. The mass was beautiful. It lasted just over an hour but had been truly inspirational. I really liked the priest and looked forward to getting to know him better. He greeted everyone as we left and seemed to know every single worshipper by name. Amazing. We walked back to the house and helped everyone to their cars. Nobody lived very far away so that was a good thing. They all promised to call as soon as they got home safely. Aunt Teresa told me to keep that boy in line and everything would be fine. I laughed and promised I'd do my best. The four of us walked back into the house and decided that a nightcap sounded like a fine idea. Tom fixed drinks and we all collapsed in the den. Lorraine told us that we had done a spectacular job on dinner. She told us, "It was magnificent! You both act like a well-oiled machine and seem to feed off one another quite well. Nobody would ever believe that you'd only just met such a short time ago." Tim told her that when you've searched for almost 40 years for the other half of you that when you finally come together it's like magic; everything just fits perfectly. Lorraine and Tom both just gleamed over his comment. I finished my drink and bid everyone goodnight. "I'm going to go upstairs with a glass of iced cold white wine, soak in a warm bubble bath, read for a few minutes and then go to sleep. I feel like I've been up for a week." Tim walked me to the landing and kissed me goodnight. "I love you, Amanda. So very much." I told him that I loved him also. "Tim, please remind your mom that she and I have a date after breakfast to go through the ancestors."

I awoke early feeling completely refreshed. I was excited about going through the foyer and getting acquainted with the ancestors. I jumped out of bed and went to shower and get dressed. I decided jeans and a tee and cardigan were perfect for a day of do-nothing. I went downstairs and heard everyone else already up. What time do these people get up? I went into the kitchen and greeted everyone, and Tim gave me a kiss and handed me a coffee. "Breakfast in 15 minutes, he said." "What are you fixing, I asked." "I'm not, Tim said, my dad has bacon in the oven, mom is ready to fry the eggs and dad is making waffles which is my favorite food in the universe!" "Really, I said, I had no idea. And, while I'm thinking about it, Timothy, I believe you are a bit of a spoiled boy." Lorraine started laughing and said, "Oh no, not our Tim." We sat down to a beautiful meal and thoroughly enjoyed it. Wow! Waffles! Who knew?

Chapter 54

The men went about their business for the morning and Lorraine, and I went to begin my tour of ancestors. Lorraine had a big book that she was extracting the information from. She told me that I was welcome to be the holder of that book going forward. Lorraine asked if I wanted to start on the Donaldson side or the Evanston side. I told her it was entirely up to her. "Ok then, she said, these are Tom's parents. His dad, Patrick Donaldson was born in Boston. He worked for the railroad here in the city. He passed away right before Tom, and I married. His mother was Sharon O'Malley. She also was born in Boston. She was a homemaker. She passed away at age 87 years. Next is Tom's granddad. Liam O'Donaldson was born in Boston. He, like his father, was a laborer who worked on the roads and the railways. He had his name legally changed to Liam Donaldson before he married. He was in a work-related accident passed away from the injuries. Tom's grandmother was Catherine (Kate) Shanahan. She was an accomplished seamstress and sewed for a group of wealthy Bostonians. She passed away at age 60. Next is the great grandfather. Peter O'Donaldson was born in Cork, Ireland. Peter was a farmer and an elder for his church. He married Elizabeth Murphy, also from Cork. Elizabeth gave birth to 10 children before dying in childbirth with son, Liam. That's about all I have of *real* information on the Donaldson side. Excuse me a moment while I go get the Evanston book." Lorraine returned shortly with another book of equal size for her side of the family. Lorraine started with her parents. My father was Alistair Evanston. He was born in Boston. My mother was Caitlin O'Toole. She was born in Chatham and her family moved to Cambridge when she was about 5 years old.

My parents married when she was 19. My father was a steel mill laborer and later became a foreman. My mother was an elementary school teacher. My dad has been gone about 20 years and my mother about 10 years. My grandparents were Broden Evanston and Elizabeth MacCowan. They were both born in Plockton, Scotland where they met and married and then immigrated to the United States. My grandfather was a fisherman and my grandmother a seamstress and day-time housekeeper for a wealthy family. My grandfather died at age 47 years and my grandmother lived another 25 years when she got pneumonia and passed away at the age of 89 years. My great grandfather was Archibald Evanston. He was born in Plockton, Scotland in 1864 and fished until he died. My great grandmother was Fiona MacCallister. She was born in Plockton, Scotland. She met and married my great grandfather when she was 20. There were seven children born to that union. That's it. There is a general write up about each of the ancestors in the two books. You may take them both with you and I'll assume that you are the caretaker of the family history." I hugged Lorraine and told her that I was thrilled to be entrusted with such important information. "These books are just beautiful, Lorraine." "You will find, she said, that birth records, naturalization paperwork, baptism records, hospital visit, immunization, death records, and such are all included in the books." "That's wonderful! I'm so excited about adding this for the annual celebration. Before I forget, would you be able to steer me in the right direction for the classes that I'll be taking when we get home? I would like to be as prepared as possible so that we don't run into any snags with my confirmation prior to our January 12th date." Lorraine thought for a moment and said, "follow me. I may have exactly what you need in the study." We walked into the study, and she started sifting through the file cabinet looking for something. "Here it is, she said. My mother was Episcopalian like you are and converted prior to marrying my father. The classes were all out of a book and I'll bet they've not changed that much over the years. You are welcome to take this with you." "I'll just look at it while we are here so nothing will happen to it, I said." "It's fine, Amanda. Whichever way you want to handle it is okay with us. Now, how about some lunch, I'm famished!" I told her that the idea was perfect as I too was starving. While we were eating our sandwich, I commented again on how beautiful the books are that she has on ancestors. "I can give you the name of the publisher that put them together for me, if you like, she said." I told her that would be wonderful as it was the ideal way to house the family information and photographs. We finished our sandwiches and cup of tea and decided that a shopping trip was a great way to spend the rest of the day. "Perhaps the men would like to meet us for dinner some place near our shopping?" "Yes, said Lorraine, I believe that would work fine. Amanda, when are you headed back to Edgartown?" "I would like to leave tomorrow after breakfast, I said, if that works for Tim. I need to get home, and I'd also really enjoy one full day to clean house, grocery shop, and what not before returning to work on Monday. My assistant, as I'm sure you're aware, underwent a terrible ordeal and left to go stay with family. I'm not convinced that she will return at all. I can't say as I blame her." "No, she said, I agree. It must have been terrifying for her. I totally understand your wanting to get home." "Lorraine, I asked, do you have any idea where the boys are?" "Yes, she said, I do. They left early this morning to meet the moving van to pick up all the office furniture and take it to your office for you. I'm hoping that you'll get an executive desk to match the lobby furniture. I never did think they went together." "Oh, that's grand, I said. Yes, I want the desk, console, bookcase and chair to match the lobby style. I'm crazy about the conference room table. I was thinking of putting his desk in the new study that he wants to add to the house and, if you don't mind, I was going to take my desk and put in Granny's house for you to have there." "Wonderful, she said. We obviously have a plan! Let's go shopping!" I called Tim and told him we were off to the Shops at Prudential Square in Somerville and asked if he had a suggestion for dinner. He said they'd meet us at Wagamama's. Lorraine opted to drive which was good because she knew where she was going. We found the mall with no difficulty, parked and headed for a boutique that she loves to browse through. "Are we hunting anything in particular, she asked." "No, I responded, but I could use a couple of cute winter dresses and I am almost desperate for a camel color winter coat. Also, does Tim need anything that you know of?" "Well, she said, I tend to always let him do his own shopping, but I've noticed that he wears the same shirts repeatedly. Let's try to find him a half-dozen new ones. Here we are. I think you can find what you're wanting in this shop. While you look and try on at your leisure, I'll go next door and see if I can find the birthday gift I'm hunting." I went into the store and started looking through the racks. I found a beautiful crème color wool dress with a cowl neck that was belted at the waist that was perfect for the office. I found another gorgeous wool dress in gray with a stripe around the round collar area that was A-line like I tend to like. I wanted something that was a bit brighter for dinners out or company. On the back wall was a gorgeous black dress with red trim, midi length with a matching red coat. Gorgeous! I took them all to try on. I had figured maybe 2 of the 3 but nope, they all fit to a tee, and I told the sales lady to ring them up! I asked her about a winter coat, and she came back with 2, both in camel color. One street length and one was midi length. I opted for the midi-length. I was just walking out of the store when Lorraine came from doing her shopping. We walked to a men's store and found six new shirts for Mr. Tim that we hoped he would like. He tends to wear a lot of gray and light blues that work well with his beautiful coloring. I found a mauve long-sleeved Henley and two other long sleeve shirts. One was dark teal, and the other was cream color. His mother found him three more that were like what I'd selected but different colors. There! We had done a great job of shopping. As we were walking to the restaurant Lorraine told me that Wagamama's has wonderful Japanese food and that Tim loves it!

<h1 style="text-align:center">*Chapter 55*</h1>

We found the bar and the boys found us a few minutes later. Tim said he told the host that we wanted at least 30 minutes drinking time before going to our table. The men ordered their drinks, and we caught up with what the other had been doing all day. Tim said the office furniture would arrive next Wednesday at my office. "I'll plan to be there to receive the delivery, he said." I told him that was wonderful and that we wanted to move his desk to the house, my desk to my grandparents and I needed to order office furniture for me to match the lobby furniture. "Ok, he said, let me take care of that. I know what I got so it'll make it easy to order the furniture for your office. Dad and I went by the condo to check on things. I contacted a maid service in the area that is reputable, and they will clean every 3 weeks and advise if anything is out of order. I also had an alarm system ordered for installation and it will connect with the local police department. When are we going home?" I told him it was funny he should ask because his mother had asked the same thing earlier. "She is sick of us, he said, but is trying not to make us feel like we need to leave." "Timothy Ryan!" Lorraine was mortified with his comment. Tim started laughing and she finally joined in but not before shaking her fist at him. To answer your question, I said, I'd like to leave in the morning. I've a ton to do and I don't know if Dolly is coming back. "You need to call her, my girl, he said." "Yes, I know I need to." Our host came in to show us to our table. Tom ordered Saki for us to sip on while we enjoyed our appetizer of crispy fried Prawns with a chili and garlic dipping sauce. Lorraine ordered the Kokoro Bowl with spicy tuna. Tom ordered the Ramen bowl with grilled chicken.

Tim and I decided to share, again, and he ordered for us; a raw salad, pork belly with panko apple bao, a small bowl of short rib ramen and Wagamama ramen with chicken, pork, prawns, mussels and noodles. Oh, my goodness! It was so delicious that I couldn't shovel it in fast enough! "That was incredible, I said." Tim smiled and said, "Yes, I know. It is one of my favorites that I still haven't perfected a recipe for. We'll work on that when we get home." Tom said that he was sorry to see us leaving but certainly understood that we needed to get home. "I'm thinking that the kitty has been missing you two." "Well, I said, I'm sure she has missed Tim. She is a rather traitorous female. She was mine for all these many years but the moment he came on the place she threw me under the bus." We had a pot of delicious tea and then decided to call it a night. Tom said he'd drive Lorraine home in her car and Tim could take Amanda in his car. Tim and I visited about his day and my meeting with the ancestors. We were both full and tired and the thought of going home was a good one. We visited with Tom and Lorraine for a few minutes and then went upstairs to pack for our trip home. I told Tim that I was going to soak in a hot bath and then hit the sack. "Are we good to leave about 9am, I asked." "Yes, he said, I think that will be perfect. It started to snow a bit so hopefully we can beat the bad weather back to Edgartown. Goodnight sweet girl. I love you." I handed him the package from his mom and me. "What's this?" "We just wanted to give you a present because you're such a sweet man. Goodnight, Tim. I love you too." I undressed and put my robe on while I packed up. I went in and drew my bath while I finished. The bath was just what I needed to completely relax. I had spent a whirlwind week filled to the brim with family and fun. They are all wonderful people, and I will look forward to seeing them for the Christmas holiday. Lorraine said that they planned to stay on until the January 12th wedding and then would head home to get ready for the big bash. Tim was going to be busy figuring out the key or keys with David, arranging the remodel of both houses, and whatever else he has in mind. I need to call Dolly on Monday and find out what her plans are. With that I decided I was tired and going to sleep.

Tim and I met on the landing and started carrying bags downstairs. We went into the kitchen following the wonderful aroma of cinnamon rolls. Lorraine handed us a cinnamon roll and coffee to keep our strength up while we were waiting on Tom to finish fixing breakfast. We were devouring our rolls when Tom set down scrambled eggs, crisp bacon, fat little sausages, and beautiful hashed brown potatoes. There were no words. The four of us attacked the food as if we'd not eaten for days. "Tom, this is just delicious. You can come to Edgartown and cook for me anytime you want to." Tom smiled brightly and said, "I hope that I've taught the boy how to do all of this. I'd hate to think that your man wouldn't be keeping you well fed." "Oh, I said, there is no chance of that. He's a very accomplished chef and I am happy to be sous chef." We finished up our meal and an extra cup of coffee and then Tim and I cleared the table. Tom told us to go ahead and get ready to hit the road as the snow was on its way. We went back upstairs to check that we'd not left anything. I stripped both beds and threw the sheets down the laundry chute. I cleaned my bathroom and Tim cleaned the guest bath. We hung new towels in both bathrooms and left the beds to be made by the lady that comes in to clean and do laundry each week. We grabbed our coats, gloves, and scarves and headed downstairs. Tom and Lorraine were waiting on the landing. Lorraine was already teary-eyed, and Tom looked the same. You could see my Tim's heart melting as he hugged and kissed his parents. I kissed and hugged them both and tried to hold back the tears. I wanted to tell them what this week had meant to me. I started to speak, and Lorraine interrupted saying, "Amanda, we love you so much and we are so glad that you're a part of our little family. God's speed in your travels home. We will see you the week before Christmas and we will call often. Timothy, call us the moment you arrive safely home. We love you both." And with that she disappeared down the hall. Tom hugged us again and waited on the porch as we got into the car and was waving as we pulled away.

Chapter 56

I could no longer hold back the tears and about a block away Tim pulled over to hold me while I cried. "I know exactly how you feel, my girl. I feel that way every time I leave those two people. I can't imagine my life without either of them." We got control of our emotions and started the journey again. "Tim, are you worried about the snow?" "Not particularly, he said, as long as the other guy stays on his side of the road." With that comment we were on our way! It wasn't snowing hard as we left the Boston city limits and seemed to dissipate as we headed toward the ferry. We visited about our wonderful week with his family and traveled along at a good pace. We ran into road construction about 30 miles away from the ferry terminal which caused a hurry up and wait kind of situation. We were finally back on the highway and the snow was all but gone. We reached the ferry terminal about 40 minutes before the new Seastreak ferry was due. There is a café of sorts there, so we went in to grab a coffee and pastry to hold us until we reached home. We walked back to the car when we saw the ferry arriving. The new ferry was much faster than the old ferry system, so we'd be on Martha's Vineyard in less than one-hour. The crossing was pleasant, but very cold. Winter had settled into our area. We offloaded at Wood Hole and began our hour and one-quarter trip home. It was now snowing again, and they were big flakes that were sticking rapidly. Tim pulled over at a gas station and put chains on the car as a precaution. We took our time and Tim's defensive driving course paid off. He maneuvered those roads like a pro! "I hope that the house isn't too cold after us being gone for so long, I said." Tim glanced over and smiled. "Well, it probably would have been if you were marrying a dummy. But since you're not marrying a dummy, he said, I thought to call David this morning. He's delivering fresh food and the cat and turning the heat up to warm the house." I just stared at him. "Do you always think of everything?" "Yes, he replied, it's my job. I have promised to take care of your every wish, and I damned well plan on doing just that. You'll need to give David a check for groceries." It continued to snow all the way to the house. Tim suggested we wait until the snow let up to worry about unloading the car and I agreed. We ran for it! It was so good to get home. Precious was on the couch, glaring at us, as we went in. We both walked over and gave her a pat on the head, but she just ignored us. The house was already toasty warm and felt wonderful. Tim immediately called his folks to let them know we made it safely. I went in and checked to see what David had left for us as we were starving for lunch. Lucy had made a beautiful chicken potpie that just needed to be popped in the oven to bake for dinner. There were fresh veggies, sandwich fixings, and fruit. David left a note in the fridge that Precious had already had her treat and her milk and had lost a full pound in our absence. It also said to look in the bread box as there was a loaf of homemade bread in there for sandwiches. I went to work on slicing the bread and getting the sandwich stuff on a plate and it was all ready when Tim walked in the kitchen. We fixed our sandwiches and drank our ice-cold milk and relished being home. Tim had called David and thanked both him and Lucy for their generous gifts to our stomachs. He had also invited them to dinner tomorrow evening… Oh, how I love this man. "What are we fixing, Timothy?" "Well, I figured we'd go to mass in the morning and stop and pick up an array of seafood and fix jambalaya." "I'm from Massachusetts, Timothy, I don't know what jambalaya is." Tim just smiled and said, "Stick with me, my love, and I'll teach you all sorts of things. In fact, are you busy? Wanna' take a nap?" We both raced for the staircase as we needed no more prompting.

We woke up to a totally dark house! Obviously, we had fallen asleep after reacquainting ourselves with one another. I turned on the lamp on the side table and Tim woke right up. "Wow! I guess we fell asleep, he said." "Yes, it certainly would appear that way. I'm starving!"

We got ourselves together and went downstairs. Precious just glared at us as we walked by her. I went in and turned on the oven so we could put the potpie in. She was fast on our heels when she heard the refrigerator door open. I found her some skim milk and warmed up some chicken for her. She allowed me to pet the top of her head but that was all. I put the pie in the oven and set the timer. We decided that cold white wine sounded like a wonderful idea. Tim made a salad and I set the kitchen bar for us to eat at. "Ok, you need to bring me up to speed on this jambalaya stuff so we can make a grocery list." "Are you serious, he asked? You've never had Cajun food? "Nope, sorry. I'm an east coast debutante. We don't travel much." "Ok, well, it's a beautiful tomatoey rice dish that is full of pieces of chicken, sausages, shrimp, mussels, and clams. I usually make a lemon aioli to drizzle over the top of it." "It sounds delightful, I said." I started making out a grocery list while Tim browsed through the cupboard calling out what we were out of or low on. It was a long list! The beeper went off and Tim grabbed the potpie out of the oven. Oh, my goodness, it was gorgeous! We dug in and ate about two-thirds of it. We cleared up and did dishes by hand and emptied the dishwasher from last week. "I want to read for a few minutes and then I'm ready for bed. How about you?" "That sounds good, Amanda. It's been a very long week."

Chapter 57

They both awoke early and went downstairs to see about some breakfast before showering and getting ready for mass. It had stopped snowing, and everything was covered with a beautiful blanket of white. They opted for hot oatmeal and toast. It was an easy clean up and it filled them up with warmth. Amanda hurried upstairs to shower and free up the bathroom for Tim. They were both ready and downstairs in less than 30 minutes. Amanda grabbed the grocery list and they headed for the car. They arrived at the church and the parking lot was packed with cars. They circled the parking lot and finally found a place where they could squeeze in. They hurried to the front entrance and went in to find a seat. It was so warm and comforting inside the sanctuary. It wasn't so very different from the church I'd been brought up in. In fact, after reviewing the information for converting that Lorraine had given me to review, I found a great many similarities in the doctrine of both churches. The only major difference I found was the act of confessing to the priest. I was still on the cusp about that one. I hadn't spoken to Tim about it, but I might. I'd like to know his thoughts on the subject. The service was lovely and the message very inspiring. We were greeted by Fr. James on our way out and he reminded me that he was looking forward to our meeting on the 2nd of December. I told him I was looking forward to it and would see him then. We spoke to several people that we knew on our way to the car. We talked about the sermon on our way to the grocery store. I asked Tim about the confessional and would he please give me his interpretation. We sat in the car and talked about what confessing his sins means to Tim. "I feel that it helps me to clear my conscious if I've offended someone or deliberately done something mean or sarcastic or hurtful. I guess what it does is to help keep me on the straight and narrow. Does that help?" "In a matter of speaking, yes, I said, but I'm still not sure I understand the "why" of it. I've always thought, and in fact, been taught, that you pray directly to God through Jesus Christ. I was unaware that I ever needed a mediator." "Well, I know what you're saying, and I think you'll have to sort it through with Fr. James because it is deeply embedded in me, and I don't know how to help you." "Thank you, Tim, for listening. I don't mean it to sound critical it is simply something that I have to get straight in my mind." "Absolutely! I wouldn't want you to react in any other way, my girl, not ever about anything. You need to have your heart and soul satisfied before making this huge step. And, Amanda, if for any reason you decide against this, we will work it out." "No, she said, don't worry about that, Tim, I'm fine with converting. I just like to ask questions is all. Tim, did you have to go to confession because of me?" "Well, not because of you, but definitely because of me. Yes, I had to confess that I had taken your virginity outside of marriage. I should have gone and sat on the cold porch, Amanda. I hope you'll forgive me for being so weak?" "Tim, you are a silly man, I seduced you! It was I who knocked on your door, remember?" "Oh, well, I might have had the thought in my head which was responsible for my guilty feelings." They went inside to do their grocery shopping. I got the essentials and Tim went straight to the fish market to get all his goodies for tonight's spectacular dish. I grabbed one of their delicious pizzas to bake when we got home. That would make the perfect lunch. Tim caught up with me and we went to the checkout stand. We loaded everything into the car and headed for home. I was starving and couldn't wait for the pizza to be hot and gooey and ready to eat! We headed home just as it started to snow again. We grabbed the grocery bags and headed for the front door to not have everything wet from the snow. We unloaded the groceries and I put the pizza in the oven to bake. Precious was starved and laying in front of the refrigerator howling. Tim fed her. I told Tim I was going to clean the bathroom and vacuum before the Adlers arrive.

Tim was busy in the kitchen, and I looked around to be sure everything was clean and tidy. I had already set the table, chosen the wine for dinner, and now I just needed to go put a cheese platter together for an appetizer and make the salad. The salad was almost a stand-alone entrée. It had butter lettuce, tomatoes, avocadoes, black olives, marinated green beans, red and orange bell pepper slices, purple onions and a rich garlicky vinaigrette. Tim's jambalaya was gorgeous. He had developed a rich tomato-base gravy that he cooked chicken thighs, bacon, andouille sausage, shrimp, mussels and clams in. He cooked the rice separately and was going to add to the dish shortly before serving it. I had prepared garlic toast to sop it all up with. I was now officially starving! I checked the time and decided that a gin and tonic was for the chef and sous chef and perhaps a 5-minute sit down prior to our guest arriving. Tim readily agreed! We sat at the kitchen bar trying to stretch and relax for a few minutes. Our lives had been on rocket speed for quite some time now. "I'm really looking forward to doing absolutely nothing strenuous for the month of December. How about you?" "Well, we need to celebrate your birthday. We are supposed to get together with Suzy and James to celebrate both your birthdays. You have 4 grueling classes to take to be confirmed by end of the year. We have Christmas to shop and plan for. My parents are arriving one full week before Christmas. I have 3 keys that David and I need to see if they work on this monster safe. Are you tired yet? I know I am!" "Good grief, I said, I think we need a vacation! We can't even have a honeymoon because we're getting married again a week later." The doorbell rang and we just started laughing as we went to greet the Adlers.

Chapter 58

David and Lucy came in and we all exchanged hugs. Precious immediately went to Lucy and wanted to be picked up. Who is this cat that they returned to our home?? Tim and David went to make drinks for everyone, and Lucy and I found a spot in the living room where we could catch up on what was going on in our busy lives. "Amanda, I'm so excited, Lucy said, to be in your Boston wedding! I was thrilled to be helping with what we're now thinking of as "rehearsal" but to be included in your wedding party! I'm just thrilled!" I told her that I was equally thrilled to have her by my side. "Have you visited the bridal shop yet? Is your dress there? Did it fit ok? Did you like it?" "Amanda, she said, it fit perfectly! They don't even have to hem it. I couldn't believe that you were able to find not only the perfect size but the perfect dress! The color on my skin is quite beautiful. When she helped me on with it, I wept. I don't remember ever feeling so even at my own wedding." Suzy's dress needs to be hemmed but other than that it was also perfect for her. "Do you know, I asked, whether the children have tried on their clothing yet?" "Yes, she said, we all met and went together which made it so fun. The details here are all coming together perfectly. They must hem the boy's trousers but then they are ready to ship back to Boston." David and Tim had joined us and brought our drinks. David said, "Yes, and my tuxedo is almost as pretty as me!" With that he smiled and winked at me. "Before I forget, I said, I must tell you that Tim was able to secure reservations at an Inn just a few blocks from his parents and the church so you're all set. Give me a second, I have something for you." I went to the hall closet and got the gift that I had purchased for them while shopping with

Lorraine. I handed the package to Lucy. "What's this for, Amanda, she asked?" "It's a thank you gift from Tim and me for watching Precious and our house, I said." Lucy opened the beautifully wrapped gift and let out a whoop! "Amanda, it is beautiful!" I had found her a lovely platter to go with her Polish dishes. It was quite lovely. "I'm so glad you like it, Lucy." "I love it, she said. Thank you so much." We finished our drinks and Tim announced that dinner was ready, so we all moved into the dining room. I went to get the salads and the cheese platter which I had forgotten to bring out to the living room. Oh well, so much for my manners of late. Everyone enjoyed the cheese and were equally thrilled with the salad. When Tim brought in the jambalaya there was an explosion of applause! I'm glad that we are all comfortable with each other because there was no holding back as we attacked the bowl of deliciousness. Lucy and I tried to eat slowly and savor every bite, but we found we were running a race with the boys. We all took second helpings and I believe there was groaning toward the end of the meal. "I didn't make dessert, I said, but we have gelato for later." Tim poured more wine for everyone, and we just sat quietly savoring the moment. "Let's take another glass of wine into the living room so we can be comfortable in our misery, I said." Tim poured wine and took another bottle in and set on the coffee table in case anyone wanted it. We all talked non-stop, and it was a thoroughly pleasant evening. Tim and David agreed to meet tomorrow afternoon to try the keys to the safe. David asked me if I wanted to be there, and I told him I did. It was snowing again so we asked them to call us when they got home so we wouldn't worry. We cleaned up the kitchen, loaded the dishwasher, and decided to read for 30 minutes and then get some sleep.

Chapter 59

I was up before Tim and downstairs eating yogurt when I heard him start downstairs. "You're up early, my girl, is all ok, he asked?" "Yes, I just wanted to get an early start for the office. Are you running in this weather?" "Yes, of course. It's invigorating. Slippery, too, but invigorating." "Well, kiss me goodbye then. I'm off to the dungeon." He walked me out to the car and made sure all was good before taking off down the road. I drove slowly to the office and was glad for my parking space right outside the door. It was cold inside as I started down the hall. I missed Dolly already. I need to get me a coffee and then call her. The heater came on and I had my coffee in hand. I called her number, and she answered right away. "Amanda, she said, it is so good to hear from you. How is everything, she asked?" I caught her up on all the news and then got the nerve to ask if she was coming back. "I'm not, she said. I'm sorry but I just can't. I'm still shaken over what occurred and I just can't come back. I hope you understand." "Of course, I do, I told her. I miss you terribly but certainly understand your position. Stay in touch with me, Dolly. I love you." I hung up and just broke into tears. I had grown so fond of her over the past 5 years. I went in the bathroom to mop up the damage from the tears and went back and called the temp agency and then the local community college in search of a replacement. I knew I couldn't do this alone. My typing just isn't that good! It was only a few minutes later that Dolly called back saying she had a favor. "If I send you my power of attorney, can you handle the paperwork on the sale of my condo?" "Yes, of course. Anything for you. Have you already listed it?" "Yes, I'll send you all the info along with the POA. Also, I'll email you my passwords right now, so you'll have them. Thanks Amanda." I hung up the phone feeling very sorry for myself. Tim called shortly after that and said he was coming by for a quick bite with me if that was ok. I called him back to bring food and alcohol that my day wasn't going very well.

Tim showed up at the door about 15 minutes later. He knocked because I still hadn't remembered to give him a key. He came in with smiles, hugs and kisses and it didn't take much for me to be smiling and feeling better. The man has that effect on me. I told him about Dolly, and he told me how sorry he was. He mentioned that he types about 90 wpm and would be happy to help until I found a replacement. Again, as happens quite often, I just stared at him. We ate our lunch and then he asked if there was a chance that I could go with him to meet David. "Yes, I put in a call to the college and the temp agency but haven't heard back. I'll collect the responses tomorrow. Let me just pick up and clean up and I'll be with you shortly." I shut down my system, put away the files that I had out, went to the restroom, grabbed my coat, purse and briefcase and met Tim at the front door. We locked up and I gave him the spare key that I had in my desk, so he'd be able to get in if he needed to. We walked to the car, and I mentioned that I'd need to come back to get my car before going home. "Yes, we will, he said, I promise not to forget." We met David at the precinct and went across the street to where the evidence lockers are maintained. We were granted entrance and escorted to where the safe was housed. "Technically, David said, the safe is not evidence, but at least it is being kept safe." We agreed with that. Tim said, "Well, here goes. David, you have the combination that opens the main door." David crouched down so he could look straight on at the lock so as not to mess up opening the door. This safe is so old and probably prone to being cranky. Success! The main door was open. Tim handed David what he thought might be the correct key. It was. The inside door opened without a problem. The first thing we noticed was that the top shelf was jammed full of stacks of money. There was another smaller box inside, and it, of course, needed a key to open it. Tim handed David a key to try but it didn't fit. He handed him the other key and it opened right up. David took the box out and set it on the table that was next to the safe. He opened the lid and found that it was full of what looked like beautiful, priceless jewels. There were several beautiful pieces that were intact and then a lot of single jewels. We tried to ascertain what we were looking at and it appeared to be emeralds, rubies, some diamonds, and other jewels that we weren't familiar with. David locked it back up so we could continue our search. There was a large ledger book on the bottom of the safe floor. David took it out and we found a meticulously kept record of every robbery that Jack Sheridan had ever committed! It contained the owner's name, address where the robbery took place and every single item taken from them. We took some other items out that seemed to be tools and such. There was one more box at the back of the safe wall. And, of course, it had a lock. David tried the one key that we had left, and it unlocked it. This contained a stack of photographs of the artwork that had been stolen and where each piece was stored. If the item was "fenced" the purchaser was named along with the date of the transaction. There were various photographs of what appeared to be about one dozen different men. On the back of each of the photographs was the person's name, address and what *job* that he had worked on. Jack left no stone unturned! David turned to us and said, "I'm going to place everything back into the safe and lock each one of the locks as we go. I believe that I should have at least two patrolmen and possibly someone from the D.A.'s office when we open this again. Amanda, if we make you copies of all the transactions and the jewelry or money that we can tie to each transaction will you be able to make restitution to the families?" "Yes, I believe so David. I'm concerned about where the paintings are being stored; the ones that haven't been sold. They are all pointing to the Highfield Hall. That is where Leonard Brice was curator, isn't it? I've never been there but I recall it being a beautiful old stately mansion that was converted into a very prestigious art gallery." David thought for a moment, and said, "Yes, I believe you're correct. I thought Leonard was too young to be mixed up with the likes of Jack Sheridan but apparently, he and his father were both involved." I muttered "what a mess" as I followed David out of the building. We thanked David for his time, and he assured us he'd be in touch. I asked Tim if he felt like going for a burger or something before heading home. I was tired and kind of cranky and he agreed that it sounded like a good plan. Do you want to take your car home first so you can drink yourself silly if you want to and not have to worry about driving? "Yes, I told him, a perfect plan." He dropped me at my car and followed me home. I parked it, locked it, grabbed my stuff and went back to his car. "I'm all set. Let's go." Tim asked me if I really wanted a burger. "Yes, one that drips down my arms when I bite into it!" "Wow, I can't hardly wait to sit across from this, he said." I just turned and smiled at him. We drove straight to Fat Ronnie's Burgertown. You could smell the burgers and fries the moment you stepped out of the car. I knew exactly which burger I wanted. The waitress brought our water, and we ordered a milk shake to share. I ordered the deluxe cheese bacon burger with fries. Tim got the bar-be-que burger with fries. We both devoured them when they arrived. Tim would be running an extra mile to get rid of this dinner! We had a cup of coffee and shared a piece of Banana Cream Pie and then headed home. It was snowing hard as we pulled into the driveway. It was more than likely going to be a slow trip to the office in the morning. We got into the house and out of our wet coats and shoes. I've got to remember to wear boots. Tim asked if we needed anything else and I told him I was stuffed to the brim. We sat down on the couch and snuggled up in front of the fireplace. It couldn't have been very long before we both dozed off. Tim awakened first and suggested we go upstairs to bed. I struggled to wake up and headed for my bed.

Chapter 60

Tim was already out for his run when I woke up. I got my shower and got dressed and headed downstairs. He had fixed breakfast, and it was staying warm in the oven. He had scrambled eggs and fixed some nice crisp bacon to go with it. I poured my coffee and sat down at the bar to enjoy my meal. Precious rubbed up against me purring loudly so I knew that Tim had already fed our fat furry friend. I was just clearing things up when Tim came in the door. "Good morning, my girl, he said. Do you want me to take you to work this morning? It's quite awful out." "That would be wonderful if you're sure you don't mind. What is on your agenda for the day?" "Well, I'm calling the contractor with hopes of going over plans for this house. You've not submitted any changes or complaints so are we good to go with my plan?" "Yes, all except the money part. I'll be pulling money out of the trust to pay for the remodel, Tim." "No, Amanda, he said. I need to pay for this. It's your house that will become our house and this is my way of claiming my share. Please, let me do this." "Alright. But I don't want you running yourself way short, Tim. We need to talk further about money, yours and mine. I would like you to consider helping me when David gets his ducks in a row. I don't want to take on this project with a temp or a college person. It is too confidential, and this is still a small community with its typical problems such as gossiping." "I agree. Yes, we will plan on it." "I must set up an appointment for the one estate that is due toward the end of December. I don't want to wait and get it hung up around the holiday. Then I have four more to settle in January/February, so our lives are going to be chaotic on many levels until next spring. I didn't see any phone message from either the temp agency or the college. I won't be happy if I need to call them a second time. I'm ready if you are. Rather than dropping me at the office I need to go to local bank first so you can drop me there. Will you be able to swing by about 3pm or so to pick me up?" "Yes, that'll work fine. I'm ready, he said, if you are."

Chapter 61

I put on my coat and boots and wrapped my scarf around my hair and shoulders. It was super cold outside! We got to the bank and Tim asked if I'd be okay to walk to work. "Absolutely. I love you and I will see you around 3pm." I went into the local bank and stopped at the service desk. I told her that I needed to speak with the branch manager. She asked if I had an appointment and I told her I did not. She went into his office, and he came back out to greet me. "Miss Bradley, it is so nice to see you. To what do I owe this surprise visit, he asked?" "Mr. Shore, it's so nice to see you, I said. May we speak privately?" "Absolutely, let's go into my office. I have coffee in there, and we can visit over a cup." "I'll get right to the point, I said. I'm closing out my business with the Edgartown Bank and I'd like to have you set up all my checking, savings, investments, trust accounts, business accounts and so on. I'll need a large safety deposit box also. Is that possible? Are you interested in taking on my business?" "Well, yes, he said, of course we want your business. I'm quite surprised is all. Is there a problem that I need to be made aware of?" "No problem. Just an untimely error on their part leaving me no choice but to change lending institutions." "How soon, he asked, are we doing this?" "Today, I said." "Okay, well do you have account numbers and so on that I can create transfers from them to us rather than you having to close out accounts? That will protect any payments or other transactions that are pending or in transit." "Yes, I have them all right here." I handed him the list and watched closely to see his reaction. He gasped before he completed the list. I must admit I rather enjoyed that part. "I'm going to see Jerry Peterson on my way back to the office. I will be advising him that sometime this afternoon you will phone him to advise him that the transfers are taking place. Is that satisfactory with you? I would appreciate you supplying me with a copy of those transfers, so I'll know the timing and that everything is concluded. I would appreciate your ordering me check stock for all the accounts. I like to have a credit and a debit card for all accounts. I need a manual check book for the trust and personal account. I need statements emailed to me on the first day of every month. I do not want a quarterly accounting of the investments and trust but rather a monthly detailed accounting. The portfolio needs to be researched and revised. I'll look to you to set that up and you'll bill me directly, rather than debiting the account, with whatever costs are incurred. Also, before I forget it, my fiancé and I are being married on January 12th here in Edgartown. We will be combining some of our accounts after that. I think that about does it. Do you have any concerns or questions of me?" "No, Amanda, he said, I think I have everything I need. I will prepare a safety deposit box for you to access the next time you're in. I don't know what to say other than thank you. We very much value you and your business and will endeavor to take good care of your holdings." We shook hands and I left.

I walked over to the Edgartown Bank and asked to see Jerry Peterson. He came out with a big smile and said, "Amanda, so good to see you. What's going on?" "Let's go into your office Jerry. We need to speak privately." I explained exactly what was going to take place and when. I honestly thought he was going to have a coronary and I honestly didn't care. "Why are you doing this to me, Amanda? What have I done wrong?" "Well, for starters Jerry, you initiated a transaction that you had no business conducting. You sold a piece of property out of my grandparent's estate without notifying me. You conducted this transaction without my signature or authority being in place. I don't want to haggle with you, Jerry. I just want to be done with you." I stood up and told him that I needed to access my safety deposit box and that I needed a large container of some sort for the contents. He went to get me a couple of large bags and opened the vault for me. I emptied the contents into the bags, told the lady that I was finished and walked out of the bank without a backward glance. Screw with me, will you? I think you should think again. I walked back to the office smiling even though the darned sacks were heavy. Wait until I tell Tim how my morning went!

I got to the office and set everything down while I locked the front door. I put everything down in my office, got my coat and scarf off and went to find coffee. I went back and checked phone messages. Both the temp agency and the college had called within the past 30 minutes. I settled in and returned both those calls. The temp agency had someone after the first of the year but not before. They wondered if it would be long term or just a short fill in. I explained that I was looking to replace my administrative assistant that was also a paralegal as she had left the area. They said they'd stay in touch and let me know if they found candidates. I called the college and got pretty much the same response. With the upcoming holidays there just weren't many choices. I decided Tim was going to be an excellent assistant. I made a couple of other calls and then called my December estate client to try and settle on a date. They agreed that they wanted to avoid the holiday rush and we settled on 10am on Monday the 9th of December. I then phoned Suzy to see if she and James were going to be available for dinner somewhere between the 10th and the 12th. We caught up with each other and then she checked her calendar, and we decided on meeting in the middle. December 11th at 5pm at the Terrace at the Charlotte. She said she'd make the reservation and that she and James were excited to finally meet Tim. I marked the event on my calendar and called for delivery for my lunch. I wanted Asian food and decided on a ramen bowl. The young man was at my door about 15 minutes later. I ate my lunch and cleaned up the kitchen.

Chapter 62

I called Tim to see where he was with his day. "I'm no place, he said. The contractor can't meet until tomorrow. What'd you have in mind?" I told him to pick me up and we'd go to my grandparent's house. "I'll be there in 10 minutes." I put everything away, grabbed my coat, briefcase and purse and went to meet Tim when he arrived. I opened the front door, locked it and ran for the car. It was snowing like crazy! I leaned over and gave him a kiss on his cheek and directed him to ***the house he'd already purchased***. We parked in front of carriage house and entered through the backdoor. Whenever I walk into my grandparent's home, I'm a mixture of emotions. I miss her so very badly and yet am so glad to be in their house because I love it so. I was only 7 years old when my grandfather passed away, but I had my granny Amanda until I was 17 years old. She and I had such fun together! She would play dolls and house with me, and we'd have grand tea parties. We shopped until we dropped and would have lunch at least weekly all throughout my school years. Tim was looking at me and I could tell he was concerned that I was okay. I assured him that I was. We took off our heavy clothes and boots in the outer porch area and entered through the kitchen. We went through every room absorbing the beauty and the love that was so evident there. The main level of the home is so beautifully constructed that it simply takes your breath away. The detail of the molding, the doors, the casings are all hand crafted and the wood just shines. The firm that comes in and cleans are meticulous in their care of the house and are paid well to insure that being the case. "This is the area I thought your parents might take as their master suite. It was originally the maid's quarter but has a lovely bath attached and there's a small alcove that could be opened and added to their quarters. What do you think?" "I think, he said, that they would love it. Nothing much to be done and the house is just incredible. I don't know how your banker allowed the sale to go through for the price that he did. This house is worth 10 times what I paid for it." "Yes, it is, I said. That is exactly why that my banker isn't my banker anymore. I'll fill you in on how my morning transpired later this evening. Let's just keep enjoying the house. We went into the living room and Tim drew in an audible breath when he saw the fireplace and the magnificent mantle. There is a 42"x36" painting of my grandparents that hangs above the fireplace that is gorgeous. We went upstairs and searched through every room. Tim said, "I think that perhaps we could eliminate the hallway and connect each of the baths to the smaller rooms and just have a 4-bedroom suite B&B. What do you think?" "I thought the same thing. I've done a bit of research in the area and found that the two master suites would go for $450-500 per night and the two smaller suites would go for about $225-250 per night. Your parents could very well be booked solid from May through October." "They don't need the money, Amanda, but they do need the chore if that makes any sense. I think they could reinvest the income in something local." I told him I thought that would be wonderful. "Your mother is very astute at your family ancestry, and I have a pretty good handle on mine. She might do well with creating a historical society here. People would come from afar to obtain her help with researching their families. There are about 45 families that were first settlers here on Martha's Vineyard. It could be a very rewarding thing to do. Did you speak with the contractor at all or just get a message?" "He left me a voice mail saying he'd be in tomorrow and would call me to firm up a date. I hate contractors as they are generally very sporadic in keeping their word, but we'll see how this goes. Some of this I could do by myself, or my dad and I could do it together. Would you be ok with me canvasing that idea? Perhaps dad and I could get a lot of what we want done and move to the rest of the project in the spring." "I'm up for whatever you want to do Tim. It's your house, too. Is there anything else you want to look at or should we head for home? Did you put anything out for dinner, or do we need to stop and get something?” “I put pork chops out to thaw, so I think we’re good. Let’s go home sweet girl.”

Chapter 63

We got home albeit slowly as the snow was getting thicker and thicker. Obviously, winter has come to Edgartown. We got in the front door to a snarling kitty. Apparently, she was hungry. Tim picked her up, against her will, and carried her into check out the fridge for her yummies. I ran upstairs to change into my sweatpants and tee and pull this hair up off my neck! I'm glad he likes it down. I went back downstairs and poured us a big, tall glass of ice-cold white wine. "Let's go in the living room so I can tell you everything I know." He asked me to give him a minute and he'd be right back. He ran upstairs and when he came back downstairs, he had on nice looking lounging pants and a fresh white tee shirt. "I'm definitely rubbing off on you!" "By the way, he said, I never did thank you and my mom for the pretty shirts you bought me. I like them and I appreciate the thought." "You are very welcome, my lord of the manor." "Ok, tell me everything you found out." "Well, first off, you'll be the assistant of choice at least through February. Sorry. Nobody is here and anyone who is does not want a job. I have my December estate scheduled for the morning of the 9th. I have left messages for the other three and we'll see where we get with them. I went to the local bank, as you know because you dropped me off there. I had a lovely visit with the branch manager and he and I have a plan in place. From there I went to the Edgartown bank and suffice to say, Jerry Peterson isn't a happy man. In fact, I'd be surprised if he still has a job tonight. Everything was transferred about two hours ago." "Everything, Tim asked?" "Yup. All of it." I thought Jerry was going to die in front of me. Come to think of it, Mr. Shore looked quite taken back when he saw the list. Because of the way in which Peterson sold my grandparent's home we are going to have to do some fast footwork with the title company as what you paid does not clear the asset. My thoughts right now are to apply what you paid the trust to the remodel of our house and leave the grandparent's house as is. It will be in both of our names after the 12th of January anyway, so what does it matter? Everything I own or is in trust to me will become half yours and all yours upon my passing. I think the important thing now is to find the best way for your parents to invest or donate the revenue from the B&B. There are advantages within the trust to leave the B&B as part of it. I have tax shelters in place for things like this." "You are correct, Amanda. I acted poorly but my intent was honorable. I'm sorry to have caused you troubles that you're having to deal with now." "It's fine Tim. Together we will get through everything and anything. I love you."

"Amanda, your office furniture is arriving this afternoon. Will I be able to set up or do you have clients?" I told him that it would be fine. I'd just plan to help him. "I'm quite excited to see your purchases anyway! You never said one way or the other, are you okay with putting your big executive desk at the house for your "office to be", I asked." "Yes, I think it is a great idea. I've just no clue where we'll store it until the office gets built." "Why don't you store it in my parent's room until you or a contractor starts work in there? You could do the back porch stretch and the office before you start upstairs." "Yes, that'll work. And I'm taking your executive desk to your grandparent's home for mom and dad to use, right? What about your conference table? Wouldn't it work in the study area?" "Oh, I said, yes, that's a great thought. Let's plan to do that." I was dilly-dallying over my yogurt and muffin and decided to just go put jeans and a sweater on and not worry about being in the office today. I could check messages and respond to any inquiries that there might be. Tim was cleaning things up and I told him I was going to go shower and dress and I'd be back in 15 minutes to help. Precious was screaming so I figured Tim would be busy fixing her breakfast while I showered. I wonder if she'd be happy if I got her a kitten to keep her company? Hmmm, I'll have to ponder that thought.

I came back downstairs to my phone ringing. I answered it and found that it was Mr. Sloan from the Edgartown Bank calling. "Miss Bradley, he said, I hope I'm not calling too early?" I assured him it was fine and asked how I might help. "Well, I've got a lot of paperwork for you to sign when you have a few minutes. Also, I have some ideas for your portfolio that I would like to present to you. Would you have time this morning?" "I'm sorry, this morning is out and I'm renovating my office this afternoon. Would tomorrow morning at 10am work for you? Also, I'd like my fiancé to accompany me as he will be on all the paperwork after the 12th of January." "Yes, that will work fine, and I'll look forward to meeting Mr. Donaldson, he said. See you tomorrow morning and thank you." I went and told Tim that we had an appointment in the morning to go over the paperwork at the bank. "Great, he said, perhaps I could get my accounts changed over to there while we're at it. Then all we'll need to do after the 12th is to add each other's names to the existing accounts." "Yes, that works perfectly. Did I remember to tell you that we have a dinner engagement with Suzy and James on the 11th of December?" "No, he said, but I knew you were trying to finalize a date so that sounds wonderful. You haven't given me any ideas what you want for your birthday or how you wish to celebrate it. Could you please give it some thought and let me know soon? I realize it won't be as spectacular as what I'm getting for my birthday, but we can try to match it somehow." "Well, let me think on that. I need to go and call your mother. I've some things I want to go over with her. Do you want me to put it on speaker and we can all visit together?" "No, he said, you go ahead and talk with her, and you can fill me in later. I've got some stuff to do before we leave to meet the moving van."

I was lucky and Lorraine answered on the first ring. "Well, hello, she said. How are you doing?" I told her that all was good here except for being snow up to our waist. "Lorraine, I have some ideas to run by you if you have a few minutes." "Yes, dear, I am all yours." "Well, I'm looking at my calendar and wondering if you and Tom can arrive on weekend of the 14th of December? If you can do that, I think you need to pack a large suitcase because we want you to stay until after the rehearsal wedding and then we can all head for Boston together for the actual event of the year." We were both laughing at the chaotic month ahead. "Yes, I think we can make that happen. Is there a reason you want us there early, she asked?" "Yes, I said, there is. I would love for you and I to be able to do all our holiday shopping together here on Martha's Vineyard. Also, we can decorate your new home and possibly even celebrate Christmas Eve there. The other reason is because I need to talk with you about some up and coming events in my office. My assistant is not returning. I was certain that she would not. I'm handling the sale of her home as she doesn't even want to return for that. We opened the safe and the contents will bowl you over. The police are working with the D.A.'s office about how to proceed with the distribution of items as retribution to the families of the people that were involved in the crimes. They have suggested that since I hold ownership over the estate that they would defer the monetary distributions to my office. I'm going to need help, Lorraine. A lot of help." "Oh my God, Amanda, that is huge! When do you think that will occur, she asked?" "Well, Tim and I had talked about it, and we figured that it would take at least 90 days in the courts to settle the how and why on all of it. We are led to believe that the paintings that were stolen are hidden somehow in the local museum. That is going to be a nightmare to work through. So, I'm hoping that you might come to work with me?" "You can count on it, Amanda. I might be a bit rusty but all my credentials, licenses, and such are all current." "Wonderful. That takes a big load off my shoulders. Also, while you and Tom are here Timothy has some ideas on how to do your private suite at the house. I need to talk with you guys about the house and the ideas going forward but would prefer to do that in person." "Yes, she said, I suspected that Timmy Bear had acted a bit prematurely on that transaction. Tom and I are expecting you to reign him in." She was laughing at that thought. "Timmy Bear? Really?" "Oh, yes, my dear, that will definitely get his attention." "Well, I'm signing off for now. We'll talk again soon. My love to you both and can't wait to see you on the 14th." I hung up feeling wonderful about my future in-laws. Tim was standing in the doorway smiling. "So, Timmy Bear, how long have you been standing there eavesdropping?" "My mother, he said, is in so much trouble! Not long. Just long enough to know that you and my mom have become fast friends and I'm ever so happy about that." "Yes, I believe she and I have a connection. You ready to go?" "Yup, let's do it."

Chapter 64

On our way to the office, I filled Tim in on my conversation with his mom. He seemed pleased that they were coming early and that his mom was willing to come back and work with me on the distributions. "I'm going to need your help through the rest of this month though on regular clients, I said." "Yes, I'm practicing up on my spelling and typing. I think I'll be ok." "You are such a Timmy Bear!" "You're going to pay big time for that one when we get home, Amanda Kay!" We arrived at the office, and it wasn't but a few minutes before the truck showed up. Tim convinced the two young men that their help in moving furniture around would be much appreciated and that a cash gratuity would be in order. They had everything moved and set up within 2 hours. Tim asked them if they would consider moving the two desks and a conference table to two different locations before leaving. They told him they'd be happy to if lunch were thrown into the bargain. I laughed and went for lunch while Tim and the guys got the two desks into the truck. I returned with enormous hoagies, chips and soft drinks. They plowed through the food like only men in their twenties can do. Tim and I locked up and led the way to Grannie's house and moved the one desk into the maid's quarters. They set the conference table in the study, and it looked beautiful in there. We then headed for the house to deliver the other desk. They had that huge desk up the stairs and in place without breathing hard. Tim asked them if they would mind taking all the furniture from the master suite and loading into their truck. He told them that if they wanted to sell it and keep the funds it was fine with us. They were thrilled! Tim gave them $100 each and they were very pleased. "Safe travels back to Boston, boys. Thanks again for all your help, Tim said." They shook hands and were off on their journey. "Well, that's done, he said." "Yes, and I'm so glad they were willing to help because I knew I wasn't going to be of any assistance at all. I supervise good, but hard labor isn't my thing." Tim laughed and said, "Yes, I knew you'd not want to mess-up your coif. So now that the furniture is gone from your parent's room, we can pick out paint color and buy new furnishings. I want to tear out everything in the bathroom, replace the existing old porcelain tub with a walk-in shower and put a free-standing slipper shaped tub in there for you to relax in." "That's fabulous! I can't wait, Tim."

Tim and I were up and ready for our meeting with the bank. I was anxious to hear his ideas for the portfolios as I felt it had gone ignored by Jerry Peterson. We parked right outside the door and walked into the customer service area. I identified myself and told the young lady that we had an appointment with Mr. Sloan. She asked if we would like coffee or tea and it would just be a few minutes. We rejected the beverage and sat down to wait on Mr. Sloan. He came out shortly and shook hands with me and I introduced him to Tim. He had set up the conference room for us to meet in, so we followed him down the hall. "Miss Bradley, I've researched your portfolio thoroughly and find that at least four of the stock choices have cost you quite a good sum. I would propose that you sell all four of those and reinvest the money in the three stocks that I have laying in front of you for your review." "I'm very happy, Mr. Sloan, that you've noticed these problems and are proposing a way of resolving them. I am most unhappy with the way my accounts were handled by Mr. Peterson. My parents and grandparents had done business with his bank exclusively and frankly, I don't think that is ever a good idea. I like to split it up a bit. Tim, what do you think about these stocks he has chosen for us?" Tim started reading the summary on each of them and said that he felt two of them were good solid investments, but he wasn't so sure about the third one. "Mr. Donaldson, what if we place one-third of the funds in a guaranteed fund while you and Miss Bradley are researching my third choice?" I took it upon myself to answer for both Tim and I by telling him that I would prefer to divide the moneys from the sale equally between the two stocks that Tim had approved. "We can always invest in others at a later date, I said." "Yes, he replied, I absolutely agree." Tim agreed as well. "Have you found any other problems in any of my accounts, I asked." "Not really, he said. I would like to propose that you authorize transfers from savings to a CD in Twenty-Thousand Dollar increments as you or I see fit. There is way too much money sitting in savings accounts that isn't earmarked for anything that I could see. Would that be something you would entertain for the future?" I told him that I had no problem with him doing that as long as there was always a minimum of Fifty Thousand Dollars in my personal savings should I have immediate need of it. "I don't mind moving funds around if I need to, but so far, I've not needed to. I draw good dividends from my great grandparents, grandparents, and parents' trust funds and am accustomed to putting those funds directly into savings. Let's consider Twenty-Five Thousand for transferring to CDs from my personal and business savings both. Will you please email me with an accounting of those transfers for my record keeping?" "Absolutely, he responded. Is there anything else that I can be of assistance with today?" Tim told him he would like to open a checking and savings account and transfer funds from his Boston bank. Mr. Sloan asked to be excused while he went to get the necessary forms. "In the meantime, I asked, Mr. Sloan, will you please get me a key for the safety deposit box that I requested and have someone open the vault for me? "Yes, of course. Excuse me just a moment, he said." While he was out of the room, I asked Tim what he thought about Mr. Sloan. "I like him. He seems thorough and he is impressed and appreciative of your accounts which I feel he should be. Humility is a good quality." Mr. Sloan returned with the forms for Tim and handed me a key for the safety deposit box. I asked Tim for his car key, and I went to get the box of items to be placed in it. I fitted everything into the box and told the lady that I was finished so she could lock up. Tim had the forms all finished and was ready to go. "Mr. Sloan, I said, will you please have the forms for joining Tim's and my accounts together by the Monday following our January 12th wedding? We'll pop in and sign things before we head to Boston." "Yes, of course, Miss Bradley. I'll have them ready for you. Mr. Donaldson, it was a pleasure meeting you. May I take this moment to wish both of you a long and healthy life together full of God's blessings." They thanked him and left. I told Tim I needed to pop by the office to check phone messages and then I was willing for him to buy me lunch, and we could then go shopping for paint and furniture. "You're such a generous person, Amanda. But I'm afraid that the contractor called, and I need to get together with him at 2pm. How about we go by the office, have lunch, go to the meeting with the contractor and if there is time left over, we can then go shopping?" "I believe that'll work, I said."

There were a couple of phone calls that I needed to return and messages to respond to and or update. The furniture looked magnificent! We grabbed a seafood salad and then headed home to meet the contractor. I didn't know him personally, but I did know his parents. We exchanged pleasantries and then showed him the house. Tim told him what we wanted to do and the order in which he thought we could proceed. The contractor, Jack Duggan, agreed with our preliminary drawings. He gave us a couple of stores and websites to visit and select the type of shower, tile, and fixtures that we wanted. He didn't think it would take more than 10-14 days to finish the master suite including painting and trim work. He felt that we could save some money, time and space by turning the main floor bathroom into a 2-piece powder room and giving the rest of the space to the new study. The existing office, such as it is, was about 10-feet wide and 12-feet long. By remodeling the bath, we would gain a full 4-feet of space making the new study 14-ft x 12-ft which we thought was perfect. Tim told Jack that we wanted built in floor to ceiling bookshelves on the inside wall and a rectangular window on the outer wall for natural light to come through. Jack told him that he would do everything except the window, and he'd wait on that until spring when he did the sunporch. I asked Tim about ordering the bedroom furniture and if he'd already done that. "No, of course not sweet girl, he said, in fact I was thinking about asking you what you thought about me building a platform bed for a California King Mattress." I told him I thought that would be wonderful. "We'll always cherish it because you made it. Will your dad help you or what?" "One of my new friends at the precinct has an out-building of sorts that he says I can use. It has a table saw and a few other things like a router that I'll need. I think it could be very special. Do you prefer dark or light wood? Making the side tables to match will be a cinch. The only thing we'll need to shop for is a dresser, chest of drawers and probably an armoire, lamps, and bedding. There will be plenty of room for two chairs and an occasional table so we can read or sit and visit when all the children are asleep." I smiled at him and said, "I sure hope all those kids will arrive soon!" I know that I teared up when I said it, but I wanted so badly to have a family with this wonderful man. I needed to change the subject, so I asked, "What about the kitchen?" "What is wrong with the kitchen, he asked?" "Nothing, per se is wrong with it but I'd like to take the wall down between the kitchen and formal dining room, get rid of the peninsula bar and have an honest to goodness island." "Oh, he said, well, we can do that! Do we want to change either of the other guest rooms or the bath while we are at it?" "No, I don't think so. I would, however, like to modernize the railing going upstairs; perhaps glass or something like that?" "Ok, let me go get with Jack and we'll be back shortly." Tim went to find Jack and told him the rest of our wish list. The men came back and assured me that this was all very workable. "Amanda, Jack said, I think that given the age of the home that glass would be too modern. I would suggest that we tear out the railings and replace them with wrought iron rather than wood, which is so ornate. Would that work for you?" "I'd like to see the detail of the wrought iron prior to committing but I believe that would be very attractive. I also want to be sure the island is large as it will be an important part of our lives together." "Absolutely, he said. Now, what do you want to do with the sunporch?" Tim said, "We want to stretch it about 6-feet, all glass on the sides, a large sliding glass door in the front and top with dark wood beams, an exit door on the left side. We would like to remove the regular back door leading out and do French doors instead." "Ok, Jack said, that is all doable as well. I'm going to work up a bid and a start-finish date for you and get back to you the end of the week." Tim thanked him, we all shook hands, and Tim saw him to the front door. "Ok, I said, let's go shopping!" "Ok, Tim said, we have about 3 hours left before stores close. How about we go select the wood for bed and side tables and the stain and from there we'll be able to choose the rest of the furniture. Ok?" "Yes, perfect." They arrived at the lumber yard and went into speak with the manager that Amanda knew personally. He was happy to help them and suggested either Walnut or Mahogany. "They stain beautifully, he said, and the hardwood last a lifetime." We looked at each other and both said Walnut at the same time. The grain was just beautiful, and we could imagine how glorious it would look on the finished product. We chose a stain called Provencal that was just beautiful. "There is a furniture store not far from here, I said. Let's go look and see what they have. Grab that sample of the stain color for us to compare." "Aye, aye, Captain, he said." I smirked at him to let him know he wasn't cute no matter what people said. We arrived at the store in plenty of time to wander around and see what they had. The first corner I turned held the most beautiful armoire that you've ever laid eyes on. It was glorious. "I want that!" Tim smiled, and said, "Ok then, let's find a chest of drawers and a dresser to match. Will that be enough storage, or do we need two chests?" "I think one is plenty." We walked up to the upper floor and found a beautiful dresser and chests that was perfect. They also had two comfy looking chairs and an occasional table with a glass top that would work very well. Two lamps, an area rug, a beautiful chandelier for over the bed, and several throw pillows later we were finished. We arranged for the furniture to be held until we called them for delivery. "There is a restoration hardware store in West Tisbury that is open until 7pm. They will have the bathroom fixtures that we want to look at. We can have dinner over there at the 19 Raw Oyster Bar. I don't think you've been there yet." "That sounds wonderful, he said. Let's go." We looked around the store and chose a tub, glass doors, the shower pan (floor), a double vanity, two sinks, a new toilet, and the hardware and faucets needed for the job. We paid for everything and told them that Jack Duggan would call to arrange for pickup of the order for our remodel. "We will need furniture for the sunporch, but I think we can wait on that until we decide exactly how we want to use it." "I agree, he said. Other than the desk and built in bookcases, what do you want to see in the study/office?" "I'm not sure, I said. I don't see us spending a great deal of time in there so perhaps a couch or a couple of chairs, and an occasional table?" "Yes, I agree, he said. So that part can wait. We made a lot of headway today, my girl." "We did. And now, I am starved!"

Chapter 65

The oyster bar is so fun because you can belly up to the bar and order oyster shooters, oysters on the half shell, oyster Rockefeller, oysters Mignonette, fried oysters, you name it. Ice cold beer or white wine is the perfect accompaniment! Tim and I looked at each other and started at the top to see how far down the menu we could continue before collapsing. We ordered the first three items on the menu and shared. Yum. We ordered the next three items and shared. We looked at each other and decided that we only had room left for one more glass of wine and one order of the fried oysters to share. There! Full! Let's go home! We waddled into the house so full we could barely move. Precious met us at the front door madder than a little wet hen. Whoops! We forgot her evening meal… Tim went to feed and console her while I went to put on something with an elastic waist. I went back downstairs and made us coffee and told Tim that I wanted to make a checkoff list so we could check off what we'd already handled and know what we still had to do. He agreed. I took coffee, pen and paper into the living room with the expectation of making a check off list. The cat curled up next to me and I apparently fell asleep. Tim woke me about 2am and suggested we both go to bed.

I woke up cranky, tired and very disgruntled. I smacked Tim on the behind and suggested we both get up and get going. I needed to go to the office today as I played all day yesterday. I showered, dressed and was downstairs within 15 minutes. Tim was close on my heels. He asked what I wanted for breakfast, but I told him I was passing. "I'm thinking of fasting today as I'm feel fluffy." "Right, he said, I had been meaning to mention that to you." I through him a backward glance, stuck my nose in the air and started collecting my briefcase, purse and coat. I walked back and kissed him goodbye and told him I loved him, and I was off to the office. I walked in and had to smile just looking at how beautiful the lobby office looked all dressed up. I locked the door behind me as I couldn't see any reason for leaving it unlocked while I'm here alone. I went into my office and was equally pleased with its appearance. Tim had done an incredible job of making everything beautiful. I hung up my coat and fixed myself a cup of coffee. I had a yogurt in the refrigerator in the kitchen and I ate it as I was starving. I had a phone message from the ADA regarding the findings in the safe. She wanted to meet and discuss the process going forward. I called her and we settled on lunch at my office tomorrow at noon. I've known her a long time and it would be nice to catch up with her. I decided to get a jumpstart on tomorrow's meeting and pulled the laws pertaining to restitution being disbursed. There were several different interpretations and care needed to be applied to following each one to the letter. I had most everything gathered when the phone rang. I answered and the person identified themselves as a counselor from the local community college. She wanted me to know that she had a possible candidate for an assistant if I was still looking for one. I thanked her and told her that the position was put on hold until the summer season. I was looking at the calendar and thinking that Tim's parents would be here next weekend! How had the time passed so quickly? I decided that a new outfit for our dinner date with Suzy and James was very much in the need. I locked up and went to my favorite boutique to see what they had that was new. I chatted with the clerk who I really didn't know, and she went in the back to get a couple of dresses that hadn't been put out on the rack yet. It didn't take long to know that the midnight blue one with the matching duster was exactly what I was looking for! It was a beautiful high-neck sheath that was made from bamboo. The duster had a beautiful flare to it and the sleeves were about three-quarter long. "I'll take it, I told her." Now, I just need shoes to match and off I went. The shoe store that I use the most often didn't have the exact color but said he could dye to match without a problem, or I could use either black or gray. I saw a pair of dark gray sling heel pumps that were gorgeous. He had a beautiful matching bag, and I took them both. I had gray gloves and a beautiful gray, blue and white scarf that I felt would work very nicely. I made my purchases, thanked him and headed for the car. I passed by the men's store and after putting my packages away decided to go back and have a look. I found a beautiful midnight blue lightweight classic neck sweater that would look like heaven on Tim. It would go beautifully with his gray sports coat and black slacks. It was time for me to go home.

Tim was already home when I arrived. He smiled and kissed me hello as he eyed the packages that I was toting. I told him they were a surprise for next week and went upstairs. I changed clothes and came back downstairs just in time to pick-up the glass of wine that he had poured for me. "Have you already started supper, I asked?" "Yep, we are having lamb chops and something to go with them." I asked him if he'd fed you-know-who and he said that he had which is probably why she was ignoring me. I sat at the bar and brought him up to date on my day at the office. "I love my furniture, Tim. I walked in and couldn't stop smiling. It is both elegant and whimsical, just like you." He laughed and said, "I'm not sure what that means exactly but I'm sure it's a compliment." "Do you realize, I said, that your parents will arrive next weekend? We need to get bedding, towels, and such, and oh my goodness, we'd better check the kitchen to see what they have and don't have and fill the refrigerator with fresh food! Should we do that tomorrow? Did you talk with Jack Duggan today? When are they starting the remodel?" "Amanda, he said, could you please try to ask just one question at a time, give me a chance to answer that, and then go to the next one? Perhaps you should jot them down, so you'll not forget anything. OUCH! That hurt!" "You big Timmy Bear, it didn't hurt you. It was just wadded up paper. You are a big baby." "I'm telling my mother, and she will be really mad at you." "Yeah? I don't think so." "Yes, I spoke with Jack today. They are starting upstairs tomorrow morning at 8am. Yes, I know my parents are coming next weekend because someone I know, and love invited them to come early for Christmas. Yes, we can go check on the grandparent's house tomorrow if you can skip work." "I can't skip work. I have a lunch appointment with the ADA to go over the restitution disbursements that will be forthcoming. Can we go at say 1pm?" "Yes, that will work perfectly, he said. I will go to the local mall and find white sheets, white blanket, a lovely comforter or quilt, white towels, cleaning products and that will get us started. We can clean the bathroom, oh wait, it is already clean because the ladies clean the place every single week. We can make the bed and hang the clean towels and we can make a list of what is needed for the kitchen and larder. We can then take that list and go to the store and purchase all the stuff, or we could wait until say next Friday. OUCH! Stop throwing things at me or I'm going to tickle you until you can't think." I took one look at him and decided to watch my Ps and Qs. "Don't burn my lamb chops, I said." I finished my wine and chopped fresh spinach to go with the chops. "How about some roasted tomatoes on the side?" "That sounds wonderful, my girl. Perfect." We fixed our plates and sat at the bar eating our delicious dinner and visiting. How did I ever exist without this man in my life? He completes me so perfectly. I'm a very lucky woman.

Chapter 66

I was ready for my meeting when Harriet (Harry) Tyler arrived. I had ordered us salads and made fresh iced tea to go with it. We caught each other up on family and what was going on in our lives before starting on the business at hand. Harry told me that she had been assigned this job after the D.A. had witnessed the contents of the safe. "We have a team, she said, of two lawyers and two policemen going through the museum trying to track down all the artworks. They have found 9 of the pieces tucked neatly behind other paintings hanging on the walls. They researched the original paintings and found photos online of several of them, so they were also able to locate the frames that they had been in when they were stolen. They have 9 of the 43 that were logged by Sheridan. Our D.A. went to the prison and talked with Leonard to see if he wanted to cut a deal and fill us in on the whereabouts of the rest of the artwork, but he wasn't interested. He pretty much told my boss to "stick it"." "Wow, I said, it is hard to believe that someone I grew up across the street from could be that type of individual. I have really had a difficult time accepting his or Lois's behavior. It is just so very foreign to me." "I know, she said, when you come from a small town you just don't expect this type of behavior out of your neighbors." We reviewed the listing of the contents of the journals, covering the cash, the jewelry, the artwork and any miscellaneous items, and cross-referenced them to their original owners. There were 7 original owners that we knew for a fact were deceased. We knew the children or grandchildren of 5 of the families. We would need to research the other two families to see if there were any heirs still living. We will have some disbursements that cover all the categories and some only one or two of the categories. The police department has counted the money in the safe, twice, and documented their findings. The D.A.'s office has counted the money twice and documented their findings. The four cash totals match exactly, and those documented reports were submitted to the sitting judge for certification, so we can deposit the money into the account that it will be disbursed from." "I need to distribute the Brice estate pdq. I paid for Lois' funeral and internment and for her cousin's internment out of the funds. I distributed a small sum of money to Oscar's sister. It's a long story, but I was within my rights to do so. One of the sisters received a bequest and the other did not. It was less than $5000 so I had that authority. I need to figure out how to tie the trust funds to monthly allotments to the prison board out of Leonard's inheritance, I feel like restitution should be made to the museum for all they are experiencing, a portion will be made to the storage facilities manager and maintenance person that was murdered. As for Lois' inheritance as far as I can tell, the only people that she owes retribution funds to would be her aunt, her cousin's mother. We need to look further into that as I don't feel good about that. Mrs. Brice had no living relatives besides her children. She was close to one of Oscar's sisters which she bequeathed a vase to. The other sister is the mother of the man that died at the scene with Lois. She can be a real pain, but I think possibly because she hasn't ever had anything but sorrow. I'm at liberty to decide but I may speak with Uncle Judge Henry before finalizing anything. Any thoughts?" "I think your idea is sound and that is exactly what I would do given the same circumstances, she said." "Mrs. Brice was always very fond of children, and I know that she made some small bequest to each of the organizations here locally that involved young people. That may be an avenue to research." We started picking everything up and she told me as soon as the judge certified their findings and signed off on everything, she would get me the information to begin disbursements. We hugged each other and promised to stay in touch. "I received a wedding invitation for the Edgartown wedding, and we are looking forward to attending." "Wonderful, I said. Would you want to attend the Boston version? If so, I'll get you an invitation mailed off." "Yes! We want to come.

Please don't forget." I checked my watch and figured I had about 20 minutes before Tim would be coming to meet me, so I called Uncle Judge Henry to make an appointment. His secretary took the call and asked that I hold for a moment. He came on the phone with a robust "Hello there!" I told him I needed to meet with him and at the same time I invited him and Aunt Lorna to dinner on Sunday the 15th so they could meet Tim and his parents. This man has been wonderful to me my entire life. "Yes, he said, we will be there. The little lady will call and get an address and find out what we can bring to the table. In the short term, I'm free at 10 tomorrow morning if you can do that." "Yes! Perfect. I will see you at 10am at your office. Thanks so much." I heard Tim at the front door, so I grabbed my coat and briefcase and ran to greet him. "Hello sweet girl. Have you had a good day?" "I have, I told him, how about you?" "Yes, mine went very well. I'll tell you about it on our way to grandma's house." I just laughed at him as we walked to his car. We told each other about our day as we traveled to my grandparent's. I told Tim that Uncle Judge Henry and Aunt Lorna were going to join us for dinner on Sunday the 15th with your parents. They will have all kinds of things in common. Aunt Lorna was a paralegal for 35 years and Uncle Judge Henry has served on both the Massachusetts Superior Courts as well as our sitting local judge. "Well, I will look forward to meeting them. That was thoughtful of you to think about them meeting my parents, he said." "Yeah, well I'm a nice person."

We arrived at the house and collected all the bags from the trunk of the car. We let ourselves in the side door closest to what would be their private space. "I think we need to have a key made for their door separate from the rest of the residence." I felt that rush of love spread through me as we walked in much like I always have felt. This house was so full of love; I miss them so. We went into the room and put the bags of bedding down near the beautiful 4-poster bed. We took the bags of linen into the bath. Tim had purchased four sets of towels which would work perfectly; two to use and two to launder. He had purchased beautiful bars of soap, shampoos, conditioners, body washes, and scented candles. I started in that room, and it was coming together beautifully. There wasn't a need of a shower curtain as the walk-in shower had a glass enclosure. I went back to help him with the bed which he was pretty much done with. He had purchased two beautiful slip covers for the chairs that were in the room. He had also purchased a large screen television to sit on the credenza that was in there. We finished up with the quilt and decorator pillows and pronounced the bedroom suite complete and beautiful. We went into the kitchen to start making a list. There was a massive double door freezer on the back porch, a double door refrigerator/freezer in the kitchen, a 6-burner stove, a double oven, and two microwaves built in and 2 dishwashers. When in the world did all of this ever get used?? We emptied out all the spices that were in the cupboard and threw away anything else that wasn't canned. The freezer was full of meat that we had no idea how old it might be. Why hadn't the cleaning people been more diligent about their duties? I would need to talk with them tomorrow. Tim went to the carriage house to see if there were large garbage cans that we could use for the freezer. While he did that, I phoned the local sanitation company and asked them to stop on their route and empty the trash. They informed me that their normal route is Thursday which I felt would be fine. I told them we'd be using their services weekly going forward. Tim came back in and announced that he'd found 3 large garbage containers. We set about filling them up. Unlike the freezer, the refrigerator was empty and clean and was the freezer in that unit. We had made a list of the spices and such that we had thrown away, so we'd be able to start replenishing the larder. We looked around at the rest of the house and decided all was good. We turned the heat up to take the chill off the room and we were on our way to the grocery store. "Wait, I said, I just thought of something." I went back into the kitchen and opened the cupboards to see what kind of dinnerware was in there. I knew that my granny's china was in the buffet along with her silverware but was unsure of the everyday dishes available. There were some miss-matched plates and cups staring at me. There was one of the cabinets that was stuffed full of beautiful big mixing bowls and pottery serving dishes, so we were good there. "We'll need to go by the mall and purchase some good everyday dinnerware and flatware. There are plenty of serving pieces and kitchen utensils, but the rest needs to be discarded." "Ok, my girl, let's be off then, he said." We went to the mall first. There was a store there that I knew would have just what we needed. I told the clerk that I wanted a set of 24 white place settings. She showed me a lovely set that was exactly what I had in mind. We looked at the flatware and I decided on a pattern that I liked, and we got 24 place settings of that. Next, we looked at 4-ounce, 8-ounce and 16-ounce glasses for tableware. We found those and she started pulling the order. I told her that I needed wine glass, both red and white, and highball glasses for the bar area. "We will come by tomorrow afternoon and pick everything up unless you have a delivery service?" She assured me that they'd be happy to deliver to us. I gave her the address and we agreed on 3pm for the delivery to be made. "Ok, let's head for the grocery store, I said." Tim asked me if I felt that the white everyday dishes would work fine for the B&B and I assured him that I did. "There is no reason to use fine china in a service-oriented business. If the pieces get chipped or broken, they probably can't be replaced any longer. Plus, they can't be put into the dishwasher, and nobody wants to hand wash that many dishes on a regular basis." "You're quite correct, Tim said. Should we think about getting my parents a set of china to use for personal dinners?" "Yes, turn around! I didn't even consider that Timmy Bear." We went back in and found our salesperson. "We need 16 place settings of fine china. I'm sorry that I was remiss in thinking of it until we were already out of the store. Can you help me find something beautiful?" She told me it was no problem and steered us toward the area where the fine china was displayed. I did a cursory glance around the room and settled immediately on the Lenox Westchester China. It is gold trimmed and absolutely elegant. "We will take that, I said. And we will need 16 place settings of the gold West Elm flatware and glassware also. She showed us the choices in glassware, and we picked one that went beautifully with the dinnerware. I paid her and she assured me that this order would accompany the delivery tomorrow at 3pm. "Ok, now let's go to the grocery store, I said." We pretty much cleared them out of the everyday spices, flour, sugar, cereal, and such. We found the canned fruits and vegetables that we wanted and got a case of each. We decided to wait until Friday to get the meats and produce.

"So, should we just leave this all in the car and unload it tomorrow when we meet the delivery truck, Tim asked." "A fine idea, I said. Are you starving? I am. Did you lay out anything for dinner?" "Nope, he answered, I thought this might very well create hunger pangs in you, so I waited to see if you wanted to go out to eat." "I do! Let's go get fish and chips! He headed for the Seafood Shanty. They put in their orders and ordered cold beer to go with it. They ate with gusto and Amanda eyeballed Tim's plate to see if he needed help. She laughed, and said, "I'm stuffed. That was so good. Did I mention that I have an appointment with Uncle Judge Henry tomorrow morning?" "I don't believe so. Is this concerning the estate, he asked?" "Yes, I just want to run it by him to see if he agrees with my thoughts on the distributing the Brice funds." Tim paid the bill and they headed for home.

Chapter 67

Amanda was up bright and early and headed downstairs to find something for breakfast. OMG, she thought to herself! I'm 40 years old today! Tim was running so she fixed some cereal and a banana and poured herself a cup of coffee. She had already showered and just had to go get dressed after breakfast. She checked her answering machine and responded to a couple of messages from friends. She was getting excited about her last session with Fr. James tonight. After this one I'll have completed my four mandatory sessions. Because I've been baptized into the Episcopalian Church and lived my life as a Christian, I will take the profession of faith to enter the church. The priest will then administer the sacrament and be given the eucharist (communion). She was heading upstairs to dress for work when Tim came in. He gave her one of his wonderful bear hugs and asked if she'd eaten already. "Yes, I had cereal. It was cold and yucky, but I ate it anyway. I've got to get dressed and get to work." With that she headed upstairs. When she came back downstairs there was a lovely smell coming from the kitchen. "What are you doing, she asked." "If you're a good girl I'll share my bear claw with you." She was all smiles as she devoured her half. "Thank you, my darling. I'm off to the war." "Not before I ask you the all-important question you're not! What are we doing for your birthday tonight? We are dining with your friend's tomorrow night, but tonight is your night!" "Hmmm, let me think on it. We've been so busy I had forgotten until I got downstairs this morning. Can we just have a nice dinner here, visit, drink, laugh, love, and we'll figure it all out later?" "You bet! Steak and Lobster, it is! See you tonight my darling. I love you."

She drove to the office and picked up the files that she needed for her meeting. It was a beautiful clear morning, so she decided to walk to the courthouse. She knocked on Judge Henry's door and he opened it with a hug and a big smile. "I'm so happy to see you, my dear, he said." "Well, likewise my dear uncle." We sat down at his conference table, and I showed him what I had and what my thoughts were for disbursing those funds. "I think it is admirable that you paid for Lois' funeral and internment and for the cousins as well. I'm sure they were grateful." "Well, I hope so. Matilda Brice is a less than pleasant person, but I'm sure, like any parent she was devastated by his death, not to mention the way he died." "I agree. I also agree, he said, with your recommendation to bestow a monthly trust to the museum. They've not only lost their curator, but they've gone through a terrible ordeal that I'm sure has stained the reputation of the museum." "Ok, so we have a monthly disbursement to the museum that I was hoping to pull from the $15,000/month from the paternal great grandparent's trust. We could use, say 25% of that or $3750/month for the term of one-year. Out of the 75% of that money that is left I thought to share it between the families of the storage unit's manager and maintenance worker. That would amount to $5625/month per family. That trust will dissolve in approximately twenty-three years. Would you think it appropriate to pay it out for the duration?" "Yes, I think that is very appropriate, Amanda." "So, I've researched the Bartletts that were murdered in their home by the gang of monsters. They had three children and I find that all are still living in Massachusetts but not in our area. I would like to contact them, and I think it would be appropriate to divide the Two-Million Dollar life insurance money equally between the three children. What do you think?" "I think that's quite a windfall and probably very unexpected. Will there be any of the artwork returned that was stolen from them?" "Possibly, but that is another case all together." I'll help the D.A.'s office in distributing the funds but this is specifically the Doris Brice Estate." "Yes, of course, he said." "I plan to pull my fee out of the $700,000 that is in the savings account. I also paid for the funeral and internments out of those funds. I would like to make a one-time disbursement to the prison for Leonard Brice out of those funds as well. I was thinking about $300,000. What are your thoughts on that? My fee right now is at $14k+ but it will go up as I put these disbursements and trusts together. Also, I'll have a monthly fee for monitoring the stocks/bonds and reconciling accounts. I paid $35,000 for Lois' funeral, coffin and internment and $14,750 for her cousin's coffin and burial. After my final bill for disbursement of the estate, let's estimate $20,000, there will be $330,250 of those funds left. That leaves the $4500/month trust from the maternal great grandparents and the dividends from the stocks/bonds which is considerable. I don't have the exact figure from the portfolio, but I'd guess at $4.5 million with the current interest. What are we going to do with that?? I'm fast running out of time on distributing these funds and am worried about being fined for being late." "Lois had no heirs, correct? Did Leonard? Did Doris have any other next of kin?" "Lois had no heirs. Leonard, to our knowledge, never married and had no offspring that has shown up anywhere. Doris has a cousin that she made a small bequest to from the original Will. We also need to deal with the eventual sale of the vacation home that is valued at $3.25 million. I haven't received any recent communication from either the fire chief or the insurance company concerning the disposition of the home that was destroyed due to arson. Mrs. Brice had me enter a clause that should I be unable to disburse the funds to her heirs that I was to do what I felt best. I think if you write a recommendation regarding the two houses that I can buy time on those. The monthly trust of $4500 for the next nine years might be earmarked for her church. She was a member of the Methodist church here locally." "Excellent, Amanda. Excellent choice." "Should I consider holding out say 3-years of my monthly fees and convert the rest of the money into stocks/ bonds in the existing portfolio? What do you think about making a monthly dividend disbursement to the homeless shelter here, the six in Boston proper for a starting place?" "I think that is again the perfect plan. I will draft a letter today and give it to you at dinner on Sunday if that's okay with you?" "Thank you. That's perfect my dear Uncle Judge Henry. I love you and now I'll run and let you get back to work." She called Tim to remind him that she had a final session at the church in about an hour and would be home after that. She went back to the office, tidied up, freshened her makeup and headed for the church.

Chapter **68**

Father James was waiting for me when I arrived. We walked back to his office where he already had tea made for us. We prayed and reviewed the catechism together. He asked if I had questions or concerns and if I felt ready to make this step and become a member of this church. "I'm very at peace over my decision, Father. I had some misgivings, questions really, over the confessional but Tim and I spoke about it and he put my mind and heart at ease. I have always followed the teachings of the Episcopalian church which isn't all that terribly different from catholic and I've always tried to obey the ten commandments. I make mistakes every day, but I've always prayed and asked the Lord to forgive me and help me to be a better person. I feel good about this decision and I'm ready." "That's good, Amanda. I believe you are, and I believe that you will be happy in your choices. I spoke with Fr. McMurry, and he can't find enough words to sing the praises of your husband to be. He knows the entire family and loves every one of them. Apparently, the family are all very active in their church, but Tim especially so; an altar boy for several years, a member of the youth choir, a member of the choir, the choir director, a member of CYO all through school and later held a director's position for the organization, and a ten-year veteran Big Brother. Quite a dossier. I hope that our parish can benefit by some of those wonderful qualities. When you attend mass this Sunday, we will welcome you into the church and you'll be able to take holy communion. You've completed your RCIA classes, and it is now official, Amanda."

I headed home for my birthday dinner. Tim was waiting on the porch when I drove up. He came and helped me with briefcase and stuff. We walked through the door and the whole living room was ablaze with beautiful candles and vases full of roses. There was soft music playing in the background. It was so beautiful, and I felt so special. I threw my arms around this man of mine and thanked him for this beautiful display of love. He helped me off with my coat and handed me a glass of champagne. He kissed me and whispered I love you as he headed to the kitchen to check on dinner. Precious looked at me, fluffed her tail at me, and followed Tim. My cat? Oh, yeah, you bet. I sat down to sip my champagne. Tim came back and sat down beside me and had a beautifully wrapped stack of gifts that came with him. "What in the world, I asked?" "Well, my sweet girl, it is your birthday, and we are going to celebrate. Come on, open them, he said." I set my glass down and picked up the first box. I opened it up to find a beautiful light gray cashmere sweater. It had a cowl neck and three-quarter sleeves and was just beautiful. I hugged and thanked him as he was urging me to continue with the rest of the boxes. There was a box that held two gorgeous antique combs for my mass of hair. I knew I was going to wear them tomorrow night for dinner. There was a tiny box that I was very curious about. I opened it up to find an exquisite gold cross on a very fine chain. Tim told me that it was my congrats gift for converting. The next box was heavy. I opened it up to find a stunning soft leather briefcase to replace my battered, threadbare one. It had so many pockets and I knew exactly what I would put in each one of them! He had my initials sewn into the front latch and the ABD looked perfect! The next box contained a nest of keepsake boxes. They were a lightweight wood, beautifully painted and just perfect for all my many treasures. The last box had a beautiful tennis bracelet with 20 tanzanite to match my ring that had 20 gorgeous diamonds. I looked at Tim and just couldn't fathom how lucky I was or how happy I was. I hugged him and thanked him repeatedly. "You know, I don't think that other than having birthday dinner with Suzy that I've had a birthday party with presents since Aunt Mamie left me." Tim told me that I'd be showered with birthday parties and gifts every year going forward. "But right now, we need to have dinner before it is ruined." Tim went to get our plates ready, and I just continued to sit and stare at all the beautiful gifts. He had given me a funny card, that made me cry, and a beautiful loving card that made me cry harder. I wonder if I'll ever get to a place where I don't weep over everything! Ha!

The table was set beautifully with candles and all. He brought out the plate and set before me and I just enjoyed the beautiful aroma of the perfectly cooked filet and the lobster tail that he had thoughtfully removed from its shell. He poured me another glass of champagne and we toasted the day. "Wow, I'm sure a spoiled girl, I said." "Really, he said! And all I'm getting for my birthday is YOU!" We laughed and visited and thoroughly enjoyed our dinner and evening together. We cleared up the dishes, loaded the dishwasher and shut down the kitchen. Tim made coffee and poured Kahlua to go with it. It had been a wonderful day, and we were grateful as we turned out lights and headed upstairs.

Amanda planned an early exit from work today so she could go have her mop of hair trimmed and her nails done for her special dinner tonight. She called Tim and asked him to remind her that she wanted to go tomorrow to Grandma's house and take down all her china and put up his parent's new pieces. She answered messages, wrote a couple of letters to clients, and finished up by noon. She walked over to the salon to get a pedicure, manicure, and have her hair cut. The salon was full, and it felt good to just melt into the crowd. She was finished up in less than two hours and headed for home. They were meeting Suzy and James at 5pm for cocktails and appetizers and then their dinner reservation was set for 6:30. It would take about a quarter-hour to get there, so they needed to be ready by 4:40 at the latest. She called Tim to tell him she was heading home. He said he was with the contractors who had apparently decided today would be a wonderful time to start tearing apart the master suite. Oh, well. I got home and told Tim that I wanted to go have a nice bubble bath and relax before getting dressed and that time was marching on. "I know, sweet girl, they should be wrapping it up with 30 minutes.

Let me go tell them that they need to finish and leave. You'll still have time. Have a glass of wine." He went upstairs to talk with the workers. I poured a glass of wine and looked at my watch. It was almost 3pm which meant I had just about 1-1/2 hours to get this all together and walk out the front door. Perhaps one more glass of wine is in order. Tim came back downstairs, followed closely by the workers who said they'd be back at 9am tomorrow morning. "Ok, you're good to go now. Have a relaxing bath. My clothes are all laid out and I've already showered, shaved and whatever so I'll be dressed when you get out of the bathroom." I hugged him and headed for the bathroom with my wine. I filled my tub with hot water and lots of bubbles and jumped in. It just feels like riding on a cloud. Delightful. I finished bathing. My hair was already done so just needed to do my makeup. I used my two beautiful combs and pulled my hair up. The combs went beautifully with my new dress. I did my makeup and pulled my hair up and immediately was pleased with my reflection. My hairdresser had used a new conditioner on my hair, and it felt soft and luxurious rather than like a tangled mess. I popped into the bedroom and slipped into a beautiful black bra and panties and a half-slip. I have been teased because I still wore slips under my dress, but hey, if there's a light between you and the public, it isn't a pretty sight. I pulled on my new midnight blue dress and struggled a little with the back zipper which I finally successfully fastened. I put my new cross on which hung ever so pretty on my new dress. I put my engagement ring on and then fastened my new tennis bracelet next to my gold watch. I looked heavily jeweled, but hey, if you got it, flaunt it! I found a scarf that would work well with the dress. I picked up the matching coat and headed downstairs carrying my new black sling heel pumps and purse to match. Tim let out a wolf whistle when I got to the landing and suggested we spend the evening at home. He's such a funny fellow. "My goodness, Tim, you must have looked in my closet because we look like matched bookends. Your shirt is gorgeous and the exact shade of blue as my dress!" "I know, he said, do you think it might be because you bought the shirt for me?" "Oh, I said, yes, perhaps that is the case. Well, at any rate, you look delicious. That shirt with your gray suit is stunning." "Well, Tim said, together we make quite a statement for a guy and his older woman. Ow! That hurt Amanda!" Precious was watching us and finally just fluffed her tail at us and turned on her heels as if to say, "Leave. I'm sick of you both." We checked the time and decided we should get started.

Chapter 69

Luckily it was neither snowing nor raining so the evening was already a success. We arrived at the Terrace which was all decked out in lights and looking festive. The valet took our car and just behind us was Suzy and James. Suzy and I hugged and sang out Happy Birthday to each other much to our men's disbelief. Suzy always makes me feel braver than I am. I seem to laugh more and say outrageous things that I normally would only think. I am uncertain whether she is a good influence or a bad one but in the short term I just love her! I introduced Tim to both her and James. I hugged James and told him I was happy to see him again. Suzy and I were talking non-stop as we walked in. The men apparently told them who we were as they were leading us to a table by the windows with a gorgeous view of the courtyard gardens. The room itself is simply magical. It is so elegantly put together and you just feel special walking into it. There was a huge bottle of champagne at our table waiting for us to enjoy. The sommelier appeared and poured our first glass and wished both of us ladies a very happy birthday. The men seemed to have made an immediate connection as they were talking and laughing together. Suzy and I played catch up on her wedding day which was just around the corner. "I wish, she said, that we'd decided on a bigger event. As it is my mom will stand up with me and his dad with him. Other than you and your gorgeous man, we've only invited 20 other people so a very small event. You will be there, right?" "Yes, with bells on. We wouldn't miss it for the world. And, Suzy, I'm so glad that you're going to be at my side, twice, while I marry this lovely man. I'm not nervous as it is exactly what my heart has hunted for all my life. When

I met him, I knew that my life was complete. Does that sound too strange?" "Not at all, Amanda. I can see it in your face and in his. I know you can't see him, but I've been sneaking looks, well because he's gorgeous, but he looks at you with such love in his beautiful eyes." "You're a funny girl, Suzy. Yes, I know, he has quite a soft spot for his older woman." We all talked at once and caught up on everything that was happening in our lives. The waiter appeared and wondered if we might want to order. We had gotten so wrapped up that we'd skipped our appetizer session and so we thought we'd best order something. The men scanned the menus and Tim took over ordering for all of us. He ordered 2 half dozen oysters mignonette, 4 shrimp cocktails and the daily fromage platter to start with. He asked us if we wanted salad, and we told him we didn't think we'd have room. He looked at Suzy and said, "beef, pork, seafood, or what?" She laughed and told him some of each was fine with her. He ordered two of the Atlantic Halibut and two of the Day Boat Swordfish and told the waiter to bring two extra plates and we'd all share. He reminded the waiter that dessert was already taken care of, and they'd want coffee with amaretto to go with dessert. We all just stared at him, and he said, "What? Have you never had someone take charge before?" James told Tim that he would like to have weekly sessions with him until he has this down pat. We all laughed and went about our conversations. Suzy asked about the remodel of the house. Tim told her what we were doing and that we were doing a mini remodel at Granny's house so his parents could move in. "Really? They are leaving Boston?" "No, well, sort of, he said. We are thinking that they can run the house as a B&B from May through September or mid-October. The rest of the time they'll be at home in Boston." I told them that I wanted to broach the subject of turning the house into a sort of gallery. We need a historical society that runs full time and has someone that can assist people with their questions and needs. Lorraine is a very intelligent, well-educated woman who is capable of most anything. Her darling son failed to sing her praises to me prior to meeting her so I had to pull it out of her myself. She headed up a law office and was a highly sought-after Mergers & Acquisition attorney. She has kept her license up and will be helping me after the first of year. The DA has asked me to handle the disbursement of funds found from the Brice/Bartlett murder cases. It is very involved and is going to take several months to sift through and finalize. "Wow. What a mess, Suzy said. I still can't believe that poor Mrs. Brice is gone and that her children turned out to be so horrible. I never knew Leonard, but it seemed that Lois was always lurking in the shadows during our growing up years." "I know, I said. It was a hard time." Our appetizers arrived and you'd have thought that none of us had eaten for a week. We devoured all of it and were anxiously awaiting the next course. We finished off the champagne and the steward brought red and white, and we all shared. The entrees arrived. The waiter had a cart and told us that the chef du jour had decided that he'd split up the plates himself so that they still appeared attractive. He set the plates in front of us ladies first and we just grinned and stared at the beauty before us. Suzy and I love to eat, and this dinner had been right up our alley. Everything was beautifully prepared and very delicious. I don't know where we were going to shove dessert as we were stuffed. What a wonderful birthday celebration! We all walked to the foyer to wait for our cars. We wished each other a happy Christmas and said we would see each other the day after to celebrate their marriage. Suzy whispered to me that next to her James she thought Tim was drop-dead gorgeous! James and Tim had already become fast friends and were setting up days to play tennis or some other athletic whatever together.

We talked about the evening on the way home. Tim confided that he had a man crush on James. "What a great guy, he said. So thoughtful and so very in love with Suzy. You sure won't have to worry about her as long as he's by her side." "I agree, replied to Amanda. He is such an open, honest fellow. Comes from a nice family and is a successful accountant. Suzy has had great success with her firm and I'm relatively sure that given time they will combine their efforts into one. I can't believe your folks will arrive in four days! Are we ready for them?" "I think so, he said. I can't think of anything we've left out." "Have you given any thought to what we'll serve for our dinner party on Sunday? Do you think your mom will be okay with my taking the helm and conducting this party at Granny's house?" "I'm sure she will

be fine with it. No, I have no idea what you want to serve. Maybe a Beef Tenderloin with Yorkshire Pudding and the trimmings? You and I need to talk with them on Saturday and let them know the changes that have been made. Unless you've already told her everything?"
"Not everything, she said, just the things I felt she needed to know."
"Funny girl, he said."

Chapter 70

The next few days were busy getting ready for *the parents*. Tim and I cleaned house all morning and then grocery shopped on Friday afternoon for our dinner party on Sunday. We also decided to have his parents to our house on Saturday evening for a simple family supper. Tim's suggestion of Beef Tenderloin struck the perfect chord, so we ordered that, trimmed, and center cut. We decided on baby red potatoes, brown gravy, orange/cranberry/horseradish sauce, and Yorkshire Pudding. We can always just have a simple scoop of ice cream for dessert. We got the groceries put away, checked everything again to be sure we were ready and collapsed with a glass of white wine. Precious crawled up in my lap and went to sleep. Stop the presses! Does this cat know where she is? I was shocked but enjoyed the opportunity to just stroke and talk to my cat. She's so beautiful and in her own way, loving. We decided that a pizza delivered was the perfect dinner suggestion. Tim called and ordered it and we set the bar to eat in the kitchen. We grabbed another glass of wine while we waited for the delivery man who arrived about thirty minutes later. Tim had splurged and ordered the meat lover's special. Wow! It smelled delicious! We ate our pizza, drank our wine and cleaned up the kitchen. Tim had a movie that he wanted to watch so we made coffee, cookies, and headed for the couch. I must have fallen asleep during the movie. Tim woke me up and said I needed to go upstairs to bed.

We were up early, got our breakfast out of the way, and set about making the lasagna for tonight's family dinner. We had bought fat Italian sausages to go in each of the three layers and it looked wonderful. I had all the veggies cut, bagged and ready for the salad. I made a lemon vinaigrette for the salad and searched through the fridge for an appetizer idea. I found a block of cream cheese and a jar of sweet pepper jelly which would be delicious on top of the cheese and surrounded by crackers. We had two loaves of Italian bread: one with garlic butter and one with butter and parmesan. There! We are all set for Tom & Lorraine's arrival. We made a big pot of coffee and put some bear claws and cookies on a plate. We were on the porch when they arrived. They both jumped out of the car, excited to see us. Lorraine opened the back door and pulled out several shopping bags. Presents for her children. Smile. There were hugs around as we walked into the house.

Precious met Grandma and Grandpa at the door swishing her beautiful tale and purring. Tom thought she was the most beautiful creature he'd ever seen. The cat curled up in his arms like an infant and he hauled her around as we showed them the house and where things were. We settled in the kitchen at the bar to have coffee and pastries and catch up as they told us about their trip. Tom was thrilled as it stopped snowing for the entire journey. "I haven't been to Martha's Vineyard for years, Lorraine said. It's just beautiful here. And your house, Amanda, is gorgeous and so welcoming." I told them that we were going to run over to Granny's a little later and give them the grand tour. "We are having dinner here tonight, I said. But then you'll know the route from here to Granny's for later. I wanted to bring you up to speed on where we are at with regards to the house. Tim and I had a long talk. Well, I talked, and Tim listened. And then we spoke with the new banker as the former banker suffered from separation anxiety. We all came to the agreement that my grandparents' house was appraised at $10.75 million about 2 years ago. For the former banker to have sold the house outright to Timmy Bear for $1.5 million left me rather curious as to how he was going to show that loss. Suffice it to say, Timothy does not own the house. The family trusts own the house and will continue to do so as long as I draw breath. We have already started the drawing for moving bathrooms and bedrooms around upstairs. I'm sure that Tim and Tom can go over those and decide if that will work or not. Our contractor is changing the door to what will be your private entry so that nobody except you will have access to that area. It already has an attached bath and is quite roomy and comfy. I've applied for the license to run the house as a B&B, and it appears that it has been accepted. Lorraine, I would really love to see you include a gallery and historical society if you're up to it. We have a need for both. With the Curator/Director of the local gallery having been incarcerated for life we have a hole in that area. It will be sometime before the museum will be able to reopen and even then, they may find that they've suffered too much scandal to be of any value in the future. There are some fabulous paintings there and I know the owners so we might be able to work a deal with them in the future. Does any of this sound like it will work for you?" Lorraine looked at both of us and said, "You two have really been quite busy, haven't you? Yes, I think this all sounds like a workable situation. Tom is very handy and is anxious to have some projects to dig into. When do you expect that you'll be needing my help at your office?" "I'm not positive. The D.A. hasn't gotten back to me, but I did talk with the A.D.A. and she feels that it will be the beginning of second quarter. That will give us all of April to work through what we can before you start expecting guest. Will that work for you? Tim starts his new job on March 1. There is just so much happening all at once that it is quite overwhelming." "Well, Tom said, don't fret. If Lorraine is working with you, I'm quite capable of taking reservations and even greeting guests should that arise. No problem." "Yes, Lorraine said, I agree. I think this will work nicely. Are you guys ready to go show us our new home?" "We are. Let's go, Timmy Bear." He squeezed my shoulder and growled at me as we were leaving. Precious was miffed because Tom had set her down on the couch so he could leave. Cats.

They followed behind us so they could unload their belongings while we were there to help. We drove up to the front entrance and got out to help them. They neither one had moved out of the car. They were just sitting there staring ahead. Tim went to the car, concerned, and asked if they were okay. Tom finally said, "My God in heaven, this is the most beautiful home I've ever seen. It is a palace." Lorraine echoed his reply as they both got out of the car. Lorraine had tears running down her face. I grabbed her and asked if she was okay. "Yes, my darling, I'm fine. It is just a bit of a shock. This certainly isn't grandma's house. I don't think that I heard you correctly when you uttered the $10.5 million parts. This house is spectacular! Take me inside, please!" We opened the front door, and they walked in and just stood and took it all in. It really is quite exquisite. I gave them the grand tour and then took them into their suite. They both commented on how beautiful the bed linen was and how comfy the room was. "It's nice and warm and just so very pretty," Lorraine said. "And, oh my, look at that bathroom!" I laughed and asked if they would please follow me to the dining room and the kitchen. The buffet was illuminated and showed the beautiful dinnerware that we had purchased for them. Lorraine knows her dinnerware and was very impressed. "Your grandmother had some lovely things, she said." "Oh, these weren't Granny's. I packed them up because they are very valuable and quite old. We bought these for you guys. I hope they match your personal taste?" "Amanda, are you kidding me? These pieces are spectacular. I am just stunned by the pair of you." "Well, let's go check out your kitchen, I said. Once again, they were just shocked by the size and the beauty of the room. I showed them that the larder was refilled with fresh ingredients. The freezer and refrigerator were full of meat and vegetables that were all freshly purchased for them. I opened the cupboard to show her the everyday dishes that we had gotten for her to use. "I think these will work fine for breakfast for guests, don't you?" "Absolutely, she said." Tom and Tim were upstairs. We followed them up so she could see those rooms and be thinking about our ideas for remodeling. "I can do a lot of this, Amanda, if it is okay with you two, said Tom." "Whatever you want to do. Just work it out with the contractor, I told him." If you guys are ready let's unload your car and get you settled in." I handed them both a set of keys, all the phone numbers for utilities, contractor, repairs, etc. We went through upstairs and downstairs so that they knew where all the light switches were, the breaker box, the switch for the generator should they lose power, and all the doors so they knew what and where everything was that had to be secured. "You have a security box with a code that is on your list I just gave you. You'll want to memorize that so you can be sure you've secured the house when you're in or out of it. It also automatically locks the coach house when you set it. If you want that changed, you'll need to talk with them." Tom and Tim went through the house one more time and then went to unload the car. I showed Lorraine the family gallery in the study. You are welcome to use this as your office. I would like to leave the photographs on the wall if you don't mind. If they create a problem for you just let me know so I can get them stored properly. "I wouldn't dream of changing a thing, Amanda. I've already made friends with your ancestors." "Before I forget, I said, the fireplace in the dining room and the study and your suite are gas, however the one in the great room is wood burning. There is wood in the carriage house and a cart that makes it easier to haul it in." The men had everything unloaded and announced that they were finished and wanting a hamburger. "Ok, I said, let's go to lunch."

Chapter 71

We took them to the Black Dog Tavern which is one of my favorites. The food is wonderful, and the service is exceptional. We all enjoyed our meal and a cold beer and decided to go by my office, so they'd know where that was also. I gave them the office tour and reminded myself that I needed to come in early Monday and finish the disbursements that were coming out of the various trusts that we had established. "Tim, before I forget, will you be able to help me here on Monday?" "Yes, my girl, I will be ready and able." Lorraine was laughing at us and said, "Really, Tim's your new secretary?" "Well, I said, according to him he out-types me by about 50 words per minute!" Tim just took a bow, and we started closing things up. We took them on the nickel tour of town and then headed back to the house to get the lasagna in the oven for our dinner. Tom and Lorraine watched TV, and I believe they cat-napped a bit, while we got dinner organized. Tim and I sat at the kitchen bar and discussed the way the day had gone. "I think my folks are really excited about this venture, don't you, Tim asked." "I do. I think they were thrilled with their dwelling, and I believe they will fit right into the community. I talked with a girlfriend of mine that I did some pro-bono legal work for a couple of years back and she has already started a beautiful website for the B&B. She's going to meet with all of us next week to give us a preliminary walk through. I hope that it will meet your folks' approval." "I'm quite certain it will. You're a busy girl, aren't you?" "Well, I don't sit around eating bonbons if that's your question. When do you want to start decorating Granny's house?" "Let's see what the parents think, and we'll take their lead on that. Who knows? They may want to do it all themselves." "Well, I don't think that will be happening. The eaves on the front of the house are probably 30-35 feet high. I would think we'll be hiring someone to assist us with this job." Tom and Lorraine must have heard us chatting as they came in looking for coffee and conversation. Tim brought them up to speed while I fixed their coffee and got them both a cookie. Precious was sitting in front of the fridge and I was worried that she was going to begin singing so I found her a treat as well. "Do we have all the lights and ornaments, Amanda, asked Tom." "Yes, they are upstairs in a cubby. Grandpa always did the lights all over the entire front of the house and granny decorated the interior like a picture book." I know that I teared up while I was sharing these memories and Lorraine came and put her arm around me and gave me a hug. "There are several boxes of ornaments and lights for the tree. There are several wreaths for each of the doors. The player piano in the great room has Christmas music that can be played. It is all quite festive when it is completed." "Amanda, Lorraine replied, Tim mentioned that you want to have a Christmas Eve open house there. Is that correct? Have you sent out invitations yet?" "I have the invitations all ready but didn't want to do that until we talked. Will you be okay with doing that?" "Absolutely. It sounds like a wonderful idea and a great chance to meet your friends." "Okay then, we will stick them in the mail on Monday which is plenty of time. I had thought a buffet dinner would be fun. We can set up the 12 small tables in the great room for people to sit at. That would comfortably seat 48 people. The room divides up very nicely with the sofas and chairs on the one side and the small round tables on the other. The tree fits exactly in front of the bay window. With the 18-foot ceilings in the great room it makes for quite a show piece." "What kind of buffet dinner are you thinking, Tom asked?" "The meat market said they could smoke 3 turkeys and do two rare beef tenderloins for us with no problem. We could add half-dozen different side salads, bread, cookies, fruit and cheese and it would be a wonderful spread of food." Lorraine asked, "How many guests are you inviting, Amanda?" "I believe that the number was 50 people. Most of these people will do a stop by and hello and leave. I wouldn't think there'd be more than 30 that would eat a full dinner from the buffet. I think that would be enough food, don't you?" "I do, Tim said. I think it would be perfect and it would be a limited amount of extra work on all of us personally." "I agree, I said. We want this to be a fun gathering not a drudgery for any or all of us. I have wonderful childhood memories of the house all decked out at holiday time and it really was quite magical." They all agreed that this would come together easily after they find someone to string lights on the front and sides of the house and the carriage house. Tim said he would call someone to do the work for them and I will call the butcher and confirm our order as you outlined. You and I can go to the market and decide on the salads. Mom and Dad can go to the bakery and pick up cookies and goodies. "Good! That's all settled, said Tom. Let's have cocktails!" Tim laughed and went to the bar to start making their usual drink of the day and asked Amanda what she wanted. "I'll have whatever they're having, she said." "Really," replied Tim. How very interesting. Gin Martinis all around coming up!" Amanda and Lorraine set the dining room table and got things ready for dinner. While they were about that task, Amanda asked if she remembered that they were having a small dinner party at *her house* tomorrow? "Yes, of course, she said. Your uncle and aunt are coming to dinner. Did you and Tim already figure out the menu? I was hoping to be able to be the bell of the ball while you two cooked." "Yes, ma'am, we have it all figured out. We thought we'd come over right after mass. Are you guys going to mass with us?" "Yes, of course. Do we know where the church is?" "Tim will draw a map for Tom. They have a 10am service that we were going to attend. It will be my first communion as a member of the Catholic church." "Congratulations my dear. I knew you were converting, and it slipped my mind when it would be official. Are you okay with everything?" "Yes, I'm quite at peace with my decisions and my plans going forward. I rather like Fr. James and I think you will also."

"Perhaps after dinner you can follow us to the house to be sure we know where we are going?" "Yes, she replied. That is a very good idea. You'll have your mental map put together in no time. Everything is relatively close, and we don't really have a peak traffic hour to contend with. Just snow. So, after mass we can go back to the house and get started preparing dinner. I've asked them to come to the house at about 4pm. We can have cocktails and appetizers and serve dinner about 5:30pm. We'll be all done and the kitchen clean and tidy by 8pm.

Dinner was delicious and the conversation was lively. Everyone pitched in to clean up and the kitchen was cleared and ready for morning in no time at all. We followed Tom and Lorraine back to Granny's house which they found without a problem. We hugged them goodnight, made sure they were safely into the house and the lights turned on, and left for home. We visited on the way home and decided we were very tired. We turned off lights, grabbed Precious and headed to bed. A good night's sleep was just what was needed.

Chapter 72

Up and showered, shampooed, dressed and ready for mass. Tim had fixed scrambled eggs which hit the spot. We grabbed the cooler and put all the groceries into it and bags as needed and headed for the car. Tim told me that he had a surprise for me later. I was curious but decided to just let it flow as it might. We arrived at the church and waited in the foyer for his parents. They arrived in record time and said they'd had no difficulty finding their way around. I had started into the sanctuary when I was stopped by someone calling my name. I turned to find David and Lucy there. "Oh, I'm so glad to see you both, I said. What brings you here? Are you changing churches?" "No, said David, we are here to support your first Holy Communion as a Catholic. We wanted you to know how proud we were of you and that we were here cheering you on." "Oh my, you sweet dears. That is just the nicest thing you could have done. Thank you so very much." We all hugged and brushed away tears and found a place for all of us to sit. Fr. James greeted everyone from the pulpit, and we all sang the opening hymn. It dawned on me that Tim was not sitting with us. Where had he gone to? About that time the choir started singing softly and then the most beautiful baritone voice that I've ever heard sang *The Lord's Prayer*. My Tim. The tears were flowing down my cheeks as I listened to this man I love sing so beautifully. His voice simply touched your soul as it sounded as if he was speaking directly to the Lord. Knowing my Tim, that is exactly what he was doing. When he finished, he came down to join us on our pew. Everyone scooted about so that he was next to me. "Please don't cry, my sweet girl, don't cry, he said." "I'm sorry, Tim. I was so moved. It was so beautiful. I love you." "I know. I love you too." I doubt seriously if there was a dry eye in the entire church. I know there wasn't in our pew.

Toward the end of the service Fr. James introduced me and one other person as new members of the parish. Shortly thereafter we all went forward to receive Holy Communion. When I turned to walk back to my pew, I noted that the entire pew behind where we were sitting was filled with our friends! Suzy and James were there. My girlfriend Patty and her husband, Patrolman James, and Cassandra and her daughter, Sheila. These folks had all come to support my decision to convert to Catholicism. I was simply overwhelmed with gratitude for these wonderful friends. When the service ended, we all gathered outside, and Tim and I introduced his parents to everyone. I found myself clinging to David Adler's hand. He's such a special friend and I cherish him and Lucy. We said our goodbyes to everyone and followed Tom and Lorraine back to Granny's house. While driving over I asked Tim how he had managed to keep this secret for so long? "What? That I can sing? I'm Irish, my sweet girl. We all can sing!" He was joking of course, but it was a typical Tim response. He doesn't like to have a lot of attention on himself even though just walking into a room brings every eye focused on him. I still catch my breath when I look at him. He is, beyond all others, the most beautiful man I've ever seen. We got to the house, and everyone helped get the groceries unloaded. The house looked beautiful. Lorraine already had everything in place for the dinner party and the house was warm and welcoming. Tim and I headed off to the kitchen to start preparing the dinner. "Tim, I noticed that the table is set for 8 rather than 6. Any idea why?" "Yes, I meant to tell you, he said. I asked David and Lucy to join us. Lucy worked with Lorna for several years and she was really missing them. I hope you don't mind?" "No, I'm thrilled. Thank you for thinking of it. It'll also give your parents a chance to get acquainted with them." The time flew by as we got everything prepared. We had already made the Orange Cranberry Horseradish sauce and the appetizers. The broccoli, cauliflower, carrots and Brussel sprouts were all ready to steam. The potatoes had been parboiled and were in the oven to brown. We had cheated on the gravy and bought a package to go with the meat drippings. Lorraine had baked two pies: a berry and a chocolate cream. I was starving and couldn't hardly wait until dinner was served. I was munching away on crackers and cheese when Lorraine came in and announced that people were arriving. Tim and I went to greet them in the foyer. I introduced Uncle Judge Henry and Aunt Lorna to Tim's parents. Lucy and David were thrilled to see them and said it had been way too long. I turned around to find Lorraine, Lorna and Lucy all involved in a conversation. So much for people getting acquainted. David and Tom and Uncle Judge Henry were headed for the bar and talking a mile a minute. Tim and I just shook our heads and went back to the kitchen. I finished up the appetizer plates and took them into the great room for people to munch on. Tom asked what I wanted to drink, and I told him lemon water. "Alcohol and coffee and I just aren't getting along these days, I told him." I took a glass of wine in for Tim to sip on while he was cooking. We took another look at everything and declared that we were right on target and had a few minutes before anything else needed to be done so we went into the great room to visit. I joined in the conversation with the ladies and Tim and David were in a discussion. Tom and Uncle Judge Henry were already fast friends as I knew they would be. Tim gave me a high sign and we headed into the kitchen to finish up. He pulled the meat to rest while I started taking up the veggies and potatoes and put them on the buffet chafing dish to stay warm. I rescued what I needed of the meat drippings for gravy, and he poured the pudding in the remainder and got it baking. Dinner would all be ready in about 15 minutes. The gravy was ready to take up and I went to pour wine for everyone. I lit the candles and turned on the other chafing dish for the gravy and pudding. The meat platter was in the warming oven ready for Tim. One last check with Tim and I went to call everyone into the dining room. Tim came in with the meat and we began serving our guests. It was truly a beautiful dinner. All the beautiful colors of winter. Everyone ate with gusto. It was so nice to see everyone so happy around the dining room table and all enjoying each other's company.

Chapter 73

After everyone had left Tim and I went to clean up the kitchen. His parents came in and were going to help but we assured them we had it. We talked about what a lovely day it had been. We were so happy that his parents had made some new friends and would feel better about settling into the community. They already had a dinner date planned with the judge and Lorna for next week. We talked about the upcoming Christmas and what each other might want. Tim told me he'd really love a money clip. "Now that I'm marrying an heiress, I should have plenty to keep in that clip." "You're such a funny boy, Timmy Bear. Such a funny boy. I want our bedroom finished. Any chance of that happening sometime soon? And, you were going to make the platform bed, is that still in the cards?" "It is finished," he said. I was going to get my dad to help me stain it and then we're good to go. I ordered the mattress, and we can pick it up when we are ready. I talked with the contractor the other day and they'll be done the end of this week so we're in good shape." "Wonderful. I'm ready to make that move!" "Did you say what you wanted for Christmas from me, he asked?" "No, I'm thinking though that I would like a two-week holiday either the end of January or first of February before you start working and prior to my being up to my neck in disbursements." "Great! I'm on it. High seas or low land, he asked?" "Somewhere warm, quiet, no murderers, no house fires, no police, lots of peace." "Ok, I'll work on it. Shall we go home, sweet girl?" "Yes, my Tim, let's go home."

In the next few days Tim had a handyman at Granny's house putting up the outside lights and wreaths. Amanda hired a couple to go in and decorate the interior per her instructions. Tim found a tree and he and his dad got that erected in the great room and made plans for the four of them to have supper and decorate before Christmas Eve. Lorraine and Amanda had lunch and did their holiday shopping. Tim and his dad stained the bed, collected all the furniture and got the master suite put together except for linens and such. Tim and Amanda shopped for linens for their bed and bath and got it all put together. Beautiful. "Let's wait until our wedding night to move in, shall we?" Tim told her that was a perfect idea. Lorraine called and asked if they were available on the Friday before the holiday to have a soup supper and decorate the tree. They all agreed and marked their calendars. Amanda met with the local ladies to be sure everyone had what they needed for the wedding rehearsal and for the real thing? With that last thing on her list, she could sit back and relax a little bit. She was having difficulty sleeping and relaxing wasn't working very well either. There was so much on her plate these days and a lot of ghosts interrupting her thoughts. She had a couple of nightmares about her parents and the concern that they were murdered by Jack Sheridan rather than the horrible accident that she had always imagined it was. In her mind she was confronting Sheridan. Perhaps that was exactly what she was going to need to do to settle it once and for all.

The day came to decorate the tree at Granny's house. Lorraine had fixed a wonderful multi-bean and corn chowder and hot biscuits. Tom had prepared tarts for dessert. The had a joyous time trimming the tree and everyone was enthralled with the breathtaking decorations that Amanda's grandparents had. When they were finished, they stood back and took in its splendor. It had snowed hard for the past two days so there was a blanket of white, glistening snow outside. They shared a cup of hot chocolate before calling it a night and heading for home. Precious was waiting on the couch when they got home. She stretched and yawned and hinted that it was her bedtime. They checked to be sure everything was locked up and cleaned up and headed upstairs with hopes of a good night's sleep. Amanda awoke about two hours after going to bed and was wide awake. This was happening way too often, and she was tired of it. Tim laid awake worrying about her but left her to do her thing. He knew that even though she shared everything with him, she was still a very private person and he respected that. He wanted her to know he was there if she needed him but didn't want to crowd her space. I vowed to myself that I would see the doctor after the wedding. Right now, I just didn't have time.

Chapter 74

The Christmas holidays came and went and were enjoyed by all. Gift boxes were everywhere in Granny's house. Lorraine had been very busy shopping. The Christmas Eve open house had gone very well. Out of the fifty people that I had sent invitations to forty-eight showed up and stayed for the entire evening. So much for twenty-five or so for dinner. They attended Suzy and James' wedding and saw them off on their short honeymoon. I was so tired by the time that Christmas was over that I could barely think. I was still suffering from lack of sleep. I knew that I was cranky and tried my best not to take it out on Tim. I vowed to sit down and try to work through this with him – after the wedding. Now I just wanted to put one foot in front of the other, get through the weddings and try to get some much-needed sleep.

Tim and I shared a quiet supper and night alone on New Year's Eve. They watched the ball drop at Time Square and headed off to bed. Tim was concerned about her but was giving her the space that she so obviously was needing right now. She'll talk to me when the time is right, he said to himself. He was sure something was bothering her but didn't know for sure what it was. I know she loves me and wants to marry me and that is all that's important right now.

New Year's morning was met with beautiful winter sunshine. I was up and dressed before Tim and was busy making breakfast when he came downstairs. "Well, good morning beautiful girl. You're up early. Did you sleep better?" "I did". I feel good and well rested for the first time in about 2 or 3 weeks. It was a very strange feelings for me to be so out of sorts and under the weather. I'm usually always perky!"

"Yes, perky! The perfect word to describe you, he laughed. What's for breakfast?" Well, I made roasted tomatoes and am in the process of poaching eggs in that mixture. It sounded healthy and delicious all at the same time. The bacon will round it out nicely." Precious was sitting in front of the fridge so Tim went to work at preparing her breakfast. She swished her tail at him and was purring loudly when he set her breakfast down. "What do you suppose your folks are doing today, she asked?" "I'm not sure. Did you want to see if they want to join us for white beans and ham later?" "Yes, let's do that. Tell your mom to bring her biscuits to go with the beans."

They enjoyed their breakfast, cleaned up the kitchen and went to watch some of the New Year's parade on TV. Tim said his folks would be there about 3pm which would work perfectly for visiting and then having a 5pm supper. "My dad is bringing a pie, Tim said." "Yum. I love your dad's pies." The parade was fun. They talked about Tim having gone to several when he was a youngster. "Mom and dad were always trying to enrich my cultural knowledge. Did it work?" She smiled and said nothing. He didn't quite know what to make of that. Tim fixed them a peanut butter sandwich to munch on while they watched the parade. Lucy called to wish us a Happy New Year and to see if I needed anything for the rehearsal. "I think we have everything under control, Lucy. I haven't had to do anything but show up. I guess I should ask you, is there anything you need me to do for you?" They laughed and decided that everything was pretty much done. The parade was over, and I told Tim I was going to go get a quick shower and get ready for his parent's arrival.

Tom and Lorraine arrived at precisely 3pm. Lorraine went to the kitchen with me to put the biscuits and pie down and see if she could help with anything. "I think we've got it. Tim soaked the beans last night and put them on to cook earlier with the ham hock. I've chopped some celery and carrots that I want to add in about 30 minutes, so they'll still have some life to them. The pie looks scrumptious! How does he do it?" "I don't know, Lorraine said. When we married, he said he liked to bake, and I just disappear while he does it. It made for a perfect marriage. You look like you're feeling better, Amanda." "I am! I told Tim that I awakened this morning feeling well rested and healthy again. It has been a horrible couple of weeks and is so very much unlike me." "Well, we're just glad you're feeling better. You've had several difficult months and earned a few weeks of feeling down." Well, I'm back and ready for dual weddings, I laughed!"

Chapter 75

Tim and his dad were upstairs surveying the work in the master suite. They had brought the furniture home, set everything up and Tim and I had made the bed and put the linens and stuff together in the bathroom. It really was beautiful. "Have you been upstairs to see it yet, I asked?" "I haven't, Lorraine said, and I'd love to see it." They went upstairs, and everyone declared that the room had become a thing of beauty. "Wow, Lorraine said, this is gorgeous. Tim, your bed is beautiful!" "Thanks Mom. I wanted it to be perfect for Amanda and she said it was, so I'm happy." Lorraine and Tom couldn't hold back the tears when they saw the way that their son looked at his intended. "I don't think I've ever seen such love between two people, said Tom, "as you two have for each other. It really is as if neither of you were whole until you found each other." "Oh, that is so very true, Tom. I've told Tim many times that I didn't know what was missing in my life. Then, from the first moment I laid eyes on him, I knew I'd found that missing part." Tim walked across the room to gather her into his arms. "I love you so much Amanda Kay Bradley." "I know. And I do you Timmy Bear." They all got a good laugh from that.

Dinner was, as always, delicious. There is just something about old fashioned, traditional suppers that do a body good. The beans were perfect with chunks of ham, carrots, onions and celery. Lorraine's biscuits were a thing of beauty. Tom's pie was, well, gone. In all, a perfect meal. I was still not consuming alcohol or caffeine as it gave me terrible heartburn and made me feel ill. "I guess I'm stuck with lemon water. A cheap date, huh Tim?" "Well, we will continue to keep an eye on you and if this continues, we'd best pay the doctor a short visit and find out why. It doesn't make much sense that you've gone from a two-fisted drinker to a tea tootler in a matter of weeks." I threw my napkins at him across the table. They continued a light conversation about the holidays and upcoming wedding/weddings. Lorraine commented that she and Tom had made a short trip to walk through the couple of museums and art galleries that were near home. "I think you're right when you say that there is a need for some assistance in gathering historical data. There really isn't a society, per se." "No, I know. And everyone is so keen on Founder's Day that you'd think they would have taken this into consideration some time back. Do you feel ready to take it on?" Perhaps after the second wedding I'll start making some notes. You and I are expecting to have a busy early Spring, so I don't want to take on too much and not do a good job at anything." "I agree. I think you and I should return to this conversation in say early May. Now that I'm thinking of it, what are your plans? Are you coming back here after the wedding or staying in Boston?" Tom said, "I think both of us will plan to move here in early March. I'll be able to answer phone calls, check messages and mail, and keep an eye out for reservations. That way I'll be here to help, and Lorraine will be here to ride herd on me."

The next week or so was busy for me at work. I had new estates that I was working on, and Tim was busy doing all my typing and preparing paperwork for meetings. I finally felt that I had the business under control again. Dolly's house had sold, and I had that to contend with also. I stopped long enough to realize that it was Thursday before my wedding. Good grief. Where had the time flown to? Tim and I went by the church to check on things. Fr. James was in his study and warmly greeted them. "Just what the doctor ordered, he said. I was needing a break from my office work. How are you two holding up?" They both hugged him and told him they were doing fine. "Not much longer now, he said. Everything seems to be in place here. Your parents came by here, Tim, and they have arranged for a nice reception in the church basement. Such very nice people." Tim thanked him and said he was glad they had figured out what they wanted to do by way of a reception. "Fr., we are having a small gathering tomorrow evening with the wedding party. We'd love to have you join us if you can." "Well, I just happen to be free and that sounds delightful. Where should I show up and what time?" I gave him the directions and time and told him we'd see him tomorrow evening. As we were walking back to the car, I asked Tim what time that Ronny and Peg were expected tomorrow. "I believe they're trying for the noon ferry, so they should be here by 2:30-3pm." "Perfect. And they are staying with your parents?" "Yes, he said, that is the plan as far as I know. Mom has everything together for the buffet dinner so really nobody needs to do anything but show up. What are you wearing? Did you buy a new dress for this auspicious event? "Actually, I did. It is just my standard A-line sheath, blood red, with a rather low round neck. I have a beautiful camisole that I believe will match the red perfectly. Black pumps, my gold cross and my beautiful bracelet that matches my engagement ring will finish the ensemble. What are you wearing?" "Well, I feel that I should wear a suit, but I've decided against it. I'm going to wear black slacks, a wine color dress shirt open at the neck, and my black loafers. I think I'll look quite charming." "I agree. You'll look very debonair." "I'm so glad you're feeling better, my sweet girl. I was quite worried." "I'm feeling wonderful. No more tiredness or depressed feelings. Tim, have your parents said anything about us living together before our marriage? Are they quite shocked by it?" "My parents? he asked. My parents think the sun get up in the sky every morning because of you. They couldn't possibly think anything but good about our relationship. They are quite cool, really, I don't think they've really given it much thought one way or the other. They just know that we love one another and are happy." "Well, I'm a worrier, you know that. I just didn't want them to think that I do something like this every day of the week." "They don't Amanda. We know the caliber of woman you are, and they respect you for it." We had arrived home and decided to have soup and a sandwich and go to bed early. We were both excited about their special day tomorrow.

Chapter 76

I awoke early to find that Tim was already back from the gym and had breakfast going. While I drank my herbal tea, I called Lorraine to double check and see if there was something I should be doing. "No, silly girl. Relax. We will see you at 4:30 sharp! And Amanda? We love you! We are so happy that you are going to be our daughter." I was smiling as I hung up the phone. Tim asked if everything was alright, and I assured him that everything was perfect. We lolled around the house all day and then about 2:30pm we decided we should start getting ready. I wanted to soak in a bubble bath before getting dressed for the evening. Tim wanted to call and visit with David about something or other before he started getting ready. I went upstairs to draw my bath with Precious close on my heels. She doesn't usually sit with me when I bathe but today, she decided to. A strange kitty. I laid my clothes out and decided that the camisole that I had thought would work didn't match so I chose a black lace instead. It would just peek up over the neckline and be ever so pretty. I finished with my bath, did my hair and makeup and went to dress. Tim walked in as I was putting on the final touches and had a box in his hand. "I found this and thought it was a perfect pre-wedding gift. I hope you like it." I opened the box to find an exquisite ring for my right hand that held my birthstone and his. It was gorgeous." There is room on both sides should we want to add any other stones in the future, he said." I hugged him and thanked him and told him it was perfect. We surveyed each other and decided we looked good and were ready to head for Granny's house. When we arrived, the house was beautifully illuminated with lights. The holiday decorations had been taken down and stored and Lorraine and Tom had replaced those decoration with magical lights and flowers. The great room looked spectacular, and people were already there to greet us. David and Lucy were the first to hug and greet us, followed closely by Ronny and Peg. We had barely taken our coats off when Fr. James arrived with Suzy and James close behind. It was a wonderful gathering of friends and family for the small wedding planned for the next day. Lorraine and Tom had obviously been cooking for a week. The buffet and sideboard were laden with food. She had a beautiful prime rib of beef and a country-style spiral ham, several salads, and side dishes. It all looked wonderful. Tom had made a fun punch to be shared by all. I avoided the punch and asked for lemon water because I didn't want to suffer the terrible heartburn that any alcohol was giving me. Lucy, Peg and Suzy were all deep in conversation and the men had gathered by the bar. Lorraine and I just smiled and looked over the group. "They are quite something, don't you agree, I asked?" "Yes, indeed. Quite the group." David came over to visit with me. "Is there a chance of us having a quick cup of coffee in the morning, he asked?" "Yes, I'm an early riser and because we are very old-fashioned Tim is spending the night here with his parents. Can you come by at say 7am or 7:30am?" "7am it is. I just want a few moments before you belong to someone else for the rest of your life. I feel that you and I share a special connection, Amanda. Lucy and I both love you, but I love you in a very special way. I believe that we are like siblings that we neither one ever had." With that he went back to join the men by the bar. I just stood there looking after him and thinking that I was probably the luckiest woman in the world. To have two men who loved me, albeit in very different ways, was quite the gift. We had a wonderful dinner and visit, and everyone was in a very festive mood as we prepared to call it a night. Suzy and James were going to follow me home and be sure that I was tucked into my house all safe and sound. Most likely Timothy's idea. I kissed and hugged him good night and told him to sleep well and I'd see him tomorrow. He walked me out to the car and told me he needed just one more hug and kiss. "Amanda, I love you so much. I can't wait for tomorrow to be here and you and I to finally be married in the eyes of our Lord." "I know, Tim. It seems we have been for some time now, but tomorrow it will be legal. You're never getting away from me now!" One more hug and I headed home with Suzy and James in my rearview mirror. James walked me to the door and waited while I checked that all was good and then bid me goodnight. Suzy was waving and throwing kisses from the curb. I picked up Precious and sat down on the couch to reflect on my day. I told Precious, "tomorrow Tim and I will be married. Perhaps someday you'll be a big sister!" With that bit of news Precious escaped to the other end of the couch. I checked my list to be sure all was accounted for. The bridal shop had delivered all the apparel to the church. I had chosen to do my own hair and makeup, but Suzy was getting her hair and makeup done early in the morning by her personal beautician. The flowers were delivered tonight, and I had received a phone message confirming that fact. The organist had called saying that she would see her there. I hadn't asked about any other music because she was quite certain that her husband-to-be had that under control. Nothing to do now but go to bed and get a good night's sleep. "Come on, Precious my girl, let's go to bed."

Chapter 77

I was up at 6am, showered, hair dried, dressed and downstairs to fix coffee and pastries for me and David. It was only a few minutes before he knocked on the door. I went to greet him and Precious was already telling him all the bad things that had occurred in her life. He held and consoled Precious as they went into the kitchen. I set down Precious' breakfast and got David's coffee. "I'm so glad you're here, I said. It was such a thoughtful thing for you to think of." "Well, inasmuch as I'm escorting you down that long aisle, not once, but twice, I thought that it was my duty to spend a few moments alone with you." I smiled at his words, and we just visited about everything and nothing. Finally, David asked her how she really was doing? "I'm good, I think. I was having some difficulties sleeping for a few weeks, but I feel I've turned the corner on that problem. Tim and I are so happy with one another. It's as if a part of me that was always missing has suddenly showed up and filled the gap. I've had some bad moments in thinking of my parents and that they possibly left this earth before their time at the hands of a monster. I had even considered going to talk with Jack Sheridan about it. I wouldn't ever do such a thing without consulting with you first, but it still plagues me." "I knew that something was bothering you. Both Lucy and I felt that you weren't always *present* if you follow my meaning." "I do, and you're right. I believe that my mind wanted to just shut down and even run away. This has been the only problem that I couldn't work through with Tim. I need to, but I haven't broached the subject with him yet." "He's worried, Amanda. He knows something is troubling you and he wants to help. You need to let it go and let him in – completely." "Thank you for sharing that, I said. I needed to hear those words and I will talk with him. I probably won't approach the subject until we get through this next wedding but then I believe he's taking me on a vacation to somewhere warm. That will give us plenty of opportunity to really talk." "Perfect, he said. And now, let me conclude by saying this. I'm here for you always. Lucy and my door is always open for you. We love you. I consider you my little sister and will, with my last breath, protect you. Be happy. Be complete. Be rid of the ghosts, Amanda. They can't hurt you and they are not here to help you. Rely on the people around you that love and adore you and let them protect you from all harm. Your new-found faith will take you to the next level of acceptance in understanding that. Let God command your life. Give Him the wheel and just sit back and enjoy the journey." With that he hugged and kissed me and said, "Get ready. It's time. See you in a couple of hours." He let himself out and I tried my best to collect my wits. How is it that such a wonderful man just showed up in my life and has made such an impact on it? Okay, girl, you need to get ready for a wedding!

I went upstairs and collected my bag that was already packed. My hair was already done. Tim likes it down, so it is down…all of it! I picked up the jewelry that I was wearing and the hat that I had found while in Boston and headed for the church. I parked in the back where Fr. James had shown us earlier and entered through the basement door. I found the dressing room without any difficulty and discovered Suzy was already in there. We greeted each other and I helped her zip the back of her dress. She absolutely looked beautiful! I did my makeup and then Suzy helped me into my granny's beautiful dress. It fit perfectly and I felt beautiful. I donned my little pillbox hat which had a wisp of a veil which reminded me of my granny's wedding photo. Suzy fastened my cross and I put on my mom's earrings which I had borrowed. I felt that my cross was new, my granny's dress was old, my earrings borrowed, so that just left something blue that I needed. Suzy handed me a beautiful blue silk hanky to wrap around the base of her corsage. Perfect! "You ready, Suzy asked?" "I am if we can find David and Tim. Please don't look at me with those big brown eyes, Suzy, because I'll burst into tears. I love you!" "I love you more, Mandy. Do you realize I'm still the only one that calls you that?" "Yes, don't let that information loose on this family!" David knocked on the door and Suzy told him we were ready. She opened the door wide, and he got a glimpse of the most beautiful woman, next to his wife, that he'd ever seen. His eyes welled up with tears and he told me how gorgeous I was. "You are simply a vision to behold. You look like a beautiful angel. Your parents are looking down and they are so very proud of their beautiful daughter." I took his arm and fought back the tears. "Let's go get me legal, I said."

Chapter 78

David and I walked out following Suzy. We waited until she was halfway down the aisle and then entered the chapel. I noticed that the chapel was full and overflowing. Where in the world had all these people come from? I spotted Tim and from then on, I couldn't see anything but him. He was so handsome in his gray tuxedo and had the most glorious smile on his beautiful face. I held tight to David as we continued down the aisle. When we reached Tim, I turned and kissed David's cheek and he did mine as well. I put my hand in Tim's and turned back to the altar. Fr. James greeted everyone and called for prayer. Tim and I knelt at the altar where they were directed. The organ started quietly, and Tim sang Ava Maria. He held my hand tightly in his as he sang that beautiful song. We went through the next steps of the ceremony and then we knelt to pray again. Tim's parents sang a duet of "We Pledge to One Another" which was so beautiful. I had no idea that they sang but certainly, I should have. They were Irish, of course. I wasn't at all surprised that this wonderful family was so talented and shared so openly with their gifts. We exchanged our vows and our rings and were pronounced man and wife! Good grief! I'm Mrs. Timothy Ryan Donaldson! We walked down the aisle to cheers and applaud from the chapel full of people. Ronny and Suzy were right behind us followed closely by Tim's parents. We went directly to the basement that had been set up for a beautiful reception. Tim's parents were hugging us and crying and laughing all at the same time. David and Lucy were in about the same shape. We just stood looking at each other in awe of what had just happened. We were married! The people started pouring in and some nice lady that I didn't know directed us to start a receiving line for the guest to come through with their congratulations. All the neighbors were there. John and Donald, our ushers for the next wedding had come with their wives. People who had served on the force with my dad were there as well as people who had worked with my mom that I hadn't seen in years. I'm quite sure that everyone that I had invited had shown up but there must have been fifty additional people that were there as well. Tim finally confessed that his mom and Aunt Lorna had put their heads together and sent off a few extra invites; for both weddings. "Apparently they all wanted to come, he said and started laughing." We continued to greet everyone, and they came through the line. Thank God that Suzy was beside me and helped me recognize everyone. It was a wonderful "rehearsal" wedding and one that I'll never forget. There was a fabulous buffet laid out and everyone seemed to be enjoying it. Tim and I looked at each other and declared that we could escape without upsetting anyone. Everyone followed us out of the church, and we noticed that the car was all decked out with paint and cans. We hugged everyone close to us as we headed to the car. We got in and looked at each other and burst out laughing. Tim said, "That was the most fun I've had in 40 years!" "Oh, my good Lord, I said, I forgot to wish you a happy birthday. I am so sorry. Happy birthday my darling!" "Well, apparently my parents forgot as well. So much for me being the most important part of this couple." We chatted and laughed on our way home. When we arrived, Tim insisted on carrying me across the threshold. Precious didn't know what to think of this sight when he set me down. She just fluffed her tail at us and went back to her couch. Tim kept telling me how stunningly beautiful I looked. "You are radiant. When you started down that aisle, I swear you looked like an angel on David's arm." "That's so weird because he told me I looked like an angel when he came to get me out of the dressing room. It's either the dress or I'm becoming transparent." "I think, he said, that it is simply the fact that you are the most beautiful woman I've ever seen, and I am so lucky that you chose me to spend the rest of your life with." I hugged him and told him how much I loved him and how happy I was. "Tim, are all those people staying with your parents or did you get them rooms?" "My parents, he said, knew that Ronny and Peg were staying with them, but John and Donald and their wives were a surprise. A pleasant one, but a surprise. Dad said that he had linen for the upstairs room, and they were making it work." "Wow. They never cease to surprise me. They seem to go with the flow better than any people I've ever known. So, we have an entire evening ahead of us and haven't made any plans. What are we going to do to celebrate your birthday?" "What would you like to do? "What would you say if I said let's change clothes and go celebrate with your folks and your buddies?" "You read my mind you sweet girl. Are you sure? We can stay here, and cuddle and we are planning on moving into our new master suite tonight?" "Yes, we are, and we'll have plenty of time when we get home tonight for cuddling. And we can do nothing tomorrow all day." They rushed upstairs to change clothes and go surprise everybody.

Chapter 79

Tim and Amanda let themselves in the back door with the idea of surprising the group. They had no more gotten the door closed than everyone was yelling "Happy Birthday Tim!" Amanda was smiling as Tim eyed her. "Are you responsible for this, Amanda Kay?" "Have you seen your mom, I asked as I walked out of the room." All Tim's buddies were patting him on the back, congratulating him on his 40th birthday and his beautiful wife. I went in to find Tom and Lorraine. Lucy was talking with them in the study. I walked in and asked if I was interrupting something, and they all assured me that I wasn't. "We were just talking about the historic society, or lack of it, said Lucy." Lorraine asked how she was holding up after her big day. "Good, I feel good. It was really a beautiful wedding, don't you think?" "It was, Lorraine and Lucy both responded, and you looked gorgeous. I seriously don't know how you're going to top this next week Amanda, said Lorraine." "Well, I will be surrounded by three gorgeous women and my dress is truly a work of art. I can't wait to wear it. It's a shame you only wear something like that once. Perhaps we'll have a daughter, and I can leave it to her for her wedding?" Lorraine and Tom were positively radiant at the thought of a granddaughter. "Do you think you'll try and have children, Amanda, or will you guys adopt, asked Lucy?" "We want to try on our own and if this old body can't handle it, we'll look at adopting. We've already decided on two children, so I guess we'd best get started soon." Tim walked into the study and encircled my waist with his arm and asked, "Get started soon on what?" "I'll explain it to you later, she said." Ronnie and the boys had set up a mock stage and invited Tim and Tom to join them. It didn't take much to get them both on stage and Tim announced that I was a lifelong Platter's fan, and this song was for me. They sang "Only You" as if they'd rehearsed it for weeks. Wait. Perhaps they had. We had a wonderful couple of hours with our friends before deciding to go home and check out that new master suite. There were hugs and kisses all around and David walked us out to the car. "I'm so happy for both of you. I just want you to know that Lucy and I are always here for you should you need us." Tim turned around and without giving it another thought grabbed David and hugged him. "Thanks David. We love you two very much!" David just grinned and waved them on their way.

We arrived home and went into find a glass of wine for Tim and a lemon water for me. I grabbed a couple of cookies on my way out of the kitchen. We sat in the living room talking and reflecting on our special day. We were now both 40 years old, settled into careers that we loved and wanted to start planning for a family. I shared the conversation that I had with Lorraine and Lucy about having a family or adopting a family. "I was a big brother while living in the Boston area, Tim said. It was heartbreaking to see those kids that were so unloved and alone. It was gut-wrenching to me to think that such a thing could happen. How do you throw a child away in favor of drugs or alcohol?" "I know, I said, I've seen it in estate planning where parents disinherit their children because of their addictions. What do you want to do, Tim? Do you want to adopt or take in foster children?" "I don't know. I truly don't. I want us to have a child together but not at the risk of your health. I also don't want to wish something on us that will take you away from the career and business that you've built. My career has always come with risks. I just want us to be sure that we are on the same page, happy with our decisions. If you decide that it is just us, I'm okay with that. Truly I am. We can always volunteer at shelters or something of that nature that would be less demanding than having a family to feed and care for. Why are you crying? What have I done? Is it something I said? Please don't cry." I sat beside him quietly sobbing while he was talking. I didn't know how to tell him that they might be a little late in making decisions. "Tim, what day is this?" "It's the 12th of January. Why?" "When were we at your parents in Boston, she asked?" "At thanksgiving time, silly goose, what are you getting at? Oh, my God, Amanda! That's six full weeks ago! You haven't had a period in six weeks! Do you think you might be?" "Well, I've had my suspicions but didn't want to say anything until we were legally married in the church, but I can't abide alcohol or caffeine, I had terrible insomnia but that is over. Yes, I think it is a strong possibility." "What are we going to do? Are you okay? Do you need to go to the doctor?" "Uh, I believe they have things called pregnancy tests at the local drug store. I thought maybe we'd get one and see what we can find out. And, Tim, I don't want to say anything one way or the other until, we are sure. Also, I don't want to say anything until after next week. I don't want to say anything until after the 3rd month to have some confidence in my being able to do this. Is that okay?" "Yes, of course, I quite agree. It will be our little secret." I looked at this man who had just become my husband and I still couldn't understand how I'd gotten so lucky. His beautiful blue eyes were watery, and I knew he was holding back a flood of emotions. He wants a family so very badly and I do so want to give him one. We went, hand in hand, up the staircase to our beautiful new master suite. Tim had moved all our clothes and things from our dressers earlier, so we were officially moved in. There was a gorgeous white negligee and robe that Lorraine had purchased for me in Boston. I couldn't wait to put it on. I told Tim I was going to take a quick rinse off and he was free to join me if he wanted. It certainly didn't take asking him twice. I hear the water running already! Their wedding night was everything that either of them could have hoped for. I was confident that our lives were going to be blessed abundantly.

Chapter 80

Tim woke me with breakfast in bed. We both sat cross-legged and fed on beautiful pastries, fresh squeezed orange juice, and herbal tea. Tim told me to grab a shower and throw on some jeans and meet him downstairs in twenty minutes. I laughed and jumped out to go follow orders. I pulled my hair into a ponytail, put on lip gloss, jeans, sweater and tennis shoes and headed downstairs. Tim was waiting for me with my coat, scarf, gloves, and a cute little knitted tam that he'd given me for Christmas. "Where are we off to, I asked?" "First, we are stopping at the drug store in West Tisbury so that there won't be any chance of gossip and then we're going for a ride, lunch, and who knows what else. I packed us an overnight bag so we may even spend the night somewhere. I checked your day timer and found that you didn't need to go in on Monday if you didn't want to. I made a tentative reservation at Christie's Inn in Oak Bluff. We'll have a water view room, and we can go for a long walk in the freezing cold. Doesn't that sound fun??" I was laughing but shaking my head yes at the same time. We headed out on our adventure. Tim went straight to West Tisbury and parked in front of the drug store. We went in and without difficulty found what we were looking for. We paid and went back and tucked it into our overnight bag. We drove to a nearby park and parked in the lot so they could drink the lemon water that Tim had put into a jug for them. He reached in the back seat and grabbed a bag of assorted cookies to go with the water. They sat munching happily and visiting about everything and nothing. Tim checked his watch and said, "let's take the long road around to Martha's Vineyard Chowder House and have lunch. Does that sound good?" "It does. I haven't been there for years. And Christie's Inn is beautiful. I can't wait to see their accommodations. Did you make a reservation for dinner yet?" "I did, he said. I thought for old time's sakes we'd eat at l 'Etoiles. Does that sound okay?" "Tim, I don't have clothes to go there. What'd you pack for me?" "I packed your red sheath, camisole, panties and red sandals. The dress never wrinkles, and you'll look spectacular as always. I put your hair comb and clips in so you could do whatever it is you do with your mop, sorry, mass of hair." "Hmm, well, it sounds like you thought of everything. Thanks. I'm getting hungry." We arrived at the Chowder House and were shown to a lovely table. We ordered a bowl of chowder each and fish and chips to share. It was a perfect lunch for our honeymoon date. We checked into Christie's Inn, unpacked, hung my dress and Tim's coats, slacks and shirt to ensure against them being wrinkled for later. We decided a walk was just the ticket. There is a walking path through the old residential area and the marina. Even though it was cold it was a crystal-clear day, and the sun was shining. A perfect day, really, for a stroll. We walked along, hand in hand, enjoying the day and one another. We talked about the small bag that was in the bathroom back in our room and decided we'd do the test before we showered and dressed for dinner. We didn't speak of it beyond that as we were both excited and nervous about the results. It was getting cold, so they headed back to the inn to get some hot herbal tea. Tim had made a reservation for 7pm so they decided they had time for a 30-minute nap before getting ready to go to dinner.

They woke up from their nap and had exactly one and one-half hours to take the test, shower, dress and get to the restaurant. They read the directions on the box together and then I excused myself to go follow the directions. I came out to sit on the bed next to Tim to wait out the 5-minutes. We stared at the instrument and then Tim started laughing and crying at the same time and I was shaking and crying and laughing. Pregnant! "We're going to have a baby, I cried!" "I know, sweet girl, I know. I'm so excited, Amanda. How on earth are we going to keep this news quiet?" "I don't know, but we must. I've read all about the problems that can occur in older, well more mature, women during pregnancy. We just want to get to the 12-week mark and then tell the world." We danced around the room and just stood and stared at one another. "We're going to be parents, Amanda. We're going to have a family." We went in and showered together and then got dressed for dinner. We decided we looked the very picture of the perfect couple.

After a wonderful celebration dinner, we headed back to the inn. "I kind of hate to go back home, Tim. This was a wonderful idea that you had, and it has turned out to be perfect." "Our lives going forward are going to be all we wished for, sweet girl. We will have many happy getaways during our lives together." We slept soundly, woke up feeling refreshed, had a wonderful breakfast and headed home. "Did we feed Precious before we left, she asked?" Tim laughed and said, "Yes, and I left her extra so she wouldn't starve. She'll be angry but she'll get over it." They had an enjoyable ride back home and spent the remainder of the day cleaning and getting ready to leave for Boston on Thursday. "How long are we staying after the wedding, Tim?" "I'm thinking we'll come home on Sunday, he said. Will that work for you?" "Yes. I've got office stuff to do when I get back and I need to speak with the D.A.'s office to see if there's any news on moving forward with the disbursements." "Yes, and I want to help get Granny's house ready for guest so we're both going to be very busy. Amanda, when do you want to make an appointment with your doctor?" "I think I'll call her on Monday after we get back. Has David mentioned anything regarding a trial date for Leonard?" "No, not a word. I've kind of backed away from asking questions until I'm officially part of the force, Tim told her."

We spent the rest of the week checking with the wedding party to be sure everyone had what they needed. We double-checked the inn reservations in Boston to accommodate the people traveling. We talked with the florist to be sure that was all handled. Tom and Lorraine confirmed with the caterers that everything was in place. I talked with my neighbors and asked if she'd consider feeding Precious while they were away. Miss Weatherby said she'd love to have Precious come and stay with her if that was okay. Precious was eyeballing me during this conversation but looked like she might be okay with this arrangement. I took care of everything at the office and talked with the ADA to see if there were any new development. She was assured that they were still on target for late February or early March for beginning the process. We packed and rechecked everything to be sure they'd forgotten nothing. We took Precious, her bed, her dishes, her food, the vet's phone number, and her blanket to Miss Weatherby's house. Precious fluffed her tail at both me and Tim and curled up on Miss Weatherby's chair. We decided she'd be okay while we were gone. We left phone numbers where we could be reached and thanked her again for her kindness. She hugged me and told me to go remarry that handsome man!

We got the car packed, walked through the house to be sure they had everything, called Tom and Lorraine to see if they were ready and were on their way. We met up with the parents on the outskirts of town and headed for the ferry landing. It would be a long day and we all wanted to get to Boston so we could unwind and relax for a full day before the wedding ceremony. After a long drive, a ferry ride, and another long drive with typical rush-hour traffic we arrived at the Donaldson home. The men got the cars unloaded and Lorraine and I went in search of food for dinner. After surveying the refrigerator, it was decided that we would call for delivery. Now we just needed to figure out what everyone wanted. Tim said Thai, Tom said Chinese, Lorraine didn't care so long as the guys paid for it and I wanted soup. Tim dug through the large selection of take-out menus and found the perfect place. They had Won-Ton Soup with chicken or shrimp, Pad Thai and all kinds of noodle dishes that would be okay with Tom. Everyone told Tim to go for it and order whatever he thought would work. It was only about 30 minutes until the delivery man knocked on the door. Tim collected the food, paid the driver, and came back into the kitchen with the evening's offerings. There was a huge bowl of Won Ton Soup with shrimp that Tim said he'd help her eat, Pad Thai for Tim and his mom, and a noodle bowl for Tom. Tim pulled a bit of the Pad Thai out for me as I was eyeballing it across the table.

We all enjoyed our dishes and sampled everyone else's' dishes. Tom volunteered to clean up and they all laughed over how difficult throwing those boxes away was going to be.

Tim and Amanda went up to the room she had used when they visited last time. "Are we still in separate rooms? she asked." "Hello, Mrs. Donaldson, we are married – remember?" "Ohhhhh, yes, I do remember something about that. Ok, so we're both in this room. Good." We unpacked and went back downstairs. I got myself and Lorraine a cup of herbal tea and asked if she had a few minutes to visit. "Of course, dear, what's up?" "I'm just wondering if there is anything that we've forgotten? I'm getting nervous that something might have slipped through the cracks. I'm usually so very organized and I haven't a clue what is wrong with me of late. I just thought that we might make a quick list of all the tasks at hand?" "Absolutely. I agree. Perhaps it was something to do with the rehearsal wedding and the rather large wedding that got to you." She was laughing and hugging me letting me know that we would get through this. We made a list and went through disbursements and invoices to be sure we had everyone taken care of. I compiled a handwritten letter, to each of my attendants, also the florist, the organist, and the priests at both churches. Satisfied that she hadn't forgotten anything or anyone, I asked Lorraine if she was up to going to the mall tomorrow with me. "Yes, of course Amanda. Do you have a store in mind?" "No, she said, I want to get a thank you gift for Suzy, Lucy, and Peg, Sheila, and Robin. And I wonder if Tim has purchased a gift for his best man and ushers yet. I'll have to ask him. Also, I would like very much to get something for Fr. McMurry and Fr. James. Any thoughts for them? "I don't have any off the top of my head, but Tom may know what kind of Scotch that our priest consumes behind closed doors. I'll ask." I went in search of Tim to ask if he'd done anything for his attendants. "I haven't. I didn't even think of it. What a bloke I am, he said." "No, just male… I'll take care of it. Your mom and I are going to the mall tomorrow morning. If you think of any last-minute things that you need or want you must speak or forever hold your piece, I said as I kissed him and walked off."

Lorraine and I decided to have breakfast downtown and then go shopping. Lorraine had a favorite place that had delicious pastries and good coffee and herbal teas. They shared a plate of assorted pastries and sipped on their beverage of choice. "This is wonderful, Lorraine. It was just what I needed." "I know, my dear, you have both been terribly busy and it begins to pull a person down after a while, she said." "Yes, it certainly does. I'll be glad when this business with the D.A. is behind us. I've told Tim that I'd love to go somewhere warm and just lay on the sand for a week or so." "That is a perfect idea, and we applaud it. Do you have any thoughts on which store we might start with?" "Well, I'm hearing that the ***Things Remembered*** has some lovely gifts to choose from. I'm thinking about gold compact mirrors for Suzy, Lucy, and Peg, chilled whiskey glasses for Ronnie, John and Donald, a pair of cufflinks for David, and a bottle of 18-year-old Glenlivet for both priests. I already have a Savings Bond for both children, but I'll need cards to put them in. I was thinking that Tim and I could write personal thank you notes in all of the cards tonight and give everyone their gifts tomorrow after the ceremony. I wrote out a check to put in a thank you card for Kathy who has been our florist genie. I already sent a thank you note and check to our florist in Edgartown. I thought a card with cash in it for the organist. Have I forgotten anything or anyone?" "Good Lord, girl, I think you covered everyone, she said. Okay, let's go get this show on the road. Do you and Tim have dinner plans for this evening or are you staying in?" "I haven't heard anything about plans so I'm guessing we're staying in. Shall we get a rotisserie chicken and some fixings on our way home, I asked?" "Perfect. I love chicken tacos." We found three distinctly different gold compacts for the ladies, beautiful square whiskey glasses for the gentlemen, a pair of gold and onyx cufflinks for David, and I added two more of the glasses to go with the Scotch for the two priests. We found a card shop and got beautiful thank you cards for everyone. "There, I believe we have everything we need for tomorrow's party. Let's go get groceries and head home. It looks like we may have another snowstorm tonight."

Chapter 81

After dinner Tim suggested that they use the office to wrap gifts and write notes. Tom and Lorraine volunteered to clean up the kitchen and sent them off to do their chores. Tim had stopped at the liquor store and purchased the two bottles of 18-year-old Glenlivet for Fr. James and McMurry and got a bottle of his attendant's favorite to go with the beautiful glasses. He also found a bottle of 21-year-old Glenlivet for David as a special token of thanks from both. They wrapped everything, filled out their cards, shed a few tears, laughed hysterically at some of their messages, and got everything loaded into a box to take to the church tomorrow. "Amanda, what do you think about staying at the condo tomorrow night. Are you good with that?" "Absolutely, she said. But will it be ready, warm, clean?" "Yes, silly girl, I have a lady that comes in and cleans every two weeks. She has filled the refrigerator with fresh fruit, cheese, juice, and desserts. She will make the bed up fresh, put out clean linens in the bath, and turn the heat up so the place will be warm. I just wanted to check with you before sending her a final phone message." "That's perfect, Tim. And then Sunday afternoon we can head home?" "We will head for home by noon on Sunday so we can avoid any bad weather," Tim said. He hugged her and told her for the umpteenth time how much he loved her and how excited he was about everything. "You still have decided we're waiting to say anything to anyone, he asked?" "I don't want to tell your parents until after we've seen the doctor. At the end of the first 3-months, I think they call it trimester now, we'll have dinner with your folks and tell them the news. Is that okay?" "Yes. It is exactly the right thing to do." They went to the study and found his folks watching the news. "Is everything okay with the world, Tim asked?" "About as good as it can be, said Tom. Which isn't very good actually. Did you guys get everything done?" "We did. It's already to load into the car tomorrow. I think Amanda and I are going to turn in. We have a big day tomorrow and we don't want bags under our eyes." They all hugged one another, and Tim and Amanda headed upstairs. They changed into their nightwear and Tim asked Amanda if she said her prayers before going to sleep at night. "Yes, of course, I always have, she replied. Why?" "I was wondering if we could perhaps pray together of an evening. It seems that at the end of each day there have been so many things that have occurred that it would be a wonderful way for us to always come together in our faith. If you're not comfortable with this idea you've only to say so. It is just a thought." "Tim, it is a wonderful thought and I think it is a perfect tradition for our family. I'm not at all shy about asking the Lord's blessing, or His forgiveness, and certainly not shy about you hearing it. Shall we take turns?" "Yes, let me put a couple of pillows on the floor next to our bed so we won't ruin our knees." They both knelt, said the rosary, and Tim began. When he was finished, I had my turn. When we were finished with our prayers, we looked at one another and just hugged and cried. Tim told her that this meant so much to him. "I've always felt so drawn to my faith. I've tried to be a good Catholic boy and I've tried to take that into my adult life. I feel so strongly that God's hand was present in my finding you and us building our lives together. It feels so right to thank Him each evening, with you, for all that He has given us. Thank you, my darling."

The four of them had a huge breakfast thanks to Tom's cooking. Lorraine volunteered to clean up. I asked Tim what time he was headed to the church, and he told me he and his dad were going to leave about 12:30. "I think we'll grab a sandwich somewhere before we head to the church. Are you riding with Mom? "I think so. Is that what we're doing, Lorraine?" "Yes, I believe that works for us. Lucy, Suzy, and Peg will all be at the church about noon as they are all having their hair and makeup done. You're doing yours yourself, right?" "Yes, my mop only behaves for me and then not all that well, I laughed." "Ok, then let's plan on sharing a sandwich here at home and then head for the church at 12:30. That'll give you plenty of time to get dressed." "Are you dressing at home, Lorraine, or at the church?" "Here at home, honey. I'll just throw on that beautiful dress you got me and run a brush through my silver locks and be done with it." They all laughed. I said that she was going to go soak in a warm bath for 30-minutes and then Tim was welcomed to the bathroom unless he'd prefer to use the one down the hall… "Yes, my darling, I'll shower down the hall, he laughed." I went upstairs and laid out the clothes that I would wear to the church. I had bought an ivory suit to wear after the ceremony. I had found a beautiful ivory colored camisole that had beautiful seed pearls sewn on the front. I placed it, along with pearl earrings that had been my mother's, and ivory pumps in a travel bag. I had decided on slacks and a sweater to wear to the church as they would be easy to place back in the travel bag to go home. I had a good soak in the tub and then got into the shower to rinse off and wash my hair. I stood in front of the mirror noticing that she was developing a slightly round tummy. Hmmm. Wonder what that might be, I smiled to myself. I studied my hair in the mirror trying to decide which way it was falling. It had grown quite long; longer than I've worn it for several years. My head covering was a simple pearl tiara with a wisp of a veil. I finally started pulling my hair up from the sides and doing a French braid down the back. It was still so long that she had to bring the braid up and secure it into a kind of loop. I looked in the mirror at the results and decided that it really was quite stunning. My auburn hair was glistening with warm blond highlights, and I was very happy with the do. I massaged a moisturizer into my face and neck and gathered my makeup together to take to the church to apply just before the ceremony. I slathered perfumed moisturizer all over my body, sprayed on my favorite perfume, and called it a day. I dressed, grabbed my travel bag and went downstairs. Tim and Tom had already left. Lorraine had made them a chicken sandwich and a glass of milk. We ate our lunch and then I cleaned up while Lorraine went to finish dressing. She came downstairs about 15 minutes later and we were ready to head to the church.

Chapter 82

I found the dressing room, greeted all the ladies, and headed for my portion of the room which was a secluded corner. Suzy asked if she might help me dress and I was so grateful for the gesture. "Yes, please. I'm more nervous today than last week. You look stunning." "Oh, this old thing? One of my lifelong buddies found it in a remnant barrel for me." They both laughed and hugged. "Amanda, are you doing alright? Are you holding up under all this excitement?" "Yes, I'm fine, really. I will admit that I'll be glad when I'm on my way home tomorrow afternoon." I applied my makeup, freshened my hair with a mist that I discovered made my hair shine a bit. Suzy placed the tiara on her head and declared it "perfect!". I had put on an ivory camisole under my slacks and sweater which worked quite well with her gown. I pulled my gown on, and Suzy fastened the back for me. "Stunning. If it is possible, you are even more radiant than you were one week ago today." I thanked her and set about getting my jewelry on. I stood in front of the mirror and wondered how it could be that I waited forty years to marry and then do it twice in a week's time. I couldn't help but laugh to myself over how my mother might have reacted to such a decision. There was a knock on the door and Suzy let David in. He walked over to Amanda and once again stood and stared at the beauty in front of him. He carefully hugged her and declared her the most beautiful bride he'd ever seen. They looked over their shoulders to discover that Suzy, Lucy and Peg were all watching them. David shook his finger at them and told them this was a private meeting. They all scampered away. David told me that I was beautiful and that once again he was so proud to have been chosen for this great honor. "Your

351

father would just be so very proud of the lovely, smart, and capable woman that you've become. He would also be very proud of the choice you made in selecting your soulmate. I love you, Amanda. Let's go get you married…again." I checked my image in the mirror one last time and started for the door. We stood just behind the entrance doors so we could see everyone as they went down the aisle before them. The ladies looked radiant, and the children were adorable. I could smell the flowers and the scent was truly uplifting. I heard the organ and knew that our cue was just a moment away. We stepped into the doorway and was stunned by the number of people that were seated there. I saw Tim which helped to calm my nerves but still, my God, look at the people. All the people stood and turned, and we started down the aisle. I reached for Tim's hand, turned to kiss David's cheek, and turned back to Tim. Father McMurry performed the opening prayer. Amanda was thrilled to hear Tom singing the Lord's Prayer. Fr. McMurry introduced the couple and asked for the Lord's blessings on their wedding day. Lorraine, Suzy, Lucy, Ronnie, and finally Uncle Judge Henry all took part in the Liturgy with scriptures they had chosen for the couple. Fr. McMurry instructed the entire congregation to stand during the couple's exchange of vows. Tim and I knelt at the altar while the organ played. We exchanged rings and Tim sang one of her favorite old tunes, "For Your Precious Love". I wasn't surprised when Ronnie, John and Donald were his backup singers. These guys really are incredible. After the song was finished Tim and Amanda sat at the side of the altar while Fr. McMurry said Mass and the congregation partook of Holy Communion. When the congregation was once again seated Tim and I took Communion. When they finished Suzy handed me a beautiful bouquet of flowers that I laid on the shrine of Blessed Virgin Mary while Tim sang Ave Maria. When Tim and I were once again standing at the altar Fr. McMurry blessed their marriage and introduced them to the congregation. We turned to a sea of people and started down the aisle headed for the reception hall. We rounded the corner and Tim grabbed me and swung me around. "We've done it, my girl, we've done it again. A perfect wedding!" "Tim, stop! Before we go another foot, I wanted to tell you thank you for singing my favorite song to me. It meant so much to me and if possible, you sang it prettier than Jerry Butler did." "Thank you, sweet girl, and before you go another foot, I want to tell you how proud I was of you when you took the flowers to the shrine of the Blessed Virgin. It made my heart soar with love, Amanda. You've settled into your role as a Catholic woman and wife with such dignity. My grandma would be so over the moon with you." We were still hugging and kissing when the wedding party found us. We all were hugging and laughing as we headed for the reception hall. When we went through the doors we gasped. It was set up so beautifully, flowers and balloons and ribbons everywhere. It was truly beautiful. There was a dance floor and a bandstand all set up for who knows what to take place. Some of the ladies from the church guild directed us to form a reception line about the same time as people started pouring through the doors. The reception line was dictated by the lady from the guild who told everyone where their place was to be; Tom, Lorraine, Tim, me, David, Suzy, Ronnie, Lucy, John, Peg and Donald. Tim introduced me to everyone that I hadn't met by that time. David helped me to remember all my father and mother's associates as they came through. We were all surprised and thrilled to see Fr. James walk through the line. Uncle Judge Henry and Aunt Lorna had brought several of my elderly neighbors to the wedding which was just so very thoughtful. I hugged them all and thanked Uncle Judge Henry for his thoughtful selection of scripture to read for the wedding. He just beamed and told me that my mother would be so very proud of me. We spent over an hour hugging and greeting our guests. Finally, Tim and I were ushered to our table. Tom spoke on behalf of Lorraine and himself. David spoke on behalf of Lucy and himself. Suzy spoke, burst into tears, and finally managed to toast us both. Ronnie spoke and as it turned out was one of the most eloquent speeches that I've heard in a long time. He managed to make both of us burst into tears before toasting us. Uncle Judge Henry spoke on behalf of my parents which just took my breath away. He told everyone that he had known me since the day I arrived in this world and had loved me for forty years. I couldn't help myself as I got out of my chair and went to hug him as he came off the bandstand. Such a wonderful man and such a wonderful friend. Fr. James came over to visit with Tim and myself as they started getting the dinner ready to serve. We thanked him for his kindness in coming all this way to celebrate our special day. He assured us that he was thrilled to be partaking of such a beautiful event. "Amanda, I didn't think it was possible that you could be a more beautiful bride than you were last week, but, well you certainly proved me wrong. Stunning."

Chapter 83

They served our dinner, which was incredible thanks to Tom and Lorraine. The band gathered and started playing some beautiful old love songs. Tim and I had picked "This Magic Moment" to be our first dance. It was perfect. We cut the cake, and everyone danced and visited and obviously had a wonderful time. I asked Suzy if she would take possession of the box that I had brought in and see to it that everyone received their thank-you gifts. She was happy to help. "We are about to take our leave. I want to change clothes and then we thought we'd come back and say something before we leave. Can you cover for us for about 15 minutes or so? "You bet. Go." We went back to the dressing room and Tim helped me get out of my gown and into my suit. We changed my jewelry, got everything back into my travel bag, took the bags to the car, and went back to bid everyone goodbye. When we walked into the reception hall everyone broke into applause. We went up to the bandstand and Tim thanked everyone for coming and making our special day that much more perfect. He thanked his parents for their love and support and thanked all our attendants for their helping hands and being there to make the day perfect. Everyone stood and applauded as we left the building.

It was snowing lightly as we left the church headed for the condo. We talked and laughed about how the day had gone. Tim commented on how wonderful it was to see so many folks he hadn't seen for a while. "I hope the photos turn out well as I feel the day may otherwise be a blur, he said." "I agree. There were so many people and so much activity that I occasionally felt as if I were encased in a cloud. I hope that everyone realized how appreciative we were of their being there." They pulled up to the condo and Tim came around to help me out. I had not changed my lovely ivory-colored pumps and the sidewalk was snowy and slippery. Tim asked me if I had more sensible shoes in the travel bag. I started laughing hysterically and he asked what in the world was so funny. "Did you pack anything for tomorrow morning? A toothbrush, clothes, shoes? I didn't. I guess I'm wearing what I wore to the church today and will brush my teeth with salt and my finger." And then I burst into laughter again. Tim just shook his head and told me to hang on tight. He got me to the foyer and went back to collect the travel bag and lock up the car. When he got in the door, he put the bag down and opened it up for me to see. There was a toiletry bag, fully loaded for them, jeans, sweaters, underwear, socks, boots and heavy coats. I glared at him and asked when he had gotten so darned smart. I stuck my nose up in the air and walked to the refrigerator to see what was in there. "Look, it's a grocery store!" Tim asked her, "Are you hungry? Seriously? We just ate prime rib and all the sides less than two hours ago." My response was a steady stare as I prepared a sandwich and one of the tasty desserts. Tim went and unloaded the travel bag and readied the bathroom. He was guessing that I'd want to take a bubble bath before going to bed so he wanted everything to be ready for me. We fixed herbal tea and went into his comfy living room to reflect on the last week's events. I asked him if he was aware of David's early morning coffee visit with her last week or his dressing room visit today. "I am not. Can you tell me what he said or was it just between the two of you, he asked?" "No, not at all. You know, he's such a wonderful human being and I believe I've known him since I was about 10 or 11 years old. He was a rookie cop and always had a nice word for me even though I was just a kid. He told me that my dad would be proud of the woman I had become. I wonder if that is accurate. My father never paid much attention to me one way or the other. He belonged to my mother." "I'm sorry, sweet girl, I'm guessing though that as he had looked down upon you and watched you grow and succeed in life that he has regretted not spending more time with you. You need to forgive him and move on." "Forgive him? Oh dear, I think you're right. I am mad as hell at them for the way they treated me and then for leaving me without my telling them I was mad." She was crying softly, but they were good tears. She needed to say these things out loud and now she'd be able to deal with them. Who knows? Perhaps this will be part of her first confession as a Catholic woman, she thought to herself.

"I'm going to go soak in your beautiful lavish soaking tub. Give me about 30 minutes, ok? "Yes, my girl, I'll meet you in 30 minutes. It's our wedding night after all, he laughed. I had a lovely soak, slathered some kind of yummy skin cream all over her, slipped into the robe that was hanging on the door and headed for the bedroom. Tim was sitting cross-legged in the middle of the bed with a bowl of strawberries and chocolates. Hmmm, that really looks good! I hopped onto the bed, gave Tim a kiss and dove into the strawberries and chocolates. He was laughing at me while I was devouring the treat. We spent most of the rest of the night exploring one another and giving thanks for this wonderful love that we had found.

Chapter **84**

Early next morning we ate pastries and drank herbal tea, called the parents, and then headed home. We were both anxious to get home to our cat, Precious, and our familiar surroundings and begin our lives together. The ride home was slow at best as it snowed the entire way with wind to boot. We finally got back to Edgartown about 6:30pm. Tim went and fetched Precious and took a thank you gift to Miss Weatherby for watching the cat. I had grabbed a lot of the groceries out of the condo fridge and brought home with us. There was plenty of deli and fruit to make for a lovely dinner. We were both tired and hungry and I got to work on fixing our plates. I had a can of tomato soup that I heated up to warm us up while we snacked on deli meats, cheeses and fruit. After dinner we took pastries and tea and retired to the living room. "I'm going to go into the office tomorrow, Tim, and see if there is anything going on. I'm also going to call the doctor and see if we can get in this week. Will that work for you?" "Yes, Tim responded, of course. Do you want me to drive you to the office or see if there's anything that you need help with? I've kind of lost track on where we are with all that's been going on." "I agree she said. That's why I want to go in. And, yes, if you're up to going with me that would be wonderful. I know there's phone calls and messages to respond to, also we have a couple of estate appointments to get on the books. Can we say we are out of here at 8:30am in the morning?" "Yup. Let's go to bed."

There was a major snowfall during the night making it a sleigh ride to work. Thank God Tim was driving! Amanda printed out and organized the messages to be responded to and gave Tim a portion of them to answer. He went through all the phone messages. He went to the post office and gathered the mail. Amanda called the two clients that she was going to put estates together for and made appointments for early February. She phoned the ADA to see if anything new had transpired. She was informed that Leonard had a court date of the 5th of February which would more than likely result in them being able to begin the distribution of funds in early March. Amanda phoned Lorraine and gave her this bit of news and mentioned that she might want to wait until late February before heading back to Edgartown. "Good, she said, that will work for me. I'll tie up loose ends here and plan on about the 22nd or 23rd of the month to return and I'm staying with you, right?" "Yes, that's correct. We'll be all ready for you and more than happy to have you. Love you both. We'll talk soon." Tim was standing at the door grinning. He had figured out that I was talking with his mother, and he was loving it. Such a good boy is he!

"I called the doctor, I told him, and we have an appointment tomorrow morning at 10am. Can you do that?" "Yes, I most certainly can. Are you nervous?" "No, well maybe a little bit, but I think more excited than nervous. I'm hopeful that she can guess when our little person will arrive so we can start planning." "I'm certain she can, Tim said. I believe they have this down to a science now." "I think it's either a blood test or urine analysis, I said, but I'm not sure. Anyway, it will be an easy test and she'll tell us what we need to do next. Let's go home. I'm tired and hungry and we have laundry to do this evening." They gathered up everything that needed to be filed and then headed for home. "What are you preparing for our supper, I asked?" "Has this become my job, Tim inquired?" "Yes, you're very good at it and I enjoy watching you cook. I do, however, miss drinking my white wine while you're doing it." "Well, lucky for you I laid out chicken. I had to thaw some for Miss Precious, so I figured we'd eat the same thing, he said. Does that sound ok with you?" "Absolutely, can you please turn it in to something piccata?" "Oh, I guess. I suppose you want pasta to go with it?" "Yes, that would be lovely, I said."

We were up early the next morning in anticipation of our doctor's appointment. I wasn't worried or nervous, just terribly excited to hear what the doctor had to say. Tim had already been on his run and had breakfast ready when I came downstairs. We were quiet during the meal and then looked at the clock and decided it was time to go. We were met with hugs and congratulations from the staff on our recent marriage and told that it would be just a few minutes and the doctor would see us. There was a new nurse working for my doctor that I'd not met before. She came and got us and took us into the doctor's office to consult with her prior to any procedures taking place. It was only a few minutes and Dr. Andrews came in and greeted both of us. "You two look wonderful! It's obvious that marriage life has settled in well for both of you, she said." We assured her that it had. "What brings you in today, Amanda?" "Well, we have taken an early pregnancy test, and it was positive. We would like to do whatever it is that we are to do with you today to confirm this." "You're smiling ear to ear, Amanda Kay. And, Tim, you are as well, she said with a smile. Let's visit for a few minutes and then we will take a blood test which is the quickest way to confirm this suspicion." "We are very excited, I said, and can't hardly believe our good fortune if this test is accurate." "Oh, they most always are, my dear, so I'm sure we'll be able to put your mind to rest shortly. How are you feeling?" "Wonderful, I told her. I was a bit off for a couple of days but that is about all. I found I couldn't abide caffeine or alcohol and to be on the safe side eliminated both immediately from my diet. I've only felt an upset stomach a couple of times but now I feel wonderful!" "Do you have the date of your last period, Amanda, she asked?" "That is where I'm uncertain. We were in Boston at his parents for Thanksgiving. I thought I'd started my period the day before the holiday, but I only spotted lightly for about 24 hours." "Well, she said, that may very well indicate that you conceived shortly after you began having intimate relations. Knowing you, I'd say that is about right, she was laughing as she said this. Let's skip this blood test and do a pelvic exam instead. I believe we'll be able to determine the results quickly. My new nurse's name is Barb. She will come and collect you in a moment. Tim, why don't you wait in the outer room until we've completed our examination and then we'll all meet back in here for the results." Tim kissed me and went to wait in the lobby area, and I went with Barb. Dr. Andrews came in and performed the exam and told me to get dressed and meet her back in her office. I was walking toward the office when Tim met me outside the door. He looked like he was ready to burst into tears which was exactly how I was feeling. We gave each other a kiss and hug and entered the office together. Dr. Andrews was already sitting at her desk grinning like a Cheshire cat. "Well, you two. Let me put your minds at ease. You are very much with child, and I would estimate you to be about ten weeks into this pregnancy. I was able to hear a strong heartbeat and we will want to do an ultrasound in about another two weeks. Are you interested in knowing the sex of your child or are you going to be surprised at his/her birth?" I started to answer her and found that no words were coming out and then I burst into tears. I looked at Tim and the tears were running steadily down his beautiful cheeks. "We are going to be a family, I said." Tim started laughing and hugged me and then got up and walked around and hugged Dr. Andrews. "Thank you so much, he told her. You just don't know how much this means to both of us." "Oh, I believe I do, Timothy, I believe I do, she said. I believe you're looking at about mid-July for this child's arrival. Amanda, are you going to have difficulty accepting that you were with child before you two married?" "You know, I said, I've thought a lot about that, and the answer is NO! People don't have the right to judge my life nor I theirs. Tim and I love one another and that's all that matters. When our child is older, should he or she asked, we will tell them the truth." "Hear, hear, said Dr. Andrews, that is just what I wanted to hear from you. I'm going to give you some prenatal vitamins to take. I want you to keep a journal on how and what you're feeling. We don't any of us want to be reckless about this. You're 40 years old and we need to implement some precaution going forward. I will suggest that you get at least 8 hours sleep each night, that you eat good, hearty meals without thoughts about weight gain, that you not travel by air for at least another 8 weeks, that you not do any heavy lifting of any kind. If you spot at all – call me immediately. If you have cramps – call me immediately. Other than that, go home, love this beautiful human being sitting next to you both emotionally and physically, and enjoy your lives together. Before I forget it, I wanted to tell you that both the rehearsal wedding and the wedding in Boston were two of the most glorious I've ever attended. God's presence was so evident in the faces of your attendants as well as yourselves. I was raised Catholic and have certainly slipped in my convictions over the years, but your wedding grounded me. I went to confession with your Fr. McMurray in Boston, Tim, and I feel renewed in my faith. Thank you. I am excited to take this journey with you both. I can't think of two people who deserve this wonderful gift more than the pair or you. Now give me a hug and get out of here. My nurse will schedule your ultrasound for two weeks from now."

Chapter 85

We did exactly as she directed and floated out about 10 feet off the ground! We almost made it to the car when Tim picked me up and whirled me around laughing, crying, and laughing some more. "Amanda, we are going to be parents. We are going to be great parents! We are going to have a family! Can we please call my folks and tell them, he asked?" "Of course, I said, I can't wait to hear their response to this news."

Lorraine answered right away saying she was glad to hear from us. "How is everything going, she asked?" Tim started to say something, kind of choked back the tears, and Lorraine was yelling, "I knew it. I knew it!" Tom wanted to know what she knew, and she told him, "They are having a baby! I knew it!" Both Tom and Lorraine were over the moon with the news. We told them that Dr. Andrews told us we were about 10 weeks so the baby should arrive mid-July. "Tom, Amanda asked, are you up to making a bed, dresser, and changing station? Oh, and a cradle?" Tom said that between he and Tim they'd get that job done! We all said how much we loved one another and hung up.

Chapter 86

We tried to make an outline of what we needed to do and what we needed to buy. We tried to look at our schedules and how we were going to move things around, so we could take time off and enjoy our baby. "July is probably going to prove to be your parent's busiest time with the B&B. By July I should have the project for the D.A.'s office over and done with. I can recommend other estate attorneys to any new clients explaining why. If I'm feeling good, I would think I could continue to work until mid-June? Don't you?" "I don't have a clue, Amanda. I don't know what we can and can't do which is why I'm going to the library to check out as many books as I can on the subject. I think we need to talk with David. I'm supposed to begin this new position in March which would mean I'd have absolutely no vacation or sick time available. I'm really torn here, Amanda, because I want to start this job, but I want to share in the raising of our child. What do you think?" "Well, I think getting the books for us to read through is a great idea. I think talking with David is also a good idea. I don't believe that I can begin to raise this child without you near me. I don't have a clue what I'm doing, and I don't want to make any mistakes. What do you think about creating a consulting business and working as a consultant with the local authorities, at least for a year or so? "Amanda, you are the smartest woman I have ever met. That is a wonderful idea and one that I think could be beneficial to a lot of people. It would mean that I could work independently with the police as well as the district attorneys or judges. That would be the ideal base for a long-term career move. Brilliant! You are brilliant!" "Well, I said, yes, that is all true. In the short term, did you lay out anything for my dinner? Ouch! You have the nerve to throw a pillow at a pregnant woman?"

We went upstairs to my old room to try and decide between it and the one next door to the master suite. We decided that the one next door, even though smaller, would be a perfect nursery and then when the child was older, we'd move him or her into my old room. We decided that painting them at the same time was a sound idea. We went into our suite and decided that the alcove where we had chairs and a table set at present time would be perfect for a bassinette. I remembered my girlfriends saying that they always kept the newborn in a bassinette near them for the first three months. We laid out a diagram of where furniture could go in all three rooms. Tim felt that he and his dad could make the perfect cradle, crib, dresser and changing station. He also said he'd like to make a trundle bed for my old room so that our baby could invite their friends to stay overnight when they were older. There! A perfect plan. We went back downstairs, and Tim called David to see if they might be available this evening for dinner or at least dessert. David said that he and Lucy had just said not an hour ago that we all needed to get together. "Let me call her, said David, and I'll get back to you in five minutes." True to his word he called right back and said that Lucy had made a beautiful beef stew, and we were invited. Would 6pm work for us? "Yes, that's perfect, Tim said. See you then. Let's go to the library." We grabbed our coats and headed out. We almost got the door shut when we heard the worse singing you've ever heard. "Whoops. We forgot to feed Precious. Go ahead and get the car warmed up, I'll just be a few minutes." We got to the library and found about a dozen books that we figured would help us lay out this plan. We headed home to get ready to go to the Adler's house.

We arrived at the Adler's, and both Lucy and David greeted us at the door. After hugs around we headed to the kitchen as Lucy had the island set up for us to eat at. We all tend to love the intimacy of a kitchen island or peninsula as it gives everyone time to really connect with the other person. It had taken forever for our kitchen, sunporch and office remodel to be done but it was worth it. We love our kitchen, and the sunporch will be a real blessing this summer. We were all talking and catching up with what was going on with each other. David asked, "Is there something you two would like to share with us?" "From the look on your faces, I said, it would appear you already have a pretty good notion of what's going on with us." David just smiled and prompted us to speak. Tim said, "Well, it would appear that you guys are going to be God Parents sometime in July." Lucy was grinning and ran over to hug us both. David, a much more conservative person, just looked at me with those big brown eyes and whispered, "I love you." He came around the island and hugged me and then hugged Tim. They both told us how happy they were for us and told us that they too had some news for us. Lucy looked at us and said, "We are due in June." Tim and I both let out a whoop and a holler and headed around for more hugs! "That is the best news ever. Our babies will have best friends! Are you feeling okay, I asked?" "Yes, wonderful in fact. No problems and we're just thrilled with the news. I've given notice at the firm that I'll be leaving to be a fulltime mom so if you still need an administrative assistant and don't mind a baby coming to work with me, I'm your girl." "Oh my gosh, Lucy. That is the best news ever!" David asked Tim what his plans were. Tim told him what we'd discussed earlier about doing consulting work. David told Tim, "I think that is a sound decision. Why don't you and I make an appointment with the captain next week and sit down and put this plan in motion." "Great, said Tim. I'll check my calendar and we can make a firm appointment to talk with him." Lucy served up a wonderful beef stew and hot biscuits and we all made pigs of ourselves. We helped clean up and then headed home. I was tired. It had been a long day full of wonderful news.

Tom was at our door early the next morning. He apologized for the early visit but said they couldn't wait another minute and arrived late last night. He had downloaded diagrams and building instructions for a cradle and a crib that he wanted to run by us. "What do you think? Would it be with your blessings that I make these items for my grandbaby?" I told him that only if Tim could assist him. "Also,

I said, could you add a changing station and a trundle bed to the order?" "Absolutely, said Tom. Do you by chance have any coffee made? I've not had any breakfast and I need something." We laughed and told him that breakfast was practically ready, and the coffee was made. Tom wanted to get an early start on the painting and furniture building. He reminded us that the B&B was getting reservations and that we didn't have a very long time to accomplish these tasks. He and Tim set up a schedule and it was decided that I would spend next weekend at granny's house with Lorraine, and they would paint the two rooms. Tim asked, "What color are we going to paint, Amanda? We don't know what we're having so something neutral?" I thought for a moment and said, "how about we paint both rooms crème color, change the trim out to bright white as well as the ceiling, and you guys figure out how to lay new wood floors in both rooms while you're at it. I would like a light color wood to be used for the cradle and then something mid-range for the nursery and bedroom. Can you do that?" Tim said, "How about we use the same kind of wood for the nursery pieces as well as the bedroom as we used in our room?" "Yes, that's perfect, I said. Can you paint the alcove a shade darker than it is presently to give more definition to that area?" "Yes ma'am, Tim said, no problem. We will move you over to granny's house but then we'll join you of an evening. We would like the upstairs master overlooking the garden if that's ok?" "I'm sure your mother will be fine with that, Tom said. Breakfast was wonderful. Thanks so much for inviting me. He smiled and raised his eyebrows up and down at us. Let's go to the hardware store, Timothy."

Chapter 87

I checked emails (I am loving this new technology!) and phone messages after the two men left for their shopping spree. There wasn't anything terribly important going on, so I decided to just relax and read some of the books that we had checked out of the library. I fixed myself a cup of tea, grabbed a cookie and headed for the couch. Precious came with me and curled up on the pillow next to where I was sitting. I told her about the baby, and she just glared at me. I told her it was going to be her little sister or brother and that she would come to love it. With that news she turned her back on me and went to sleep. So much for bonding with my cat. I read for a while, and then looked outdoors to see what the weather was like. It was sun shining beautifully so that meant it was super cold. I called Lorraine to see what she was up to. She answered right away and said she was just doing some tidying up. "Have you seen Tom? I've not a clue where he ran off to." "Well, I said, it so happens that he and your son are at the hardware store shopping. He was on my doorstep before breakfast. Do you think he's excited?" "Oh, my goodness. Shame on him, she said. He should have called you first." "It's fine, I said. He was so cute and so hungry. We really enjoyed his early visit. I was wondering if you might like to go shopping and then have lunch?" "Sounds wonderful. Are we shopping for anything in particular?" Well, I said, I think a layette would be in order and we might as well buy some clothes while we're at it. I have a sneaking hunch that this child is a male and I'm tempted to just go with my suspicions. What do you think?" "Well, I knew immediately that Tim was a boy. We had a special connection that only a mother and son can have so I'd say, "go with your gut". "We are supposed to have the ultrasound in 2 weeks and I'm thinking that we can asked for the sex of the baby at that time. Do you think we should or is it better to wait for the surprise?" "Well, she said, these options weren't available when I was carrying Tim, but I would say that if it doesn't harm the baby I'd want to know. That way you begin speaking to him or her by name while you're carrying him." "That's such a sweet idea. And Tim could sing to him which I know he would love. That's a perfect idea. Thank you, Lorraine. You always know what to say. I'll pick you up in twenty minutes."

We went to the local children's store and bought bedding, quilts, mobiles, everything needed for the changing station even cloth diapers. I had already decided that I would use diaper service and use cloth for my child. Lorraine filled a shopping cart to the top with every article of clothing imaginable! "Do you want a baby shower, she asked." I don't, I told her. I want my two or three best buddies to join you and I for lunch before the big event. And your sister if you'd like to invite her. Other than that, I'm good with just us. Did I tell you that Lucy and David are expecting in June? "No, she said. Oh, my goodness. I need another cart!" And she was off to find one. I was laughing when she returned and warned her that they didn't know what they were having so it was going to have to be unisex stuff. Lorraine filled the cart with blankets, quilts, unisex onesies, mobiles and toys for infants. She'll have a wonderful time wrapping to get them ready to give to Lucy and David. We went to the café down the street and had salads and tea for lunch. I ran Lorraine home and then headed back to the house to see if Tim was home yet. He and Tom had unloaded the truck already and had the paint and accessories upstairs. They had unloaded the wood in the sunporch. They were both excited to show me the paint color and the wood they had purchased. They hoped it met with my approval. "It's beautiful and it's perfect. Thank you both so much." Tom hung around a little while longer and then headed for home. Tim fixed himself a peanut butter and jelly sandwich and a glass of milk. His dad had forgotten they needed to eat as he was "on a mission".

The two weeks went by very rapidly. I completed an outstanding estate and had received all the necessary paperwork and contract from the D.A.s office to begin that process. The new nurse at Dr. Andrew's had called and let us know where and what time our appointment was. Tim and I were both anxious and excited as we readied ourselves for the appointment. We arrived at the radiology clinic, and they told me what I needed to do. I asked if Tim could be present and they said, "of course". I changed into the gown, and we waited for the technician. Dr. Andrews showed up, quite unexpectedly, and asked us if we minded if she stayed during the ultrasound. "No, we both said, of course not." The tech started her procedure and turned the monitor so that we, along with Dr. Andrews, could see what was going on. There was a gurgling sound and a lot of activity on the screen and what looked like a baby. It must have been a shadow or something because it looked like two babies. Dr. Andrews let out a whoop and said, "I knew it! I was sure I heard two heartbeats. You guys are having twins!" I couldn't say a word and I was afraid that Tim was going to faint. His color was totally drained out of his face, and he was just staring open mouthed at the screen. Dr. Andrews asked if he was alright and he finally said, "I think so." Tim looked at me and said, "My God above, Amanda, we are having two babies; twins." At which time he burst into tears. I couldn't take my eyes off the screen. Two babies and they looked little but perfect. I finally got up the nerve to ask Dr. Andrews if she had an idea what sex they might be. "Well, she said, we can't be positive yet, but the heartbeat sounded like boys. And these are not fraternal twins, these are identical twins. Do they run in your family, Tim?" "I don't have a clue. The subject has never, ever come up that I'm aware of. Amanda, two babies." I found myself trying to comfort Tim as he was really shaken by this whole event. "It'll be ok, I said. We may have to build another crib and another trundle bed, but it'll be okay." The tech congratulated us and told me to get dressed. Dr. Andrews told us she'd see us in two weeks and left. Tim and I just looked at each other and he helped me to get dressed because I found that I was shaking like a leaf. We walked out of that clinic absolutely stunned. I turned to Tim and said, "can we please go to your folks? I need your mom's hug badly." Tim drove to granny's house, and we went in through the back door. Lorraine and Tom were in the kitchen and heard us come in. They started to say something to us and then they both burst into tears. "Is something wrong? What'd you find out.?" We looked at them and finally my Tim said, "We are having twins, and they appear to be identical twins and Dr. Andrews thinks they are boys." Tom tried to find a chair to sit down in and Lorraine just stood there with her mouth agape. "Two babies," she asked. Two identical babies?" "Yes, I said, that is what they think. And judging from the ultrasound they are active little rascals. Probably just like their father." "Dad, Tim said, I think we need more wood." Tom started laughing and said "yes, I guess you would be right about that." We all just sat and silently tried to digest this news. I said, "Wow, I'm probably really going to need to go on a diet for the first time in my life after this."

Chapter 88

My MIL and I went to work on distributing the funds from the stolen items. We had contacted two of the Bartlett children and had their addresses. We had the addresses for the two families of the manager and maintenance worker at the storage facility. In some cases, the people who had been robbed were still living and would simply have their treasures returned to them. The judge had decided that all money was to be divided equally among the heirs. One of the equal shares would be sent monthly to the museum. I would be responsible for the distribution of funds, the balancing of bank statements each month to maintain a reconciliation of the monthly distribution checks. This would continue until either the money was expended or until I relinquished responsibility for handling the trust distributions. In that case another estate attorney would need to be appointed by the courts. Leonard was found guilty of all charges and would go to jail for the rest of his life. His uncle and cousin both got twenty-five years.

The next few months were filled with readying the two rooms and the alcove, building the furniture, sanding and staining the furniture, and me sleeping a lot. I found that I was more tired than anything else. By the end of May I was hoping that this blessed event would occur sooner than later. Dr. Andrews was correct, together with my MIL, we were having boys. Tim and I argued back and forth about names and finally settled on Daniel Andrew and David Alexander. Daniel and David were good strong biblical names, and these would be good Irish Catholic boys. The rooms were painted, and furniture installed and dressers and changing stations filled and ready. The cradles were the most beautiful things you've ever seen. They were lovingly manufactured by father and grandfather and dressed by grandmother. The nursery, when the babies were ready were adorable. Tim had found decals to go on the walls that were whimsical and enchanting. Perfect for our sons.

We had an end of May visit with Dr. Andrews who determined that I was doing wonderfully. I had gained a total of 28 pounds which, she said, was remarkable for housing twins. She was estimating that the babies were at about 3-3/4 pounds each at present. She wanted desperately for them to achieve at least 5 pounds before delivery. She also had questions. "Tim and Amanda, I need to know what you two are thinking. Are you going for natural childbirth or are we doing a C-section? We looked at each other and I said, "we are having natural childbirth. God willing, He will get me through this without too much trouble. I'm ready and I believe, able. Tim will be at my side and will give me strength to continue and get through this." "Ok, she said, then here is what we must do for you to be able to do that. You must get off your feet and stay off your feet except to use the bathroom. No stairs. Can you do that?" We looked at one another and said, "yes, we'll manage. I'll move into the sunroom, and we will be fine. Tim and I want to be together, just us, through this last bit of time. We want to be able to share in this experience without interruption or intrusion. We will tell everyone, including his parents, that our home is off limit until the babies make their debut." "I think that is smart, she said. I believe that is just what you need to do to get through this next bit of time. Do your best to make it another two to three weeks at least. The fatter these boys are the better their chance of survival. I don't mean to frighten you, but this is what it comes down to. Eat good healthy food. Lots of fruit and nuts and protein. Keep your strength up and your attitude in check. This isn't the time to be feisty or ornery. Rely upon each other. Rely on your faith. Ask your God to see you through this difficult time because, Amanda, it will be difficult. This is two babies and you're now going on 41 years of age.

Tim and I went home and talked about everything. Tim went online and ordered a twin bed to be delivered ASAP. "I'll sleep on the sofa in the sunroom he said." "You most certainly will not, I retorted. We will sleep together as we have since making this commitment, Timothy Ryan." "Well, then I best change the order to a queen size. I'll be right back." They got everything moved into the sunroom and I settled myself down to be waited on hand and foot until my delivery time. To say I was bored beyond reason would be an understatement. Tim brought me books, moved a TV into the sunroof, brought me magazines to browse through which were all looked at by 9am every morning. What am I supposed to do the rest of the day? I ate, I complained, I whined, and I cried. This needs to be over I screamed at Tim! On the afternoon of June 21st my water broke, and Tim called 911 to take me to the hospital. I really don't remember much after the paramedics came in and relocated me to the ambulance. I remember being scared to death and writhing in agony from contractions. Dr. Andrews was waiting at the door when we pulled up and she and a team of people swiftly moved me to what I think was an operating room. I remember bright lights, lots of conversations, Tim holding my hand way too tightly telling me everything was going to be ok, and then a feeling like "swoosh" and a crying baby, a little breather, another swoosh and another crying baby. Tim was laughing and crying as they brought me two screaming babies and laid them on my chest. They were the most beautiful babies that were ever born. We looked at each other and like magic, they nestled into me. I couldn't stop staring at them. Dr. Andrews asked me how I was doing, and I think I told her I was fine. They took my babies to clean them up and swaddle them and then brought one each to Tim and me. We looked at each other through tears and laughter and both said how they were so beautiful and looked exactly alike. The nurses told us that they were going to take the little ones for a few minutes while they got me relocated to a room and then they'd bring them to us. They wheeled me into a private room, gave me a lovely sponge bath and a nice clean, soft gown and settled me into my bed. There was another bed in the room for Tim, so he didn't have to leave. Dr. Andrews came in to check on us. "The boys are in wonderful condition, she said. Baby

#1 weighed in at 4 pounds 13 ounces and baby #2 weighs 4 pounds 9 ounces. They are both exactly 20-1/2 inches long. They look good, they sound good, and I would say you have two healthy little boys. Do you have names? Tim told her that Baby #1 was Daniel Andrew and Baby #2 was David Alexander. "Your parents are here, and they need to see you as soon as possible. They both look like they may expire at any given moment. May I show them in?" "Yes, of course I said, but before you do, please explain what happens now." "You did a great job, Amanda. There was no tearing and little or no problems that were apparent throughout the ordeal. I would like to keep both of you and them both until they are at a full 5 pounds. We want to be sure they aren't either one jaundice. I am estimating a five-day stay. During that time our nurses will assist you in learning to nurse them properly, will teach you to pump any extra milk which will help you out, teach you to bathe them, swaddle them, and all things to watch for when you take them home. As a rule, babies are resilient, but at the same time they need to be monitored 24/7s during the first three months. By then you're all into a routine and life gets easier. I say that with a smile on my face. I will go get your parents now. I will check back with you every day that you're here. If you have questions, write them down so you don't forget them. If you need me, you know the number. Use this precious time to begin a schedule and a routine that will work for both of you. And, Amanda Kay, try to remember that these are Tim's children also. They are his equal responsibility, and he needs to share in all phases of the boy's upbringing. Got it?" "Got it, I said, thanks so much for always being there for me. I love you." With that Dr. Andrews gave Amanda a hug and kiss on the cheek, threw kisses to Tim and was gone.

Chapter 89

Tom and Lorraine came in and gave hugs and kisses to both of us and then sat down to wait for their grandsons to arrive. The nurses wheeled in their little beds and put them close over by their grandparents. They were both crying and laughing as they stared at these two precious gifts from God. "They are just gorgeous, Tom said." "Yes, echoed Lorraine, and they really are identical. How are you going to tell them apart?" Tim said, "We are having #1 and #2 tattooed on the bottom of their feet so we'll know who's who." His parents just glared at him. "Seriously, I said, I think I saw a mole on one of the baby's necks. Of course, I don't know which one but perhaps their bracelets identify which one is which. Tim, can you look please?" Tim checked out their bracelets and sure enough their full names were filled out. And the mole was on Daniel's neck and not on David's. There! An easy way to tell them apart. Lorraine let out a small yelp and said, "I almost forgot. Lucy went into labor about two hours ago and they are somewhere here having their little one." "Tim, I said, you've got to try and find David. He may need moral support. We'll be fine but please, go find him and find out how Lucy is doing." Tim gave me a kiss and told me he'd be back shortly. True to his word he and David showed up about ten minutes later. David came in and hugged and kissed me and told me what a wonderful job I'd done. He then went to see his God sons. "Oh my, Tim and Amanda, they are just beautiful. They are perfect and quite big for newborn twins, aren't they?" "Yes, I think they made the doctor a very happy woman.

"How is Lucy doing, I asked?" "She is doing very well. They are estimating about another 2-3 hours, so all our wee ones will share a birthday." "That's right, I said. I hadn't even thought about that. They will always have each other in their lives." David gave everyone a hug and said he'd best get back to Lucy and give her a rundown on what the boys look like. I believe I have their little faces memorized for that reason." Later that evening a tired David came in to let us know that his daughter, Alicia Marie, weighed in at 6 pounds 4 ounces and was 20 inches long. She had an entire head full of black hair, big brown eyes, and dimples to boot. "Perhaps we can talk arranged marriages for the future, he teased." Lucy was doing good, and he was going home to get some rest and would be back tomorrow to take them home.

The 5 days passed quickly. Tim and I learned to feed, bathe, swaddle, cuddle, rock, burp and watch over our sons. We learned that one of us rested while the other was alert. We had lots of visitors, and everyone thought our sons were gorgeous. We were packing up our suitcase and getting ready for the trip home when Dr. Andrews came in. "I wanted to see how you were fairing. Are you feeling healthy and strong enough to begin this journey?" "Yes, I feel good. I've been able to sleep. I've eaten everything set before me. I feel comfortable with the babies, and I feel like we will do okay. Thank you again for everything."

Tim went out to bring the car around the front and to be sure the infant seats were installed correctly and ready for his sons. Lorraine and Tom were taking turns staying at the house for another week to help cook, clean, rock babies, etc. Tim came into get me and the boys and we bid everyone goodbye on our way to our new adventure. Tim got us all strapped in safely and headed home. I felt like he was driving about 3 miles per hour. I'm sure he wasn't, it just felt like that. Tom and Lorraine came out to the car to help us all into the house. Tim carried Daniel and Tom carried David. Tim and Tom had discussed the situation before I came home and decided that the stairs might be too much for me for a few days, so they moved the two cradles into the sunporch. They had it toasty warm and waiting for us. They had rearranged the furniture so that we had a conversation area around the babies. Very smart grandparents. Lorraine was taking the first duty, so Tom bid us farewell and headed back to granny's house. Lorraine had made a big pot of homemade chicken and dumplings for our dinner, so we had that to look forward to.

By the end of the week Tim and I were ready to take our home back. I felt wonderful. I had lots of energy, had almost returned to my normal weight and was feeling strong. I had even answered some emails and letters and worked on one of the upcoming estates. I had received a letter from the Bartlett heirs and the manager's family both thanking me for my part in their settlements. Tim and I had worked out a good schedule between us and we both felt that we were helping the other which was important. The babies responded well to either of us. You could already see little characteristics that they had that were different from each other making it easy to tell them apart. I swear that Daniel hummed along with Tim when he sang to them! He sings lots of little tunes, but they love "you must have been a beautiful baby". When I rock the boys together, they lay on my chest and kind of cuddle me. I tell them stories about me growing up or a funny story about their father. They seem to love it when I just "talk to them'. One day Tim was humming a beautiful song that I wasn't familiar with. I asked him about it, and he told me he hadn't even realized he was humming. He thought about it for a few moments and said, "I think the name of it is "Now is the Hour". He looked it up on the internet and found that his remembrance was correct. He sang the song while reading the lyrics and both boys began sobbing. Their little lips were quivering, and they were really crying! We each picked up a boy and comforted them until they quieted down. I made Tim promise he'd never, ever sing that song again. "Not even so people can see how cute they are when they cry like that, he asked?" I threw a big pillow at his head!

Chapter 90

Weeks turned into months and months became a year. The boys turned one year old! They were both trying desperately to walk and were just about there. I understand from my friends that this is when our fun begins for real. We, along with the Adlers, had sent out invitations to our one-year old's birthday bash. We were having the festivities in our backyard complete with all the yummies things that one-year old babies eat. Alicia was already walking and was very good at teasing the boys. David was always trying to catch her but couldn't crawl fast enough to get to her. The party was a big success, and the babies all seem to have a good time. Lucy and I were picking up after everyone left and looked over in time to see David and Alicia kind of cuddled up together in the corner. They seemed quite content with one another. Both Daniel and David look exactly like Tim and Tom. The only difference that was obvious was eye color, which we understand is very rare. Daniel had his grandfather and father's beautiful blue eyes. David's eyes tended to be more greenish or hazel. I wasn't surprised by that at all. It seems to be a trait of the Donaldson men. I asked Lucy if she was still considering coming to work for me and she answered immediately. "Yes! I can't wait. I'll have to bring Alicia for the first year but after that I'll put her in day care. When do I start?" I laughed and told her we'd talk in a week or so.

It seems when you're raising two rambunctious boys that time just seems to fly by. I used to try to keep a daily journal but of late I can't even find the journal! Lucy has begun working for me and she is simply a delight. She and Alicia brighten my day every day. Tim has started his consulting business and has two county judges that he is working with, the Sheriff's department as well as our local police department. He's loving his work and I know is a real asset to all his clients. The boys are growing like weeds. They are so funny! They have big personalities and have a language all their own which is hysterical to listen to. The expressions on their little faces while they are "visiting" is just adorable. We have concerns about David and Alicia as they seem to be quite inseparable. We find them in the corner of the room, snuggled close together and sometimes even holding hands. It'll be interesting to see how this situation progresses as they grow up. Daniel is a mini-Tim right down to his beautiful blue eyes. He has his father's twinkle and some of the exact expressions. He is also a serious boy. David tends to laugh much more often than Daniel, but Daniel is the one that loves to be rocked and cuddled. David's hair is black like Tim's, but he has big green or hazel eyes, more like his mama. They are both children of our hearts.

Tim and I were spending a quiet morning together over the lovely breakfast that he had made us. The boys were napping, and we had some time to ourselves. I was enjoying the pancakes that he had made when he inquired if anything was new. "Well, I said, I'm pregnant. I guess that is new." Tim almost fell off the bar stool. "I'm sorry Amanda, he said, perhaps I misunderstood what you said. It sounded like you said pregnant." "Yeah, I sort of did. We apparently are having another child in about 7 months. I haven't called Dr. Andrews yet, but we probably should." "Amanda, oh my God, Amanda! Tim jumped up and came around the island to hug me. Another child. Are you okay? Do you feel alright? Is there anything I can get you?" "Yes, I said, more coffee would be good. I don't seem to have a caffeine problem with this one." Tim stared at me and said, "You don't seem in the least upset or worried or anything about this situation. Am I missing something?" "Well, the boys are 14 months old and in seven months they'll be three months short of two years of age. I'm a little stressed out over that, but I'm sure it will be fine." "Three children under 2 years of age, he said. Is it too early for a drink?"

As it turns out I was able to make an appointment with Dr. Andrews for the next afternoon and she confirmed my suspicions. She felt I might be a tad off on my calculations as she thought I was closer to 12 weeks than 8 weeks along. "Oh, goody, I said. That helps a lot." Dr. Andrews was laughing and assured me that it would all be okay. "What's one more, she said, and laughed." We stopped by his parent's house on our way home to give them the news. I swear that they both stared at us like we had committed a mortal sin. "Another child, Lorraine said. Amanda, are you feeling alright?" "Yes, I'm fine and Dr. Andrews seems to think I'll get through this pregnancy without a big problem. I've done everything I was told following the twins. I'm at my normal weight. I eat right and exercise daily. Well, maybe not daily, but I have exercised a couple of times. It'll be fine. We apparently only have about 6 months before meeting this new person, so we don't have a lot of time to fool around here. Tom, I need to move the twins into their little trundle beds that you haven't built yet. Can we do this soon so I can have the nursery for this new one?" Tom smiled and assured me that he'd get right on it. Tim offered to help but Tom knew for a fact that he was up to his neck in contracts and babies, and well, Amanda. After the initial shock the grandparents seemed to be happy about another child. Tim and I went home feeling a little slighted but figured it would be okay after the shock wore off.

Tim's parents finally got on the happy train about the baby once they got over the shock of it. Lorraine said they were nervous that it was going to be too much for us. We laughed at them and told them "What's one more baby". We got the boy's bedroom put together and Tom did an outstanding job building the trundle beds. We purchased some cute linens for their beds and Tom painted their names on the closet doors, so they knew which side of the closet was whose. They each had toy boxes with their names and they both had chest of drawers also. Tom also painted their bathroom while he was at it. Each boy has a hook for his towel, his toothbrush and personal items. Might as well train them while they're young!

It seemed that Tim was always busy with his business. I couldn't remember the last time we had an entire day together. I'm sure I was just feeling sorry for myself with two busy boys and bigger than a house with baby number 3. I suffered a kind of meltdown one evening and he came in and found me crying my heart out. He comforted me and we talked about it, but I still felt very lonesome. The smart side of me knows that he's trying to establish himself and make a living for his family. The stupid, immature side of me doesn't understand that and simply wants him to stay home and cuddle with me. Hopefully I'll get over this hump soon. I need to snap out of it, apologize for making him feel badly and get on with my life. I called Tim to invite him to an early-morning breakfast on Saturday morning from 7-8:30am. He responded saying that it sounded wonderful. I planned on having the boys fed, being up and showered and dressed before our breakfast "date". It would be fun, and we needed some fun.

I was up early and showered, did my hair and makeup, put on a pretty dress and fed the babies. We played for a while and then I put them in their playpen and started our breakfast. I set the island with pretty dishes and made a delicious frittata and crisp bacon. I poured juice and just started the coffee when I heard Tim come downstairs. He came into the kitchen and pulled me into him, hugging me and telling me how much he loved me. "Tim, I said, I am so sorry that I've been such a baby. I was just missing you terribly. I've grown so used to you being with me all the time that I hate it when you're away from me. Can you forgive me?" "My sweet girl, he said, there is nothing to forgive. I've missed you so badly, but it seems that the work just keeps piling up and I'm drowning in it. I'm going to have to hire a secretary to help me through this." "Well, that's easy, I said. I'm only using Lucy part time and she would love to work with you. Call her!" "That's a great idea he said. I will give her a shout later and see what she has to say about the idea. Breakfast smells wonderful. You smell better, but I'm hungry. I need to go hug my boys and I'll be right back to help." Tim came back with both boys hanging on him. So much for our quiet breakfast together. I smiled as I looked at of them. What a wonderful family I have.

Tim did, indeed, phone Lucy and they seem to be bringing it all together. She is a happy camper working with him. They are using my office which makes perfect sense. Tim and I have talked about changing things around so that we both conduct our businesses out of the same building. Another chore for Tom to help with! We are considering 9-12 for Lucy and me to work together and 1-4pm for her and Tim to work together on Mondays, Wednesdays and Thursday. This will give her a good 8-hour day, a schedule she can rely on. I have tended not to take on a lot of extra work. Managing the trust distributions for the Brice estate and the monthly transactions for the D.A.'s office has been plenty to deal with. I still want my Friday-Sunday time off as I have things to do, and so does Mr. Tim.

Chapter 91

I'm still kind of off kilter regarding Tim's parents' reaction. He feels that they are just concerned about our age, our health, our jobs, and our rather full plate. I'm sure he's right but that doesn't really ease my feelings. I need to take Lorraine to lunch and tell her how I feel. I called Lorraine and invited her to lunch tomorrow. She seemed thrilled and asked if I was bringing the babies. "No, Tim is going to babysit so you and I can visit without interruption, I said." "Ok, well perhaps I can stop and play with them afterwards." "Absolutely!" I fed the babies and put them down for their nap and went about cleaning and figuring out dinner for us. The boys decided they wanted to play for a while after they ate their lunch, so I browsed through magazines while they played. David slapped Daniel and they were both crying so now it was nap time. Tim came home a couple of hours later and it was nice to just sit and visit with him. I reminded him that he was babysitting tomorrow while I was at lunch with his mom. He frowned at me but said, "yes, he remembered." I thought about it for a minute and then asked him if he had a problem with caring for the boys alone for a couple of hours. "No, it isn't that he said. I thoroughly enjoy being with them it's just that I'm always scared I'll do something wrong." "Tim," I said, take it from your clumsy wife, short of dropping them they are pretty resilient. I never carry the two of them downstairs at the same time because I feel a need to hang on to the railing when I have them in my arms. That is my one and only suggestion." "Gotcha, he said. That is good information." We were sitting and talking when suddenly, I kind of jumped. "Are you okay, he asked?" "Yes, I'm fine, I said. This new one just kicked the heck out of me is all." "Really? Oh my gosh, that's so exciting Amanda. Do you think I can feel it?" "I don't know, I said. Try and see if you get any action." Tim put both hands on either side of my belly and waited patiently. Bam! He jumped further than I did! We were both laughing. "Well, I said, that is one rambunctious baby." "Why, Tim asked, do I feel just a bit afraid of that fact?" We were still laughing and then heard the babies hollering that they were awake and to come and get them.

I met my MIL at the Seafood Shack for lunch. We had a great meal and a wonderful visit. I really feel that she was afraid we were pushing ourselves too thin and they were just worried. I told her that Tim and I had a good schedule worked out, both at home and at the office. He was much happier now that Lucy was helping him and that was working out very well. "I think both of us are in good health and that our bodies physically do not reflect people in their forties. We are both physically and mentally strong and with the wonderful support system we have around us we are happy with this addition to our family. We hope you are too." "Oh, Amanda dear, she said, it never occurred to us not to be happy about this newest addition to our family. Tom and I were just feeling guilty about being back in Boston six months of the year and not being on hand to help you more." "Oh, my goodness, I said. Don't even think about that. You two have your lives to live, same as us, and we'll all make this work. Soon as these kids are older, I'm shipping them to you for the winter!" We both laughed and were just glad that we had met and cleared the air. I brought her up to date on how active this child was and had a hunch that "she" was going to be a handful. "Really? You think this one is a girl, Lorraine asked." "Yes, I'm positive she is. She's totally the opposite of the boys and I already feel like she thinks she's in charge. If you're ready you can follow me back. Tim just called saying that the boys are awake and waiting for grandma to arrive." Lorraine and the boys had a wonderful hour together playing, singing, and rocking. She even managed to get in a quick story that they listened to very attentively. She seemed much happier when she left for home.

Tim asked how it had gone with his mom and I told him what was bothering them. "Wow. I wished they'd have just come clean to begin with rather than us feeling badly over their initial reaction. I guess I understand their concerns, but we will be fine whether they are here or in Boston." "Yes, I absolutely agree. Also, it is good for us to only rely upon each other for raising our children. When they are older perhaps there will be opportunities for us to have a short break; a weekend or such away from them. Nothing any longer because I personally couldn't stand it." "Yes, Tim said. I can't imagine being gone any longer than that from those little rascals. So, you really think this one is going to be a girl?" "I do. This pregnancy is totally the opposite from carrying the boys. Also, I've monitored some different things that go on to be sure I wasn't losing my mind. When you and I are being intimate with one another, even just cuddling, this baby is doing somersaults. If I'm relaxing, she's doing pushups. If I want to go shopping or something like that, she just lays dormant as if she's pouting. I swear she's a girl and she's going to be a handful." "That is scary, Amanda. Were you like that?" "No, I said, but I'm betting that my mother was exactly like that."

Chapter 92

The boys were growing like weeds. They both run through the house, not walk mind you, but run through the house at break-neck speed. They chatter between one another constantly, but as far as real talking goes, they have a vocabulary of about 12-15 words. No is amongst their favorite words. They are funny and loving and feisty which are all characteristics that I like and respect. Lucy was a Godsend for both Tim and me. She just seemed to read our minds and get the job done. She and I worked closely on the month end procedures so that, if necessary, she'd be able to monitor that part while I was on maternity leave. What a joke. Maternity leave doesn't really apply when you're the entire business.

I found that I was craving every food that was out of season and cranky when Tim couldn't find it for me. I hated myself for being a grouch but didn't seem to be able to curb it. I tended to apologize a lot. I talked to my MIL almost every day. She and Tom had returned to Boston, and I was really missing her. I tried not to say that to her because I didn't want her to feel guilty for being back in her own home. She asked if I needed her to return when the baby arrives and I couldn't help myself, I admitted that I needed her to be there. She laughed and assured me that she would be on hand for however long I needed her. We talked about her staying for two full weeks. I thought I could rally by then. I had a streak of energy and seemed to be cleaning everything from top to bottom. I even cleaned windows and I hate that job. I was busy doing laundry when my water broke. I called Tim to come home but the pains were coming very close together. I called David and he was at the house practically before I hung up. He had already called 911 and they had paramedics to take me to the hospital. David got both boys' coats on and got them loaded into my car so he could follow me to the hospital. In the short-term Tim had texted me and gotten no response, so being a very smart man, he phoned David who gave him the news. Tim said he was on the way to the hospital and would meet us there. The paramedics got us to the hospital first and Dr. Andrews was waiting for us. The pains were coming very fast, and she got me right into the OR. I was frantic because Tim wasn't there, and I didn't know where David and my babies were. I was crying and very upset when Tim magically appeared at my side. He reassured me that there were a couple of nurses helping David with the boys and Lucy and Alicia were on their way. Dr. Andrews told me to push, and I swear the baby just kind of appeared. I don't really know if it was that fast, but it certainly felt like it. I heard a screaming infant and then they laid her on my chest. She continued to scream at the top of her little lungs. She was getting no comfort from me whatsoever. We both said she was beautiful and then the nurse took her to clean her up. She was still screaming and very red in the face. Dr. Andrews looked at both of us and said, "Good luck with this one. I believe you're going to have your hands full." I heard her laughing as she left the room.

The baby finally stopped screaming. She weighed in at 8 pounds 14 ounces and was 21-1/2 inches long. Good grief. Isn't that like half-grown? She was very healthy, and I was feeling fine, so it was decided we'd spend the one night and go home tomorrow about 10am. Tim called his mom, and she was on her way back to Edgartown. David and Lucy brought the boys in to meet their sister. She looked at them and then feigned sleep. David and Lucy commented on how beautiful she was. "Yes, I said, she is very pretty." Lucy told us she was going to take my car so that the boys would have their car seats. David and Alicia would follow, and they were all going to go back to our house for the night. "Thank you so much for being such wonderful friends. I don't know what I would have done without David's help. I completely forgot to call 911. Please feed Precious. She hasn't had her afternoon meal yet and I'm sure she's in a bad mood."

Tim and I settled down to acquaint ourselves with our daughter. We had pretty much decided that we were calling her Debra but hadn't settled on a middle name. We finally decided that Lorraine would go beautifully with Debra and so the girl child was officially named. We tried picking her up and cuddling her, but she simply wouldn't have any of it. She didn't mind being held, but not close. She hated being swaddled and much preferred being able to stretch and breathe. I tried nursing as the boys had taken to it without a problem but not this girl. Nope, just pump it and put it in a bottle. "I really feel like she doesn't like us, Tim, I said." "I know, he replied, but that's ridiculous. She can't possibly have those kinds of feelings, can she?" "I don't know. But I'm thinking we're going to need therapy before she's much older."

Lorraine arrived early evening and came straight to the hospital. After hugs and kisses for Tim and me she went over to the baby in the crib. We heard a soft gurgling sound coming from Debra that we hadn't yet experienced. Lorraine picked Debra up and sat down in the rocker next to the crib. Debra snuzzled into Lorraine, cooing, and then drifted off to sleep as if that were the exact place she was meant to be. We stared in total shock at each other. Tim told his mom that she wouldn't cuddle with either one of us but seemed very happy with her. "I've been waiting for her, Lorraine said, and she knew it. Debra and I are going to be best friends."

We were all ready to head for home at 10am. Tim brought the car around and had already run home and gotten the baby car seat. He was laughing when he came in as he had a cute story to tell me. "It seems, he said, that David and Lucy didn't want to sleep in our bed. Why? I haven't a clue. Anyway, they pulled out the trundle bed and they slept on the bed portion and put Alicia on the trundle portion so she wouldn't roll off onto the hard floor. David said that when they woke up this morning Daniel was in bed with them and Alicia and David were on the trundle cuddled up together. I really think we may have a problem when they get older." He was laughing so hard though that it was hard to think of anything other than how cute that must have been. Tim got us in the car, and we headed home with our newest charge. Debra seemed to enjoy the ride home as rather than sleeping like most newborns she was watching the shadows on the interior roof of the car. I tried talking to her, but she seemed oblivious to my very existence. David was watching for us and came out to help get everything into the house. Lucy was standing at the door with the twins in tow. The boys and Alicia were jumping up and down and shouting our names. At least they were glad to see us. We all got into the house, hugged everyone and set Debra's infant seat down on the coffee table so the boys and Alicia could tell her hello. She immediately starting cooing for them which delighted the boys. Lucy and I went into the kitchen to get a cup of tea and visit before they left. Lucy asked how I was doing and before I could utter a word I just started sobbing. She hugged me and asked, "What's wrong Amanda? Are you ok? Is Debra ok?" "Yes, we are fine, Lucy, it's just that she doesn't like either one of us. She won't look at us or respond to anything we say or do. She stares at us as if we were invisible. You saw how she responded to the boys and Alicia? Well, you should see her with my MIL. She can't get enough of her. I don't know what to think or do." Lucy seemed really perplexed and said, "My goodness. I can't imagine why she would be like that. I mean, she's 24 hours old." "I know. The thing is, she looks exactly like my mother and seems to have come ready-made with my mother's personality." Lucy just stared at me. "Really, she said. I mean that child is breathtakingly beautiful. Was your mother like that?" "Oh my, yes, she certainly was, I told her. You see that beautiful dark chocolate brown curly hair? My mother. You see those bright green eyes? My mother. I'm going to work through this the best I can. I just hope that she warms up to us as she gets older." "I know it will, Lucy said. This is weird but I know it will pass. She is absolutely a beautiful child and I'm sure we will all be blessed to have her in our lives." "I hope you're right, I said." Tim came in the kitchen and noticed that I'd been crying. He put his arms around me and hugged me tight telling me it would all be ok. He knew, instinctively, exactly why my heart was breaking.

Chapter 93

We took our tea and went back to the living room to find David holding Debra and the three children surrounding him talking to her. I swear she smiled! She was cuddling and cooing up a storm. Lucy just held my hand as the tears slipped down my cheeks. Please God, let me connect with this precious little girl you've loaned us. I swear she was looking right at me. David, Lucy and Alicia all hugged everyone goodbye and took their leave. Our David looked longingly out the front window waving at Alicia who was weeping. They are just too cute. I picked up Debra, who I swear stiffened when I did, and carried her upstairs to the nursery. I sat down in the rocker and tried humming to her and talking to her like I'd done while I carried her. I asked her why she didn't like me, but she just feigned sleep. We had tried nursing in the hospital, but she wouldn't have any of it. Tim had a small microwave on top of the fridge so I could warm her formula. I laid her in the bassinette while I warmed a bottle for her. I leaned over the bassinette to pick her up and she was staring at me with those damned green eyes. I decided to just ignore this whole bizarre situation and get on with life. I fed her, changed her, and laid her down in the bassinette to sleep. I decided I'd sit close by and read rather than leaving her unattended upstairs. Debra slept for about an hour and one-half and woke up stretching and yawning. She didn't cry. Just stretched and waited for someone to do something. I gave her a warm bath, toweled her off, put on a pretty onesie and started to wrap her up in a pinning blanket. Now she was screaming! Fine. No blanket. We went downstairs to find Tim and his folks visiting in the kitchen. "We didn't want to disturb you two, so we just waited until you appeared, Tim said." "May I hold her, asked Lorraine." "Yes, of course, I told her." I wanted to say "you can have her" but I didn't. I handed Debra off to Lorraine and she immediately began cooing and gurgling. Lorraine and Tom told her how beautiful she was, and she was loving it. I just looked at Tim. "I'm not nursing, Tim, so I would love a large glass of white wine." Tim got up to get it for me but not before looking at me with an "are you ok" look. "I haven't had wine or any alcohol for almost 2 years. I may pass out after I drink this." Lorraine just laughed and told me if I did, she would catch me. Not to worry. It's nice to know she has my back. I will talk with her about Debra as things go forward.

I drank my wine and must say I thoroughly enjoyed every drop of it. Lorraine had brought a beautiful lasagna to put in the oven. "That was so thoughtful, I said. Let's make a salad and some French bread to go with it, shall we?" Lorraine told me that they didn't need to stay but I insisted. "We can visit and play with the boys and I'm sure Debra will enjoy having you here, I told her." The boys were growing restless. We keep them enclosed in a playpen on the sunporch so that we can keep an eye on them. They move way too fast to be loose very often. Tom decided he was going to go play with the boys while Lorraine and I got supper going. Tim took Debra and went upstairs to change her and to lay her down for a rest. He kissed me and told me that he would do some book work while she rested. She was screaming bloody murder when he took her from Lorraine. She continued to scream while he walked upstairs but he stuck it out. Finally, Lorraine asked me, "What is going on Amanda? Why is she behaving like she does with you and Tim?" "We don't know. We are just as baffled by it as you are. She acts like she detests the very sight of us. It is difficult on both of us as we were so excited to have her." I was weeping and Lorraine was trying to comfort me, but she too was crying. Lorraine hugged me and said, "Amanda, sometimes these things just happen. I've heard about it from other parents. You guys just stay with it and keep telling her you love her. It is going to sink in sooner or later. Also, Tom and I will be diligent about enforcing that information whenever she's with us. Don't you worry. It'll be okay."

Chapter 94

As time passed, we recognized that Debra was very bright. She was more alert than the boys were at that age. The boys were crazy about her. If she cried, they were right there beside her. They loved to hold her and give her a bottle. She continued to bond with her grandmother. Lorraine thought the sun got up every morning because of Debra. Tim and I worked hard to tell her that we loved her every single day. We made it a point to rock her and talk to her whether she enjoyed it or not. He and I discussed the situation and agreed that like it or not she was stuck with us. Even Precious was high on her list. The cat always laid at her feet; being very careful to never get up around the baby's face. It was as if she'd been told not to, but to this cat, well, it just came naturally.

We were getting ready to plan the boys and Alicia's second birthday party. Debra would be 4-months old when the boys turn 2 years. What were we thinking? Our office looked more like a day-care than a busy professional office. We turned the conference room into a playroom for Daniel, David, and Alicia. Debra was still too young to join in their romps so we kept her in an infant seat or her swing or a playpen so we could watch over her more closely. The boys and Alicia still napped after lunch until about 4pm. Depending on what we had going on it usually worked better for Tim and Lucy to work mornings when the boys were awake so that I could keep an eye on them at home and Lucy would only have Alicia to contend with during that time. Then the boys and Debra and I would go in at lunch time, feed all the children and put the older ones down for their naps while

Lucy and I got my work done. It seemed to be working and for the time being I just wasn't adding to my workload. I felt I had enough to handle with the children.

Tim's consulting business was growing rapidly. I knew it would as he works well with all kinds of people and his knowledge of justice and law enforcement making him an asset to all. I was maintaining where I wanted to be for the time being. I figured when the children started school I could expand if I wanted. Otherwise, I was happy just taking care of the clients I had. Lucy and I had a plan for the kid's 2nd birthday celebration. We made a list of what we needed and then divided it between us. The weather had been kind of gloomy so we decided to use the sunporch for the event and that way the children would be warm and out of any possible rainstorms. The boys love balls so that became our theme. Big, colorful soft beach balls. We hung crepe paper streamers and lots of colorful animated artwork. Each child would have their own cake to devour. We have friends from the community that have children the ages of ours, so we'll have about eight 2-year-old for two hours! What fun! Tom had been busy in his workshop and made the boys and Alicia rocking horses. Hers was very girly and the cutest thing you've ever seen. Tim bought them all western wear, so they'd be appropriately dressed when they ride off into the sunset.

The morning of the party I picked up the cakes and stopped at the deli who were kind enough to make 11 each peanut butter and jelly, tuna fish, and bologna sandwiches, minus the crust for the children's lunch. I had made a couple of pitchers of juice that was mom-approved, and we splurged on potato chips to go with the sandwiches. Paper plates, paper cups, lots and lots of napkins and we're good to go. The deli prepared 6 beautiful chef's salads for the moms. There! That is the perfect party. Lucy arrived early to help me get things together. We made sure our kids had clean faces, that their hair was combed and that they were looking presentable. Tim had taken the boys to get real haircuts a couple of days before their birthday. We all cried, but they really looked adorable. Just way too grown up. Alicia's hair was gorgeous. It parted in the middle and just fell into place on its own. She is really a beautiful child and just as sweet as she is pretty. Debra's hair was a mass of chocolate brown curls. I loved to brush it and wind the curls around my hand. I would weave ribbons through the curls, and she looked so adorable. If only she would act adorable all would be so much better. She seemed to react to everyone with a positive attitude except for Tim and me. She just tolerated us.

Tim and I had talked about perhaps seeing a psychologist about our situation with Debra, but he felt strongly that things would get better as she got older. I made him promise that if by the time she started kindergarten that she was still ignoring us as if we were invisible that we would seek professional help. He agreed. In the meantime, we continued to pray about it hoping that God would direct us on how to proceed. It was very stressful for me, and I cried about it all the time. She seemed to sense that, and I felt like she enjoyed knowing that it hurt me so badly. I'm sure that this precious little baby wasn't capable of some thoughts, but nevertheless, the look on her face said otherwise.

The party was a raving success, and the boys were officially 2 years old! Everyone had a good time and helped clean up before they left. Lucy and I grabbed hot tea and headed for the living room. We just collapsed and started laughing. "Would you have ever thought that a 2-year-old birthday party could take that much energy? She asked." "I know. Just think, we only will have to do this about 100 more times! We were both rolling in laughter as Tim came in with Debra and the boys in tow.

Chapter 95

It had been a long, tedious day and we all went to bed early. About 12:30am I came fully awake and instantly knew something was wrong. I checked on Tim and he was resting comfortably. I checked on the boys and they were sawing logs. I went into the nursery to check on Debra and she was awake, not crying, and burning up with fever. I grabbed her into my arms, yelled for Tim and headed to the bathroom where I started filling the tub with cool water. I took her temperature, and it was 103.4. I wasn't comfortable putting her into the cool water so quickly, so I got into the tub with her in my arms. I carefully started immersing her in the cool water to bring the fever down. I asked Tim to please call the doctor and get her advice on how to proceed. Both boys were standing in the bathroom door softly crying. I assured them that sissy would be okay and that they should go back to bed. Daniel told me that, no, they needed to be there to help. Tim came back upstairs and said that we should keep up the cool bath for about another 15 minutes, check her temp, and if it hadn't come down to bring her to the E.R. I couldn't help but notice that Debra was cuddled into my arms and staring at me with those big bright green eyes. I kept assuring her that we were going to be fine, and that mommy loved her very much. I didn't even realize that the tears were streaming down my face and bouncing off her. Tim and the boys just stood at the door anxious to help however they could. Tim told me that the 15 minutes was up and went to get the baby thermometer. We saw that her temperature was still about 101 degrees. I asked Tim to call the doctor back and ask what to do. He came back and said that Dr. Andrews felt like things were returning to normal. Tim said, "She said to wrap Debra in warm blankets and then in about half an hour to take her temp again. If it hasn't changed or has gone up then bring her to E.R. otherwise, bring her into the office tomorrow at 10am."

I handed Debra to Tim while I got out of the tub and dried off. He was drying her off and wrapping her in warm towels. We got her into a clean diaper and warm clothing, and I went into her room to rock her while we kept an eye on the clock. Tim warmed a bottle and I fed and rocked her while quietly humming and assuring her that all would be ok. Tim got the boys tucked back into bed and came to join us. He sat quietly on the floor in the corner of the room. I knew he was praying for both of us. About 4:30am her fever broke, and her eyes took on a clearer, brighter look. Her skin was cooler to the touch, and she was cooing softly as I rocked her. She hadn't let go of my finger for several hours. I believe we turned an important corner during this very long night. I fed her again, changed her diaper and clothing and tucked her into her bed. She was asleep before I walked out of the room. Tim said he would sit guard duty so I could go get some rest. I slept until about 6:30am and went to check on them. Tim was rocking her and humming softly to her. He said she had awakened about 5:30am and wanted to cuddle. They looked so sweet together that my heart just burst. I went down to make coffee for both of us and by that time I heard the boys rustling around in their room. Tim came downstairs with everyone in tow. Debra truly looked like she felt a lot better. We would keep that 10am appointment to be sure all was okay. I fixed breakfast for everyone, and we sat at the breakfast bar while we ate and visited. The boys were so glad that Debra was feeling better! She was in her infant seat parked on the side of the bar where they could talk to her. She was smiling and cooing and seemed to be genuinely enjoying her brothers. Precious ate her breakfast, puffed her tail at all of us and went into the living room. I had been concerned about her of late as she seemed less nasty than usual. Perhaps she was mellowing in her old age.

Tim and I got everyone ready for the doctor visit. We all piled into the car and headed off to see Dr. Andrews. The nurses and receptionist all had to talk to the kids and comment on how adorable they all were. Dr. Andrews didn't keep us waiting as she seemed anxious to see how Debra was doing. I gave her a full report and after she checked her over, she said, "Well, I think we had a bout with the flu. She seems ok right now. All her vitals are good, and her eyes are bright and alert. You did a fine job, Amanda. You instinctively knew exactly what needed to be done." I thanked her and gave her a big hug. "It was terrifying. We were so worried, and the boys even stood by the door to be sure she was ok." "It's their baby sister, she said. They have a stake in her well-being." We thanked her for her time, collected Debra and the boys and headed for home.

We watched her closely for the next few days to be sure she was okay. The fever was gone, and her appetite had returned so we felt all would be okay. It was like a huge turning point between Debra and Tim and me. She warmed up to us, cooed and snuzzled, and seemed genuinely happy to be with us. Thank you, Lord! The entire family seemed to be happier. Debra smiled and cooed and laughed out loud at the boys. The boys learned many new words and were growing taller and bigger every day. Tim's work was super busy, and I tended to just do what I absolutely had to do at work. My thoughts were that when the kids started to school, I would get more involved in increasing my workload. Until then I was content at being Mom.

It seemed that one day became a week and a week became a month and before I knew it, Debra was one-year old! And walking! She, very clearly, says momma, daddy, brudder for both boys, kitty, granny, gramps, and NO! She stomps around the house, twirling, and reminds me of Shirley Temple in her old movies. She's adorable and she knows it. Since being so ill she has had a total change of disposition with Tim and me. She seems thrilled at being in our family. We told her we were having a family party with cake and hats, and she is thrilled. We don't have any friends with one-year old children, so this was our best bet on having a party.

The boys helped us make cupcakes, frost them and arrange them like a tower. They put all the sprinkles on each one and had the best time ever. The boys said that Debra wanted tuna fishy samwiches, with sweet pickle (where did these children come from?), and potato chips. We made some PB&Js just in case someone wanted something different. Debra wanted orange juice and chocolate milk to drink, and the boys wanted Hawaiian punch. We fixed three punch bowls to accommodate the various taste buds. We made invitations and sent to Uncle David and Aunt Lucy, Granny and Gramps, and Alicia was to be a separate invitation. Debra also wanted invitations for her brudders. We colored the invitations and put stars and confetti on them, placed them in envelopes that the kids decorated and mailed them off. We decided on Saturday at 11am for the party. Debra wanted to wear her party dress. I asked her if she'd like to get a new one for her birthday, but no, she likes her old party dress. She picked out clothes for her brudders to wear and we are sure they'll look very handsome.

Debra and I were up early on Saturday to get ready for the party. We hand curled her freshly washed hair and put on her party dress. It took some convincing for her to change out of her cowboy boots into pretty shoes, but I finally convinced her that it looked better. She has a stubborn streak like her grandmother did and at one year of age she is already as verbal as most two-year old children. Her vocabulary was growing daily and so was her stubborn streak. She would stomp her little foot, jut out her chin and narrow her eyes at you thinking for sure she was scaring you to death. It took everything that Tim and I had to not laugh out loud when she did it.

Everyone arrived on time, dressed in party clothing, ready to bestow gifts upon our princess. Granny, of course, brought her a tiara and a wand. Always such a helpful MIL. Debra helped serve lunch by grabbing hands and pulling them into the kitchen to fill their plates. All her guests were thrilled with her sandwich choices and fun was had by all. Debra went to each guest, hugged them and thanked them for her present and for coming to her party. Her gramps practically dissolved in tears over her gesture. It really was very sweet and both of us were very proud of our daughter. We had already told her that we were going out for pizza at dinnertime which is one of her favorite foods in the world.

Chapter 96

The next couple of months were quiet ones. It was hard to believe that the boys would be three years old in a couple of weeks. They were very independent, and they always had Debra join in whatever they were doing. I don't have a clue how she managed to keep up with them, but at one year old, she did. Her vocabulary was growing daily. I occasionally would take her to day care when I had clients and Tim was busy with his workload. The day care was always commenting that Debra needed to be enrolled in a program that would enhance her learning as she was very advanced. Tim and I talked about it and decided we just wanted plain ordinary children rather than gifted ones. We felt that all three were gifted in their own way and that was enough for us.

Our entire life was rushing away. Summer came and went, and then the holidays came and went, and months turned into years, or so it seemed. Debra turned 2 years old, and the boys were just 4 months away from being four years old! How had that happened? Just yesterday they were so little and totally dependent on us and now, they figure a lot of stuff all on their own. It seems that our lives have taken such a different direction than what we originally intended. I hadn't expected to be absent from my firm so much, but it was apparent that the children needed me at home with them as much as possible. Tim's business was flourishing. Between he and Lucy they were barely able to keep up. Tim was considering hiring someone to help him. I was very happy for his success, but I must admit that I was a little bit jealous of the excitement that he was experiencing while I was changing diapers.

I sat with a cup of coffee and mulled over what I was thinking and decided that I was a very normal woman of 40-plus years tending to three toddlers and so I felt much better.

David and Lucy had agreed to take our three children for a sleepover so that Tim and I could make a quick trip into Boston. We wanted to spend the night at the condo and try to decide if we really wanted to keep it or if we should sell and buy a vacation home for the entire family to enjoy.

Tom and Lorraine seemed to be spending more and more time at the B&B and less time in Boston. They had made so many friends that it was hard to book dinner with them! They were busy all the time. Tom had mentioned that they were considering selling the house in Boston. We had considered asking them to watch the kids but figured they'd be busy, and that David and Lucy were the better choice. I called my MIL to let her know that we'd be gone from Friday afternoon until Sunday evening so she wouldn't worry if she discovered we weren't at home. I asked her to stop by and feed and visit with Precious while we were gone, and she assured me that either she or Tom would do that. She told me to have a wonderful getaway and that she had to hang up because her friends were there to pick her up for lunch. So much for the doting grandparents.

I packed the children's overnight cases, their bag of goodies, and delivered them all to Lucy. I told her that either Tom or Lorraine would come by to feed Precious and spend a little time with her. Both David and Debra gave me a haphazard wave as they ran off. Daniel looked up at me with his big blue eyes shining with unshed tears and asked if I'd be okay without him. I scooped him up and assured him that I would count the moments until we were together again. I must admit I had a huge lump in my throat as I turned to leave. Lucy assured me all would be okay, and of course, I knew it would be. I drove by the B&B to see if either Tom or Lorraine were at home. As it turned out they both were. I had a quick cup of coffee with them, filled them in on all the most recent events regarding the children, hugged them tight and took my leave.

I hurried home to pack for Tim and me so we could get on the road to catch the last ferry. We wouldn't arrive in Boston until late evening, but the cleaning lady had warmed up the condo and filled the refrigerator with goodies for us.

Tim arrived home just as I was finishing up the packing. He carried the suitcase and cosmetic bag downstairs while I took one last look to see if I'd forgotten anything. We met on the landing, turned down the heat, checked the backdoor to be sure it was locked and headed for the car. We chatted all the way to the ferry landing. The wind was rather brisk, but the sailing was without incidence. Depending on the traffic the trip from the landing to our condo is about 2 hours as we're a few minutes beyond Boston proper. We stopped at a diner and split a burger and salad for our dinner and were back on the road within 30 minutes. The traffic was picking up and I was getting more and more anxious to reach our destination. Tim understands my discomfort in traffic and tries to keep me occupied with cheerful conversation during such times. We were stopped at an intersection waiting on the light to turn green. The car ahead of us shot forward the minute the light changed just in time to be broadsided by a pickup truck that ran the red light. Tim and I saw the truck smash into the car in front of us, flip and then it was moving straight for us out of control. I remember the impact. I remember looking at Tim. I remember thinking about the boys and Debra.

And then nothing.

9 7 9 8 8 8 9 4 7 9 1 7 9 1